JOHNNY QUARLES

"BRINGS A FRESH APPROACH TO THE
CLASSIC WESTERN, WITH INTRIGUING
CHARACTERS TWICE BIGGER THAN LIFE
AND FOUR TIMES MORE INTERESTING."
Elmer Kelton

"PROVIDES AN EXHILARATING PICTURE
OF THE UNTAMED WEST."
Kliatt Book Guide

"IS A PLEASURE TO READ"
Clay Reynolds

"MASTERFULLY BRINGS HIS COLORFUL
CHARACTERS TO LIFE, SPINNING A DARN
GOOD TALE IN THE PROCESS."
Youngstown Vindicator

"IS THE GENUINE ARTICLE . . .
HE JUST KEEPS GETTING
BETTER AND BETTER."
Terry C. Johnston

Other Avon Books by
Johnny Quarles

FOOL'S GOLD
NO MAN'S LAND
SPIRIT TRAIL

JOHNNY QUARLES

Shadow of the Gun

AVON BOOKS ◆ NEW YORK

SHADOW OF THE GUN is an original publication of Avon Books. This work has never before appeared in book form. This work is a novel. Any similarity to actual persons or events is purely coincidental.

AVON BOOKS
A division of
The Hearst Corporation
1350 Avenue of the Americas
New York, New York 10019

Copyright © 1995 by Johnny Quarles
Front cover art by Maren
Published by arrangement with the author
Library of Congress Catalog Card Number: 95-94429
ISBN: 0-380-77657-X

First Avon Books Printing: November 1995

AVON TRADEMARK REG. U.S. PAT. OFF. AND IN OTHER COUNTRIES, MARCA REGISTRADA, HECHO EN U.S.A.

Printed in the U.S.A.

RA   10   9   8   7   6   5   4   3   2   1

1

CLAYTON CRIST was tired. He sat bare-chested, smoking one last fixin' before he went downstairs. He took a deep pull on the cigarette and started to cough violently, as the strong smoke scratched and abused his lungs. His swollen stomach jumped and jiggled. It looked like a big, ripe mellon, he thought unhappily. Once he'd stopped coughing, he wiped the water from his eyes and took another pull on the smoke. This time, it felt more soothing.

When the smoke was finished, Clayton snubbed it out, got up, and pulled on his shirt. Then, as if it were a part of his body, he strapped on his pearl-handled Colt, a short-barreled .45. The trigger guard was cut away for faster and surer access. Before he tied it down, he followed the routine of gently taking the pistol with his fingertips, lifting it from the holster, and letting it slide back down. Satisfied the motion was smooth as silk, he tied the holster to his leg.

He started down the hotel stairs, taking each step with a slowness that he found aggravating. He cursed his aching legs and feet. Why, he must look like an old man to all those observing. He surely felt older than his age. His thoughts shifted to what the date was. He couldn't even remember. Was it the sixteenth or the seventeenth? Or maybe it was the eighteenth. He wasn't sure. The more he tried to remember, the more confusing it was. Clayton grasped the stair rail and cursed again. What was happening to him? His body was already falling apart, and now his thinking was becoming muddled, too.

At the foot of the stairs, he gave up on wondering what day of the month it was and looked around the room. The desk clerk glanced at him nervously, then turned to a man and a woman who were there to inquire about a room.

Clayton squinted at the pretty woman. His once-powerful vision was becoming fuzzy, like his mind. Some days, he could see pretty well, while other times he'd get a headache from straining to focus on something. It came and went. As of late, though, he hadn't been able to do any book-reading at all.

He stepped out onto the hotel porch and leaned against a post, taking in a deep breath of the morning air. He noticed the people up and down the street looking his way. It didn't surprise him any when they began to crowd into open doorways and disappear down the nearest alleys.

Three women were standing directly across the street, watching Clayton. They made no move to go inside.

"That's him!" Sheila, the whore, said. "I seen him in Dodge City." She shook her head admiringly. "He's the prettiest man I ever saw."

Celeste strained for a better look. "I don't know," she said hesitantly. "From the looks of his paunch, I'd say he's had too many beers."

"Honey, his eyes are as blue as the sky on a clear day," Sheila said. "If you ever looked into them blues, you'd pay him for the pleasure."

Another whore named Mary pushed past them and stepped to the edge of the street. After several seconds of scrutiny, she said, "Sheila's right. He's handsome, all right. Does he pay for it?"

Sheila shrugged. "I'd like to say yes, but the truth is, I don't know."

Across the way, Clayton's eyes lingered on the whores that were huddled together across the street, talking amongst themselves. This morning, his eyes couldn't quite make out the women's fine features. But they looked interesting. Maybe, he thought, he'd take a closer look later.

Clayton was still watching the whores, when the voice of Delbert Parker called out from somewhere down the street.

"This way, Crist! I'm still waitin'!"

Clayton let his eyes linger a few more seconds on the three whores. He surely wished he could see their faces better. All three were of medium height. Two of them had dark hair, and the third was red. He had a fascination with red hair. It had been too long, he thought. Yes, he would take that closer look later, when he had time.

"You gonna stand there and gawk at them whores, or are you gonna fight?" Delbert Parker yelled, drawing a laugh from his two companions, Stinky Wahl and Leonard Bailey. They were standing next to a hitching post in front of Buckminster Mercantile.

Slowly, Clayton stepped from the hotel porch. He walked a few paces, to where he was facing Delbert Parker and his friends.

He didn't know Parker—had never seen the man before this day. Parker was bigger and younger than his brother, Sherman. Almost four months to the day, Clayton had killed Sherman, down in the Cherokee Outlet. Since that time, he'd heard on several occasions that Delbert Parker intended to avenge his older brother's death. He had finally caught up with Clayton here in Platt's Crossing. This morning, Clayton had been heavy in sleep when Stinky Wahl pounded on his door and said that Delbert Parker was out on the street, waiting.

Clayton tried to forget about the awful pain in his feet and legs. He walked to where his eyes could see Parker's face. His blue eyes were cold and serious, while Parker's were wild with excitement.

"Looky here, boy. It ain't too late to walk away," Clayton said in a solemn tone.

"You crazy?" Parker snapped, taking one last glance at his two friends. "I didn't come this far to walk away, and you *sure* ain't about to!"

Delbert Parker had barely ended his sentence, when he pulled leather. He was pretty fast. With a fluidlike motion, he whipped his gun from the holster at his side. He almost had the barrel of his pistol pointed at Clayton, when he saw the smoke coming out of Clayton's Colt. The arrogant grin slid from his lips as the .45 slug knocked him backward.

He dropped his pistol and clutched his chest.

"God, it hurts!" Parker said. He turned to his friends. The excitement was gone from his eyes, and he stared at them with a fearful look. They stared back.

Parker turned his gaze skyward. "God, it hurts," he repeated, then dropped dead.

The Colt felt hot in Clayton's hand. He turned to the hitching post in front of Buckminster's and waited for Parker's friends to make the next move. His eyes had hardened into icy blue orbs, and the tired body had turned young again, ready to fight.

Stinky Wahl raised his hands in surrender. Leonard Bailey, who moments before had given the oath that, if Parker's first shot didn't kill Clayton Crist, then he wanted to finish the job, dropped to his knees.

"Please don't kill us! It was Delbert's fight, not ours!" His voice cracked.

The confrontation was over, and there was no need for any more killing. Clayton holstered the Colt and turned away. Slowly, he walked to the saloon across the street and pushed through the swinging doors.

The interior was dark. He couldn't see, but he could hear the whispers—the same whispers he'd heard so many times before.

"That's him! That's the Gunny! Clayton Crist!" a man said.

"I know!" another said. "I seen him drop Taylor Lewis in Coffeyville three years ago."

Clayton waited for his eyes to adjust. He saw the silhouetted heads. It seemed like half the town was there, faceless heads talking in hushed voices about him. They were all watching him, waiting to see what he was going to do next. He was used to it. It was always this way. Every town, every gunfight.

He looked around for the whores. He intended to buy one of them a drink. And if they looked as good up close as they did at a distance, he might buy more than that. Finally, his eyes adjusted to the room, and he noticed them, still together, standing at the opposite end of the bar.

He walked toward them amongst the hushed whispers.

"It's the Gunny, all right."

"Can you believe it? Here, in Platt's Crossing!"

Clayton heard the words, but they'd long ago lost their meaning. He walked up to the bar, next to the whores, and asked the barkeep for a drink.

Up close, he took a look at the three women. None was beautiful, but they were pleasant enough. The redhead caught his eye most favorably.

"You hungry?" he asked her.

She giggled nervously. "I reckon I am. You offerin'?"

He nodded. "Let's us go across the street to the hotel. We'll get somethin' to eat and take it up to my room."

She looked uncertainly at the bartender. "Well"—she hesitated—"We could go upstairs here, I guess. George don't allow us to take our business nowhere else."

Clayton followed her gaze. "Oh, I don't reckon George gives a damn whether it's here or across the street. Do you, George?"

"No, sir," George the bartender said, his eyes wide-open and friendly.

The whore just stood there, nervously watching the bartender. Clayton understood, and leaned over the bar to speak in a more confidential tone.

"Looky here, George," he said. "I'm takin' the lady across the street to my hotel room, and I don't want her to get into any kind of trouble later on. So, if you've got any objections, let's hear 'em right now. You understand?"

George nodded furiously. "Yes, sir, I do! You go on now, Sheila. Take care of Mister Crist. It's on the house!"

"That ain't what I'm askin' of you, George. I'm sayin' I don't want you dealin' the lady no grief after I'm gone. 'Cause if I hear you do, I'm gonna come back. You hear?"

"Oh, of course, Mister Crist! There won't be no trouble. I swear!" the bartender said. He held up both hands to validate the fact.

Clayton held his icy gaze on the man for a moment, then picked up his drink and downed it with one swallow. The whiskey burned all the way down. He needed its warmth.

He wasn't necessarily a drinking man; in fact, he'd only been drunk three or four times in his life. But there were times when the whiskey had a calming effect, and this was one of those times. He ordered another and drank it quickly down, then turned to the redheaded whore.

He offered her his arm. Surprised, she took it, and together they left the silent saloon and went into the street.

The undertaker's wagon was parked outside. As they walked past, Clayton avoided looking at the thick blood that lay pooled in the dirt. He ignored the whispers that followed him to the door of the hotel.

At the desk, he ordered steaks to be sent up in one hour. Then, he climbed the steps with the whore on his arm.

Even with the delightful thoughts of what lay ahead with Sheila the whore, Clayton still couldn't think away the tiredness that had returned to his legs and feet.

2

CLAYTON LAID his head on the whore's thigh, facing her. He had never seen such red hair before. His mind was preoccupied with such, when Sheila broke into his thoughts.

"Are you sick, or somethin'? I mean, you're sweatin' somethin' awful!"

She reached down and rubbed his forehead. It was wet and clammy. He felt hot, yet the weather was cool outside and the room felt cold.

"No, I ain't sick. Not that I know of. Outside of feelin' tired and havin' a few aches and pains, I'm healthy enough, I guess," Clayton said. He raised his eyes and looked past her breasts at her face. She was prettier than he had first thought. "Have we ever met before?" he asked.

"Once. In Dodge City. I seen you. I didn't think you noticed me."

He thought a moment, but he couldn't place seeing her in Dodge City. Still, there was something familiar about her. "What's your name?" he asked.

"It's Sheila. I thought you knew that."

"That's not all the name you've got, though."

She smiled and rubbed the back of her hand on his cheek. "You've surely got the prettiest eyes I've ever seen," she said. "My name is Sheila Ann Weeks. Nothing special. I always thought it to be a plain name."

Clayton closed his eyes. He could go right to sleep, he thought, but a knock sounded at the door and the food arrived.

Sheila ate ravenously. She didn't even bother to get dressed. Clayton didn't mind. It had been a while since he'd been with a woman. He toyed with his food while his eyes took in her shapely body. He waited until she was finished, then motioned for her to come to him. They frolicked once more, and then he did fall asleep, lying next to her.

He awoke a short time later with a burning in his bladder. He got up to relieve himself. It was the third time since they'd arrived in the room that he'd felt the need.

"You sure do pee a lot," she commented.

"Sometimes."

Sheila frowned. She got up and picked up her dinner plate. "I want you to do somethin'," she said. She wiped the plate clean with a rag, then handed it to him. "Here. Pee a little bit on this plate."

He looked at her, wondering if he was supposed to laugh. "Well now, that's the strangest request I ever heard," he said. "But as much as I'd like to oblige you, I'm afraid I don't have the need to go again."

"Come on," she urged. "Just a drop or two."

"Are you crazy or somethin'?" he asked. "I ain't pissin' on no plate!"

Sheila shook her head. "No," she said kindly. "I ain't crazy, but I think you might be sick. Please, just dribble some on this plate."

Clayton looked into her serious hazel eyes and saw the compassion. There was something about Sheila that he liked. It wasn't just her special talent at frolicking, or the fascinating red hair that drew him to her. It was the sincerity in her eyes, and the way she showed her sense of humor, smiling easily and laughing out loud, without reserve. He needed that.

But, going in a plate? It was the craziest thing he'd ever heard of! Crazy or not, though, he found himself giving in to her coaxing.

He forced himself to make a few dribbles of water.

Sheila took the plate from him and reached out to touch the urine. He grabbed her by the wrist.

"No!" he hollered. "What do you think you're doin'?"

She shook his hand away and dipped her finger in the

urine, then touched it to her tongue. She made a face and spit.

"Well, it ain't what I thought," Sheila admitted, looking up at him. "I was afraid it would taste sweet."

"What do you mean, sweet?" Clayton frowned.

"Well, you see, my daddy, back in St. Louis. He's a doctor," Sheila explained. "I used to help him, before I left home. Those folks with sweet pee have a sickness, and when you said your feet and legs hurt, and you'd been sweatin' so, I was just sure you were gonna have sweet pee."

Clayton frowned, and she went on.

"Haven't you ever seen a horse wastin' away, and how the flies gather around its pee?" She shook her head. "Well, anyways, I was wrong. I guess you just need to take better care of yourself." She looked him over. "You could stand to lose some of that belly. I ain't complainin', but my daddy used to say that any man got as much belly as he's got chest, he ain't gonna feel right. I'll bet you never get enough sleep, neither."

Clayton sat on the bed and pulled her next to him. They leaned back against the pillows, with her head on his shoulder.

It was quiet in the room. Clayton closed his eyes and was just about to doze off again, when Sheila stirred from his shoulder. She raised herself up to look at him.

"Why did you kill that man? What did he do?" she asked.

"Nothin'."

"What do you mean, nothin'? You killed a man for no reason?" Sheila sounded more matter-of-fact than disapproving.

"It's a long story," Clayton said, and let it drop at that.

Sheila thought a moment, then said reflectively, "I don't think I could just *kill* somebody. Not unless they was tryin' to kill me. Oh, I could name a few cowboys I felt like killin' one time or other. See this?" She pointed to a small scar on her eyebrow. "That's what a drunk cowboy gave me, once he'd had his good time. He didn't have no money, so he hauled off and hit me. If I'd had a gun, I woulda killed him, for sure. There's been others, too.'' Her eyes narrowed into slits. "Some men like to get rough. I can't tolerate roughness.''

"Why do you do it?" Clayton said. "Couldn't you find work doin' somethin' else?''

Sheila shrugged. "I could, if I wanted to. I'm just not sure I want to. Some Saturdays, I can make twenty dollars in one night.'' She paused. "Why shoot, I can make eight or ten a night during the week. And those cowpokes spend themselves in three or four minutes, so you can't say it's hard work. Besides that, it can be right pleasurable, sometimes.'' She rubbed some sweat from his forehead. "Have you killed a lot of men?" she asked.

Clayton studied her face and decided there was no malice in her question. "Oh, a few, I guess,'' he said.

"More'n a few, I'll bet. I've heard people talkin'. They say you've killed a *bunch* of men. One fellow said you killed thirty or forty." Sheila considered such a thing. "Don't it ever bother you none?''

Clayton had never really *enjoyed* killing, but he had to admit it had bothered him more when he was younger than it did now. Still, he'd just as soon not kill any more men. A quiet, peaceful life, keeping to himself without the bother of others, seemed like a reasonable way to live out his life. But that didn't seem to be his lot. It seemed like there was always somebody waiting, ready to creep up on him and offer a challenge. Clayton could hardly enter a saloon, when someone didn't try to lay claim to his reputation.

"Well, does it bother you?" Sheila pressed.

"Sure, it does,'' Clayton said. "There's nothin' pleasurable about it. After all, it's always some mama's son, or somebody's daddy.''

"Well, why do you do it then?" Sheila asked.

He was tired of her probing, but then, hadn't he asked the same of her? He let her questions linger in the air and stared past her, toward the window. "You know,'' he said wistfully, "I have a place up in Ness City, Kansas. I used to work a few beeves there.''

"Couldn't you go back to raisin' cattle, instead of killin' folks?"

Clayton didn't answer. He couldn't answer. He had tried working an honest life several times, but it seemed like trouble had always followed him everywhere he went. He'd grown fond of Ness City and the folks around that part of the country. They had pretty much accepted him the way he was. Oh, there'd been a curiosity, but the Ness Citians had let him be, and he had likewise left them alone.

Just as he'd gotten comfortable in his surroundings, though, someone had come to town, looking for trouble. Looking for Clayton. It wasn't good for him, and it wasn't good for the community, so he'd packed up and left.

What followed was one job after another. Clayton found work on several ranches down in the Cherokee Outlet and throughout Kansas. The jobs were always the same. Pleasant enough work, and Clayton was a willing hand, but his employers always wanted more. They wanted his gun. It was never long before the job was done, and he was no longer needed. Not many ranchers were willing to pay for a gun once the problem was eliminated. So, he moved on. Every so often, he returned to Ness City. Someday, he told himself, he'd go back and settle down for good. Maybe then trouble would stop looking for him.

He caught himself daydreaming about the past. Sheila was watching him. "Sure," he said. "I guess I could settle down and just raise cattle. Someday, I hope to."

"Have you got a house in Ness City?"

"Not much more than a dugout. I always planned to build a nice house someday. Just never did."

"You got any family there?"

"Nope. There's a man named Martin Frusher that runs a few beeves on my land, but no family." He shook his head regretfully. "There's just me, and I reckon it'll always be that way."

"I'd say that's surely a shame," Sheila said, enjoying his clear blue eyes.

3

CLAYTON AND Sheila had been asleep for about an hour. The sun was about to set when there was a tap on the door.

"Wake up," Sheila said groggily. "Somebody's here."

Clayton opened his bloodshot eyes, then suddenly he was sitting up. In the blink of an eye, he held the Colt in his hand.

Sheila saw the tension in his face. Wide-eyed, she shrank against her pillow and pulled the covers up over her, watching him.

"Throw somethin' on and see who it is," Clayton said.

Sheila took the top blanket from the bed and wrapped herself in it. The hair tingled on her body as she walked barefoot across the cold floor. Clayton was sitting behind her on the bed with his Colt pointed at the door.

Sheila forced herself to grab hold of the doorknob. Getting slapped around by cowboys was one thing, she thought, but standing there in the line of fire was altogether different, and it was apparent that Clayton expected trouble. Still, as frightened as she was, Sheila felt an excitement running through her. She glanced back at Clayton. If it had been anybody else sitting there with a pistol drawn, she would be downright scared.

She opened the door and quickly stepped aside, out of harm's way, then gasped at the man standing there.

"Why, Alcie Bryant! What are you doin' here?" she asked.

"Have you forgot, Sheila? I'm the sheriff," the man said. "I need to see Mister Crist."

Sheila waved him inside with her arm.

Sheriff Alcie Bryant stepped inside the room and looked straight into the barrel of Clayton's Colt, which was pointed directly at him. The sheriff lifted his hands in a defensive posture. "No need for that, Mister Crist. I didn't come here lookin' for no trouble. Just want to talk, is all."

Clayton silently reached up to retrieve his holster from the bedpost and laid it in his lap, then eased the Colt inside. Taking that as an invitation, the sheriff stepped farther into the room. He was nervous and didn't try to hide the fact. Still holding his hands up, he cleared his throat before he spoke.

"Just need to ask you some questions, is all. Like I said, I ain't lookin' for no trouble. They don't pay me enough around here for that. Not with you, anyway," the sheriff said with a small chuckle.

Clayton glanced at Sheila. She gave him a crooked smile. She looked like she was enjoying herself. He wondered what all was behind that smile. Maybe this sheriff hadn't always treated her so nicely.

"Well," he finally said. "I'll try to answer anything you want to know."

The sheriff nodded. "Well, you see, it's like this. I was over in Starnsville this mornin', and when I got back, I heard that you'd shot a man out front. Killed him. Now"—he paused and took in a deep breath—"several folks have told me that it was the man that called you out and pulled on you first. I mean to say, Mister Crist, that I heard it was a fair fight on your part."

The man was so nervous, he was sweating. Clearly, Clayton thought, he didn't have the stomach for being a sheriff. He felt a little angry at him, but more than that, he felt sorry for Sheriff Bryant. Clayton had seen dozens of men like him—men who needed money, so they strapped on guns and got paid to keep the peace, thinking it entailed no more than locking up an occasional drunk. Some of them got by just fine. Clayton recognized that just because a man acted a little nervous, it didn't mean he couldn't do his job effectively. Most sheriffs just asked their questions and went on, but those who tried to be heroes often met their match and went on to early graves.

Clayton tried to sound as humble as possible. "Looky here, Sheriff. I ain't wantin' no problems, either. Me and Sheila, here, were just gonna go get us a bite of supper. In the mornin', I'll be goin' on my way."

Sheriff Bryant nodded his approval. He'd finally dropped his hands. "That's fine. I'm not wantin' to stir up anything nasty. But you just killed a man, right in the middle of our town. You know, Mister Crist," he went on philosophically, "the days of shootin's and street fights and such are comin' to an end. People are more concerned with buildin' towns with churches, schools, and social clubs. They're even buildin' colleges in the bigger cities. We're workin' on makin' it a nice place to raise our families and such. I just wish you hadn't killed a man in my town, is all." He paused and glanced at Sheila. "But, if you figure on leavin' out in the mornin', I'll be much obliged to you." He took a deep breath, looked nervously around the room once more, then left.

"Well, I'll be doggoned," Sheila giggled as she closed the door. "Those things I heard about you havin' a reputation must be true. Ol' Alcie acted like he was talkin' to a ghost!" She shook her head and giggled some more, then jumped into the bed beside him, causing the bed frame to squeak. "Yessir," she said, "it did me some good to see him squirm like that."

"Why? What do you have against the sheriff?" Clayton asked, amused at her behavior.

"Oh, nothin' personally. It's just the way he throws his weight around over at George's. He likes to beat up on some of the fellers that come in and get drunk, but he ain't never had to deal with any real gunplay before. I heard he shot the Widow Brockelhurst's husband, four or five years ago. That was before I got here. I heard Alcie shot him with a double-barreled shotgun. And they say the widow's husband only had a pocketknife on him!" Sheila smiled at Clayton with admiration. "But boy oh boy! Was he scared of you! I wish George coulda seen it! George hates Alcie!"

Clayton was only half paying attention to Sheila, but he enjoyed the attention she so generously gave him. She made him feel good and occupied his mind, so he could forget about feeling bad.

Sheila's face grew serious.

"Killin's easy for you, ain't it?" she asked. "Who was the first man you ever killed?"

"I don't know. It happened a long time ago," Clayton answered honestly. He felt surprised at how quickly he answered her personal questions.

Clayton lay back, falling deep into the pillow, and stared up at the clapboard ceiling in the room while he thought back, to so many years before.

He was in Tennessee, at Camp Cheatham, on a hot July morning in 1861. As he stood in front of a long line of boxcars, the knapsack on his back was heavy, filled with rations. He carried two pistols, his rifle, and a bowie knife. The enthusiasm was so strong inside him, he couldn't stop himself from grinning. He gazed out at all the other soldiers that stood out on the platform. It was the grandest sight he'd ever seen.

Clayton could still remember climbing atop the boxcar, and the long and noisy ride toward Nashville. He remembered staring down at the ladies in every town, as they stood alongside the tracks, waving as the train passed by.

He was a member of the First Tennessee Regiment, which was traveling with the Third and Eleventh regiments. All of the young men were new. They were excited about going to war and "whipping some Yankees." They were on their way to Manassas, about to burst with the excitement of getting there and joining the fray, but when they reached Manassas Junction, the battle there was over. The disappointment could be felt all through the regiment.

From there, they moved on to Staunton, Virginia, then to Warm Springs, Virginia, climbing across the Allegheny Mountains. After Warm Springs, they were sent on to Big Springs.

Before long, it seemed like all they had done was march from place to place and stand picket duty. They stayed in

the Big Springs area until August. It had been the coldest
August anybody ever remembered, raining off and on for
days. It was there, at Big Springs, that Clayton killed his
first man.

He'd been on a scouting patrol, when he came upon five
Yankees. The rain had soaked everything. Clayton examined his supply of gunpowder. It was wet, too. He wasn't
sure if he could even get off a shot. He hunkered down
behind some bushes, where he knew the Yankees would
walk by. As he waited, his heart pounded in his chest.

When the first Yankee's boot splashed water not more
than two feet from where he lay, Clayton nearly wet himself from fear. The second, third, and fourth Yankees
passed. When the fifth had just gone by, Clayton rose up.
His legs trembled, and his hand shook so badly, he was
sure he would fail at the last minute. But the big bowie
knife remained clutched in his hand as he crept behind the
last Yankee.

So many times, Clayton had tried to think back to that
moment, but he just couldn't put the pieces together. One
second he was standing there, shaking, and the next second
his hand was cupped over the Yankee's mouth with the
bowie knife plunged into his body. A tremendous fear had
come over him, but there was also a great pumping of
adrenaline in his veins. The Yankee, though mortally
wounded, managed to pull free from Clayton's hand and
hollered for his companions. They turned and tried to fire,
but their powder was wet, too, and their caps just popped.

Clayton turned loose of the Yankee, who took one step
and fell to his knees. The other four Yankees were desperately trying to put in fresh caps. Clayton realized the danger, so he ran. Wet tree limbs cut into his face and ripped
at his clothing. The ground was soggy and sucked at his
feet, but his fear kept him running. When he decided he'd
run far enough, he stopped, his chest heaving. He sat down,
holding his rifle in one hand, the bowie in the other.
Through the gray sky that cut through the treetops just
enough to see, he stared at the blade. Rain and blood
dripped from it. Why had he done it? Why had he taken
the chance? He'd only been sent ahead to scout. He'd never

been able to figure it out, all these years later.

Back at the camp, everyone wanted to hear about his meeting up with the Yankees. Gathered around him, the boys he'd grown up with all wanted to hear the story, over and over. How'd he done it, they wanted to know? How'd he killed the Yankee? Clayton told the story again and again, and each time, a little of the excitement went away. Eventually, he got to where he was sorry he'd killed the man in the first place, although he'd become somewhat of a hero to his fellow soldiers.

The next evening, the regiment had a surprise visit from General Robert E. Lee. Clayton was sitting with two boys from home, Andy Bishop and Burgess Monroe. They were making him retell the episode again, looking for new details, when Lieutenant Fisk came and singled Clayton out.

Clayton was taken to the commanding officer's tent. There, standing out in the evening mist, was General Lee.

He was impeccably dressed and stood with his hands behind his back. Clayton was struck by his commanding presence and manner. He was still staring, openmouthed, at the old gentleman warrior, when Lieutenant Fisk formally presented him. General Lee gave a gracious salute.

"At ease, son. Clayton R. Crist, isn't it?"

"Yes, sir," Clayton said.

"Crist, I have been informed of your bravery, and I would like to shake your hand."

The general's grip was firm, but gentle, like the man himself. Their eyes met, and Clayton stared openly. He had never seen eyes that held a more childlike honesty and forthrightness. Though the face was mature and wrinkled, the eyes still carried a sparkle. Clayton felt a warmth go through him as he stood there with the general, with all of the officers in the regiment watching.

General Lee put his hands back behind his back and took a step forward. "Come, walk with me," he said.

Clayton found himself stumbling along behind.

"None of that," the general said. "Join me." He stopped and waited for Clayton to reach his side. "How old are you, Crist?"

"Seventeen, sir."

"Ah, seventeen. You may not believe this, but I can remember being seventeen years of age, almost as if it were yesterday. Do you have family back home?"

"Yes, sir. I have a mother and father back in Beartooth Flats. Got a little sister named Wendelin, but my mother was expectin' when I left home."

"Oh? Do you have any preference?" the general asked kindly as they walked through the wet undergrowth.

"What do you mean, sir?" Clayton asked, confused. He wanted so much to be able to converse intelligently with the great man, but he was nervous to the core.

General Lee smiled broadly. "Whether it's a little brother or another little sister! Any preference which?"

Clayton thought it a queer question, coming from such a worldly man. But, at the same time, he realized how great he really was, to care about a private's unborn sibling.

"Well, sir, Wendelin has been a mighty fine sister, so I wouldn't mind another girl, but I guess it'd be pretty grand to have a little brother, too."

They had walked under a heavy growth of trees, so thick it was too dark to see the general's face clearly. He turned and faced Clayton.

"Son, what you did, being the first to bring down the enemy, was a brave thing. But, at the same time, it most likely brought the realities of war home to you and your fellow soldiers. I know it must have been a traumatic experience for you, but it was one that a soldier must live with in times like these. There will be more rough times ahead for you, and you shall be in my prayers."

Clayton strained hard to hear every word from the soft-spoken general, but he strained even harder with his eyes to read the man's emotions. Big droplets of water fell down from the trees, splattering on the undergrowth below. Clayton looked at the shadows of the man's face, and at the whites of his eyes.

"Are you a praying man?" General Lee asked.

"Sometimes," Clayton stammered, not wishing to disappoint the general.

"Ah, yes, you're seventeen," the general said, his words sewn in kindness. "I suggest that you pray often to our

Maker, for it is only through His generosity and kindness that we stand here and talk. You see, except for the grace of God, that fellow that you killed today could be the one standing out in this evening, having this conversation." He fumbled for something in his jacket. "Take this, my son," he said. "It's a Testament. Read it, and find wisdom in the words. I pray that it shall not be so, but I sometimes think that this war could last a long time."

Clayton took the Testament. It was warm from the general's pocket. He wanted to say something, but he couldn't. There was a hard lump in his throat. Together, they walked slowly back to camp, both quiet. Once, Clayton glanced sideways at the general. He was taken at how the man could look so old from the side, but have such a youthful presence when one gazed directly into his eyes.

Just before they reached camp, General Lee turned and said, "May God be with you, Clayton R. Crist. Please remember me in your prayers tonight, as I remember you."

When he returned their final salute, Clayton had felt overwhelmed and tired. He had just killed his first Yankee, followed by a one-to-one meeting with the greatest of all commanders. He wanted to be alone to think and let it all soak in. But he knew that wish was folly.

When Clayton had returned to his friends, Andy Bishop and Burgess Monroe, others were waiting there with them.

Andy Bishop said, "They say you've been with General Lee. Did he make you a lieutenant or a captain? 'Cause if he did, he'll make me a general for all the Yankees I'm gonna kill!"

"Aw, behave yourself, Andy," Clayton said.

"Clayton's right," Burgess Monroe said. "I don't reckon killin' one Yankee will make a lieutenant out of you. It might get you promoted to corporal, though."

Clayton gave a tired laugh. "Sorry to disappoint you fellas, but I'm still just a private, like you."

Still, they all wanted to hear about the general, and the questions and discussion went on until they rolled into their bedrolls that night. Only then did Clayton find the quiet to think back over the events of the day. By then, though, it had started to rain. He went to sleep hunkered under his blanket, still wanting to think through the day.

After Big Springs, all the way to the Gauley River and down through the Kanawha Valley in West Virginia and back, Clayton was asked about the killing. Now, everyone wanted to hear about his visit with General Lee. Time and time again, they complained to him that the war would be over any day, and Clayton just might be the only private in the regiment who got to kill a Yankee.

They all agreed they had no intentions of going back home until they'd done likewise.

4

IT WAS a beautiful Sunday morning in Shiloh. The harsh cold of that dreadful January in Virginia was gone. Clayton had never been so cold in all his life, as he was during that time. Often, he'd thought he might freeze to death, especially at night when he was walking picket. Some men *had* died. He'd seen their bodies, lying stiff on the ground before they were taken away, frozen as hard as stone.

This Sunday morning, he stood outside enjoying the sunrise. Off in the distance, he heard the roar of the cannons and the popping of rifles. It seemed so peaceful where he stood, yet gritty reality lay ahead. Since the day he'd killed the Yankee and had the visit from General Lee, the men still talked glowingly about him, flattering him to the point where he was embarrassed. There had been other skirmishes, but Clayton couldn't actually say for sure that he'd shot anybody.

A strange feeling crept over him. This morning, orders had been given for the entire army to advance and to attack immediately. The First Tennessee had been instructed to support a brigade from Alabama. Clayton thought about his mother, a God-fearing woman who had always read the Bible to him and his sister. His own father had been a tirelessly praying man. This Sunday morning, though, the foremost remembrance Clayton had of his mother was how she had preached about keeping the Sabbath sacred. This was to be a day of rest, she'd said. But there would be no

rest today. *No rest for the wicked*, Clayton thought to himself.

Hurriedly, his regiment assembled and moved forward.
The roar of the guns grew louder. As the Alabama brigade
began to retreat, the First Tennessee was ordered to pass
them by and head right into the middle of the fray.

Clayton ran alongside Andy Bishop. Minié balls were
whizzing through the air around them, like big drops of
rain. Men were dropping everywhere. Clayton was trembling as he ran. His mind ran in circles. He wondered if he
would be able to aim steadily enough to kill a Yankee. The
bodies were lying in his way. He had to jump over the dead
and the wounded, who cried out for help. Clayton gritted
his teeth and started humming. He mustn't cry or show fear,
he told himself. After all, he was a hero of sorts to these
men. But he was scared to death.

He glanced at Andy Bishop, who was still running beside
him. Andy was small, about five-six, no more than a hundred thirty pounds, and athletic. Both of his parents had
been small people. He was a faster runner than Clayton,
and soon had outpaced him. He looked back over his shoulder and grinned wildly. Clayton tried to force a smile in
return.

"If they could just see us back home!" Andy hollered.

He was still looking at Clayton, smiling, when a ball
struck him above the right ear. At first, Clayton didn't realize his friend had been hit. It was the way his eyes lost
their excitement, then turned to shock, and then went vacant. He took two more steps, then fell, facedown.

Clayton stopped and stared down at Andy's body. The
air was growing thicker with balls. One clipped the collar
of Clayton's shirt. It felt like a bee sting. He reached and
grabbed at his neck, thinking at first that he'd been shot.
He gave one last look at Andy Bishop, his friend, before
moving on.

A few seconds later, Clayton got his second kill. A Yankee lieutenant, walking among some bushes to the right
with his saber drawn, caught his eye.

Clayton thought about Andy Bishop and all of the other
men he had counted as his friends, who now lay dead at

the hands of the Yankees. An anger filled his heart, and he cursed out loud as he fired his gun.

The lieutenant had not seen Clayton, and he never knew what hit him. Clayton's shot struck him dead center, in the heart.

He reloaded and kept firing, as fast as he could. Some other force had overtaken him. The fear had left him, and he could only think about ridding the earth of the men in blue. He couldn't kill enough Yankees. As the battle raged on, he had no idea how many men he killed. The Yankees began to retreat, but Clayton would have none of their quitting. He followed after them, firing and reloading, again and again, as fast as he could. He stepped and stumbled over dead Yankees that lay everywhere, sometimes stacked two deep.

An order was given to halt, but Clayton refused to stop charging. By the time he had totally spent himself and his anger subsided, he stopped to realize that he was chasing the Yankees all by himself.

He dropped to his knees, exhausted, and took several deep, trembly breaths. Tears were running down his cheeks as he wondered what all of his eager young comrades were thinking, now that they had had a taste of the real thing. For months, all the members of the First Tennessee talked about was having a chance to kill Yankees before the war ended. Well, what now? he wanted to scream. Had they had enough?

Slowly, he climbed to his feet and headed back toward his regiment. It was hard to find a piece of ground that wasn't littered with the dead. Everywhere lay bodies, twisted and bloodied. The sounds of cannon fire, missiles and minié balls that had filled the air were now replaced by the cries of the wounded and those desperately dying. Wounded horses lay thrashing and whinnying on the ground.

Clayton's feet were heavy as he walked back toward his line. All about him, young innocent faces filled with pain and terror called out to him. He came across one man whose side had been ripped open. His guts lay beside him.

The man cradled an arm around them and begged Clayton for help.

That evening, Clayton sat by himself, contemplating the day. He hadn't tried to be brave. Gallantry had been the last thing on his mind. There had only been anger in his heart. Still, once again his heroism was being praised all throughout the First. Burgess Monroe was alive, and Clayton was grateful for it, but he grew tired of hearing Burgess talk of Clayton's deeds and had sent him away. Out on the battlefield, litter bearers were hauling off the wounded, while a good number of Clayton's regiment were out, moving about like scavengers over the dead Yankees. They secured rations, guns, and ammunition. Federal greenbacks were everywhere. Even though most of the Confederates considered them to be useless, now that they had their own money, some of them still gathered up the greenbacks. They took personal items, watches, boots, and anything that glittered or shone.

One Negro servant, who had followed Captain Hawkins into the war, brought in a whole handful of greenbacks, watches, and gold pieces. He offered them to Clayton.

"These be fo' you, Massah Clayton," he said respectfully.

Clayton shook his head. "Thanks, but I have no room in my knapsack for such things. You keep 'em."

"No, suh!" the servant said. "Beggin' yo' pardon, suh, but Cap'n Hawkins would be right happy if'n you would take all of it."

Clayton smiled. "Tell you what. You tuck 'em in your britches. Tell him you gave them to me."

The Negro servant gave up his argument and reluctantly left, cradling the booty in his arms. As he was leaving, Burgess Monroe reappeared. Clayton wished he would go away. He couldn't stand the thought of hearing Burgess talk about his bravery all over again.

But Burgess had other things to talk about. "Have you heard, Clay-boy?" he said. "Them Yankees killed General Sidney Johnston. They also say General Gladden is nearly dead."

Clayton looked at him, but said nothing. He felt no more

remorse for the two generals than he did for any of the thousands of soldiers that had perished on both sides.

"Captain Connelly said you killed at least two dozen all by yourself, Clay-boy. He called you a fightin' son of a gun!"

Two dozen? That was absurd, Clayton thought. He only remembered killing the lieutenant. After that, he'd just fired at figures, never looking to see if they fell or not. Anger had been the only thing on his mind, dark and blinding anger that gave him a surge of strength that was over-powering.

Clayton ran his fingers through his damp, sweaty hair. His lips curved into a half smile. "Burgess," he said softly, "remember back a long time ago, when you and me and Andy were all trying to court Abigail Beecher? Remember how me and you both snuck up to her house, and neither one of us knew the other was there? When we got there, we found her with Andy, down at the spring drinkin' but-termilk!" He laughed out loud. "Boy, that Andy was fast!" He had to stop and swallow back the lump that had formed in his throat. "He—he sure was fast and fancy with that Abigail Beecher," he said again.

Burgess smiled and nodded his head. "Yeah, he was fast, Clay-boy. That Andy had a tongue full of honey. I wonder if he ever talked Abigail out of anything."

"I don't guess anybody'll ever know that now, but Abigail," Clayton commented.

That was the last time he or Burgess ever mentioned Andy Bishop. As the days and weeks passed, they saw many others die, just as Andy had. Sometimes, they'd talk about it, but mostly they just tried to get by. And life in the war moved on.

Clayton's feet hurt. In fact, the pain in the right foot started at the bottom and went all the way up to his knee. He turned over to look at Sheila. Her eyes were closed, but he could tell that she was awake.

"Ready for some supper?" he asked, not too loud in case he was wrong.

"You must have lots of money, honey," she said softly.

"Nope. I'm just hungry."

"I don't know if I'm wantin' to set foot outside," Sheila said. "I'll bet George is as nervous as a settin' hen with a fox in the coop."

"The hell with George. It's you that counts."

Clayton reached into his britches and pulled out some money. "Reckon twenty dollars would satisfy George for the night?"

"That would do it," Sheila said quickly. "Except George likes to have us around, so the cowboys'll spend more on drinks. But, in your case," she added, "I'm sure he'll understand."

Clayton felt relieved that Sheila was going to stay. Her body felt smooth and comforting next to his. She was good to talk to.

And he didn't want to be alone.

5

CLAYTON SLEPT with Sheila lying on his shoulder. Even though he'd always had trouble sleeping on his back, it still felt good, having her fragrant and womanly body touching his. He kept his head bent next to hers, so he could sniff her hair whenever he felt like it. His hand was wrapped around her shoulder, holding her baby-soft skin.

His rest was erratic. When he did fall into moments of deep sleep, he dreamed about his past.

This had been happening more and more often as he grew older and more tired in life. One of his most disturbing dreams took him back again to Shiloh and Andy Bishop's dying eyes. Sometimes, it left him feeling scared. Most often, he'd wake up feeling like the loneliest man on earth. He sought comfort in taking to a whore's bed now and then, but that companionship was only of a fleeting nature. Most of the time, he was simply alone.

But now, Sheila was there with him. And she gave him a special feeling. Clayton pulled her tighter against him and rubbed his hand up and down her back. He could never remember feeling more content or needed than he did with her. He let his hand slide down to explore her backside. It was colder than the rest of her. He squeezed the softness in his hand and patted her lightly. Her eyes still closed, Sheila turned her face up to his and kissed him, then put her hand over his on her backside. She smiled at him drowsily, and in seconds, her breathing was deep again.

Clayton let himself relax into the soft feather bed and drifted back to sleep.

"Wake up, Crist! Lieutenant Rice wants to see you," Corporal Hedren said.

Clayton sat up in his bedroll, rubbing his eyes. It took a while to realize that he was at Shiloh.

"Now!" the corporal barked.

"What time is it?" Clayton asked. It usually didn't take much to get a soldier rousted out of his bed, but for some reason, Clayton had fallen into such a deep sleep, he was having trouble getting oriented.

"Almost four in the morning," the corporal said.

Ten minutes later, Clayton stood in front of the officer.

Lieutenant Thurman Rice wasn't much older than Clayton, himself. He was a painfully thin man of the nervous sort. Most of the men made fun of him, for of all the men in the regiment, he looked the least likely to be a fighting man.

"Sir, you wanted to see me?" Clayton said.

"That's right, Crist. I'd like for you to scout out the Federal lines. We think Buell's army has arrived. We've been hearing a commotion on the river since yesterday evening. Seeing as we're the advance outpost, we need someone to take a look-see. Lieutenant Fisk has highly recommended you for the job. He, himself, has gone upriver to look around."

Clayton felt a sickening in his stomach. Like everyone else, he had assumed Confederate victory at Shiloh. It had been a nightmare, but hadn't they all seen the Yankees turn tail and retreat, running in all directions for their lives? He had fallen asleep, thinking that the worst was over—that they would simply take care of the dead and the wounded, regroup themselves, and move on. How could this be?

Surely, Clayton thought to himself, God would allow some sort of reprieve. But, as he listened to Lieutenant Rice's instructions, he knew that the worst was not over. He was turning to leave, when the lieutenant stopped him.

"By the way, Crist, as of this morning, you've been pro-

moted to corporal. May I be the first to offer my congrat-
ulations.''

"But sir, I don't wish to be promoted," Clayton said
truthfully. He had considered such a possibility when he
had signed up, but now he didn't want the responsibility.
Or the grief.

The lieutenant gave a small nod of understanding. "But
it is *our* wish," he said. "Let me tell you something, Crist.
You've been catching the attention of the big boys. That's
no secret. In fact, Colonel Reese wanted to promote you to
lieutenant." He gave an ironic smile.

"But sir—"

"I'm afraid there's no buts about it, Corporal Crist. You
have your assignment. Now, be off." Rice saluted briefly
and turned his back.

The night sky was dark, but Clayton's eyes quickly adjusted. He entered the vast void in the war, the neutral
ground that separated the two adversaries. Behind him lay
the First Tennessee and the advance outpost for the Confederacy, while before him lay the enemy. He felt open and
exposed as he crept silently across that void, praying that
he wouldn't be detected. The fallen bodies were black silhouettes, scattered like macabre rocks all throughout the
void.

Clayton had to stop often to get his bearings. He
crouched down low behind the bodies for cover. It made
him think about Andy Bishop. He prayed that God would
guide him away from his fallen friend. He tried to remember where Andy's body might lie, but in the darkness,
everything looked the same.

It took nearly a half hour before Clayton worked himself
into a good enough position to see the Federals' location.
Lieutenant Rice had been correct. General Don Carlos
Buell had arrived with reinforcements. Lots of them. Clayton thought of the ant colonies he'd studied as a boy in the
woods. That was just what Buell's troops looked like, down
below, as they prepared to join Grant's army. Clayton felt
his heart pounding in his chest. The rumors he'd been hearing lay confirmed below him. Confederate intelligence had
been insisting that Buell's troops wouldn't make it here

before the Rebels had a chance to rout General Grant's unsuspecting army. But here they were, come from Nashville and Savannah by foot. The Tennessee River was full of gunboats and transports ferrying Buell's army to the fracas.

The eastern sky was turning a pink tint on the horizon when Clayton returned to camp. He reported his findings to Lieutenant Rice.

"Just as I thought," the lieutenant said, drawing his skinny face into a grimace. More to himself than to Clayton, he shook his head and added, "We shouldn't have stopped yesterday. We should have run those Yankee bastards right into the river."

Clayton knew it was useless to go back to sleep. He lay down in his bedroll, until the orders came that they would advance and meet the enemy—to the last man, if need be. And, in Clayton's eyes, that was just what it would come to. The First Tennessee moved forward to meet the enemy. It was Monday morning, April 7, 1862.

Clayton was on the front line. His stomach lurched and churned as he steeled himself for the sudden rain of balls.

He took his first long shot at a Yankee who was running forward, holding his weapon loosely in his hand. He reminded Clayton of a young boy off squirrel hunting out in the woods and not quite ready to take aim. The Yankee fell instantly, and the butterflies calmed in Clayton's stomach.

Artillery fire shook the earth, and men from both sides began to fall like dead leaves from a tree. From his dangerous position, Clayton knew that his life was strictly in God's hands. His fear was gone. He was no longer the innocent young soldier who took his first Yankee on that day in the Virginia woods. Quickly, death on the battlefield had become as common as breathing itself. Life was there to be taken, none more special than another.

Clayton and his fellow campmates had dropped their airs of false bravado, but it wasn't fear they showed. It was a solemn acceptance that life's table had been set. This exact day, this war, was their moment in life, to live through in victory or to meet their Maker.

Clayton had heard all his life that no one ever escaped

death, but it had never given him a moment of concern. After all, dying happened to other people. It was something to be pondered when you got old and sickly.

But he had never pondered war, either. Now, today, death was the single reality that dominated every man's thoughts on that battleground.

Clayton briefly glanced down at the men who fell around him, looking to see if there was anything spiritual about dying that he could see with his eyes. But there was nothing. They just fell. Some never blinked again, while others took their time to pass to the next world. Always, the end was the same. They lay still and quiet, the fear and emotion gone from their faces.

Clayton was no more than twenty yards from the advancing Federals when he heard the order to retreat. He wasn't ready to turn back, and it made him angry. Why should they give up, he thought? Was it better to die anywhere else than here in the morning sun? Was another kind of dying any easier? He stopped and looked back at his own army. The soldiers had turned tail and were running, the same as the enemy had done the day before. Would the Federals go back to their camp today and laugh and tell stories about the cowardly Rebels, as the Confederates had done yesterday?

Clayton turned back to face the enemy one last time. He raised his rifle and took a shot at a faceless Federal, then hesitantly turned around to run for his own life.

Minié balls cut through the air around him, so thick, he expected to join Andy Bishop and the others at any second. He began to pray, but then realized that his Maker already knew everything. He knew who was going to live and who would die today. It had already been decided. With relief, Clayton felt the fear escape him. He started smiling as he ran.

Zip zip zip zip. Thud thud thud. The sounds of war were in every part of his brain. Why he hadn't been hit? God only knew. Clayton raised his face to the sky. He had feared God all of his life. Not a day had gone by in the Crist household when his mama hadn't read the Bible, or his papa hadn't spoken of fearing the Lord. Where was the sting of death? It almost made him feel guilty.

In a loud voice, he spoke to the sky, "Ain't it my time, Lord? Just what is my purpose here?"

He laughed with God, the great player. Why, this wasn't between the Conferates and the Federals, he thought. Nor was it between Johnston and Grant, or Beauregard and Buell. Politicians liked to talk about the Puritans from Plymouth Rock versus the Cavaliers of the South. Everyone called it a politicians' war. They said as how the Northern states wanted to help everybody by overseeing them like the kings and queens of Europe. The Southerners, on the other hand, preached their own style of brimstone, declaring that the states in the South wanted the right to govern themselves.

"But you know, don't you God?" Clayton said aloud. "The politicians can do and say all they want, but this is your war, ain't it? You have the final say on who dies and who lives another day!"

Clayton wished his army hadn't turned and run. They should have stayed, fought to the last man, and got it over with. After all, God had already decided who would live to tell the stories to their grandchildren.

"Let's don't prolong the agony!" he said. "Let's settle things now! Ain't that right, God? You know who's gonna make it. Why punish us along the way? Let us either go back to our families, or die here like men. Let life go on!"

Sheila's voice came up from the deep and into his dream, pulling him awake.

"Hey! Hey! You're havin' a nightmare!"

She shook him by the shoulder and gently patted his face.

It took Clayton several seconds before he realized where he was. She stroked his forehead and kissed his cheek.

"What is it, honey? You were thrashin' about and moanin' somethin' awful!"

"I'm sorry," Clayton said. "I didn't mean to wake you up." He felt embarrassed. He often dreamed about the past, but he usually slept alone. "It wasn't nothin'," he added.

"You're all wet and clammy," Sheila said. She took a cloth from the nightstand and gently rubbed his face dry.

"Well, whatever it was, it's all right now. Mama Sheila's here," she said softly. "I'll take care of you." She crawled on top of him.

Soon, the war was forgotten.

6

IT WASN'T yet light outside. Someone was knocking at the door. Sheila sat up.

"Who is it?" she called out sleepily.

At first there was silence. Then, "It's Solon Johnson. Is Clayton Crist in there?"

Clayton recognized his friend's voice. He and Solon had traveled together, off and on, for fifteen years. Solon was a lot like Clayton. He'd never settled down, partly because he'd never had anyone to settle down with. Solon was sometimes a heavy drinker, and it was usually after he'd fallen into one of his drunken stupors that the two men would part ways. During the time when Clayton had worked his place in Ness City, Kansas, Solon had shown up from time to time, stayed a couple of weeks or a month or two, then left. Clayton had never minded when Solon left, but he was always glad to see him again.

"Let him in. He's a friend."

Sheila lit the lamp and opened the door.

Solon Johnson was in his late forties, but he looked a good fifteen years older than Clayton. He stepped inside the room and glanced nervously at Sheila, who had the blanket wrapped around her. Her bare shoulders caught his eye. Then he peered into the shadow on the bed.

"That you, Clayton?"

"It's me, Solon."

"I got into town and heard you was here. I'm on my way to Caldwell."

"Well, damn! You-all get around early in the mornin',
don't you?" Clayton remarked.

Solon twisted the brim of his old hat in his hands and
glanced again at Sheila. "You know me, Clayton. Shoot, I
never could let the light of day get too high. Never was
worth a dern if I didn't get up."

Solon went on talking, filling Clayton full of information
about his latest whereabouts. Clayton lay back on the bed
and listened patiently. He was used to Solon's ways. The
man could talk forever, Clayton thought. He had learned
just to let him go on, while he went about his business and
caught enough of the conversation to know what Solon was
talking about. He reckoned Solon was the only man who
could talk for five minutes about the simplest subject.

Sheila crawled back into bed, and in doing so, dropped
the blanket she'd been wrapped in. Solon caught a brief
glimpse of her flesh as she pulled the covers up. His eyes
blinked a time or two and he twisted the brim of his hat so
hard, he rolled it into a scroll. For a second, he forgot to
talk.

"Give me my tobacco off the table there, would you?"
Clayton said to Sheila. He rolled a fixin', licked it, and lit
up. A piece of the paper fell to his chest and stung his bare
skin. "What're you goin' to Caldwell for?" he asked.

Solon was still watching Sheila. His knuckles had gone
white from clutching his hat. He shuffled his feet and swallowed.

He said, "There's a man name of Bassinger. Needs some
freight drivers. I was figurin' I could hire on 'til the harvest
starts and work right on through. A feller told me up in
Dodge that the work would be good for two or three
months. Then, there's cattlemen down in the Outlet that
could use some hands through the fall. To tell you the truth,
I need the work. I've been workin' for a man name of
Shorty Gillis on the west edge of Dodge. You know Shorty,
don't ya?"

"Yeah, I know him," Clayton said. "How in the world
did you manage to get along with Shorty?" Shorty Gillis
was a fine carpenter in Dodge City, but he'd never been
able to keep help. He was a worrier, and no one could

please him. In fact, most folks referred to him as Nervous Shorty Gillis.

Solon shrugged. "We just did. Oh, you know how Shorty is, Clayton. John the Baptist himself couldn't do right in Shorty's eyes. I just had to close my ears to his frettin' and complainin'. After a spell, though, it kinda got to me. I couldn't close 'em tight enough no more. Besides, there wasn't much else happenin' in Dodge. So, I decided to quit. That's when this feller told me about Bassinger over in Caldwell. I just stopped in here for the night." He paused long enough to take a breath. "I heard about what happened yesterday. Heard up in Dodge about that boy's brother, Sherman Parker, pullin' on you down in the Outlet. Those were bad boys, Clayton." He shook his head. "Bad boys."

Solon had the greatest of respect for Clayton, and throughout the years, he'd always justified Clayton's gun-play, whether it was a gunfight in the street or Clayton's gun for hire.

"You had breakfast yet?" Clayton asked.

"Ain't et a thing since yesterday noon."

Clayton knew Solon was broke. He always showed up with his pockets empty. Clayton, himself, still carried nearly three hundred dollars, left over from a job for a rancher out in far western Kansas.

"Well, looky here, Solon. You let me and Sheila throw on some clothes, and we'll go down and have some breakfast. What do you think of that?"

"Sure," Solon said, nodding. "I'll wait outside."

Clayton waved at him. "Go on, then." He knew if he didn't send him out, Solon would stand there, talking, while they all starved to death.

When Solon had left, Sheila giggled. "By gosh, I think that's the most nervous man I ever saw! He acted like he'd never seen a woman before."

"Is that so?" Clayton asked matter-of-factly. He wished he hadn't been awakened so early. He'd wanted to sleep in and spend the morning with Sheila, eating his breakfast in bed. But Solon was hungry, and Clayton knew there'd be no breakfast in bed with his old friend in town.

As they washed up and dressed, Sheila took her time.

She was thinking about her evening with Clayton. She couldn't remember a better night. In a way, it made her sad. She wished she wasn't a whore. She wished she could have met Clayton like other ladies met their fellows. Not that whoring was altogether bad. Quite the contrary. The pay was quite good, and she couldn't care less about what people thought about her.

Sheila had grown up in St. Louis, the daughter of a wealthy family. She could easily have been spoiled and turned socially toward the privileged folks, but her father hadn't allowed it. He'd been raised poor. His folks had saved every nickel they could for his education. Like them, he was an average-thinking person, practical and careful, and he had taught Sheila and her two brothers to be the same.

To her way of thinking, whoring was as necessary for her as opening up the store each morning was for a grocer. She provided a service that her customers needed. It was Dodge City where she had turned her first trick. She'd gone there with a man named Ervin Sandefer. At one time, they had talked about getting married, but then Ervin had gotten himself shot and killed. He'd always been an arrogant sort, and had gotten away with it back in St. Louis. In the mean saloons of Dodge City, though, it was a different story.

After Ervin's death, Sheila had had nowhere else to turn. One day, she let a rancher named McHendry talk her into frolicking with him for two dollars. It hadn't been altogether unpleasant, and she soon found herself working in a saloon that McHendry had money in.

A few weeks later, she'd heard about George and how he treated his whores fairly decent, so she gathered up her belongings and moved to Platt's Crossing. George was a good enough sort, except when he thought the whores might be getting out of line. She had never seen a gun in George's hand, but she had seen him whip an unruly cowpoke before the man even knew he was in a fracas. The other women had told her that he sometimes took a belt to the whores. It had never happened to her, but she knew she would leave if it ever did. George must have known it, too, because he'd always left her alone.

Sheila adjusted her dress at the shoulders and looked at Clayton. He was a pretty man, she thought. She wished it had been him instead of Ervin Standefer that she had left home with. Ervin had originally promised to take her to San Francisco, but then he'd decided there was money to be had in Dodge City. He'd told her they would stay there a while before they went on west.

Other whores, like Celeste and Mary, complained almost constantly about how they hated the drunken cowboys—how someday they would make enough money to leave the profession. Sheila couldn't understand why someone could hate something so badly and still do it. Both of them seemed to hate men, down deep inside. Sheila was just the opposite. She enjoyed the company of men, much more than that of women. She could talk to them about anything. She reckoned she enjoyed their attentions before and after frolicking more than during. In fact, most times there wasn't much to the frolicking. The usual customer was three-fourths drunk and ready to explode before he even started.

Still, Sheila longed for the day when she could marry and settle down. Clayton Crist was the first man whose company she enjoyed enough to think about such things. Yes, things might have been different with Clayton. Sheila pondered the idea. He surely didn't seem like a man who carried much baggage with him. He was a nicely proportioned man. He was kind of tall, maybe five-ten, she guessed. He was muscular and, except for his paunch, mostly trim. And he was breathtakingly handsome.

When they entered the hotel cafe downstairs, Solon was already seated at a table, drinking coffee. He jumped up and knocked his cup over. Coffee spilled across the white tablecloth.

Sheila giggled at his awkwardness. "Are you always this nervous?" she asked.

Solon just blinked at her, then looked at Clayton. "Dad-blamed coffee. Had the cup too full. Never could understand why they'd fill a man's coffee so full. And it's hot. I swear, they must've boiled it for an hour. Burn a soul's lip off!"

"Oh, a little spilt coffee won't hurt nothin'," Clayton said. "What's good to eat?"

"Ain't never had breakfast here," Sheila said. "I usually ain't up before noon. Sometimes, I sleep 'til two."

"Well, I declare," Solon said. "I couldn't do that. Good gosh! Two o'clock, you say?"

Sheila shrugged. "We usually just fix somethin' over at George's."

They ordered bacon and eggs. Talk was scarce as they ate. Solon dug greedily into his food, his eyes scarcely leaving his plate. Clayton could tell that Solon had a lot on his mind. Of course, he was always pondering something, and he loved to share his ideas. But this morning, he was especially nervous around Sheila. It wasn't that Solon didn't take a whore on occasion, himself. He usually fidgeted around about the whole idea, then mumbled something to Clayton about needing to go talk to a man about a saddle, before he took off for the nearest brothel. It never took him long. Solon was usually back in twenty minutes.

Clayton thought about it, but he could not remember ever seeing Solon sit down to a meal with a woman. Solon usually complained about females and their lack of serious communication skills. "All they know is silly gossip," he'd say.

As Solon ate, some egg yellow ran down his mouth and caught under his bottom lip, hanging there like spittle. Once they'd finished eating and were drinking their coffee, he said, "Where 'bout you headin', Clayton?"

"Oh, I think I'll mosey on up toward Ness City. I ain't been there for a spell. I keep thinkin' I'll fix the place up. Now might be a good time," Clayton said.

"You know, a feller could have a right nice place there if he worked it long enough," Solon said. He wiped the egg from his chin with his hand, then licked his fingers. "Me, I don't think I could stay in one place long enough to fix it up. Though I gotta admit, when a body gets older, he gets tired of movin' from place to place. How long you reckon you'll stay this time?"

Clayton stared into his coffee cup. He thought about Solon's question. It seemed like every time he'd headed back home, he'd always intended it to be for good. Several times, he might have stayed, if trouble hadn't always found him. Or a job offer hadn't come along with a sizable sum of money attached.

He reached for his cup and held it between his hands, with his elbows propped on the table. The woman who waited on them had just filled it. Solon was right, he thought. This was the hottest coffee he'd ever drunk. He blew at it, and the steam rose up and tickled his nose.

He said, "Oh, I'd like to stay this time. I'd like to be there long enough to put in some crops, maybe add to my beeves." Clayton didn't usually allow himself to think out loud, but then Solon had always been easy to talk to, when he wasn't talking, himself. And Sheila was surely one of the few women he'd ever felt this comfortable with. He put down his coffee cup and stretched, talking through a yawn.

"Yep, I'd like to get around to building a nice house. Maybe I'll do it this time." But suddenly he felt tired again. He couldn't understand this new feeling. It happened a lot lately, when all he felt like doing was sleeping.

"Well, why don't you do it?" Sheila was saying. "It would be sort of exciting, building a house and all. You know, doing all the little things, like decoratin' and such. Makin' a home."

Clayton finished yawning. "You're talkin' about a fancy place with a woman's touch, but I'm afraid my house is just gonna be a one-room affair with a privy out back."

"Oh no!" Sheila broke in. "You'd want somethin' nice. Two or three sleepin' rooms, at least! Who knows, you might even have young'uns someday! And you'd want a kitchen, separate from the sleepin' rooms. And what about a front room where you could sit in a rocker. Wouldn't that be nice?"

"Sounds like you've given a lot of thought to the subject," Clayton said.

"We all have our dreams." Sheila gave a small smile. "You need a woman's touch, Clayton, and that's a fact."

"Are you offerin'?" he asked her.

"You never know," Sheila said lightly, sipping her coffee.

She might have been teasing, but whether she was or not, an interest developed in Clayton. He could get used to sleeping with her, sharing everyday life with her. He hadn't allowed himself to think about settling down with one woman. But, these were silly thoughts. His interest died as quickly as it had come.

They all three finished their coffee in silence, as if too much had been said already. Finally, Sheila pushed her cup to the center of the table.

"Well, as much as I've enjoyed you boys' company, I haveta get back and clean up for work tonight." She smiled at them both and left.

Clayton absently swirled the dregs of coffee in the bottom of his cup, staring intently at it. He felt empty inside, and as lonely as he'd ever felt.

"You weren't serious about settling down with that whore, were ya?" Solon said.

Clayton pulled out his tobacco and rolled a smoke, then tossed the bag to Solon. He lit up and took a few pulls.

"Ever feel a need to settle down?" He paused, watching the smoke curl up past his face. "I mean, have you ever given any real thought to gettin' married and quittin' the trail?"

"I suppose," Solon said. "But, it's kinda like fartin'. I think about that occasionally, but once I've farted, the wind catches it, and then the smell's gone. I guess that's how I feel about gettin' married. My goodness!" He briskly shook his head. "I can't imagine havin' some female struttin' around, tellin' me what to do. You know, my mama used to drive my pap near crazy. Made him drink, I swear! Why, a wife'd be wantin' me to go to church, put me on top of the house in hundred-degree heat, fixin' the roof, and Lord knows what a body would have to do to keep a conversation goin' with one! Most women dern near talk your ear off! Oh, I suppose it's all right for some ol' boys. Me, I like my freedom. I like to come and go when I want. Say." Solon stopped and grimaced at the sad look on Clayton's face. "I believe that whore's done turned your head, boy!"

"Don't call her that," Clayton said.

"Well, I declare," Solon said. "If she ain't got to ya! I didn't mean nothin' about that whore business. 'Sides, who am I to judge what they do? I swear, if I ever did take a woman, I'd want her to be a whore. That's what they all oughta be in the first place, I reckon. Seems to me the only good women around are whores. At least, you can see 'em comin' and they don't make no bones about askin' for what they want. Give somethin' back in return, too. Hell, a wife can keep ya picked clean! You remember Augustus Clodfelter, down in Texas? Hell, a while back his wife just up and killed him. Caught him in the head with one of his own bottles, and he died."

"Why, hell, if I remember right, Augustus used to slap her around like she was a dog. Can't say as how I blame her for killin' the bastard!" Clayton said.

"Oh, Augustus wasn't a bad old boy. Certainly not bad enough to get killed over. Just goes to show ya." Solon let the subject drop. "So, you're sure enough goin' back to Ness City?"

"That's what I'm figurin'. You want to come along?"

Solon nervously crossed his legs, uncrossed then recrossed them. He frowned as he mulled it over. "Gosh, I'd like to, for dern sure. Always liked the folks around Ness City. You know, if a body was to settle down, it would be a fine place. But, I guess I pretty much have my mind set on that freight-hauling job in Caldwell. To tell you the truth, I ain't got much more'n a dime to my name."

"If it's money you're worried about, I got a little," Clayton said. "Frusher owes me a little, and I got seven beef cows. At least, I had 'em last year. Kirby Wiggins tried to buy 'em from me. Maybe I could sell off a couple. We could get there in time to plant us a big vegetable garden. Remember Whitey Golenback? He's always got pigs to sell. If we buy eight or ten sucklings, shoot, we can see ourselves through the winter. Next winter, we can plant wheat, too." He stopped a moment, feeling the fatigue wash over him. Maybe it was all too much for him, too. He looked sympathetically at Solon. "But, you've got that job in Caldwell waiting for you, and the stuff I got waitin' in Ness City is mostly my folly."

"I wouldn't say that," Solon said. "Why, we could go up there and fix the place up in no time. There ain't a better fence man around than me. And I like that idea about the pigs, too. I knew a boy down in the Outlet. He started out with maybe a dozen, and the last time I was through there, he was up to three hundred hogs. Told me he was gonna take 'em to Caldwell and sell 'em. About all profit, he told me. And them damned old filthy hogs'll eat anything!" He leaned forward across the table. "You know where you've got the dugout? I've always thought you could build a house on that little rise north of there. Won't have to worry about any high water, that way. You still got that scrap lumber from a couple of years ago, don't ya?"

Solon grew more excited as he talked. It was the same conversation they'd had a dozen times before, always working themselves into a high state of enthusiasm. Clayton, though, realized that this time, he really did want to go back for good. Something told him he needed to.

Just then, Sheriff Alcie Bryant walked through the front door. He looked the room over, then his eyes slid to Clayton. Behind him stood two nervous-looking men with shotguns. The sheriff walked up to the table and tipped his hat.

"Mornin', Mister Crist. I don't mean to be pushy, you understand. But you-all promised me you'd be leavin' town this mornin'. Now, I ain't wantin' no trouble."

Clayton looked hard at the sheriff. "For a man that ain't lookin' for trouble, it looks like you brought a little trouble with ya." He glanced toward the two backup men. "Those fellers are liable to get nervous and shoot. They might even hit you, Sheriff. I've seen it happen before. Ol' boys carryin' their big shotguns and rifles, get excited and shoot the wrong feller." His gaze slid back to Bryant. "Now, I told you that I was leavin' this mornin'. So you listen up. Don't be crowdin' me. You understand?"

Sheriff Alcie Bryant's jaw twitched. His face turned red. "Are you threatenin' me? 'Cause if you are, you better remember that this here badge says I'm the law around here!" He pointed to his chest. "You're not talkin' to me. You're talkin' to this badge. I told you once that I ain't wantin' any trouble. As good as I've heard you are, I guarantee one of these here shotguns won't miss if you try anything fancy.''

Clayton was surprised at the sheriff's words. He hadn't expected the man's challenge. There was something in his eyes that Clayton had seen in other men before—men who tried to put on a show of strength in front of others. A lot of men had sought Clayton out, with the desire to try their hand with a six-shooter and the reputation that came from killing a man like Clayton Crist. Most often, though, they'd show up all full of themselves, only to get nervous at the last minute and want to back out. Clayton always let them walk away with their dignity.

He had no want or desire to kill anymore. Only when he had no choice in the matter would he draw on a man. But, a lawman was a different situation. Clayton had always walked easily around the law and kept his distance. Though he wasn't proud of his past killings, they were mostly justified, not only to himself, but to everyone else. Killing a lawman would offer little justification, no matter what the situation.

''Give me an hour, Sheriff, and I'll be gone,'' he said.

Sheriff Alcie Bryant rubbed the day-old stubble on his chin. ''You know, I'd like to believe you, but I thought you would already be gone by now,'' he said. ''I guess I'll give you that hour, but if you're not gone by then, I might have to turn these shotguns loose.''

Clayton looked past the sheriff at the two men standing behind him. They didn't seem quite as confident as deputy lawmen should. When Sheriff Bryant turned on his heel to leave, the two shotguns followed behind, so close they nearly bumped into each other.

''Pissant sheriffs,'' Solon remarked. ''Why, if you'd said 'boo,' those two auxiliary deputies woulda shit their britches! That sheriff feller is just a low-down snake, I can tell. He was over at the saloon last night, runnin' at the mouth. That's how I first found out you were in town. He was goin' on about how he was cleanin' this town up. I figured it was just talk. You wanta watch a feller like that, though. He's the kind that'll sneak up on ya. Remember Garland Terrell, over in Coffeyville? He shot that Douglas feller, about a year ago. Fair fight if I ever seen one. I remember he was riding out of town, when that damn Sheriff Tim Crites put a bullet in the back of his head, then propped poor old Terrell up in the middle of town for everybody to look at. Ol' Crites stood there like he'd done somethin'. That's what this old feller Bryant reminds me of. I'll tell ya, I ain't got a lot of use for a lot of them so-called lawmen. I think most of 'em are ex-bandits, themselves. Mind if I have another one of them smokes?'' He smacked his lips and rubbed his mouth.

Clayton tossed him his tobacco fixin's. ''Well, looks like I'll be leavin' town shortly,'' he said. He looked at Solon. ''You goin' to Caldwell or comin' with me to Ness City?''

''Doggone it, Clayton! You done got my thinkin' mixed up here! Shucks, you know me. I always did fancy the idea of raisin' all those hogs.'' He shuffled his feet on the floor and rubbed his eyes. He pulled on his chin. ''Hell, boy! I reckon I'm goin' to Ness City with ya.''

''Well, I'm goin' across the street for a few minutes. I'll be back in a little while. You get our horses saddled.'' He paused and turned back. ''Hell, there ain't nothin' wrong with us bein' a couple of pig farmers, is there?''

''Don't reckon,'' Solon said.

7

CLAYTON STEPPED out onto the hotel porch. He felt pangs of guilt for not telling Solon his intentions of asking Sheila to go with him. But then, after all, how could he? It had been a rash decision, maybe not even a wise one, but he intended to ask her, just the same.

He watched the people going by on the street, then looked over at the saloon. His mouth felt dry, yet he was sweating. He was thirsty all of the time. What if he did have that disease that Sheila had talked about—the kind horses got? What did that say about his future? All the years he'd walked this earth, yet he still felt young inside.

He thought about Sheila. What was it that had drawn him to her so quickly? He'd enjoyed being with her, and not just for frolicking. It had been a long time since he'd been with a woman whose company gave him so much more than a few pleasurable moments in bed. There had been one other woman, years ago. It had taken a long time before he had erased Jolene Summers from his every thought. He could still see her standing there, as he hurried away from her Kentucky farm.

After Shiloh, the First Tennessee had moved to Corinth, Mississippi, to reorganize and fortify against the advancing armies of Grant and Buell. Rations were low, and disease was prevalent. It seemed like as many men were dying from chronic diarrhea as from battle. The war had become a game of cat and mouse. First the Federal sharpshooters picked off Confederates while lying in hiding, then the Confederates' own sharpshooters returned the favor. It was a vicious little game played out by both sides.

The fighting soldiers who sat low on the ladder of rank always had to be on their guard. This was tough, especially since they'd been told to relax and reorganize. But the danger of sharpshooters was all around them. Not only were they dodging Yankee minié balls, but they'd barely been able to survive the bad bouts of diarrhea. When they finally left Corinth, they were jubilant. Corinth had been as much a hell to endure as the fighting itself.

From Corinth, they moved to Tupelo, where they did manage to get reorganized without the Federal army disrupting the effort. There, they spent what to them was a leisurely summer. The drinking water was better, and the diarrhea that had weakened so many of the men was clearing up. Feeling like a fresh army again, they moved from Tupelo to Mobile, then to Atlanta and on up to Chattanooga. Then they marched the soles off their shoes all the way to Kentucky. It was there, in Perryville and in the midst of war, that love first pierced Clayton's heart.

The First Tennessee was at Harrodsburg, a few miles north of Perryville. He'd been sent ahead to take a looksee, his customary assignment since Lieutenant Rice had singled him out as the regiment's most proficient scout. General Buell and his army were camped on the other side of town. On hearing that the Confederates had arrived, most of the citizens of Perryville had left town. Clayton couldn't get out of his mind how strange war was. Here, in a little Kentucky town, thousands of Yankees and Rebels had converged.

He'd come across a farm, where a young woman was carrying milk toward the house. They were both startled to see each other, she because he was a soldier, and a battle in the town was imminent, and he because she was the most beautiful woman he'd ever seen. Her face was that of an angel, blue-eyed and fresh, with a perfect nose and a full mouth. If she had been a Yankee spy or sympathizer, she surely could have killed him on the spot, the way he stood there, dumbfounded by the sight of her.

Clayton's mouth hung open. He was speechless. All through the various towns the regiment had passed through, there'd been pretty Southern women to greet them. They'd offered up food and drink and sometimes more to their fighting men. More than once, Clayton had felt his heart start to flutter, but all he'd ever managed to do was take the food and drink and offer a sheepish thank-you. He'd envied the other men their ease with the women, taking them off on strolls and tucking the small, soft hands under their arms.

But now, here he stood, alone, with the attentions of a woman who put those other Southern ladies to shame. She had an easy smile, and after her initial reaction of panic had passed, her face had relaxed into a soft, sweet smile. She seemed to be flattered by the fact that Clayton was struck dumb by her beauty.

"Why, I declare! You've come to save me from them dreadful Yankees!" she said. Her voice was clear and fluid, like a bell.

Clayton just stood there, his mouth still open. He wanted to speak to her, but he was sure he'd say something ridiculous, and she would laugh so hard, she'd spill her pail of milk.

"My my! I do believe the cat has got your tongue! My name's Jolene Summers. What's yours?"

"It's Clayton Crist, ma'am," he managed to say.

"Come"—she motioned to him—"carry my pail for me. I'll bet you're hungry. There's roast beef inside, and fresh biscuits with honey, still warm. Potatoes, too. Do you like potatoes?"

Clayton took the pail of milk and followed the Kentucky angel into her house. He was surprised to find that there was nobody else inside. She smiled at him.

"Just set the milk down over there, if you would. Thank you kindly," she said. "You-all can sit down at the table. But get rid of that rifle. Put it by the door. The milk's good 'n cold for drinkin'. I just fetched it from the spring."

Clayton sat down. He looked around at the kitchen. It smelled good, like fresh-baked bread.

"Where's your family?" he said.

"Gone. All of Perryville is gone. They all left. The blame Yankees are on the other side of town. Did you know that?"

Clayton nodded. "Yes, ma'am. That would be General Buell's boys. Your family was smart to leave. You should have gone, too." He paused. "Why didn't you?"

Jolene put a couple of plates on the table and busied herself dishing up food for them both. "We didn't want the Yankees here," she said. "They took most of our food and grain. Everybody was scared enough, but I guess we could have lived with that. It was when we heard that you Southern boys were just a few miles away that everyone panicked and left. Now I guess they'll wait until the two sides have their war right in the middle of town, then come back and pick up the pieces."

"But, why did you stay?" Clayton asked.

Jolene looked solemn. "Where are you from, Clayton?" she asked him.

"I'm from Tennessee, ma'am."

"Is this the farthest you've ever been from home?"

"No, ma'am. I reckon I've been to Virginia, and West Virginia, back to Tennessee and Mississippi and Alabama, and now I'm here in Kentucky."

"Well, I've never been more than a few miles outside of Perryville," Jolene said. "I've lived on this farm all my life. My mama died when I was born, and my daddy took sick when I was eight. Just before he died, he asked my Uncle Harry and Aunt Esther if they'd come live here and take care of me 'til I was older. 'Marry her off to a good man,' he told them. 'Somebody who'll watch over our girl and take care of the farm when you're both gone.' Well," Jolene smiled, "that's just what they did. They've treated me fairly. They're good folks, and I don't begrudge them for runnin' away. But as for me, well, I just decided I'd rather die than run off and hide. This is my home. So, I just decided to stay here and watch over what's mine."

Clayton felt mighty glad about her decision, foolish as it was. Since the day he'd left home, he'd not felt this good about anything.

"Well, you wanta watch yourself around them Yankees,'' he said. ''I've heard they're not always gentlemen.''

''You-all don't worry about that,'' Jolene said. She poured him a large glass of fresh milk. ''I've got no desire to be takin' up with no Yankee. Although, I think it might be excitin', havin' a man fancy over me. The most excitement I ever have is milkin' ol' Jezebel.'' She smiled broadly at her own joke.

Clayton started to take a drink of milk, but he stopped when he saw Jolene bow her head.

''Dear Lord,'' she prayed, ''let us be thankful for the bounty You have set before us. We pray, oh Lord, that no harm will come to this house or to this man of the South, or any of his fellow soldiers. Forgive us, Lord, of our trespasses, as we forgive those who trespass against us. In His precious name we pray. Amen.''

At that moment, Clayton fell in love. He had never heard such a well-worded prayer. The fact that this woman, who was as beautiful as an angel on high, would sit across the table and pray for him with such warmth and sincerity in her voice suddenly stole his heart and pushed the gravity of war aside.

Jolene dished up his food, serving him a large piece of the best-looking roast he'd ever seen. She heaped potatoes on his plate, then split and buttered a biscuit. She waited on him like an honored guest in a European palace. Clayton had been so hungry for so long, the food was like a treasure, second only to Jolene herself. He had no more taken his last bite, when she refilled his plate with more food. Surely, he thought, she was an angel of mercy, and nothing from Heaven could be any nicer. It occurred to him that maybe he'd been hit by a sharpshooter. Maybe he was dead, and this was Heaven. After all, no one had any inkling of what a man woke up to on the other side. He turned his head and listened, but there were no sounds of gunfire to be heard. It was only the two of them, him and Jolene, sitting in the kitchen of the Kentucky farmhouse. He had before him the best food he'd ever eaten, and the most beautiful angel Heaven could offer praying over him.

Finally, Jolene cleared away the plates and poured him another glass of fresh milk.

"I'm afraid biscuits with butter and honey will have to be your dessert," she said. "If I'd known I was going to have company, I'd have made a pie." She looked him over and said, not unkindly, "I'll bet it's been a while since you had a good soak in a tub. I'll tell you what. Eat your biscuit and drink your milk. While you're doing that, I'll fetch some water from the spring and heat you up a nice bath. And, let me launder your clothes for you. I'll make them clean and soft to the touch. It'll do you good."

Yes, Clayton thought, he had, indeed, fallen victim to a sharpshooter. Only an angel would care so much for a dirty, bedraggled soldier. "You don't have to do all that," he said meekly.

"Oh, but I do. I want you to be strong and healthy. You see, our country must not fall to the Yankees. If it does, I've heard tell that none of us will be in charge of our own destinies. No, Clayton, you are a guest in my house, and a very important one to me and all that I care about. I couldn't think of anyone I'd rather serve than our Southern boys. Now, if you'd be so kind as to remove your clothes." She handed him a blanket. "Put this around you until I get the water warm."

Clayton felt just as he was, naked, sitting there in her kitchen with a soft quilt draped around him. Jolene filled several pails of water and set them on the wood stove. Soon, steam began to rise into the room. She took up his clothes and said, "When you think it's hot enough, go ahead and fill the tub." She went to the door, and added, "There's soap over there by the stove," before she left.

Clayton stared at the water. What if he hadn't died, he thought? What if Lieutenant Rice was to show up right now and find him standing, stark naked, in the home of an angel, instead of out scouting for the Confederacy? He guessed he'd be shot, right where he stood. After a little more thought, he chose the sharpshooter theory. Even if he wasn't dead, this was too much like Heaven to pass up.

He touched his finger to the water. Satisfied it was just right, he emptied the pots into the washtub and climbed in. His body odor rose up with the steam and struck his nostrils. Clayton grimaced. Everything else in Heaven had been

such a transformation, he couldn't believe he had gotten so
filthy. He lathered himself well, washing away the weeks
of sweat and grime that had built up on him. He took particular interest in washing his feet. The bottoms had a thick
layer of callused skin from the miles upon miles of walking
that the First Tennessee had done. Clayton was amazed at
the abuse his body had taken. There were bruises and
scratches on his arms and legs. His tired muscles slowly
began to relax in the warm water.

He was lathering his right foot when Jolene walked in.
Quickly, Clayton pulled his knees together and tried to
cover himself.

"I've hung your clothes to dry," she said evenly. She
paid him no mind as she walked by and busied herself with
washing the dishes.

Clayton sat there, watching her uncertainly, until the water began to turn cool. Finally, Jolene turned to him.

"If you like, I'll wash your back," she offered.

"That's all right," Clayton said, unsure of what else to
say. It was the first time in his life he'd been naked around
a female, except for his sister, and that had been when they
were both very young.

"Well, I'd like to."

Jolene took the soap from his hand and lathered his back.
Then she began to rub it gently with a cloth. It felt so good
and soothing. Clayton smelled her fragrance and began to
relax. He no longer minded that she was in the room with
him. Then, she had him stand with his back to her, as she
began to dry him.

Softly, she asked him to turn around, and their eyes met.
There was a flame burning inside him—a sensation he'd
never known before. Jolene began to unbutton her dress,
and then they embraced. No words were spoken.

It was Clayton's first time with a woman, but it could
have been his tenth, or his hundredth, for he knew that no
one would ever come along again that was perfect for him
as Jolene was. They ravaged each other's bodies, two people caught up in a desperate time and situation, as if both
of their lives had been waiting for this chance meeting.

All of the killing, the marching and starvation was behind him, as Clayton's flesh joined hers. In turn, Jolene, too, was escaping from her own imprisonment. She was a beautiful woman, left alone in a town that faced an uncertain future. Her right to dream of faraway places, of palaces and kings and all the things one wishes for, was now riding in the hands of the soldiers of the North and South.

Clayton and Jolene took their stolen time for all it was worth and gave fully to each other.

They stayed in each other's arms, neither wanting the moment to end, until the sun had set, and darkness covered the earth.

8

CLAYTON'S CLOTHES were still damp when he pulled them from the line. He kept a careful lookout, sure that if anybody saw him, he'd be shot for dereliction of duty. After all, he'd been sent out to scout the enemy's position, and he'd been gone, what was it? He tried to think. It was after midnight. Had he been here for more than six hours? Feeling a small panic, he hurried into his wet clothes. Before he left the farm, he took a last look over his shoulder at Jolene, and saw her silhouette in the doorway. He didn't mean to holler quite so loud, but his words filled the air.

"I love you, Jolene Summers."

He could barely hear her response. "I love you, too," she said. "Don't get yourself killed."

Clayton raced toward Perryville, running like he'd done the night the Yankees chased him at Big Springs. He stumbled into the middle of the little town and came to an abrupt halt when he heard his name called out.

"Is that you, Burgess?" he asked.

Burgess grinned. "Where in the hell you been, boy? Or, I mean, corporal," he said. He'd teased Clayton ever since his promotion. "By damn, we thought some Yankee had got you. Lieutenant Rice has been lookin' high and low for you."

Clayton walked over to where Burgess stood in front of a little community store. He didn't answer, but looked sheepishly back at Burgess. He could feel his face turning a deep red, but he tried to act as nonchalant as possible.

It was then that he noticed the three Yankees. They were

sitting on the steps of a church, directly across the street, watching him and Burgess.

"What in the hell's goin' on?" he asked.

Burgess shook his head. "Ain't this somethin'! That son of a bitchin' Buell is here. As you can see there, he's brought some of his pissants along with him and stuck 'em right across the street from us. In fact, there's pissants scattered all up and down the street. I got half a mind to pick one of 'em off, but I guess as long as they ain't shootin' at us, there's no need to start nothin'. Might as well live as long as I can."

One of the Yankees stood up. He hollered out. "Hey! Johnny Reb! How about we go in that store, there, and see if they got any licorice whips or peppermints. I'm hungry. 'Sides, I can wait until tomorrow to kill you!"

Burgess grew excited over the challenging words. He licked his lips. "I wouldn't be so all-fired convinced about that killin' idea," he shouted. "I was sorta figurin' on killin' you first."

The Yankee just laughed.

Burgess turned to Clayton. "What do you think?" he said. "Can we believe them sons of bitches?"

"I suppose if they intended to do any shootin', they already woulda done it," Clayton commented. "Tell 'em to come on over."

Burgess nodded. He turned back to the Yankees. "Well, I reckon if you-all wanta come on over real slow, we might see what we can find. That is, if'n you promise you won't be tryin' to trick us or nothin'."

"Oh shucks, Johnny Reb! My sweet tooth's got too big a hankerin' for what might be in that store. We're comin' across now, so hold your fire."

"All right then. You Yankees come on over."

Wordlessly, the three Yankees walked across the street, and joined Burgess and Clayton at the door of the community store. One of the Yankees, a redheaded one, broke the clasp off the door, and they all went inside. At first, Clayton felt a terrible guilt over it, but then he decided the store was apt to be blown to bits tomorrow, anyway.

"I ain't never been this close to a live Johnny Reb before," the redheaded Yankee said. "Where are you boys from?"

"Well, Yankee, you're talkin' to the First Tennessee. What about you? Where you Yankees from?" Burgess asked in a friendly tone.

The same Yankee spoke up. "We're all three from the First Corps. Army of the Ohio."

With pleasantries out of the way, the men went about pilfering through the store. The Yankees seemed to have a special fascination with a crate of eggs. They filled everything they could with eggs—their hats, knapsacks, and down inside their shirts.

"You want some of these eggs, Johnny Reb?" A bucktoothed Yankee asked.

Clayton shook his head. He studied the three Federal soldiers. They didn't look any different from the thousands of boys serving the Confederacy, he thought. Their faces were full of youth and mischief. There was a braggadocious sense about them, but all three looked like decent fellows from decent families. There was no way to justify war, he thought. Tomorrow, they'd all be trying to kill each other. Suddenly, he couldn't look at them anymore. He didn't want to know them.

When the three Yankees had their fill of everything, eggs, soap, bacon, tobacco, and lots of candy, they quickly made ready to retreat.

"You Johnny Rebs sleep good," the buck-tooth said. "My aim's going to be good in the morning."

The redheaded one stepped toward Clayton. The silly grin was gone. "Look," he said. "I wish you both a long life. I hope God in Heaven puts a shield around both of you." He nervously offered his hand.

They all stood there, suddenly awkward. There was no bravado in the Yankee's voice, only sincerity and a bit of sadness. Clayton reached out and took the hand. They shook somberly.

Clayton said, "I hope you have a whole passel of young'uns and grandkids to grow old with."

Silently, they all shook hands, then the Yankees hurried outside. As soon as they were gone, Clayton and Burgess closed the door tight and returned to the street.

"Burgess, where did you last see Lieutenant Rice?" Clayton said, knowing that he still had to give an accounting of himself.

Burgess pointed. "About a mile or so north," he said. "He was headed to that farmhouse that sits on the hill, yonder. Said they're gonna try to secure it for a command post."

The hair bristled on Clayton's neck. He excused himself and headed back toward Jolene's farm.

In a panic, he searched his memory. Had anyone seen him leaving the farm earlier? He'd left in such a hurry, he could easily have missed seeing anyone. Clayton thought about how close he'd come to being discovered, sitting naked in Jolene's washtub. They'd have shot him, for sure. Cursing under his breath, he forced his trembling legs to move quickly toward the farm. He was sweating profusely.

In the darkness of night, he reached the foot of the hill at the edge of town. From there, he could see many horses and the silhouettes of men, all standing around Jolene's house.

"Halt! Who goes there?" a voice called out.

"It's me!"

"That you, Crist?"

Clayton recognized Lieutenant Rice, who appeared out of the darkness. "By damn, we've been looking for you! We thought for sure you'd been captured," the lieutenant said.

Clayton was afraid to speak, for fear that Rice would somehow figure out exactly where he had been.

"Come closer so I can see. Are you all right, Crist?"

"Y-yes sir."

"Where in thunder have you been?"

Clayton blurted out, "Yankees are all over the place, sir. They're downtown, not more than a mile from here. They're standing right across the street from our own troops."

"Yes. Peculiar isn't it?" Rice commented. "Well, come with me. General Cheatham has set up a command post here. I got something I want you to do, and you're the only man I trust to do it."

He took hold of Clayton's elbow and led him toward the house. "Corporal Crist," he said, "there's a young lady livin' here. She's all alone. Far as we can tell, her family's all gone, along with everybody else in town. What I need is for you to watch over her. It's been a good while since the men have even seen a woman, and this one is a fair sight to behold, believe me. Stay close by at all times. I don't want any of our boys botherin' the lady, if you understand my meanin'."

Clayton was speechless. He wondered if his ears were playing tricks on him. Just minutes before, he'd thought his fate was sealed—that he'd been found out and might even be shot. He accepted his new orders with a subdued "Yes, sir," as Lieutenant Rice took him up to the farmhouse.

The quiet kitchen and front room were now busy with Confederate officers. Jolene had fetched a pot of fresh coffee from the stove, and was pouring General Cheatham a cup when she saw Clayton. Their eyes locked, and Clayton felt his worries wash away.

Introductions were made, then the lieutenant and Clayton went back outside. Rice pointed to the barn.

"Miss Summers will sleep in the hayloft. There's a little room up there, and she'll be comfortable enough." He followed Clayton's gaze to the dusty hayloft and grimaced. "War is a hellacious thing. As bad as it is for us, I think it's even worse for the people whose towns are beset by our battles and invasions." He turned sharply and faced Clayton. "You know, Crist, my Uncle Roy and his wife, Rose, live in Pittsburg Landin', there by Shiloh. I went over to visit their place that Sunday evenin'. Down deep, I was hopin' they wouldn't be there."

Lieutenant Rice was about to cry. Clayton thought of the ridicule and criticism that the men voiced toward the lieutenant behind his back. He made jokes about the man, himself, on occasion, but he wasn't laughing now. He didn't begrudge the man his tears; in fact, he looked respectfully away.

"But they were," Rice went on. "When I got there, m-my Uncle Roy was lyin' dead, there in the kitchen. He'd just sat down to eat, when a stray bullet hit him. While he was eatin' in his own kitchen! My Aunt Rose was kneelin' by him on the floor.'' Tears ran down Lieutenant Rice's face. ''She didn't even know who I was. She just sat there, cradlin' Uncle Roy's head in her lap.''

The two men stood there in silence for a couple of minutes. Finally, Rice took in a deep breath and composed himself. ''Forgive me, Crist,'' he said simply. ''Anyway, as I was sayin', this war is hell. Unfortunately, the young lady has to sleep in the hayloft, while our general occupies her bed. Security, you know. Some of these Kentucky folk are Yankee sympathizers. We just couldn't take the chance of havin' her in the house with us.''

He excused himself, and left Clayton standing there in Jolene's front yard. He sat down on a grassy patch to think things over, feeling his eyes being drawn to that hayloft over the barn.

It was nearly one o'clock in the morning when Lieutenant Rice and Colonel Patterson came out the front door. Colonel Patterson slapped his gauntlet several times against his thigh. ''Corporal Crist,'' he said, ''Lieutenant Rice, here, says he would entrust his own sister to your watchful eye. He claims that no man would dare speak a slang in her presence with you nearby. That's a fine recommendation.'' He nodded approvingly. ''You make sure no harm comes to Miss Summers during the night.'' He slapped his leg with his gauntlet, and added, ''By the way, Crist, General Bragg will be here tomorrow. He has talked with General Cheatham and Colonel Feild. They would like for you to take the commission of lieutenant. I must say that I agree. Your bravery under fire has been noticed by all, throughout the Tennessee Army.''

''Well, Colonel, I'm afraid the only problem is that Crist, here, doesn't want a promotion,'' Rice said.

Colonel Patterson flapped the glove again against his thigh and frowned at Clayton. ''Well now, that's something we will have to discuss later. You think about what I told you. You mustn't disappoint General Bragg.''

Later, Clayton escorted Jolene to the barn. They walked silently in the dark across the yard. At the door, she quickly stepped inside. Assuming she had hurried up the ladder to the loft, he followed inside and stood there uncertainly. It was so dark, he couldn't see a thing.

"Do you need a lamp?" he started to call up to her. Just then, he felt Jolene's arms around his neck, and she was pulling his face to hers. She kissed him long and deep. He started to resist, but the darkness around them made it seem so safe, like they were far away from the rest of the world. The war and the duties of war were forgotten as he gave in and pulled her against him.

Finally, she pulled back and took his hand. "Follow me," she whispered. She led him to the ladder and he climbed up behind her.

Jolene was giggling. "Poor Lieutenant Rice and his honorable decision to appoint me a guardian! I wonder if he's ever heard the story about the fox in the henhouse? Well, at least I have to admit he made a good choice! Why, I don't even mind havin' to sleep in my own barn. Not if I've got you to cozy up to." She giggled again and pulled his head to her bosom.

Jolene fell asleep naked, with her body curled next to Clayton's. He eased himself away from her and covered her with a blanket, then dressed and climbed back down from the loft. The night passed, more slowly than any time he could ever remember. He couldn't get life's contradictions out of his mind.

And tomorrow, he would hurl himself at the enemy, with only God knowing whether he would live or die.

9

DAWN APPROACHED, and Clayton was hovering between wakefulness and falling asleep. He was seated on an overturned bucket, leaning against the steps to the loft.

There was a rustling overhead, and he jerked his head upright. The straw sifted down onto his face. He yawned and stretched.

"Good mornin', Clayton Crist. It's cold up here without you. Won't you please come up?"

Her voice sounded husky with sleep. Clayton's body tingled all over. In his chest was a swirling that made him light-headed.

But they'd taken enough chances. Clayton knew he surely couldn't push his luck much farther. Barely above a whisper, he said, "I can't. If the lieutenant were to come in and find me with you, they'd shoot me for sure."

"Why, the rooster ain't even crowed yet. I imagine everybody's asleep. Come on. Please," she coaxed him.

Clayton shifted about and deliberated.

Life was short, he thought. Every time he went into battle, he knew it might be his last day on earth. In fact, the odds were stacked in that direction. His mind played back and forth. Finally, he decided, it came down to one question. What difference would it make whether he died out there, like Andy Bishop did, or got himself shot for being with the woman he now loved? The choice came quickly. He climbed the ladder to the loft, and again, they took each other, body and soul.

Afterward, Jolene lay with her head on his shoulder. She was hugged up tight to him, but her usual gaiety was gone. Instead of gently touching the locks of his blond hair and kissing on him so lightly, shivers ran up and down his body, she just held him and trembled. He felt her tears on his shoulder.

"Don't cry," he whispered.

"Oh, but I must! Tears are all that I have," she said. "I'm not given in to foolish hope. You'll be leavin' here soon, and you'll never come back! Clayton, I have to confess something to you." She paused and let out a shuddery breath. "I've never given myself to anyone before. I wanted to save myself for the right person. But now you're going to leave me."

Clayton squeezed her tight. "Please don't cry. I will come back, if it's God's will." He buried his face in her hair and breathed in her sweet womanly scent. "You're my first, too," he said softly, "and I pray that you'll be my last. Would you wait for me?"

"You won't come back." Her shoulders shook as she cried. In the darkness, he felt her hand begin to stroke his face with her fingers. "Let's leave," she said suddenly. "I've got good horses. Uncle Harry races them. Your General Cheatham offered to buy them last night, and he said General Polk will surely procure them, anyway. We could ride to Canada or someplace far away from here. You're about Uncle Harry's size. I could sneak in and get some of his clothes for you—"

Clayton put his finger to her lips. "I could never do that, Jolene. Why, we could never face ourselves if I was to desert. 'Sides, they'd catch us, and then what? No," he added, "I'll come back to you. I promise."

Outside, the rooster crowed. Reluctantly, Clayton pulled himself away from her and crawled down the ladder. A couple of soldiers were walking about outside, and the farmhouse was becoming astir. He had once again escaped from being caught with Jolene, but the idea gave him little hope or happiness. He went about his duties, and never got a chance to see Jolene again that morning.

Across the way, on a hill, the Yankee line was drawn.

Clayton and his fellow Confederates formed their lines, and the two enemies readied to engage themselves.

Soon, a calm fell over the men. Some joked and seemed to be laughing at the gravity of the situation. Some looked eager, while others were in thoughtful moods. Both armies stayed put, eyeing each other, until midmorning.

It was strange, Clayton thought. There'd been some scattered musketry fire since early morning, but nothing of significance. Now, both armies sat, watching each other like they were all in a trance. The eastern sun was shining in his eyes, and he felt them grow heavy. He nearly dozed off on several occasions. He would get to thinking about Jolene and lying with her in that soft yellow hay, only to have some soldier's laughter wake him back up to what was really happening.

It was nearly ten-thirty when the whole Yankee army started shifting their position to their left. Orders were soon given for the Confederates to shift right. This cat-and-mouse game was played out until almost two o'clock, when the North finally unleashed their thunder.

The Federal cannons ripped into the beautiful Kentucky landscape. The whole ground shook as if the earth had split right open and the devil had turned serene Perryville into hell on earth. Order was given to return fire, and the two enemies commenced toward each other.

Suddenly, Clayton's legs grew heavy. It surprised and scared him. In every previous battle, for some reason that was more of a mystery to him than anything else, he had dashed forward with a vengeance. At first, he had always felt a revolting sickness in his innards, but then, it was as if some magic hand was placed upon his back, pushing him into the fight. The rage would fill his heart and take over, turning Clayton into a killing frenzy. He had never understood the change that came over him. It made no sense to him, because when the battle or skirmish was over, he would nearly collapse with horror over what had happened.

He had tried to think it out in his mind. Why had he been allowed to live through such impossible acts? So many of his fellow soldiers had died along the way. He had seen the minié balls come rushing toward him so hard, it

was like rain turned sideways. Yet he hadn't received a
scratch. Sometimes, he wondered if he was invincible. How
else could he perform such distinguished acts, when he felt
such a powerful fear inside before the battles commenced?
It puzzled him deeply. He hated the fighting and prayed
daily for the war to end, while all around him, his fellow
soldiers whooped and hollered before battle. It reminded
him of a circus atmosphere. They couldn't wait for the killing to start, but then, when the cannons began to roar or
the shooting filled the air, these braggadocious, eager soldiers' faces would suddenly turn white with fear. They
would make little effort to fight, and sometimes they turned
and ran. Clayton had seen men drop to their knees and bawl
like little boys attached to their mothers' apron strings.

But Perryville was different. The hand wasn't behind his
back this day. That mysterious urgency that pushed him
forward through incredible odds was gone. Clayton hadn't
gone more than ten steps forward, when men on either side
of him dropped. But Clayton's gait stayed the same. He
was within fifty yards of the advancing enemy, and he still
hadn't put off a shot. He sweated profusely. His eyes darted
about.

He could see the enemy from their chests up as they rose
up to fire, the smoke from their musketry swirling everywhere like clouds. By this time, he should have been out
in front of his own line, firing and reloading, firing and
reloading, but his rifle was silent.

He looked around in all directions, feeling the alarm rising up inside. Surely, he knew, he couldn't just dodge bullets all morning. But he couldn't fire back. He found
himself ducking and wincing as he heard the balls ripping
into his companions with sickening thuds. He listened to
their cries as they fell to the earth. Milt Brewer, whose folks
lived on a farm in Tennessee six miles from Clayton's,
dropped to his knees, at Clayton's right. A big shell from
the Federal artillery had ripped his right arm off, shoulder
and all. Clayton's legs felt weak as he ran to Milt Brewer
and stared at the horrific sight. Milt had been one of those
braggadocious soldiers, who always made the comment before each skirmish, "It's a great day for a fight. I think I

will kill ten Yankees today.'' Now, that arrogant face was frozen into a look of bewilderment. His tongue darted in and out of his mouth, but it was his eyes that made Clayton nearly turn and run. Milt was looking at Clayton, but there was no life left in them. They were blank and dull, as if they had a coating of death on the surface.

Clayton started to reach out for his fallen friend, but then Milt fell forward. His head struck Clayton in the chest and knocked him to the ground. The two men went down together, and Clayton fell underneath, with Milt draped over his legs. He felt Milt's blood flowing out like a stream, and panic swelled up inside him.

''Get him off!'' he screamed out hysterically. Milt's blood was warm as it soaked heavily into Clayton's trousers. ''Get him off!'' he screamed again. He sat up and took hold of Milt Brewer's head with both hands. He tried to push him away, but then Milt's left hand reached up and grabbed Clayton's shirtsleeve.

Clayton's terrified scream pierced the air. He yanked his sleeve away from the dying man's grip and managed to pull himself free. But then another body crashed into Clayton from behind. The ground shook from artillery fire. Clayton began to cry.

It was the first time he'd cried since he was a little boy. Clayton looked out over the macabre scene of death. He watched the two battle lines as they became one. The shooting war had turned into a deadly fight of hand-to-hand combat. Both sides fought savagely with their bayonets affixed to their rifles.

Clayton couldn't stop thinking about Jolene Summers and her fears that they would never see each other again. He stared at the dead and dying around him and wished he had climbed upon her uncle's horse and ridden away with her.

He knew then why that hand was missing from his back. It was Jolene. He must live for her. A ball struck Milt Brewer in the back of the head, but he had already died seconds before. Another ball snapped the limb off a small tree at Clayton's left.

On his knees, he looked skyward. ''Is it my time, Lord?''

he asked. "You know, I almost forgot that this is Your battlefield. You make the decisions. Is Milt there yet, Lord? Do you see him? Is he smiling? That boy had a heck of a smile, Lord."

Suddenly, Clayton felt that urgency return. It filled him up. He nodded up at the sky one more time before he rose to his feet and tried to shake the blood from his pants. Then, he ran hard to the fight in front of him.

Two Yankees had broken through and were in his path. Clayton shot one and killed the other with his bayonet, as the Yankee tried to reload. He looked closer and recognized the redheaded Yankee from the night before at the store. Clayton could still feel the firm handshake and hear the words he'd spoken. He remembered the Yankee's kindness and the warmth in his eyes.

Turning away, he cursed Lincoln and Davis and Buell. He cursed Hood and Cheatham, and Grant and Bragg. He cursed the dead as well as the living. He cursed Milt Brewer and everyone he could remember that had talked of war and the glory of it. He wished he could pull the bayonet back. He looked down at the redheaded soldier from the First Corps of the Army of Ohio. The man looked like he was asleep, except for a twitch in his neck.

"I'm sorry," he said, and turned to the fighting ahead. That hand was back, pushing him forward, and Clayton threw himself into the battle with more vigor than he had ever before mustered.

Clayton thought the fighting would never stop. All around him, men fought to the death, while another Federal line in the distance kept the musketry fire going. Clayton forgot about living and dying. He stopped wondering who was falling or who was winning. Blood dripped from his bayonet like water from a tree after a heavy rain. It ran down the stock of his rifle and covered his hands. He could feel the stickiness between his fingers. But he kept on killing.

It wasn't until someone who made such decisions ordered the two armies to separate and regroup, that Clayton drew himself out of his killing rage.

Later, he stumbled out into the middle of the Chaplin

River and sank, exhausted, into the shallow water. He tried desperately to wash off the blood from his arms and legs. All he could think of was Jolene. He must go to her.

He climbed out of the little river and walked past the dead and wounded. A Yankee grabbed at him and begged for water. Clayton pulled his leg free and moved on. He spotted Colonel Patterson. The colonel was still wearing his gauntlets and looked like he was dressed for a wedding. Only he was stone-cold dead. Clayton thought briefly about their talk the night before, but his mind refused to dwell on it.

For the first time in his life, the death around him failed to spark any emotion at all. It was Jolene he cared about. Soldiers died every day.

10

THE CITIZENS of Platt's Crossing eyed Clayton openly as he crossed the street. Some carried a wary fear of him, while others were just curious. He ignored their gawking and murmured comments as he stepped into the saloon.

There was no one inside except for George the bartender. He was washing glasses behind the bar.

"We're not open yet, Mr. Crist. I should've locked the doors," George said.

"I'm here to see Sheila," Clayton said.

A glass slipped from George's fingers and shattered on the floor. It was plain that he was nervous, and he wasn't about to offer any challenge. He nodded toward the stairs.

"Third room, top of the stairs," he said meekly.

Clayton tapped on the door. Sheila seemed surprised to see him. "Good mornin' again," she said. "Did I leave somethin' behind?"

"Just me," Clayton said. He stood in the doorway, avoiding her eyes. I was wonderin'—" he began. "Well, it ain't much, you understand. It's nothin' but a dugout right now." He searched hard for the right words. He had never had any trouble conversing with women, but then he'd never asked one to come and live with him, either. "I was wonderin'," he began again.

Sheila took his hand and pulled him into the room. "Yeah, I know," she said with a smile. "You were wonderin' if I would come with you. The answer is no."

Clayton opened his mouth to speak, but Sheila put her

68

hand over his lips. "Don't think it's nothin' against you," she said, " 'cause it sure ain't. It's just that I don't think things would work out. You're like all the cowboys, Clayton. You were lonely last night, and I'm—well, as you cowboys like to say, I'm just a whore. If I went with you, you'd wake up someday and realize that's all I am, and then I'd be stuck somewhere, on my own."

"You're wrong as rain," Clayton argued with her. "Why, I don't feel that way, a-tall! Who am I to judge what you've done? Looky here! I've never asked anyone to share my life with me before—"

She touched his cheek. "You don't want me," she said. Her gaze fell on his eyes. "You're too pretty. You could mess up a woman's thinkin' with those blue eyes of yours. And don't think I ain't tempted. No," she sighed. "You just came along at the wrong time in my life. I'm makin' a good livin' here with George." She pulled his head to hers and kissed him. "You want to diddle one last time? It would be on the house."

Clayton angrily pushed her hand from his face and shoved her backward. "That ain't what I want, and you know it," he said. "You can just save your diddlin' for your other customers."

He didn't notice the sadness in her eyes as he abruptly turned away and left her.

Solon was waiting for him on the steps. He followed Clayton to where their horses were tied.

"I don't mind tellin' you I'm ready to leave this place," Solon said. "That blamed sheriff gives me the creeps."

Clayton silently swung atop the roan and gave spur to the horse. They rode at a steady lope, quickly putting distance between themselves and Platt's Crossing. Solon tried several times to offer up a comment for a topic of conversation, but Clayton only answered him with more silence.

Solon let two hours pass before he finally blurted out, "Doggone it, Clayton! I know I ain't no sparky conversationalist, and it's okay if you don't wanta say more'n one word every few hours, but you're gonna kill these horses before we get to Dodge City."

Solon was right. Clayton pulled rein on the roan. He

climbed down from the horse and took a big drink of water. His mouth felt as dry as cotton.

"I bet we're gonna have a hot summer," Solon said. "Anytime we have a cold winter, we have a hot summer. I felt like I was about to freeze this mornin', and it's spring-time. Must be that cussed wind. I ain't never got used to the wind. Down in Texas, we got some wind, but not like Kansas." He shook his head. "Wind can make a bad day seem ten times worse. You just wait. In a couple of months, the temperature will be over a hundred, and when that cussed wind starts blowin', it'll be like you're standin' next to a campfire."

Clayton unsaddled the roan. He dropped the saddle next to a dead tree stump, then sat down and leaned against it. He reached for his canteen and took another long drink.

Solon stood next to his horse, watching Clayton doubt-fully. "We ain't fixin' to make camp here, are we?" he asked. "Truth is, I'd like to put more distance between us and the sheriff. I just don't trust that fellow."

Clayton said, "I'm tired. Seems like I'm tired all the time, anymore."

"You're just gettin' old," Solon said. "It gets worse, you know. I'm a lot more tired now than I was at your age. Remember when we was workin' for Jess Breedlove? Remember how he walked around with that cane?" Solon laughed. "Hell, I just thought the man was lazy. But now that I'm his age, I think sometimes I could use a cane."

They sat there into the afternoon, Solon talking and Clay-ton drinking his water. Clayton tried to sort out his thoughts. He felt silly for asking Sheila to go with him. That would be a story she could tell for a long time, he thought. It would make a fine joke.

He didn't know what had come over him. But, it had somehow seemed like a good thing to do. He knew now that it was a lucky thing Sheila had refused him.

But why did he still feel so miserable and lonely? Solon had been talking since they'd stopped to rest, but Clayton felt as lonely as if he were sitting there all by himself. He guessed that, deep down, he knew why he'd made such a fool out of himself and invited Sheila along. He'd been smitten by her. His thoughts drifted back to Jolene. It had been the same way with her, only he'd known right away that he loved her, deeply and everlasting. He surely didn't feel as strongly about Sheila, but he was smitten, nonetheless. She'd been good to him and shown sympathy over his illness. Maybe that was it. Maybe this was more of a gratitude for her kindness. Whatever it was, he couldn't get her out of his mind, and he couldn't help feeling sorry that she wasn't with him right now.

Solon was in the middle of one of his one-sided discussions. Clayton broke in. "Do you ever think about your past?" he asked.

Solon looked surprised. He had to mull it over a moment. "Yeah, I suppose I do," he finally said. "Like I've told you, Clayton, you're gettin' older. Lookin' back on what's been, or what might have been—that's one of the signs. You remember ol' man Fox?"

Clayton nodded.

"Remember how he was always tellin' those stories about early Texas? I believe the man was just gettin' old. Dwellin' on his memories." Solon frowned. "I always heard that, when a body gets old, he turns back to like he was when he was a child. By dern, ol' man Fox was a livin' testimony to that theory. You thinkin' about your past, Clayton?"

"Yes, I am. Seems like I've been thinkin' about it a lot lately," Clayton said with a note of sadness. He pulled out his tobacco and rolled them each a fixin'.

"Well," Solon said cheerily, "don't let it worry you none. You know what they say. 'What's done is done.' A body couldn't change things if he wanted to. The Widow Tucker used to tell me that all the time. She was always tryin' to give me religion, you know. Come to think of it, I don't think that was all she was tryin' to give me." He chuckled at the remembrance. "Anyhow, she had these theories in life, and one of them was how you just can't change things. What's done is done, and that's that. I reckon it would drive a body crazy if they spent too much time worryin' about it. As for myself, I can't help but think about some things. Just this mornin', I was thinkin' about

Shorty Gillis and how hard he was to please. I swear, if
that man dies and goes to Heaven, he'll find somethin'
wrong with the place. God didn't do this right, or God
didn't do that right!'' He stopped and took a long, contented draw off the cigarette. He noticed that Clayton was
staring off, looking even more unhappy. Solon added
kindly, ''I wouldn't be worryin' about things, Clayton.
Those were fair fights you were in.''

''Oh, I don't know about that, Solon,'' Clayton said in
a tired voice. ''I mean, given the choice, I would just as
soon not have killed anybody, but you ain't always given
the choice. No, what I was wonderin' about was life itself.
Seems like lately I can't close my eyes that the past ain't
there.''

Solon nodded and stared off into the distance. He had
his own burdens, but he certainly didn't have to wrestle
with the demons that plagued a man like Clayton Crist.

''Well,'' he said, ''if you're askin' me if it's normal, I'd
say most likely. Heck, it might even be good. Maybe that's
how we learn.''

Clayton pulled his hat over his eyes and wished he was
back in Platt's Crossing. Hard as Solon was trying to be
good company, he would have felt a lot better with Sheila
sharing his bedroll.

He let his memories carry him off to sleep, with Solon's
voice an unlikely lullaby.

11

PERRYVILLE HAD been vicious and bloody. The horror of war had turned the peaceful little town into a canvas of man's brutal ability to destroy. Clayton had become separated from his outfit, but instead of looking for them, he headed for Jolene's farm. His thoughts were too muddled. He had to see her, to talk to her and straighten everything out in his mind while he held her in his arms. He needed to tell her that he wanted her forever.

He was thinking about what he would say to her. The images of the battle kept crowding into his thoughts, and he tried to brush them away and concentrate on Jolene. It made him feel a little guilty, not wanting to think about the war and the fine boys who had been lost that day, but what good would it do, anyway? He was still wrestling within himself when the farm first came into view.

From a good distance away, he could see the destruction. Clayton walked faster, then broke into a run. ''No!'' he cried out, his breath catching in his throat.

The house had taken artillery hits, almost dead center. It was destroyed, with only three walls standing. Clayton searched frantically through the rubble, calling out her name, but there was an air of eerie silence. Panic-stricken, he raced to the barn and climbed up to the hayloft. Even in the darkness, he could see that there was no life there.

Like a child lost from its mother, he ran back to the ruins of Jolene's farmhouse. Again, he dug through the debris until his hands were cut and bleeding. There was no sign of her anywhere. Clayton sat down where the kitchen had once been and cried. He cried like he had when he was seven years old and his grandpa had just died—unashamed. He stayed there half the night, crying until his eyes were swollen and his head pounded with pain.

It was three o'clock in the morning when he left the farm. He wandered about, waking soldiers from their sleep to ask if they'd seen Jolene. Most of them had no idea who or what he was talking about. Finally, he found Lieutenant Rice, who informed him that he hadn't seen Jolene since early the day before.

Morning was on the horizon when Clayton stumbled down to the spring and called out her name. His voice was hoarse and nearly gone. He fell down there, and finally cried himself to sleep.

Jolene had vanished, almost as if she had never existed.

When the First Tennessee left Perryville, it almost left without Clayton. It was the hardest decision he had ever made to leave the little farm behind, not knowing what had happened to Jolene. The army headed for Camp Robinson, where they drew rations, before moving on to Cumberland Gap, and then to Knoxville.

Soldiers griped and complained all along the way, and with good reason. Food was in short supply, and the men were so hungry, even the songbirds in the air weren't safe from their guns. The Confederate Army was in desperate need of provisions. The men's clothes rotted on their bodies, and their bellies clung to their backbones. Clayton thought he would be eaten alive by the scourge of ticks, fleas, and lice.

He had joined the army strong and healthy. Standing five-ten, he'd weighed in at 178 pounds. Now, his weight had dropped to 140. Not only was it the hunger. It was the chronic diarrhea that also deprived his body of its size and strength. It had gotten so bad, he'd had to throw away his filthy, threadbare drawers and go without. The lack of nutrition had turned his skin a pallid gray. Dark circles ringed his eyes.

It offered him no comfort to see that the other men were suffering as well. Most of them were complaining of the diarrhea, and a spirit of depression had settled over the army. Clayton kept his mind focused on only one thing. His memories and hopes of seeing Jolene again kept him alive and moving. It was at Knoxville where Lieutenant Rice summoned Clayton to his tent.

A deep snow had fallen, and the lieutenant's tent was about to cave in from the weight of the snow. Lieutenant Rice was nervous and full of concern. He knew there wasn't a better fighting man in the regiment—perhaps the whole army—than Clayton Crist. But that fighting man looked to be at death's door. Rice worried about all the men. He knew they were sick and battered and tired. Not a day went by that he didn't grieve over the losses and curse his superiors for the leadership that had brought the men to this. He'd been taught that war was a noble thing, but Rice had seen nearly as many men die from disease, accidents, and suicides as from the battles themselves.

"Men become hardened to the atrocities of war," Colonel Feild had told him. "It has to be that way, Lieutenant Rice, or we would all go crazy."

The colonel's observations did little to convince Rice. He couldn't stop worrying over the welfare of every single man who fought for the Confederacy. He prayed for them constantly.

But the lieutenant carried an even more special feeling for Clayton Crist. Not only was it a personal fondness, but he had a respect for Clayton above all the other men.

In his tent, he looked Clayton over. "I'm worried about you, Crist," he said. "You look like walking death. I can't have you sick. I don't want to lose you. Now, this army's heading for Chattanooga. Hopefully, we're going to quarter there through the winter. Here." He handed Clayton a folded paper. "I spoke with Colonel Feild about this, and I want you to take a leave. Go see your family, get rested and well, and meet back up with us at Chattanooga. Colonel Feild is going to loan you the use of Captain Reardon's horse. As you know, the captain was severely wounded at Perryville, and is hospitalized."

Clayton's eyes remained fixed on the lieutenant's face. His expression stayed the same. He was too weak to feel any joy in the lieutenant's words. "But sir," he said, "all these Tennessee boys are sick. They need to see their families, too. It ain't right that I get to go and they don't."

Lieutenant Rice was nodding his head. He said, "Of course, you're right. And if I was the big monkey in charge, you can bet I'd let many go home. At least, I'd make darn sure they were all properly fed. But, that's not the case. Colonel Feild thinks you should get well again, and I agree." He pulled a cigar from his pocket and handed it to Clayton, then lit another for himself. "General Bragg's aide gave me a handful of these cigars. He's a distant cousin of mine. It's good tobacco. Fine Kentucky tobacco." He puffed a few times, then took the cigar out of his mouth and examined it closely. "I can't justify sending you and none of the others. I can only say that it's been given a great deal of thought, and losing you, Crist, would be like losing twenty or thirty good men. We need you healthy, and that's that. You know," he added, "they want you to take another promotion. Colonel Feild says it's inevitable."

Lieutenant Rice's words seemed distant and fragmented, as if he were talking to someone else. Clayton said nothing, but nodded his head occasionally, mostly out of respect for the man himself. He had little regard left for the war.

"Here, Crist, let me light your cigar. Go ahead and have a smoke. As I was saying, Colonel Feild—well damn, *everyone* in the whole Tennessee Army—has noticed your bravery under fire. Colonel Feild said you were the most fearless man he's ever encountered. I'm afraid your promotion to the rank of lieutenant is imminent. It's Colonel Feild's opinion, and mine too, that these men would follow you through hell itself. Your own fellow soldiers hold you in awe. I don't need to tell you, but as men become hardened to war, that's quite a distinction." He paused and took a pull on his cigar. He blew out slowly, studying Clayton. "Do you know what they say about you? The men you fight with, that is. They say you have an angel with you when you go into battle, protecting you. At first, I thought it was poppycock, but I'm starting to believe it, myself."

Angel. Where was this angel when Jolene had been taken from him, Clayton thought? If he really did have an angel to protect him, then why didn't it protect his heart, too?

Clayton's body shook as he mounted Captain Reardon's big brown mare. He felt guilty as he rode through the camp, even when the men came up and gave him encouragement and words of advice on how to get home safely. Burgess stopped him and stuffed some letters into his hand.

"Take these to my folks, would you, Clay-boy? There's one for Abigail Beecher, too." He gave an embarrassed grin.

Clayton looked sadly down at his friend. Burgess had been a strong and well-built man when he joined the army. Even as a child, he'd been husky and full of health. Now, his face was hollow and sunken. His powerful arms were much leaner, and the cocky gleam in his eyes was gone. His tattered clothes were too thin to keep the cold from his body. Clayton swallowed hard. "I'm sorry," was all he could say.

Always full of himself, a man who could laugh at anything and usually did, Burgess took hold of Clayton's hand and squeezed it hard. "Don't you be sorry, Clay-boy," he said kindly. "Ain't a soul in this whole damn army begrudges you. Go on now." He smiled again. "You tell Abigail Beecher that I'm gonna win this war for her. I'm gonna bring a Yankee general's sword home as a present. You tell her that, Clay-boy. Tell her that for me."

Clayton shook his friend's hand, then pointed the mare toward his home and slowly set out.

Ever since the first shots had been fired in the battle at Perryville, Clayton had ceased giving any thought to his own safety. Since the war started, there had been one battle after another, and he had fought with the same impersonal fervor. He'd given in to the fact that it was all up to the great General in the sky to decide when Clayton was ready to die.

But now he was facing a different kind of battle. Clayton had serious doubts about whether or not he could make it home without food or decent clothes to protect him from the cold. As he rode along, he began talking to his Maker, asking for the strength to stay alive, even if it was just long enough for a last glimpse of his home and family.

At night, when he crawled down off the mare and fell into his bedroll, he would lie there and wait for death's door to open. The hunger gnawed at his insides so bad, he was too miserable to mind if it was his time or not.

Then, he saw the deer. It was early morning, and Clayton had just gotten up to relieve himself, when he noticed the animal, not twenty yards away. Quickly, he grabbed his rifle and shot. He nearly cried out with relief when the deer jumped, took two steps, then fell.

He stayed there for two days. Fearful of drawing attention with the smoke of a fire, he ate the deer meat raw. Still, it was a feast to him. Like an animal himself, he protected the carcass with a vengeance. Once, he angrily shot a starving dog that had been drawn by the smell.

The deer saved his life. When he was ready to leave, he packed over thirty pounds of deer meat to take along with him. He felt better and seemed a little healthier. The diarrhea had finally stopped. Clayton began to feel positive again and grew excited about seeing his family. He could close his eyes and let himself see Beartooth Flats in his mind—remember the feel of the water between his toes while playing in the creek south of the house. He could still see the fishing hole where he, Andy, and Burgess had spent so much time together in their youth.

He thought briefly about Abigail Beecher. Once, he would have looked forward to calling on her, but not anymore. It was Jolene who filled his heart with excitement. He promised himself that he would see her again.

Then, finally, he was on his parents' farm. Wendelin was out in the field. She had a goat by the horns and was trying to pull it along as the animal shook its head back and forth. Clayton almost didn't recognize the grown woman as his sister. She would be sixteen on Christmas Eve, he reminded himself.

He sat there on the mare, watching her for a moment, the lump growing huge in his throat. Then she saw him.

She let go of the goat and ran toward the house. "Mama!" she yelled. "Get Papa's gun. There's a soldier comin'!"

Clayton laughed out loud. "Wendelin! It's me, your brother, Clayton! Don't be shootin' me!"

Wendelin stopped on the porch and shielded the sun from her eyes with her hand. "Clayton!" she shouted. "Oh, Mama! It's Clayton! He's come home to us!" She ran to him and grabbed him around the leg, nearly knocking him down as he climbed from the mare's back.

Clayton's mother, Flossie, stood on the porch and began to weep. She held her arms out to him. When Clayton hugged her, he felt her body tremble.

"I've prayed for this day, as hard as a mother could," she said in a whisper.

Together, they all three held each other, then Clayton pulled back and smiled down at them. "Where's Papa?" he asked.

Flossie's smile faded a little. Her wet eyes blinked. "You didn't get our letters, did you?" She pointed toward a tiny cross on the hill. "Papa died last spring, son. He was plowin' over yonder, in the cornfield. Just fell, all of a sudden. He was gone when I got to him."

Clayton stared at his mother. The news shocked and saddened him, but he accepted it calmly. He hugged her again. "I'm sorry, Mama."

"Clayton," Wendelin said softly, "you have a new baby brother. Born late November last year. His name's Joshua."

"Joshua," Clayton repeated the name. "Where's he at?"

"He's asleep, son," Flossie said. "He looks just like you." She patted his cheek. "Come on. I'll show you your papa's grave."

That afternoon, Clayton sat in a rocker on the front porch. The clothes he was wearing were clean and comfortable, but they hung on his thin frame. Just a little over a year and a half earlier, they'd fit him like a glove, he thought. Now, they looked like they belonged to someone else. But they felt wonderful and soothing to his abused body.

He leaned back and smelled the aroma of his mama's chicken and dumplings on the cookstove. She was a gifted cook. He couldn't believe that he was about to enjoy one of her fine meals. As a boy, he'd taken her for granted, but he never would again.

But Clayton's thoughts didn't linger on chicken and dumplings, nor the fine feel of the clothing. He was studying the proposition of going back to Perryville, Kentucky, instead of returning to Chattanooga. He had to search Jolene's farm again. He would search until he found her, whether she was alive or dead. Clayton tormented himself with the idea that he'd failed Jolene. He could scarcely close his eyes without seeing a picture of her, lying underneath the rubble of her house, clinging to her life as she waited for someone to dig her out.

Supper was a big event that night. Clayton dug into his plate like a starving man.

"These are surely the best chicken and dumplings you ever made," he said with his mouth full. "Is this a new recipe?"

Flossie Crist hadn't smiled for a long time, but now she laughed, a soft, gentle sound.

She had survived the grief of losing her husband, Narvel, but she missed him dearly. Especially at night. Narvel had been a curler. When they'd first been married, she'd had the hardest time sleeping with her new husband all wrapped around her, his leg over hers. Over the years, though, she'd become adapted to her husband's sleeping style, and now she missed it something awful. Wendelin had started sleeping with her, and baby Joshua was a blessing. Life had gone on, and day by day, the pain slowly began to ease.

And now, Clayton was home. Flossie reckoned if the truth was known, she'd always loved her son more than anything else in life. She spooned more dumplings onto his plate. "I baked a pie, too. We've got good apples. You know, your daddy loved apple pie." A hint of sadness showed in her eyes. "But no, hon, I don't have a new recipe for my chicken and dumplings. I just bet you haven't et good food since you've been gone. That's why this tastes extra special."

Clayton held Joshua on his lap as he ate. He rubbed the baby's head against his cheek. It seemed like he'd been around nothing but smelly soldiers all his life, and he couldn't get enough of the little boy's sweet scent.

"Isn't it funny how Joshua's taken to Clayton so quick?" Wendelin said.

"Nothin' funny about it," Flossie answered. "I believe young'uns have an instinct about their family."

That evening, Clayton sat in his father's rocker, holding Joshua. Wendelin sat on the steps and Flossie was in her rocker next to Clayton. The air was crisp. The homestead was peaceful and appeared content, but burdens lay in the heart of each of them.

"Andy Bishop's folks have near grieved themselves sick," Flossie said sadly. "You know, I liked that boy. Always had a smile for everyone, and so polite. Some of these other hooligans around here could use some of Andy's manners." She reached over and shook Joshua's toe and cooed at him. "How is Burgess?"

"He's as fit as possible," Clayton said.

"This cussed war!" Flossie exclaimed. "I declare! Haven't we lost enough boys from around here? Mister Yates came over here from Columbia yesterday and told us about the boys in Kentucky. I was so grateful to God that your name wasn't on the list of casualties." She sighed. "I don't know what I'd do if something happened to you. Mister Yates said some boys get out of the army when they're needed back home." She gave him a worried smile. "We need you, son. Do you have to go back?"

Clayton kissed the top of Joshua's head and thought about Jolene. "I'm afraid so, Mama," he said. "I'm supposed to meet up with my outfit at Chattanooga next month."

He saw the despair in his mother's face and felt guilty. His dear mother was heartbroken. She needed him at home, yet, given the choice, he knew he couldn't stay. He had to find Jolene first.

That night, Clayton drifted off easily for the first time in his memory, but sleep did not come peacefully. His dream turned into a nightmare.

He was seated in Jolene's kitchen. She was across the table from him, smiling. Suddenly, a faceless Yankee appeared and took after them both with a large knife. Clayton fired his rifle at the man, then his pistol, but he couldn't kill the Yankee. Terrified, they ran from room to room with the Yankee right on their heels. The shiny blade was raised and ready to strike, when Clayton came awake with a start.

He shot up in bed, breathing in gasps and drenched in sweat. His shoulder and neck felt stiff. The dream had seemed real. Shakily, Clayton got up and walked out onto the porch.

The night air was cold, but it felt good on his sweaty body. He leaned against a post and smoked a cigarette while he tried to calm himself.

There were footsteps behind him. "Is that you out there, son?" Flossie said. "Goodness, you'll catch your death in this night air. Here, put this quilt around you. Would you like a cup of coffee?"

"No, Mama. You go back to bed."

She watched her son for a while. "When you were a little boy, your papa and I always knew how to help you," she said thoughtfully. "I wish I could help you now."

"I know, Mama. I know."

The days passed, and Clayton found the horrors of war were beginning to fade, little by little. His mother was determined to build up his strength again, and with her expert cooking abilities, Clayton quickly put on weight.

It was easy to adjust to life on the farm, and Clayton was more than willing to put aside thoughts of returning to the war. He again began to pray that the war would end. Then, he wouldn't have to go to Chattanooga. He could go back to Perryville and find Jolene.

☜ 12 ☞

CLAYTON WAS starting to feel better physically. He'd thought a lot about his childhood memories of days spent with Andy and Burgess at the fishing hole. One day, he rose early and dug up a batch of worms, then headed for the water.

It was a bright, peaceful day. The sun was out to warm things up a bit. Clayton put his line in the water and settled back on the bank to wait for a bite.

He hadn't been sitting there ten minutes when a female voice surprised him.

"There you are!" Abigail Beecher drawled. "Your mama said I'd find you here. I'm utterly shocked that you didn't come and see me, Clayton Crist! And sending Wendelin with Burgess's letter wasn't very friendly." She put her hand on her hips and tried to pout, but she wasn't very convincing. Clayton just smiled.

Abigail sat down beside him, settling her skirts on the ground around her. She turned her large, dark eyes on him.

"Oh, Clayton, tell me all about the war. I *must* hear about it firsthand from someone who's been there."

She was the prettiest girl in Beartooth Flats, and all of the boys had loved her deeply, Clayton among them.

He had entered the war like all the rest: young and curious about the ways of romance. He'd been eager to learn firsthand, but unlike most of the boys, he'd resisted the allure of the prostitutes that waited in every town. As the war progressed, the number of ladies grew, and Clayton became almost consumed with the desire for womanly company. Before long, venereal disease was running rampant. Clayton knew at least a dozen boys from his outfit who'd gotten gonorrhea. Two had syphilis. He was glad he'd resisted temptation, but he still carried his desires, until the day he met and fell in love with Jolene. She had made all the other women fade like dried flowers.

Now, he found himself wishing Abigail would go away. Clayton couldn't look at her without seeing Jolene's face and remembering that he had a mission to find her.

"There's nothing to talk about, Abigail," Clayton said impatiently. It wasn't his way to be rude, but he wanted to be left alone. He stared out at the water, avoiding Abigail's demanding eyes.

"Well now! I just can't believe that! Over in Columbia, everybody's talkin' about our boys! They even wrote about you in the paper, Clayton. Didn't your mama show you? General Cheatham said you are a hero." Abigail demurely touched his arm with a small white hand, trying to lure his eyes to hers.

"I ain't no hero," Clayton said.

"Why, of course you are! We're all so proud."

She stroked Clayton's arm gently while he wished she would give up and leave. He had no desire to hear about the war, and he certainly didn't want to talk about it. All he wanted to do was to be left alone with his thoughts of finding Jolene.

"Remember when we used to go swimming, here in this little water hole?" Abigail said dreamily.

"Yeah, I remember."

"Don't you just miss it? If the water wasn't so cold, we could just take off our clothes right now and jump in!" she teased.

"Guess we could," Clayton said. "But you're right. The water's way too cold," he added, more kindly. It occurred to him that Abigail was just trying to be friendly. After all, they'd been friends all their lives. He got angry at himself for not being nicer.

"Andy had told me he was going to kill a hundred Yankees in his first battle. That Andy!" Abigail smiled. "He always did have a flair for sayin' things. And now he's gone forever. It's so sad. But you''—she looked at Clayton—''you never said much at all. Always just went about your business, so quiet and sure. And now General Cheatham says you're a hero.''

Clayton stiffened at her words. It had always been accepted by everyone that she and Andy Bishop would someday get married, and Abigail had just mentioned his name without so much as a waver in her voice.

''It must've been a shock, learnin' about Andy's death,'' he said.

''Oh, yes. I swear, I cried my eyes out when I got the news.''

''Well, it looks like you got over it awful quick,'' Clayton said coldly.

Abigail put her hand to her chest and gasped. ''Why, Clayton Crist, I'm surprised at you! Of course, I was devastated, but what's a girl supposed to do? Go hide in a cave somewhere? Dress in black for the rest of my life? No, I tell you, I was deeply hurt. Who wouldn't be? But, there's nothing I can do or say to bring him back, is there? It's just a terrible thing. Why, there isn't a man left of courtin' age! They've all gone off to war, and I know a lot of them won't be comin' back. The same's true in Columbia. I've been there to stay with my sister, Laurina, and there aren't any fellas there, neither!'' She reached over and ran her finger around the outline of Clayton's ear. ''That's why I'm so everlastin' happy to see you!''

He pushed her hand away. ''Don't do that. It ain't right.''

Abigail only snuggled closer. She said, ''I guess it's right if I want it to be! Look here, Clayton Crist! I'm a woman and I have womanly feelin's. If you think I'm supposed to hide those feelin's because a boy's got himself killed in war, then you got another think comin'. Besides, Andy and I didn't have much more than a puppy love, is all! I know the war's been a terrible ordeal for you and Burgess and all the boys, but what about me, Clayton? Sometimes I crave havin' a fella to sit down and hold and talk to. Surely I do! Why, I'm about to go crazy with lonely desire!''

Her eyes filled with tears, and Clayton immediately felt

guilty. Who was he to judge, he thought? He guessed it
must be hard for the womenfolk to be left behind, to wait.
He thought about his mama, left all alone with Wendelin
and the baby on a farm that was in bad need of repair. He
had seen the pain in their eyes when he talked about leaving. Yes, he thought, the folks left back home had their
own misery to deal with. He guessed that had been too
easily forgotten by himself and the others who'd gone off
to war. It was the least he could do to fix the place up and
help out before he went back to Chattanooga. He felt embarrassed, too, for having put Abigail on the defensive.

"I'm sorry, Abigail. Really sorry. You've been my
friend all my life. That was very rude of me," he said.

"Don't be sorry. I know you, Clayton, and there was
never a nicer boy in Beartooth Flats than you."

Her finger was back on his ear. It sent goose bumps over
Clayton's body. He tried to brush her away, but she persisted.

Abigail reached up and kissed Clayton on the cheek. He
jerked away.

"Please don't do that," he said, more to himself than to
her.

Abigail moved closer and put her arm around him. Clayton's voice wavered. "Don't, Abigail. I have to tell you.
There's somebody else that I love," he said.

Abigail paid no attention. She touched her lips to his, a
soft but lingering kiss. Clayton didn't respond, but he didn't
resist either. "Didn't you hear me?" he said. "I love
somebody else."

Abigail's breath quickened. "I don't care," she said in
a raspy voice and kissed him again.

Clayton pulled back. "But I do care," he said, but his
words lacked conviction.

Abigail pressed against him. Her hands began to explore
under his shirt. He grabbed her wrists, but she twisted them
free and reached down lower. Clayton's body responded,
and soon he was swept up in her passion.

Afterward, Clayton felt great shame. He was a Judas, he
thought, a man so weak, he lacked any willpower whatsoever. They were lying naked on the dry grass. He was

on his back, with Abigail's head on his shoulder. His eyes drifted down over her shapely backside. God had not spared His artistry in making Abigail, he thought. But what gave him the right to partake of her, when he loved someone else, and there were other men who held a stronger desire for Abigail's affections?

It wasn't fair, he knew. But Abigail held an allure that he couldn't resist. She was like an aphrodisiac, calling to him.

During the days that followed, he told himself over and over that he was strong enough to resist her, but by each afternoon, he'd find himself grabbing up a pole and heading off to the fishing hole. She was surely pleasurable in her frolicking, and even though the passion wasn't the same as it had been with Jolene, Abigail had the ability to make him forget for a short time.

The fishing hole became their regular meeting place for the rest of his stay. By day, Clayton was caught up in Abigail's attentions, but at night, he lay in bed and cursed himself for giving in to her pleasures. Jolene had been the first woman he'd lain with, and he would have been satisfied if she'd been the last as well. He thought about how he would like to have married her when the war was over. They could have settled down and had children together. But, if and when he should ever be lucky enough to find Jolene, he knew he had already betrayed her. This hero on the battlefield, he thought, was a coward in a woman's arms.

It wasn't long before Abigail began to talk about love. She had promised herself to Andy, she explained, but Andy was gone, and Clayton had filled that terrible void. Now, she said, she couldn't imagine loving anyone more. Her words were lost on Clayton. He had to admit that she had made his life good on that grassy fishing bank, and the war had seemed far away, but that was only a temporary happiness. He didn't love Abigail like a man should love a woman and he tried to tell her so, but Abigail wouldn't hear a word of it.

The time grew nearer for Clayton to leave. It made him feel gloomy. With the exception of wanting to find Jolene,

he had no desire to be anywhere but home in Beartooth
Flats. It filled him with regret to think of leaving little
Joshua. He wanted to be there to watch the boy grow. He
wanted to teach him how to hunt and fish and do all the
things that his papa, Narvel, would have taught him if he
were still alive. It saddened him to know that he might not
be there when Wendelin found her own man to marry. Who
would give her away and be there if the new groom didn't
treat her right?

The thought of dying loomed on his mind as it never had
before. What if he never returned? Who would be there for
his family? He had seen the color return to his mother's
cheeks at his return home. How would she keep things running without him, and knowing that she would always be
alone?

Clayton found himself imagining how he would go back
to Perryville and find Jolene. They would return to Beartooth Flats and marry. She was the type of woman that any
man would choose for a mate, he thought. She would love
Wendelin and Joshua and his mother, and they would love
her. He could take her to Columbia and watch all the boys
watch her walk by. Her stunning beauty would be the talk
of the whole county. He longed, too, for the time when
they would have a family together. He could picture himself
with Jolene, as they watched their children playing games,
running through tall stalks of corn, splashing and laughing
in the creek. It would be a perfect life.

He wished the carnage would stop. Right now. But he
knew it was not to be. Clayton liked to walk through the
valleys and hollows, and sometimes he'd come by the home
of one of his fallen mates. It grieved him to see the shattered families as they went about their lives in a catatonic,
empty state. He felt guilty just for being alive and able to
smell the crisp October air. So many others would never
get that chance again.

Like Jimmy Decker. Jimmy had been cut down by a
direct hit of artillery fire at Perryville. His father, Hiram,
stopped Clayton one day and had questions about his son.
Had Clayton talked to Jimmy, before he was killed? What
had their last conversation been about? Was he there when

Jimmy died, and had he said any last words?

Clayton gazed at the poor man before him with his twisted arthritic hands and eyes that had lost some of life's spark from the grief of his loss. He couldn't tell Hiram the truth. He couldn't explain how he'd seen Jimmy Decker's body lying there on the battlefield, cut into two pieces, dead before he knew what had happened. He could only shake his head and assure Hiram that Jimmy had been brave and unselfish and that he had saved the lives of others. Hiram hugged him tight and thanked him, and Clayton walked away from the Decker farm with a heart full of sadness for good folks like Hiram and Jimmy Decker.

One day, Emma Lacewell invited Clayton to stop by for a piece of pie and a glass of cow's milk. They sat together on the porch, and as Emma watched Clayton eat, her eyes filled with tears. Clayton knew what she wanted from him, but he couldn't begin to mend the agonizing pain she felt. He didn't know how. Finally, she did allow herself a good long cry on that porch, while Clayton swallowed back his own tears and tried his best to comfort her. Like Hiram Decker, Emma didn't know how her son had died.

Clayton knew. He would never forget Robert Lacewell, yelling and pleading for help. His nose had been shot off, and he walked around for several minutes before a ball ripped into the side of his head and ended his pain. Clayton prayed to God, as he sat there on Emma Lacewell's porch, that no mother would ever have to see the horrors of war.

Homer and Althea Castleberry had seen their twin sons, Tom and Tim, off to the war. Both boys were lost at Shiloh. Timmy's body had never been found, but his mess kit was located a few feet from where an artillery shell had exploded. Not fifty yards away, Tommy had died at the hands of a Yankee bayonet.

There were many others. Friends who were shot dead while they were fighting or eating or telling a story. Young men with their faces shot off, limbs ripped from their bodies and left to die slow, painful deaths. Eventually, Clayton stopped his walking and stayed on the farm, away from the reminders of where he had been and where he would soon have to return.

He didn't want to think about it anymore. He didn't want to think about anything. All he wanted was another afternoon with Abigail Beecher at the fishing hole.

13

WHEN THE day finally arrived for Clayton to leave and join his outfit at Chattanooga, a sadness fell all over Beartooth Flats. It was almost like a wake, Clayton thought, when folks come to bid their last farewell and there's so much crying and sorrow. He stood on the porch and looked out at the crowd that had gathered. Abigail was there, along with Parson Black and almost all of the Beartooth Flats Baptist Church congregation. One at a time, they offered him their best wishes and bid tearful good-byes.

Captain Reardon's mare was loaded down with sacks of food and clothing and any sort of supplies that Clayton might need. A late arrival, Mrs. Annabelle Grimes tried to find a place on the horse for her contribution. When she saw there wasn't room left for her sack, she just handed it to Clayton.

Abigail approached him with a sad, yet sensual look. She took hold of his hand and held it between both of her own.

"I'll be waitin' for you, Clayton," she said. "Truly, I will." She pulled a letter from her skirt and handed it to him. "Please give this to Burgess. I feel I owe it to him."

At last, Clayton turned to his mother and pulled her tightly against him. She was trying hard not to cry, and he felt her body shaking with the effort. In a whisper, he told her he loved her. He kissed Wendelin and his new little brother, then mounted up to leave.

It was hard getting situated on the laden horse, but he was soon ready to go. He tugged on the mare's reins. As

he rode away, Parson Black spoke once more, his words
bringing the war back to the forefront.

"You be mighty careful, son! The Yankee army is in
Nashville, you know. We'll be prayin' for you," he called
out.

Clayton didn't look back, but raised his hand in a final
wave good-bye. All was quiet, except for the women's crying.

When he arrived at Chattanooga, the First Tennessee was
there. The men greeted him warmly. Clayton was shocked
to see his fellow soldiers again. They were as ragged and
desperate-looking a bunch of soldiers as he'd ever seen.
Their clothing had nearly rotted away. Many were barefoot,
and the weather was wet and cold. He felt guilty and con-
spicuous, riding in with the mare so loaded down with provisions. He surely expected that someone would try to steal
from him, but nothing was touched, for it was a fact that
Clayton commanded a respect that few others could boast.
These were desperate times, though, and Clayton knew
he'd have to keep an eye on his booty while sleeping or
on picket.

Clayton unloaded the mare and delivered some packages
that had been sent along for a couple of the boys from back
home. There was a package for Burgess, too. Clayton also
handed him the letter from Abigail Beecher. Burgess's face
lit up.

"How did she look, Clayton? Still as beautiful as a summer rose, I bet."

Clayton nodded, but he couldn't look Burgess in the eye.

"Did you tell her to wait for me? Did you say that I was
gonna come a-courtin'? Did you tell her that?" Without
waiting for an answer, Burgess added, "What did she
say?"

Clayton hesitated a moment. "I reckon she'll still be
there when you get home," he finally said. He turned away
to leave.

Burgess's eyes narrowed with suspicion. "Hey, wait a
minute. Somethin' don't smell right. You didn't court her
whilst you were home, did you?"

Clayton wouldn't look up. He didn't know what to say.

After all, Abigail had been Andy's girl before the war started. He didn't know how to tell Burgess that this courting talk was all in his own mind, not Abigail's. Still, that fact didn't keep him from feeling guilty for doing something behind Burgess's back. He felt his face redden. "Ah, Burgess, go on," he said. He pointed to the letter. "You got some readin' to do, so I best leave you be."

"What kind of answer is that, Clay-boy?" Burgess called after him, but Clayton had hurried off.

The war kept up its momentum. With news that the Federal army was in Nashville, General Bragg moved his troops to Murfreesboro. It was December 1862. Clayton and the other men spent Christmas tramping in the rain. The storms seemed as if they would never end, and soon the tension among both armies was at a peak. On the night of December 30, there wasn't a man on either side who wasn't cold, wet, and hungry. Conditions were so miserable, even the men's prebattle bravado was missing. Both sides were spent. Across the way, the Yankee band began to play "Yankee Doodle," followed by "Hail, Columbia." When they were finished, the Confederate band played "Dixie" and another Southern tune.

There was a quiet moment, and then a lone musician began to play "Home Sweet Home." The Confederate band joined in, and then the Yankee band began to play, too.

Soon, everyone was singing together, men from the North and the South, all united for a brief moment in a common wish that this war would come to an end. Clayton sat under a tree with not a dry spot on his body, listening to all the men's voices singing about their homes and families. It was so peaceful in that strange, small bit of time, it was hard to imagine that more death and destruction lay ahead of them.

December 31 brought more rain. The hungry soldiers, exhausted beyond reason, fell into battle again, fighting and killing without thinking. The price of life was as cheap as a penny in good times. For three days, the battle raged on, so heavy and intense that the water in the creeks soon flowed as red as wine from all the blood that had been shed.

By the time the fighting stopped, almost fifteen thousand Johnny Rebs were dead, wounded, or missing. Twelve thousand Yankees had met the same fate.

Once again, Clayton had distinguished himself, fighting at the front like a man possessed. He'd done it so many times before, it was an accepted fact. Fellow messmates had taken to walking by and rubbing his head or asking him to touch a keepsake for them to carry for luck. They thought he was unkillable.

Another name to be singled out was General Cheatham. Never had a general shown more courage than he had during the battle of Murfreesboro, leading charge after charge on the Wilkerson Turnpike. His actions had turned an army that wanted to give up and retreat into men who fought like heroes.

Clayton was told that his name would be added to the Roll of Honor, which the Confederate Congress had enacted a few weeks before. The Roll of Honor was a list of names published after each battle to recognize gallantry, heroism, and courage under fire. The list was to be published in newspapers to specially recognize the men's fine efforts. Lieutenant Rice also informed Clayton of Colonel Feild's comment that, if the Roll of Honor had been in effect at the war's onset, Clayton's name would have been on the list each time.

But being a hero brought no privileges. Clayton was put in charge of a burial detail at Murfreesboro. Even in the cold winter air, the bodies quickly swelled. Some bloated up to almost twice their original size. The men had to be careful, just picking them up, as the flesh would pull off in their hands. The terrible smell was something Clayton knew he would never forget. He vomited so many times, he got the dry heaves. Killing was something you could get used to, but this detail was far more terrible than anything he'd had to do on the battlefield. The bodies looked like something a person would dream about in his worst nightmares.

As a boy, Clayton had loved to hear his papa tell him stories about Davy Crockett and Daniel Boone. He'd told about the Indian wars and the Mexican War. His papa had made it sound so exciting. Clayton spent his boyhood years playing war games in the hollows of Beartooth Flats. It all seemed so grand, that when the time came, Clayton had been more than anxious to take up the Confederate cause.

But there on that bloody battlefield at Murfreesboro, Clayton found out that the only romance connected with war was written by men who had never fought in one. There were men from newspapers who viewed the carnage from a distance, then rushed in like vultures to a kill to write their stories and take their pictures. One reporter from Nashville told Clayton that the folks back home wanted to read about the war and see for themselves what was going on. Clayton shook his head over the idea. No story in a newspaper was going to give this war its due, he thought. A man couldn't capture something so grisly on paper.

Standing there amongst the dead, the odor so thick it nearly choked him, Clayton wondered exactly how much the people really wanted to know. How accurate were the reporters, and how much detail were they giving? Every reader should come to this spot, he decided. Then their curiosity would surely be satisfied forever. His was.

After Murfreesboro, the army moved to Shelbyville and Tullahoma to set up winter quarters. It didn't take long before Clayton was again as threadbare and undernourished as his campmates, but at least he was still in Tennessee, and the time seemed peaceful. He enjoyed being located by the Duck River, where he'd fished as a boy. It was his favorite diversion to sit by the water, tossing rocks and thinking about canoeing down through Columbia, then parking the canoe and walking to Beartooth Flats. The river made him think of the fishing hole and Abigail Beecher. That, in turn, made him think of Jolene and how he had betrayed her. It was during winter camp in Shelbyville that the boredom set in. Day after day stretched by with nothing to do but look forward to someday fighting another battle. Clayton began to think about deserting.

Perryville wasn't that far, he figured, and it shouldn't take him any time at all to get there. His inclination to go back was so strong, he even packed his knapsack and headed out one night after midnight. He made it a mile outside of Shelbyville before he stopped to consider his situation. The night was cold and his feet had grown almost too numb to carry him. He was moving so slowly, he'd surely get caught and shot for desertion. Realizing his foolishness, he turned back for camp.

Clayton wasn't the only man who suffered. Foraging became a main concern among the men. Unlike the Federal army, the army of the South was full of poor, uneducated volunteers. Supplies were always short and food was scarce, so they had to eat anything they could find. Parched corn was usually the ration of the day, but even that was scarce. Throughout the war, the men raided the dead from both sides, looking for morsels of food left in the knapsacks. At times, they had nothing more to eat than boiled leaves or grass, and some outfits were so hungry they resorted to eating rats and pieces of leather. Green corn was a delicacy. Sometimes hungry soldiers would find a field of green corn and eat themselves sick. Orders were given against pilfering the civilians' crops, but the men no longer cared about anything but staying alive, and such orders were forgotten. At Shelbyville, Clayton found himself eating anything that crept or crawled, robins and sparrows or green apples. The men even boiled the bark from the trees and tried to drink the bitter soup.

From Shelbyville, they worked their way to Chattanooga, with Bragg and Rosecrans trying to outwit each other all the way. First one general had the upper hand, then the other. In the end, it looked as if Rosecrans held the trump cards. His army was better outfitted, and their numbers were larger. By now, Bragg's own troops were openly doubting him. Stories and rumors of his harsh disciplinary measures were stirring up a fear of their own leader. He'd had so many of his own men shot, desertions were taking place almost daily. Reinforcements were what the Rebel army needed.

At Chattanooga, Bragg was to fortify, but soon Rosecrans had nearly surrounded him and had taken the high ground at Lookout Mountain. Bragg ordered his army south into Georgia. The Federals outnumbered him nearly two to one, but word spread that reinforcements were coming.

General Lee's top commander, General Longstreet, was on his way from Virginia, along with General Hood.

Rosecrans thought Bragg to be moving all the way to Atlanta, a deadly mistake on his part, for Bragg was playing possum with his army along the Chickamauga Creek.

None of this made any sense to Clayton. He couldn't understand why they hadn't just turned around and fought at Chattanooga. He wanted this war to end, one way or the other. He was tired of seeing so many die. He wanted to go home, to be able to find Jolene, to leave this place and never think of war again.

Clayton discussed his thoughts with Lieutenant Rice, who quickly defended General Bragg's move. Once the Yankees were on top of Lookout Mountain, he pointed out, it would be disastrous to try to fight them. "Don't ever try to take the enemy when they have the high ground," he said. "We'll fight them, all right, but it'll be on Bragg's terms, not theirs."

Still, Clayton was disturbed. He guessed he just didn't think like an army general. That was one of the reasons why he didn't like to hear their talk of promotions. He despised being a corporal. War had lost all of its grandeur. He'd yet to be in a battle that made any tactical sense. At Shiloh, they'd had the Yankees on the run, but instead of pressing harder, the Confederates had been ordered to pull back. The next day, they had been whipped good. To Clayton's way of thinking, you attacked and attacked until the enemy was exhausted. If that wasn't possible, you would lie in hiding, catch the Federals unsuspecting, then strike and run.

But that was not the way of generals. Their idea of strategy was to line the two enemies up, facing one another, and watch the carnage begin. It was a battle of attrition, fighting man against fighting man until one line would break. Some of the poor boys who made up that line were barely fourteen years old and away from their mamas and papas for the first time. A lot of them had wives and little ones back home. They all went out together on to the battlefields, getting themselves shot up and twisted and mangled, while the generals sat up on the ridges with their field glasses, observing. Their talk of courage and heroes seemed hypocritical. What did bravery mean to these poor boys who left their guts out there on some field they'd never even heard of before? What glory was there in being dead?

There was no glory, Clayton decided. It was just two armies made up of innocent boys, spilling their blood for ideals that most neither understood nor cared about.

Clayton decided that he would answer the general's call. He would fight until there was no fight left in him, or he got killed, himself. He would do his best to help his fellow soldiers, and he would do it for the honor of the South.

But he would not be the one to lead these men to their deaths. That was better left for Bragg and those like him.

14

TRAVELING OUTSIDE of Dodge City, Clayton and Solon met up with Jerome Billings, who seemed excited to see them.

"I'm glad you fellers are comin' to town," Jerome said. He gave a handbill to Solon, who passed it over to Clayton.

"You know I can't read," Solon said.

Jerome Billings talked while Clayton tried to read the handbill. "They're puttin' on a medicine show tonight. Gonna be a big event. Kid Martin's gonna perform, too. You know about Kid, don't ya? Bills himself as the fastest gun alive." He looked sheepishly at Clayton. " 'Course, I know it ain't true 'bout him bein' the fastest."

Solon rubbed his chin. "Kid Martin? Seems like I heard tell of him."

"I wouldn't be surprised if'n you did," Jerome Billings said. "He just played in Delano, over by Wichita. They say he pulled down on Rowdy Joe Lowe. Folks say ol' Rowdy Joe should be six feet under right now, 'cept Kid Martin didn't kill him." He shook his head, duly impressed. "The man that hired me to pass out these handbills says the Kid is fast as lightnin'."

"That don't surprise me none," Solon said with a bit of arrogance. "Why, ol' Rowdy Joe ain't no gunny! He might could bend a barrel over a dead man's head, or shoot you when you ain't lookin', but he ain't no fast-draw."

Jerome Billings looked like he wanted to argue, but his quick glance at Clayton Crist showed that he wasn't about to stir up controversy in such dangerous company. He quickly bade them farewell and rode on. Solon gave a sarcastic laugh.

"What's that piece of paper say?" he asked.

"Just an advertisement for their little show."

"Can you imagine that boy tryin' to impress us with that sorry little story?" Solon shook his head. "Why, that weren't nothin'! Ol' Rowdy Joe Lowe's just like that sheriff back there in Plattsville. He may of killed a few men and whupped a few, but he did it when they were drunk. You can bet your bottom dollar on that! Remember the last time we saw Rowdy Joe? He was so full of himself that day, why, I don't think he could see straight!" He looked at Clayton. "But he knew who you was, and he would've loved to have gotten you all drunk so he could shoot ya. He wasn't about to mess with you sober! No sir, he knew better'n that!"

When they reached town, Clayton said, "Let's get a room at the Dodge House."

"You mean we're gonna stay here the night?" Solon asked. "Hell, we still got seven or eight hours of daylight."

"I suppose we'll stay," Clayton said. He didn't really want to stop when the day was only half-over, but he was already tired and his legs felt heavy and achy. "Let's get us somethin' to eat, too. I'm hungry."

Dodge City was bustling like a Fourth of July. There were handbills posted all over town, featuring Kid Martin's shooting and fast-draw exhibition.

When they reached the Dodge House, it was all booked up. When they inquired about other lodgings, the hotel clerk told them there wasn't a room to be had in town. Besides the Kid Martin show, there was a bunch of ranchers gathered in the town for some sort of cattlemen's convention. "Might try Ham Bell's Livery Stable," the clerk offered.

"Hell's fire," Solon said as they stepped out onto the street. "There ain't no need for us to sleep with horses tonight! Let's go over to Tracy O'Brien's place. She was married to a feller named Pug O'Brien. That is, until he got himself killed by his horse. At least, that's what the verdict was." Solon went on, remembering out loud. "Pug and I was both workin' for Shorty Gillis, and Pug had been havin' trouble with a couple of cowhands from Texas. They was always givin' him what for, and he told 'em more than once that he was gonna send 'em both outa town. I think they beat Pug to death, but old Doc Hopkins made the rulin' that Pug's horse kicked him." He shook his head. "I used to tell Pug that damn horse needed the hell beat out of him. He was always buckin' Pug off or bitin' him, but sorry as that dang horse was, there ain't no way he kicked Pug to death. Pug was beat up too bad." He sighed. "Anyways, let's go to Tracy's. Her place is west of town a ways. You'll like her. She ain't more'n twenty-five or twenty-six years old and a good cook. I know she could use the money."

"Are you sure it'll be all right?" Clayton asked doubt-fully. Sometimes, folks didn't know Solon nearly as well as he claimed to know them. Solon had a tendency to talk to just about anybody who would hold a conversation with him. He'd leave thinking that they were good friends, but there'd been several occasions when they'd meet up again later, and that other person wouldn't have any recollection of Solon, at all. More than once, he'd talked Clayton into an embarrassing situation with his so-called acquaintances.

"Dern right, I'm sure," Solon said. "Before Pug died, I et with him and Tracy so many times, we're almost family. She's good folks, I'm tellin' ya."

Tracy O'Brien was in her yard, hanging out her washing on a clothesline, when they rode up. Behind her stood a small frame house with a little picket fence around it, both painted white. Off to the side was a sizable garden area, arranged in neat rows. The place was clean and well tended.

Solon said softly to Clayton, "Poor Tracy. Pug was a good ol' boy. Got him a nice start in life with this place." He shook his head. "Dern worthless drifters! I should've shot those sons of bitches, but then I reckon I'd be in jail, myself, if I had. And that ol' Doc Hopkins was about as worthless! I don't think he even had no schoolin' to be a doctor. Had a cowboy tell me once he saw Hopkins about ten years ago, workin' for a rancher in south Texas. He was doctorin' stock.''

Clayton would have made a comment, but then Solon began to wave his arm at Tracy. She waved back.

''Is that you, Solon?'' she called out. ''I thought you was headin' to Caldwell.''

Solon took off his hat and wiped his forehead on his sleeve. ''I was, but I got sidetracked,'' he said. ''This here's Clayton Crist. We've cowboyed together and been friends near twenty years. We're on our way to Ness City, and thought maybe we could stay here the night. There ain't no rooms in town.''

''Well, climb down off your horses, then, and make yourselves at home,'' Tracy said. She smiled politely at Clayton, then dropped her eyes.

Clayton could tell she was a shy woman, but what surprised him was her beauty. He had somehow expected to find a squat, heavy, cherub-cheeked woman. Tracy O'Brien was tall, perhaps five-six, and slender yet shapely. Her light brown hair fell down her back, long and curly. She'd pinned it back from her face with a bow. The smile that lit up her face showed in her eyes, too. She was pretty beyond words. Clayton had never known Solon to have much of an eye for beauty. Once, he'd bragged about some woman he knew in Fort Worth who was supposed to be the object of every man's affection within miles. He'd talked about that lady the whole winter, and by the time they finally got to town, Clayton was about to burst with excitement over seeing her.

But instead of excitement, Clayton got disappointment. The woman, Elizabeth Stewart, had turned out to be the ugliest woman he'd ever encountered. She'd stood nearly six feet tall and was at least that big around. What teeth she had left were blackened around the gums. She'd been a boisterous sort, too, with a loud, hearty laugh that reminded Clayton of one of those monkeys he'd seen once in a circus. But, Solon had held a real fancy for Elizabeth, and Clayton had never said anything that might hurt his feelings. It seemed funny that Solon had never mentioned Tracy O'Brien before.

"You can unsaddle your horses and put 'em in the shed out back," Tracy said. "Put some oats in the trough for 'em, too." She turned to Clayton. "I've heard of you, Mister Crist. Solon has talked about you. You're the one they call 'the Gunny.' " She blushed and quickly cupped her hand over her mouth. "Oh, I'm sorry," she apologized. "I shouldn't be so forward! I sure didn't mean nothin'. It just kinda slipped out."

"No apologies necessary," Clayton said. He looked around. "You have a very nice place here. I'm sorry to hear about your husband."

"Thank you," she said. "I'll bet you men are hungry. I'll fix up somethin' while you're tendin' to your horses. Since Pug's been gone, I rarely cook much."

"Well, you don't have to cook much for us, neither. In fact, we can eat in town," Clayton said.

"I wouldn't hear of it. It would do me good to have some men to cook for. Besides, I feel beholden to Solon. He's been awful good to me. Why, when Pug died, Solon brought his pay and gave it to me. I tried not to take it, but he made me." She smiled fondly at Solon, but he only looked away in embarrassment.

Once the horses were settled in, Clayton and Solon went into the kitchen and found Tracy frying bacon and potatoes. She smiled shyly at Clayton and motioned toward the table.

"Have a chair," she said. "Are you-all goin' to the big show tonight?" Tracy said.

"What for? To see that Kid Martin feller? I reckon not," Solon said. "He ain't nothin'. The best gunhand to be found is sittin' right here with us."

"I wish you wouldn't do that," Clayton said. He looked embarrassed.

"Well, it's true. I've seen those shows before," Solon went on. "They call themselves trick shot artists. But you ain't like that, Clayton. You don't shoot at cans and nickels and such silliness. No sir, you're the real thing. I'll betcha one thing. If that Kid Martin really did make a monkey out of Rowdy Joe Lowe, he just better watch himself. Every time he goes to sleep or turns his back, he better be expectin' Rowdy Joe to appear some day and surprise him.

It wasn't no trick shot, him gettin' a jump on Rowdy Joe, and it ain't gonna be forgotten. No sir! That Kid Martin better watch his beans!''

"Do we have to talk about this at the table?" Clayton said. "I'm sure Mrs. O'Brien is used to a little more delicate talk over supper."

Tracy touched Clayton's hand lightly with her own. "Don't worry about my ears none. One can't live in a wicked place like Dodge City this long and have delicate ears." She smiled softly at him. "But thank you, just the same."

Clayton felt a searing run through his body when she touched him. He looked at her pretty face and soft womanly body. Life had to be a struggle for her, he figured. Dodge City had always been a wild and woolly town. He couldn't recall seeing any place in his entire life that lent itself more to man's folly. Maybe it was from all the rough cowboys who rode into town with their herds of cattle, ready for some excitement. He'd rarely been to Dodge, when he didn't see many fistfights and even a few gunfights. He'd been involved in a couple, himself. It occurred to Clayton that Tracy O'Brien was the first respectable woman he'd come into contact with there. He'd never met any of the regular citizens before. He'd always known there had to be law-abiding residents somewhere in the city, but his stays in Dodge were usually short, and he rarely got away from Front Street. He liked to do a little gambling at one of the saloons, or maybe find a room at one of the hotels.

That evening, after an enjoyable supper in one another's company, they sat on the porch. From the distance came the sounds of a town in celebration. Gunshots sounded, and loud voices could barely be heard. The three of them sat, looking off in the direction of Front Street, where all of the activity was taking place. There wasn't much said. Even Solon, who could talk to anybody on just about any subject, fell silent for as long as he could stand it.

Finally, he let out a deep sigh and clapped his hands together. "I guess that Kid Martin is puttin' on his show right now," he said. "There's too many gunshots bein' fired off, even for Dodge City. Yep, I guess that's what he's doin', puttin' on his show," he repeated. "I wonder if ol' Shorty Gillis is there. 'Course, I ain't got no hankerin' to see him, anyway."

Clayton watched Solon fidget, smacking his lips and rubbing his mouth. He knew what was on his friend's mind, and that he was broke.

"You need a couple of dollars, Solon?"

Solon pretended to think the question over for a spell. Finally, he nodded. "You know, if Tracy here don't mind, I might just wander on into town and have myself a drink or two. Might even take a look at this Kid Martin feller. I'll tell you what, though. That Kid better watch himself when he goes to sleep. Why, Rowdy Joe is apt to be in town right now gettin' all drunked up."

"Oh, Rowdy Joe's too busy makin' money to be worryin' about some kid," Clayton said. "I suspect he's in Delano."

Solon pulled himself up out of his chair. "Could you make it ten?" he asked.

"What?"

"Ten dollars. Could you lend me ten?"

When Solon was gone, Clayton smiled at Tracy. "His appetite needs a good whettin'," he said.

Tracy smiled at his comment. "Could I interest you in some coffee?"

"I wouldn't want to put you out now."

"You're not puttin' me out. There's still some left on the stove from supper. It may make your clothes stand up, but I kinda like my coffee strong, anyway," she said.

Clayton thought the comment unusual. He could sense Tracy's soft and feminine ways. Her silhouette was dainty in the evening dusk. It didn't seem natural for such a woman to drink coffee, and it was even more strange to hear her preference for strong coffee.

When Tracy returned with the coffeepot, she sat down to pour. "Well in any event, Solon didn't go to whet his appetite, at all," she said. "It was Big Ears Wanda he was wanting the money for."

Clayton stopped the coffee cup halfway to his lips. He stared at Tracy. "Who's Big Ears Wanda?" he asked.

"Just a prostitute. She works at the Lady Gay Saloon on the south side of Front Street." Tracy shrugged. "Maybe he shouldn't of, but Pug told me about her. Anytime Solon's got money, he always goes to see Big Ears Wanda."

Clayton couldn't tell if Tracy was disapproving, or not. He hoped she didn't blame him. He said, "Look Mrs. O'Brien, maybe I shouldn't of given him the money. If I embarrassed you by doing so, I'm sorry."

She laughed, a light airy sound that attracted him to her even more. "Don't be! And please, call me Tracy. It makes me feel old, when you call me Mrs. O'Brien." She leaned back comfortably in her chair with her coffee cup on her lap. "Solon tells me you have a place up in Ness City. He says you're goin' there to build a house and raise some livestock."

Clayton noticed a note of sadness in her voice. He nodded. "That seems to be our plan, but Solon and I have a way of gettin' sidetracked." He laughed softly. "Maybe someday we'll get that house built."

"You need to do that. Build you a house and buy some stock. Get yourself a home and settle down around decent folks," she said. There was a tremble in her voice.

"It must be hard on you, since your husband's death," Clayton said.

"Nobody knows how hard it's been," Tracy said. "I envy you and Solon. You've got dreams to look forward to. I don't dream anymore." She wiped her eyes.

Clayton felt awkward, sitting there watching a woman cry. "Look," he offered, "I could help you out with some money. I ain't got much, but I could give you fifty or sixty dollars. I need to save a little back."

Tracy started shaking her head back and forth, crying harder. "No, no," she said. I'm so sorry to be carryin' on like this. No, I don't want your money, Clayton, although it's terribly sweet of you to offer. It's just that I'm so unhappy these days. So terribly unhappy. Do you know what the main occupation is in this town?"

Clayton felt an urge to take Tracy in his arms. He wanted to make her stop crying and feel better. But he knew better than to be so forward, and he certainly didn't want to add to her pain.

Tracy went on. "Prostitution. Seven or eight percent of the population of Dodge City is prostitutes! It may be even higher than that," she said bitterly. "There's more than a dozen saloons, and then there's all the dance halls! I swear, I never liked it here, even when Pug was alive." She dried her eyes and took a drink of coffee. "I'm sorry, Clayton. I must look a mess. But sometimes I wonder if it's all worthwhile. I tend my garden to sell some of the produce off, I take in people's washin', and I work at the Wright Beverley Store three days a week. All to just get by. And that's just what I'm doin'. I got plenty to eat, but I have no life."

Clayton felt a genuine pity for her. He thought about all the widows and mothers back home in Tennessee and the rest of the South who grieved over their loss and loneliness. He guessed he'd seen plenty of folks like Tracy O'Brien after the war—women who'd lost husbands and sons. Part of their own lives were dead forever. "Don't you have any family here with you?" he asked.

"No. I'm from Chicago. Pug was, too. We went to school together. He came out West as a cattle buyer. Oh, what big dreams he had," Tracy remembered out loud. "He planned to ship cattle back to Chicago and make lots of money, but," she sighed, "it never worked out. He had to go to work for Mr. Gillis."

"I'm real sorry, Mrs.—" Clayton stopped himself. "I mean, Tracy."

Tracy smiled sadly. "I know you are, and I appreciate it. When Pug wasn't working for Mr. Gillis, he was usually down on Front Street, trying to make friends with the cowmen. Poor thing. He never got over wantin' to make money in cattle."

Nothing was said between them about romance, but sometime during the evening, Clayton and Tracy found themselves in each other's arms. Silently, she led him inside to her bedroom. It seemed like a natural thing for both of them, and their desire for one another rose to a fever pitch. Tracy was as aggressive as Clayton. They took from each other in a demanding and passionate way. There was a need in both of them that drove them over the edge. The frolicking went on all through the night, neither wanting it to stop.

Clayton had always suffered from a weakness for women and a yearning for love. He had never been vulgar or unduly forward, but since Jolene ending up in bed had always come as easily to him as breathing the air around him. Sometimes, he mulled it over in his mind. It was like fighting in the war had been, he often thought. All these years later, he still couldn't understand how he had managed to go into a battle and lose himself to the fighting. Afterward, even if he sat down and thought hard about it, he still couldn't remember doing all of the killing that the others claimed they'd witnessed. It was a puzzle he still carried.

His relationships were just as puzzling. Clayton had been with so many women, he knew their every move beforehand. Nothing much surprised or shocked him anymore. He could almost fit each woman into categories in his mind. Some were shy and reserved and quiet as a mouse. Others would be passionate and loud in reaching their ecstasy. Some were submissive, while others were dominant. Some wanted tenderness, while some wanted it strong. Clayton had been involved with so many women, he sometimes had trouble remembering their names.

He had no idea what made it so easy for him to find a woman who was willing. He had even less of an idea how to find a love that would last.

But Tracy O'Brien was as full of need as he was. Not just for love, but for full possession of another spirit. Clayton's back stung from her fingernails, his lips tingled and burned from her hungry mouth.

They lay there in the darkness together, their bodies wet, catching their breath. Soon, Clayton heard Solon's horse approaching. He started to jump out of bed, but Tracy stopped him for a moment. "Later, when Solon's asleep," she said, "come back to my bed."

15

IT WAS strange how something could just pop into a man's life when he least expected it. Clayton certainly hadn't been expecting to meet up with a female in Dodge City. But, fate had a way of making life interesting. He'd come to town to get a haircut, stop by Wright, Beverley and Company to buy a few necessary items, then be on his way to Ness City. Now, due to other circumstances, he was having a hard time leaving.

It was high noon. He and Solon had been in Dodge for less than twenty-four hours, yet he and Tracy had already been together four times. Clayton felt like a kid again, all excited and silly over frolicking with a woman. And poor Solon, he thought, must feel like some kind of errand boy, the way Tracy kept sending him away. Twice already, Solon had been to town, once to pick up a copy of the *Dodge City Times* newspaper, and then to buy coffee. Solon had gone willingly enough, but not without the observation that there was already a full can of coffee sitting open in the cupboard.

Clayton had thought he'd known women in the past who shared his enthusiasm for frolicking, but Tracy gave a whole new meaning to the word enthusiastic. She made him feel young and old at the same time. The stirrings that she aroused in him were so pleasurable, he could forget about the aches and pains that had plagued him of late. Her youthfulness seemed to pass on to him for a spell. But, for that same reason, he realized that he was getting old. As full of desire as he was, he could barely keep up with her. Never before had he concentrated so hard on keeping up with a woman's energies.

In the kitchen, Tracy placed fried bacon and potatoes on the table. She smiled apologetically at Clayton and Solon. "I'm sorry," she said, "but this is all I've got in the house to eat, besides eggs. I need to get some groceries." She smiled with her eyes at Clayton and then said to Solon, "Maybe after lunch, you could pick us up a few things."

"Nah, Solon, you don't have to do that," Clayton said. "This afternoon, we'll all go buy some groceries. Tonight, we'll eat at Delmonico's."

After the midday meal, they all three walked the length of the farm together, then Clayton and Tracy returned to her room until it was time to head to town. Solon occupied himself by mostly staying out of earshot, lest Tracy might think of someplace else to send him.

That night at Delmonico's, Clayton ordered steak with all the trimmings for himself and Tracy, and liver and onions for Solon. Clayton looked across the table at Tracy. She smiled pleasantly back at him and said something to Solon. Clayton remembered her tousled hair and fiery kisses in the bedroom and wondered how she now managed to look so calm and proper in her high-necked blue dress.

They were just beginning to eat, when a small man walked up. He looked like a frail schoolboy, except for the fact that he was packing twin pearl-handled Colts.

The man looked the three of them over, then stared down at Clayton and said, "You're the Gunny, Clayton Crist. I heard you was in town."

Clayton had just put a piece of steak in his mouth. Calmly, he chewed his food and examined the man's cold eyes. They didn't seem to go with his youthful face, he thought. Clayton had seen eyes like these before. They were menacing, fearless, dangerous eyes—eyes like his own. He knew that to be true, for he'd never found a man that he couldn't cause to look away in short order, until now. These eyes bored right back, returning the stare with a challenge. Clayton could see an emptiness behind them, too, and he knew this to be a dangerous man. He continued to slowly chew his steak, then swallowed.

Finally, he said, "I'm Crist. Who in the hell are you?" The words came more harshly than was his nature, but there was something about those eyes that irritated him.

"I'm Jeremy Martin. Folks call me Kid Martin," the man said. He took a chair and turned it around and sat backward on it. "You don't mind, do you?"

"I don't believe you were invited," Solon said. "You got a lot of gall, I'd say."

Kid Martin acted as if he hadn't heard a word Solon said. Instead, he folded his arms on the back of the chair, then rested his chin on his arms. He smiled crookedly at Clayton, but his eyes stayed as serious as a heart attack. "All my life I heard you was the best, and now, here you are, sittin' right across from me."

Moments before, the restaurant had been astir with noisy customers and busy sounds. Now, a silence fell over Delmonico's. The waiters walked softly around Clayton's table, cutting a wide berth. People at the other tables talked in hushed tones and stole nervous glances at the table.

"I don't quite know what to say," Clayton said.

"Well hell! Don't say nothin'. Take it as a compliment if you will," Kid Martin said.

"I'd appreciate it if you'd watch your foul language in front of the lady, here," Solon said, annoyed at the intrusion into their meal.

The Kid glanced only briefly at Solon, then tipped his hat to Tracy. He smiled broadly. "Pardon me, ma'am. I didn't mean to offend you." He laid his hat on the floor. "Those steaks sure do look good. Would you folks mind if I joined ya for somethin' to eat?" The coldness had relaxed in his eyes, and they smiled with the rest of his face.

Solon started to protest, but Clayton stopped him. "It's okay," he said. "You're welcome to eat with us."

He had a bad feeling about this Kid Martin, but he knew it was better not to rile him any. He was definitely a dangerous sort, and no matter what Solon thought to the contrary, Clayton knew it wouldn't take much to provoke trouble—the same kind of trouble he'd seen in the past.

There were ordinarily two kinds of men that had contributed to Clayton's reputation. The older ones, anywhere from thirty to forty-five, were more deliberate and calculating. They were also more accurate. What separated the older men was that small, thin instant of calculation. A man had to draw fast and shoot precisely. The older men didn't lose their nerve at the first shot. After all, they'd been there before. Clayton had witnessed the more experienced men take mortal hits, yet still rise up to kill their adversaries before dying themselves. Older men were also more resourceful, and a man didn't dare turn his back on them. Clayton had had the time to learn that the only satisfaction in a gunfight was the fact that the other person was dying. It mattered little how pretty or fair it was.

But it was the younger men who gave Clayton the most concern. They were arrogant, full of bravado, and too ignorant to leave well enough alone. Their own immortality seemed to be their creed in life, and they were harder to shake and discourage than a hive of angry bees. Once you crossed that line with a young one, a fight was almost always inevitable. Clayton could recall several occasions when he'd been able to talk an older man out of a fight. But the pups apparently had too much to prove to call it quits. The pup who now sat across the table looked as deadly as Clayton had ever encountered. He hadn't really believed the story about this Kid Martin pulling leather on Rowdy Joe Lowe, then living to walk away without killing him. He suspected that Rowdy Joe must have seen the same thing, himself, in Kid Martin's eyes, as he stared into the Kid's gun barrel. Men knew, even the bad ones. That was why Rowdy Joe hadn't tried to kill this pup.

Kid Martin relaxed and appeared to enjoy their company. Clayton was pleased that everything was settling down. The Kid turned out to be a talkative sort, and soon he and Solon were exchanging stories as they ate their food. Clayton had been around Solon long enough to know what kinds of folks he liked and didn't like, and he knew for certain that Solon didn't care for the Kid one bit. But, Solon could talk to anybody. In fact, Clayton had never met anybody who enjoyed a conversation quite like Solon did. He couldn't help himself.

Clayton could feel the Kid's eyes on him. Even though the Kid was conversing with Solon, it was clear that he'd come to see Clayton. He seemed to be seeking Clayton's approval, glancing his way when he made the point of whatever yarn he was telling. Clayton was grateful that Solon was there to distract the Kid's attention by trying to tell the better story.

Finally, Kid Martin pushed back his plate and drained his water glass. He stood up and said, "Well, folks, I've got a show to do. There's free tickets for you if you want to come."

Clayton nodded and smiled, but no one said a word.

This seemed to make the Kid angry. His eyes turned dark and dangerous at Clayton. "I know what you're thinkin'," he said. "You're thinkin' that I'm some kind of freak, that I ain't for real."

Clayton stared hard at Kid Martin and said, "Don't be tryin' to do other folks' thinkin' for them. We've got other plans for tonight, that's all. Nothin' more, nothin' less. You just go on and do your show."

Kid Martin stood there, hovering over them. He was grinding his teeth and the anger burned in his eyes.

"I heard about you when I was a little boy," he said. "They call you 'the Gunny.' Say you was fast and deadly. For that, you have my respect. But you know what I think now?" His lips turned up into a cold grimace. "I think you've been livin' on that reputation for way too long. Why, you're nothin' but a worn-out old man."

Clayton didn't appear to be impressed. "You said you have a show to do, Kid. Best get to it and we'll just leave things be," he said.

Kid Martin's face flushed a deep red. His jaw twitched, and his hands, hanging just inches from his pearl-handled Colts, opened and closed. His words spit out like a fire that's meant to burn its victim.

"They say you're the best, but I say that was a long time ago. I say your days as 'the Gunny' are over."

Solon couldn't sit quiet any longer. "Let it drop, Kid,"

he said. "He'll kill ya, boy, and he'll do it without blinkin' an eye."

The restaurant quickly emptied. The patrons, accustomed to such occasional confrontations, hurried outside to wait until they could return to their meals. Silence filled the room, as Clayton sat and waited for the Kid to make his move.

Slowly, the cocky grin crept back onto Kid Martin's face. His hands relaxed.

"You're right, I do have a show to do. Maybe we'll meet again." He stepped backward, then turned slowly and left the hotel.

Solon was mad as a hornet. "I've never seen such gall!" he said. "You want to watch that scoundrel, Clayton. He's gonna fool around and git himself kilt before he even shaves good!"

Kid Martin's presence hung in the air like a bad odor and seemed to have spoiled the mood for everyone. They'd finished eating, but they remained sitting silently at their table, until Tracy mentioned that the hour was getting late. Solon borrowed five dollars from Clayton, muttering that he had to see a man about something. Clayton and Tracy watched him as he hurried off toward the Lady Gay Saloon.

Back at the farm, Tracy made coffee, then she and Clayton sat on the front porch. "Is that how your life goes, Clayton?" Tracy asked. "I mean, do you run into men like that Kid Martin very often?"

"More often than I care to think about," Clayton said softly. He wished he hadn't even come to Dodge City, but the thought left as quickly as it had come. The fact was, Tracy made it all worthwhile. He was more than glad to have her company. He enjoyed the way she made him feel.

Tonight, though, facing Kid Martin had been a different experience for him, far more unsettling than just facing a man's challenge.

For a long time now, Clayton had wanted to put his gun away. There had never been any excitement for him in killing another man, but in the past, he'd grown so used to hiring out his gun, he'd grown passive. He'd been able to shut it out of his mind. Now, as he grew older and more tired, it sickened him when money grew short, and he would have to hire on with some rancher to get rid of cattle thieves or take care of another hired gun. It pained him to think that all he knew how to do in life was kill.

Before, no man had been too mean or tough for Clayton to handle. It wasn't that he didn't get nervous. Even back in the war, he'd always gotten anxious before a battle, but he'd always known that the hand would be there to push him onward. He'd never had a doubt what his reaction would be to the situation.

But Kid Martin had scared him, and scared him bad, and what was worse, he hadn't felt that hand's presence. Clayton remembered how his legs had quivered under the table, and how he'd stuck his hands on his thighs so the Kid wouldn't see them quivering, as well. He could still feel that fear, sitting there on the porch with Tracy. Maybe Solon was right, he thought. Maybe they were getting old. One day, he might just be too scared to pull on the likes of a Kid Martin.

Clayton's legs had stopped shaking and his hands were steady, but at this very moment, he could feel the blood in his body vibrating.

Tracy put her arm around him and pulled his head to her chest. She rubbed the side of his face. Her voice was soft and kindly.

"Solon used to tell me stories about you. I had a picture of you in my mind as being bigger than life and as mean-lookin' as a snake. I guess I pictured you as being some kind of monster." She pulled his head up and kissed him. "But that just ain't true. You're not a bad man at all. I know you're not. I hope you and Solon do build that house, and raise those hogs. You deserve that."

Clayton leaned against the warmth of her body. He put his arms around her and let her cradle his head against her bosom. He pretended she was his mama. He wanted her to hold him and chase away the fears. Tears began to roll down his cheeks.

Tracy ran her fingers through his hair. "I could love you," she said, so softly he could barely hear. "I could take care of you."

They both cried, their tears mingling as they shared each other's pain like two empty hearts, bringing comfort to each other.

They were asleep when Solon came in. He called out their names and woke them, but neither made any pretensions of getting up. Tracy snuggled tighter against Clayton, nestling her head against his shoulder. Clayton held her with both arms.

They drifted off again, Tracy falling into a deep, peaceful sleep.

But Clayton's nightmares returned.

16

SEPTEMBER 1863. The night turned bitterly cold. That day's fighting in the north Georgia wilderness had been a treacherous bloodbath for both armies.

Clayton had never seen land more to his liking than that around Chickamauga Creek, Georgia. Early that morning, it had been so peaceful and beautiful, it was just as he imagined the Garden of Eden must have been. Except for a few scattered farms, everything seemed untouched and perfect. It was a forested area, with thick undergrowth. Squirrels ran about overhead in the trees and birds filled the air with their songs. Clayton had thought that surely the big General in the sky would intercede this day. After all, He had made this lush wilderness. Its beauty ran deeper than any of man's thoughts or foolish disagreements.

Clayton had considered writing about it to his mother. He'd actually started the letter the day before. ''You would just love it here,'' he'd written, but after that sincere opening, he couldn't find the proper words to do it justice.

Now, in the late evening, Clayton sat atop the thick undergrowth, his back arched against a tree. His hands and feet were numb from the cold. He tried to recapture the tranquility of thoughts he'd enjoyed that morning, but it seemed the gates of hell had opened up, spewing brains, guts, and blood all across his Garden of Eden. He was tired. The fighting had been as brutal as any he'd been involved in.

Off in the distance, in that void between the armies,

Clayton could hear the litter bearers moving around in the total darkness, trying to locate the wounded. Pickets from both armies kept the musketry roaring in the night. Their nerves must still be on edge, Clayton thought. Usually at night, after a day's hard fighting, there would be a merciful period when both armies would cease their fire.

Normally, Clayton did his heavy praying at nightfall, especially when the storm of battle was still raging. Tonight, though, he felt too angry to pray. The musketry fire exploded again and again, filling his head with its sounds. To make matters worse, there had been an order given that there would be no fires tonight.

"Where is your mercy, Lord?" he finally said angrily. "Isn't it bad enough that the men are hurt and dyin' out there? Do they have to freeze as well?"

Something broke into Clayton's thought. It was a familiar voice. He raised his head and listened intently, trying to cipher through the hundreds, maybe thousands, of voices. The sounds of the wounded overtook the night, as powerful as a field full of frogs and crickets making their familiar night crying. Clayton strained so hard, all the sounds eventually ran together.

Several minutes went by. Clayton thought maybe he'd just been hearing things, when he heard it again. Somewhere out there in that dark void, among the gnashing of teeth and the moaning, Clayton heard Burgess Monroe's voice.

He'd been so exhausted, Clayton hadn't realized until now that he hadn't seen Burgess for some time. He pulled himself up to stand. His feet felt like raw bones, stiff and aching, as he started toward the voice. There were so many bodies, he stumbled over them in the darkness. It was another terrible nightmare, as outstretched hands grabbed at him as he walked by. He stopped to listen, trying to put the pain and suffering of the others out of his mind, as if they didn't exist.

He heard Burgess's voice again, off to his left. The litter bearers were hurrying to their duty as the distant flashes of musketry fire could be seen in the night sky.

Clayton found Burgess leaned against the body of a dead Yankee.

"Burgess!" he called. "I'm here."

"Is that you, Clay-boy? I can't see. Oh my God! I can't see a thing!"

Clayton sat down beside him and put his canteen to Burgess's lips. Burgess's hands shook as he wrapped them around Clayton's. "If you could just get me to the light, Clay-boy. I think I'll be all right."

"Do you think you can walk?" Clayton asked.

"I don't know. I can't feel nothin'."

Clayton's eyes scanned the darkness around them. "Hey! litter bearer! Over here! I need your help! Over here!" he called out.

One of them hollered back. "Keep your patience! You ain't the only one who needs us!"

Burgess reached up and felt Clayton's face. "Please don't leave me! I'm so cold! Take me to the light."

Clayton could see the silhouettes of the litter bearers all around him, their litters full as they worked their way back to the lines with the wounded. "I'm gonna pick you up, Burgess," he said. "Hold on."

It took all of his strength to gather his friend up in his arms and start out across the dark void. Clayton felt warm blood from Burgess's body. He tried to quicken his pace, but his legs trembled under the weight. His feet felt numb and as heavy as stones. His arms began to ache. Pain shot through his lungs with every breath.

When at last he reached the tree, Clayton laid Burgess down and made a bedroll for him. He broke up twigs and brush, anything that would burn, and soon had a fire going. He sat down and cradled Burgess in his arms, like a mother would a child. The light of the fire shone on his friend, and the sight brought a horror that would forever be embedded in Clayton's mind.

A ball had caught Burgess from the side and gone through both eyes. His nose hung grotesquely from his face. There was a bloody canal where both eyes had once been. Clayton could see back into the inner flesh of Burgess's head. He had also been shot once through the stomach, and his left leg was bleeding badly.

A sergeant whom Clayton didn't recognize came up and kicked at the fire. "Don't you know the orders?" he said sternly.

Clayton looked up at the sergeant. "You get your ass outa here and leave us be, or I swear, I'll kill you dead."

A voice off to the right called out. "Ain't nothin' he hates worse'n sergeants."

Another voice said, "Shoot 'im, Crist."

The sergeant stood there in confusion as all around him, other men chimed in. Lieutenant Rice came up. "What's going on?" he asked.

The sergeant pointed at Clayton and said, "This man got a fire going, and I was trying to put it out." His voice wasn't as sure as before.

"I'll handle it, Sergeant," Lieutenant Rice said. He stepped forward and felt the warmth of the fire on his own stiff legs. He felt like being rebellious, himself. It was a stupid order, he thought, to forbid the fires. There came a time when a man would rather be warm than safe from an enemy's gun.

He looked grimly down at Burgess Monroe. The sight didn't shock him. He'd seen too much to be shocked. Still, that didn't cause him to be unsympathetic. He had to muster up the courage to follow his orders.

He said, "The sergeant's right. I-I wouldn't be doin' my duty if I allowed this fire."

Clayton glared at Rice and shook his head. He and Burgess Monroe had been little boys together. They'd watched each other grow into young men and had been sweet on the same girl. They'd shared lives full of fun and discovery. Now, here he sat, looking down at his friend, who lay there like some monster with his handsome face distorted beyond recognition. No, Clayton thought. Enough was enough. His line was drawn.

Burgess's body shook, and he sank against Clayton like a scared child. His chest was heaving up and down as his breathing grew more difficult. Clayton wondered how he could possibly still be alive.

Several men from their company walked up with their blankets. One covered Burgess's body. The others took their blankets and held them up, end to end, to form a wall around him.

"Sir," said Private Benjy Barnhart from Ashwood, Tennessee, "we'll block out the fire."

"That's right," Private Will Scott of Columbia, Tennessee, said. "We'll stand here all night, with your permission."

Lieutenant Rice gritted his teeth together. He mustn't shed tears in front of the men. He knew that many of the men made fun of him behind his back. He'd heard their catcalls and jokes, the insolence in their voices. He'd never felt a part of them. Even so, each night, when he was by himself, he would pray and shed tears for the very men who made him feel like an outsider. At first, he'd tried to tell himself that they were just private soldiers who weren't happy if they weren't griping. But, as he watched the other officers over the course of the war and saw their relationships with the men, he'd come to realize that he didn't hold the same respect. As a youth, he'd never been accepted by the tougher boys. He'd been prone to a life of thinness and frailty, but he'd always believed that, in time, and especially during the war, that things would change. It could have filled him with a bitterness toward his life and fellow man, but his mother had taught him too well for such pettiness.

Way back, when he was but ten years old, Rice had come running home one day, crying. The other boys had run him off, calling him a sissy. To this day, he could still remember his mother's words. "Pray for them, son," she'd said. "They mean you no harm, really."

He had tried to live by those simple words, and even though he didn't like the men for their cruelty, he still prayed for their safety. As Lieutenant Rice looked around him at the men whose hearts were reaching out toward the dying soldier, a different feeling came over him, a feeling unlike any he'd experienced during this whole God-forsaken war. He gave in completely to his mother's wisdom, and reached out to take a corner of a blanket. At this moment, he loved these men. He loved them all.

A short time passed, then Clayton felt Burgess die. He felt the body give a little shudder and heard the half breath. Then Burgess lay still, gone to join the others who had so bravely given up everything they had. Clayton prayed that God would accept Burgess and give him a fine new body.

He glanced upward. In his mind, he saw Andy and Burgess together at the fishing hole, with his father, Narvel, smoking his pipe and watching them. Clayton remembered how many times his father had stood on the hill above them, tending the cows, and how Narvel had stopped, smiled, and waved his hat at the boys as they splashed and played in the water. Clayton could see his father now, waving at Andy and Burgess with his pipe in his hand. A strange longing came over Clayton. He longed to ascend upward, into the heavens, with Burgess. He could almost feel the water splashing in his face and hear Andy's giggle and Burgess's voice.

Clayton pulled himself out of his wishful thoughts, and, in the cold of night, he dug a grave for his friend. Behind him, in the void, the cries of the wounded and the dying continued.

Orders were given and passed along. They would attack at daylight. General Polk would command the right wing, General Longstreet the left. But as in most battles, that day-break attack order was delayed until midmorning. When at last the Confederates' cannon fire shook the earth and the musketry fire followed, Clayton delved into yet another battle. As he fought through the volleys of musketry fire, his mind was emptied of the awareness of what he was doing. Occasionally, he became aware of thinking about that scene at the fishing hole and his longing to be there with Andy, Burgess, and his father. Once, Jolene's face flashed before him, but flew from his memory as soon as it had come.

The carnage that day was as ugly as any battle before. Salvos of canister ripped away limbs and mangled bodies right before Clayton's eyes. Soldiers died like raindrops falling from the sky. Not ten feet from Clayton, Harlan Rutherford, a man of forty from back home with three children not much younger than Clayton, had his head taken off by a big shell. Clayton watched without blinking as Harlan Rutherford's headless body took a step before collapsing.

The bloodcurdling Rebel yell was heard all throughout the width and breadth of the Chickamauga Valley. On the left, Longstreet had Rosecrans on the run, with the Federals crawling atop each other at the narrow mouth of McFarland's Gap. Polk's right wing, though they faced more resistance, soon had the Federals on the run as well. It looked to be a Confederate rout. Even after the Federals had retreated, running back toward Chattanooga with their tails between their legs, the Rebel yell could be heard above all other sounds on earth that day.

It wasn't until the next morning that Clayton found out that Lieutenant Rice had taken a ball in his right leg. Clayton sought him out, and finally found him on the surgeon's table. He took Clayton's hand.

"We beat 'em good, didn't we, Crist?" The lieutenant looked down at his leg. "They're gonna have to take it off. I guess the war's over for me." He tried to smile, but the pain wouldn't allow it.

Clayton nodded. It was a hell of a way for it to be over, he thought. He had a hard time hiding the bitterness that he felt toward the war, or the sadness he felt for the lieutenant. "Can I do anything for you?" he asked.

Lieutenant Rice said, "Yes. Take that promotion, Clayton. Take my place. This army needs good men." He paused as the surgeon, Dr. Eli Coulson, approached and began to cut away his pant leg. "You see, General Polk tried to talk sense to General Bragg last night. He and General Longstreet wanted to go on and destroy Rosecrans's army, now and forever. But you know Bragg—" Just then, in the middle of his thought, he let out a bloodcurdling scream and grabbed Clayton by the arm. Dr. Coulson had begun to saw on his leg. Rice held on to Clayton until he passed out.

Later, Clayton wearily left the field hospital. He wanted to get off by himself, away from the stench of war. Everywhere he looked, though, dead and broken bodies covered the earth. He walked, faster and faster, until he found himself all the way back at Chickamauga Creek.

A Federal sergeant was leaned against a tree, his bloody hands gripping his stomach. At first, Clayton thought him to be dead. The sergeant's eyes were stony and cold. He jumped when the Yankee sergeant blinked and said, "Could you give me a drink, Johnny Reb?"

Clayton sat down beside him and put his canteen to the sergeant's lips.

"You killed me, Johnny Reb. At least, one of you did."

Clayton stared down at the man's belly. "I suspect a surgeon will come along and fix you up, Sergeant," he said.

"It's not to be, Johnny Reb. I'm a dead man. Could you do me a favor before I die? In my sack here. Would you get my paper out and write a note to my missus? She's in Scottsburg, Indiana."

Clayton found the paper and wrote down the sergeant's words:

Dear wife,

I'm here in Georgia and I'm dying. But, while there is breath left in me, I want you to know how much I love you. I'm sorry to leave such a burden on your shoulders. There is an irony to war, for you see, dear wife, a Johnny Reb is so kindly writing these words for me. I pray to God that He will watch over you and our sons. Do not weep for me, for we all have a chosen time to die. My only regret is that I could not spend my last hours with you and our sons. Tell them to mind you and that their father loved them.

Until we meet on the other side of that river, I bid you farewell and give you all of my love.

He had Clayton sign the letter, "Your devoted husband, John Collingswood."

"I'll see that this is sent to your family," Clayton promised.

"Have you got any tobacco?" Sergeant Collingswood asked.

Clayton rolled him a cigarette and put it to the man's

lips. The sergeant looked down at Clayton's feet. "We look to be about the same size," he said. "Your boots look like they've barely got another mile left on 'em. Mine are barely broke in. Would you accept them as a gift for your kindness? I can go to the next world feeling like I've done something good for my fellowman."

Clayton thanked him. Satisfied, the sergeant closed his eyes and smoked his cigarette.

A Confederate private came by. Clayton had seen him a while back, digging through the knapsacks of the dead soldiers. It was a common sight, to see such opportunists after each battle.

The private leered at Clayton. "Whatcha doin'? Waitin' on the sumbitch to die? Hell, take whatever ye want now. Ain't gonna make no difference to him, anyhow." The private reached down and started to unbuckle Sergeant Collingswood's belt. "By damn! This is a fine pistol-riggin'," he said.

"Leave him be," Clayton said.

"You can kiss my ass, feller," the private snapped.

Clayton pulled his pistol. "I said leave him be, and I mean it."

The private looked at Clayton, his face devoid of any emotion whatsoever. He snarled and his nostrils flared. "Unless you wanta eat that pistol, you better put it away," he said. He reached back down to loosen Sergeant Collingswood's belt.

Clayton didn't flinch as he fired. The ball ripped through the private's temple. His eyes froze forever in death, and he went on to the next world without Sergeant John Collingswood's fine pistol-rigging.

Clayton stayed with the sergeant, giving him water and listening to the man's last words. When the moment of death came, he laid his head back against the tree and glanced toward Clayton. He opened his mouth as if to speak and took in a breath. But no words came. A peaceful look came over him then, and he was gone.

Later that day, Clayton learned that Lieutenant Rice had died two hours after his leg was amputated. There was hardly any time for remorse or sadness, for the Confederate victory had stirred up a great rejoicing. They had captured thousands of Federals, along with over fifteen thousand small arms and many artillery pieces.

Chickamauga had been a major victory for General Bragg and the Confederates, even though the Rebel casualties stood at almost eighteen thousand men, among them nine brigade and two division commanders. The Federal casualties neared sixteen thousand.

Chickamauga Creek had finally lived up to its Cherokee name: "River of Blood."

17

CLAYTON HAD intended to make his stay at Dodge City nothing more than a brief respite on their way to Ness City, but he hadn't counted on meeting Tracy O'Brien. She was as comforting to him as a rain shower in August, and her needs were well matched to his own. Clayton had never enjoyed being in Dodge City so much. In fact, he'd never really considered Dodge City to be of any great importance. He'd heard cowboys from Texas to Montana talk about what a fine place it was to kick up their spurs and have a good time, but Clayton had always thought it a town of weariness. He found it hard to relax in the saloons, always having to watch for some drunken cowboy who might want to gain an instant reputation.

Now, thanks to Tracy, Dodge City would always bring Clayton happy memories. After being with her, the rowdiness of past experiences faded in the distance. Clayton found his only concern to be Solon's frequent trips to see Big Ears Wanda. Five dollars here and ten dollars there was starting to mount up. Besides that, Clayton had given Tracy fifty dollars, bought her groceries, and taken them all out dining. If he didn't make a move soon, he knew there wouldn't be any money left to set up his place in Ness City.

Kid Martin had left town, taking his show to some other location, but not before he left word with Solon that he hoped to meet up with Clayton again. Clayton paid little heed to such a common threat, but he was glad the Kid was gone, nonetheless.

Though his heart wasn't in it, he knew he had to leave Dodge City and Tracy O'Brien. With a painful slowness, he was preparing to pack his bedroll, when he heard a horse ride up.

"You in there, Clayton Crist?" a voice called.

Clayton put on his shirt and walked out onto the porch.

"Remember me? I'm Shorty Gillis."

Clayton nodded. "I remember you, Shorty. How are you?"

"On a normal day, I'd say fine," Shorty said. He looked solemnly down at Clayton. "You need to come with me, Clayton. Solon's got himself arrested, and it looks serious."

"Arrested? What for?" Clayton looked puzzled.

"Kilt a cowboy down at the Lady Gay Saloon," Shorty Gillis said.

"Give me a minute. I'll be right with you," Clayton said.

He had a hard time fishing any information out of Shorty, who was so excited to be the bearer of such news, he'd forgotten the details. Clayton did manage to find out that some cowboy who'd ridden into town with a herd had been arguing with Solon for the last couple of nights over a whore. Beyond that, all Shorty could say was that he'd gotten news of the fight from a paperboy. Solon, he said, had been locked up.

They rode straight to the city jail. Clayton frowned when he opened the door and recognized Deputy Marshal Dave Mathers, sitting at the desk. He didn't like Mathers, and he knew the feeling was mutual.

"I'd like to see Solon Johnson," Clayton said. "I heard you've got him here."

"He's here, all right, but you ain't gonna see him. Not 'til in the mornin', anyway," Mathers said.

"Why the hell not?" Clayton asked.

Dave Mathers twisted on a corner of his mustache with his fingers. At the same time, his tongue was trying to dislodge a piece of meat that had gotten stuck between his teeth at supper. He stood up. He was a tall man with stooped shoulders. "For starters," he said, "we got him on a murder charge. And secondly, I don't feel like walkin' back there. You can come durin' regular office hours."

"Has he been charged yet?" Shorty Gillis asked.

Clayton touched Shorty's arm. He tried a calmer approach. "Looky here, Dave. Let me talk to him and give him some tobacco."

Dave Mathers succeeded in prying the meat loose from his teeth. It went flying, and attached itself to Clayton's pant leg. He stared at it a moment, then said, "If you don't get out of here and quit pesterin' me, I'll lock your ass up, too. You and this fat man with you."

Shorty Gillis got red-faced. Beads of sweat had already formed on his forehead and upper lip. "I don't know that I like you sayin' a thing like that," he said. "This man's got a right to see Solon Johnson if'n he wants to. I do a lot of work in this town. Do a lot of work for the marshal, if'n you know what I mean. You best let Mister Crist see the man."

Dave Mathers's eyes widened as he stepped forward. Hatred had taken up residence in them. He took a long finger and poked it hard into Shorty Gillis's belly, causing Shorty to make a grunting sound.

"Like I said, sowbelly. You come at visitin' hours. I might let you see the prisoner then." He gave an extra push with his finger, backing Shorty up a step.

Shorty Gillis looked at Clayton. "Are you gonna take this?" he asked, a little breathlessly.

Dave Mathers pulled his glare from Shorty to Clayton. "He ain't gonna do nothin'. Not unless he wants to end up on Boot Hill. That 'Gunny' reputation don't scare me none. Now, I'm losin' my patience with you sowbellies."

The barrel of Clayton's Colt was suddenly jammed inside Dave Mathers's mouth, before he could move.

"You worthless piece of shit," Clayton said through clenched teeth. "You've bullied people long enough. I could kill you as easy as killin' a mad dog, and you'd be a forgotten man in a heartbeat. You think about that, you low-down piece of horse shit."

Clayton's finger was firm against the trigger. His eyes were cold as ice, and his voice had dropped low. He thumb-cocked the Colt, and its message filled the air.

Something wet dripped down between Dave Mathers's boots. His bladder had let loose. His eyes, so full of hatred just seconds before, were now frightened. He blinked rapidly. When he tried to speak, his teeth bumped against the Colt's barrel. Clayton shoved it deeper into his mouth and he almost gagged.

"Get down on your knees, you sorry bastard," Clayton said, pressing harder with the Colt. His breathing quickened.

Dave Mathers knelt carefully to the floor. Clayton pulled the Colt from his mouth and stuck it against his forehead. "Ever see a man carryin' his brains all over his shirt?" he said. "If'n you don't want to, you apologize to Shorty here, and do it right proper."

Dave Mathers's eyes swam back and forth in his head. He tried to look away from the Colt to Shorty. "I'm real sorry, Shorty. I swear I am. I didn't mean nothin' by it. Look, why don't you ol' boys go on back and see Solon? Here"—he fumbled around for his keys, feeling with his hands—"go on in and talk to him."

"Nah. We'll come back tomorrow. Durin' visitin' hours," Clayton said. Slowly, he pulled the Colt back and holstered it. He took a step backwards. Dave Mathers started to get to his feet, when Clayton stopped him.

"Not so fast. I ain't through with you yet." He let go a kick, as hard as he could. His boot caught Dave Mathers in the chin, snapping his head and knocking him to the floor on his back. Clayton drew back to kick him again, but Dave Mathers was out cold.

"You better watch yourself, Clayton," Shorty said. "That Mathers is a wicked man. He won't fight you fairly, you know."

"Most don't," Clayton said.

They climbed atop their horses, and Shorty adjusted his hat. "You take care of Solon, there. He's a pretty good man when he wants to be. By damn, that was pretty, Clayton!" He turned and started riding away, but Clayton could hear him, still talking to himself.

"Damn! The bastard peed his britches!" Shorty let out

a whoop and put his horse into a hard lope for home.

The next morning, Clayton showed up at the jail early. He was expecting more trouble but was led right to Solon's cell. Solon was sitting on his bunk. He jumped to his feet when he saw Clayton.

"I sure am glad to see you," he said.

"I'm pleased you ain't dead," Clayton said, showing concern. "Word has it you might be charged with murder. Tell me what happened."

Solon paced in the cell. "Well, Clayton, there ain't that much to tell. This Texas cowhand pulled down on me. Would've kilt me sure as the world, too, except he was all drunked up. The only thing he hit was a billiards table." Solon rubbed his face with his hands. "The next thing I knew, he was dead, and that turd, Mysterious Dave Mathers, threw me in here without so much as askin' one question."

His gloom started to lift as he thought back on what had happened the night before. "That son of a bitchin' Mathers is as worthless as tits on a boar hog!" He nodded. "I could hear you-all last night. You showed him up good, didn't you, Clayton? I'll bet Jack Bridges would've arrested you for it, except he couldn't get nothin' out of ol' Mathers. The son of a bitch is too proud to admit he got his comeuppance!" Solon's eyes narrowed. "You know what they say about Mathers, Clayton. You'd better watch out for him. He's mean as a two-headed rattlesnake."

Solon suddenly stopped talking and stared past Clayton. Clayton turned to see a man standing there watching them.

The man looked tired and rumpled, like he'd been up all night. He rubbed the stubble on his chin. "I'm Jack Bridges, City Marshal," he said. "You must be Clayton Crist."

He seemed nervous. His eyes were bloodshot and watery. Clayton simply stared at him.

"Look, Crist. I heard this mornin' that Johnson was in town with you. Now, I got more problems than a man deserves already."

"You can relax," Clayton said. "I'm just here to help out in any way I can."

"I'm grateful for that," Marshal Bridges said. "If you have a minute, we can step out in my office and talk."

"You got anything to smoke, Clayton?" Solon asked.

Clayton handed him his fixin's and followed Marshal Bridges to his office. Bridges took a seat behind his desk, but Clayton remained standing.

"I hear tell you-all plan to charge Solon with murder," he said.

Nervously, Bridges rubbed his chin. "That's a possibility."

"Looky here, Marshal," Clayton said. "I've known Solon Johnson for a long time—long enough to know he's a man of good character. He talks too much and even exaggerates at times, but I've never known him to lie to me. He says the other feller pulled his pistol and shot at him first. That don't sound like murder to me."

Marshall Bridges had rubbed the stubble on his chin so much, the skin had turned red as a mosquito bite. His face was pulled up and tense. He nodded his head. "I know," he finally said, "but listen to me, Crist. If he is indeed charged and goes to trial, he'll most likely be found not guilty. Then he'll go free." The pained look returned to his face. "You gotta understand. He didn't kill just anybody. The victim's name was Avery Love. He was Ben Love's boy. Ben brings up some of the biggest herds from Texas."

"What's that got to do with anything?" Clayton said, getting angry. "Since when can't a man defend himself?"

He noticed the look in Marshal Bridges's eyes. The lawman plainly wasn't in disagreement with him. He looked like a man who was under the pressure of someone else.

"Maybe you'd best tell me what's goin' on," he said.

Bridges poured himself a cup of coffee and offered one to Clayton. He took his cup back to his desk and sat down.

"Do you know what it's like to be marshal of Dodge City, Crist? At this very moment, I've got Wyatt Earp and Bat Masterson, and half a dozen other men from all over, here in my town. And it's all on account of Luke Short." He explained, "Short and another feller own the Long Branch Saloon, and A.B. Webster owns the Alamo Saloon."

He paused and sipped his coffee. "To make a long story short, there's been trouble between the two from the very beginning. Webster being the mayor, and Luke Short having a temper to match his name, it's been an impossible situation for me to control. Luke starts thinking the whole town is against him, so he brings in all these gunhands." Marshal Bridges started rubbing his chin again. "I don't mind telling you, Crist, that I was once a United States Deputy Marshal, and I had far less headaches than I've got now. I don't want no trouble with Earp or Masterson or Luke Short, and I sure don't want no trouble with you."

Clayton cut into Marshal Bridges's speech. "I understand what you're sayin'," he said, "but what I'm needin' to hear about is Solon Johnson. Tell me what you've got on him."

Marshal Bridges nodded. "The barkeep over at the Lady Gay said something's been brewing for a couple of days. It seems it all had to do with a whore by the name of Big Ears Wanda," he said. "I guess your friend, Johnson, and Avery Love both set their sights on the same female. Well, last night, they were arguing over who was going to buy her a drink. The barkeep says Johnson told Love he was going to whip his ass, and Love went for his pistol." Marshall Bridges shrugged. "Reports say he fired, but Love was so drunk, he couldn't have hit the side of a barn. Well"—he gave a long pause and stared out toward the street, as if he wished he was out there, doing something else—"Johnson took his knife to him." He stopped again and grimaced. "Have you ever seen what a knifing looks like?" He shook his head. "Give me a shooting any day over a knifing. That Love boy painted the floor red at the Lady Gay with his own blood."

Clayton thanked the marshal and left to pick up a few things for Solon at the general store. He was crossing the street when someone called his name. It was a voice he hadn't heard in a long time.

"Clayton Crist. I heard you were in town," Wyatt Earp said.

They had crossed paths several times over the years, and always on good terms. Clayton had no reason to think otherwise now. He nodded at Earp and walked toward him. They shook hands.

"Come over to the Long Branch, I'll buy you somethin' to drink," Earp said.

Clayton motioned down the street. "I was just headin' to the store to pick up a few things. Maybe we can have a drink some other time."

"I think you better come now, Clayton," Earp said. "You see, I know they're gonna try to charge your friend, Solon Johnson, with murderin' that cowhand last night. Maybe we can help your friend Johnson out." He motioned his head for Clayton to follow.

Clayton didn't feel any particular fondness for Earp, and they had never been close. Socially, though, he held nothing against him, and he was definitely interested in what kind of help Earp was offering Solon.

It was too early to be open for business, so they entered the Long Branch through the back door. Inside, Clayton was surprised to see a group of men sitting together, drinking at that time of day. He recognized some of them. He had met Bat Masterson and Luke Short, and even though they'd never been introduced, he knew one of the men to be Doc Holliday. Clayton had heard that Holliday was crazy, but then, he heard a lot of things about a lot of men.

Wyatt Earp led Clayton to the table. "Let me introduce you to everyone," he said. "The good-lookin' man is Neil Brown. You know Bat, of course. This big feller, here, is W.H. Harris. The man in black is Frank McClain. The other big rascal is Charlie Bassett. I think you know Luke, here. This fellow, who sports the menacing eyes and worldly charm, is Doc Holliday. And, that fellow next to Doc is Billy Petillion." Earp patted Clayton's back. "Gentlemen, this here is Clayton Crist. I'm sure the name is no stranger to any of you."

"Pull up a chair," Bat Masterson said. "We heard what happened to your friend, Solon Johnson. In fact, that's what we"—he waved his arm at everyone at the table—"are here for. But, it's not just about your friend. It's about what's goin' on in Dodge City. The powers that be are trying to change Dodge, and"—he shrugged—"this damn place could use some changes for the better. To begin with, maybe we can stop some of the needless killin's that are goin' on. The only trouble is, some of these so-called do-gooders are pickin' and choosin' who and what they want to change.'' Masterson paused a moment and looked at Clayton. ''I heard your friend, Johnson, killed Ben Love's boy in self-defense.''

''What Bat's trying to say,'' Wyatt Earp broke in, ''is that we're all in town to help Luke, but while we're at it, we want to straighten out a few other things, too.'' He smiled that Earp smile. ''You might call us the 'Dodge City Peace Commission.' '' He grew serious. ''You let us get your friend Johnson out of jail.''

''I'm surprised they haven't arrested you, too, Clayton,'' Bat Masterson said. ''They got them a new city ordinance, you know. Ordinance Number 70. It's designed to stop all vice and immorality.''

Clayton looked at the men who sat around the table. Several of them were dandies, but none was so fine as Bat Masterson. He was fairly handy with a sidearm, and he could get drunk with the best of them, but he was mostly an amiable sort. Clayton felt comfortable in his presence.

''What kind of vice or immorality am I posin'?'' he asked casually.

Masterson frowned and tipped his glass. ''Them do-gooders are talkin' mostly about me,'' he said, then smiled. ''Me and Luke, that is. They'd like to get rid of us 'slick gamblers,' and, of course, the fine ladies who reside across the tracks.'' He studied Clayton for a moment, then said, ''No, the ordinance they'd most likely get you on is Number 71. Vagrancy.'' He looked pleased and drank his whis-key.

Doc Holliday appeared as if he was already on his way to getting drunk. He sneered angrily, ''Them no-good sons of bitches, wanting to bite the very hand that feeds 'em! After all, what would Dodge City be if you took away the gamblin' and the whores? What would all the cowboys do that rode through? Why, this town would dry up in a heart-beat! It would be gone like a fart in the wind.'' He laughed at his own joke. ''That's what Dodge City is in the first place! It's a big fart. You take the smell out of it, and it's nothin'.'' He laughed again, then went into a violent coughing fit.

For some time, Clayton had heard rumors about Doc Holliday's condition. He looked like a man who was nearing death's door, instead of a man who carried an infamous reputation.

Doc waited until his coughing settled, then regained his composure. He looked defiantly at Clayton and said in a raspy voice, ''They keep me out of sight, you know, 'cause I'm likely to just kill them sons of bitches.''

Throughout the morning, the group of men in the Long Branch went through two bottles of whiskey. Most, with the exception of Clayton and Wyatt Earp, were feeling good from the liquor's effects. What surprised Clayton the most was Doc Holliday's apparent tolerance for whiskey. He had appeared to be intoxicated that morning, and had matched the other men drink for drink for nearly three hours. Still, he didn't appear to be any more inebriated than when Clayton had first joined them.

It was noon when Clayton finally stood up and said, ''Gentlemen, if you'll excuse me, I promised Solon I'd pick up a few things from the store.''

''Oh, sit down and have another drink,'' Bat Masterson said. ''Wyatt and I are supposed to be meeting with Sheriff George Hinkle at this very moment.''

''That's right, Clayton,'' Wyatt Earp said. ''We're helpin' Hinkle keep his nose clean. He's gonna let Bridges create his own mess, before he steps in and cleans up.''

Doc Holliday's bloodshot eyes were staring hard at Clayton. ''I've heard you're the best pistoleer there is,'' he said. ''They call you 'the Gunny.' Why, with your reputation, I'm surprised they just didn't open up the cell and let your friend out. I bet they're real scared of you.''

Luke Short sat down next to Doc Holliday and squeezed Doc's shoulder. ''You heard right,'' he said. ''Clayton didn't know me then, but once in Leadville, I saw him drop Hank Jones and Ralph Bombeck, after both men pulled down on him.'' He smiled respectfully at Clayton. ''And there wasn't a meaner pair in Colorado at the time.''

Doc Holliday was still staring at Clayton. Clayton stared back.

"Oh, Doc didn't mean anything," Wyatt Earp said. "Did you, Doc?"

Doc Holliday smiled and leaned back in his chair, "Why, hell no, I didn't mean nothin'. You didn't think I meant nothin', did you, Clayton?" Twice, he touched the handle of his Colt as he sat and smiled.

Again, Wyatt Earp spoke up. "Now, let's everybody settle down. Don't pay him no mind, Clayton. Doc's just havin' a little fun with ya."

"Sure. That's okay," Clayton said. He gave Doc Holliday a friendly smile and turned his attention elsewhere.

Doc Holliday had had plenty to drink, and he also just might be the most likely to become easily provoked. Clayton noticed the wild look that flitted in and out of the man's eyes. When Holliday wasn't hacking and coughing, he was smiling, but it wasn't a friendly smile so much as one of self-indulgence. Clayton had known a few wild men like Holliday, men who seemed to have a keg of dynamite inside where their soul was supposed to be, with a short fuse attached. He had steered clear of such men most of his life, not because he was fearful of them, but because they were too unpredictable to be anything but trouble. Holliday was a nice-looking fellow, and it was said that he was educated. Maybe, Clayton thought, it was the sickness that made him the way he was.

Whatever, Clayton wasn't one to pass judgment. To his way of thinking, most people ended up being the way they were because something drove them to it.

Suddenly, Doc Holliday dropped his stare. "Wyatt is right," he said to Clayton. "I was just funnin'. Let me buy you a drink. In fact, I'll buy everyone a drink. Drinks are on me!" he yelled out.

"Why, you rascal," Luke Short said. "I reckon drinks are free, seein' as I own this place."

Every glass was filled, and the tension was gone out of the room as fast as it had entered.

Wyatt Earp stood up and raised his glass. He said, "Boys, you've all heard me say sterling things about Clay-

ton Crist, and I'll tell you why. There ain't a one of us in
this room, with the exception of Clayton, that hasn't made
a livin' either at the tables or behind the badge. Most of us
will flip-flop between both. I used to think a man couldn't
wear the badge if he hasn't lived on the wrong side a few
times, but Clayton, here, is different. As far as I know''—
he paused, looking at Clayton—''you ain't never worn a
badge, nor run a gamin' table, nor had a string of whores.
I always admired you for that, Clayton. Outside of hirin'
your gun out, which I think everybody in here has been
guilty of at one time or another, I always thought you to
be a decent man.''

Clayton blushed. ''Well, I don't know if all that's true
or not.'' He paused a moment, then asked Wyatt Earp,
''Did you say *runnin'* a string of whores, or *sleepin' with*
a string of whores?''

Clayton brought down the house. Doc Holliday laughed
the hardest. When the room quieted down, he generously
tipped his hat.

''You're gonna be my friend, Clayton Crist.''

18

WYATT EARP and Bat Masterson held a meeting with Sheriff Hinkle who, in turn, called in Marshal Bridges and the Dodge City mayor. Within an hour, Solon Johnson was released. Clayton was still in the Long Branch Saloon with the others when the three men walked in.

Clayton hadn't put a lot of faith in their so-called peace commission, and it truly surprised him to see Solon standing there.

"Well, I'll be damned," was all he could say. He stood up to shake the hands of Earp and Masterson. They were both plainly pleased with their accomplishment.

Earp smiled. "It took more doin' than I thought it would, but hell, even if it would've went to trial, I'm pretty sure Solon would've been acquitted."

"Was there a fine?" Clayton asked.

"One hundred American dollars," Bat Masterson said. "Wyatt paid it. Hell, there shouldn't of been a fine, but it was either that or have Johnson here await trial."

Clayton started digging in his pocket for the money. He was getting close to being cleaned out, and his plans for a new life at Ness City were looking dim. Still, he willingly handed Earp the money.

Earp folded the money without counting it and slid it into his pocket. "I'm afraid there's more," he said solemnly. "They've stipulated they want Solon out of town. Even provided him with a ticket to catch the Santa Fe. It's good all the way to Topeka." He laid the ticket on the table. "I don't figure he needs it, though. Didn't you both ride in by horse?"

Clayton nodded.

"I'm afraid Solon was the victim of another one of this misguided city's town ordinances," Bat Masterson commented. He gave a sarcastic smile. "Ordinance Number 83, I believe it is, whereby no one shall have a dance hall in Dodge City, or in any of its surroundings, where lewd and nasty men or women shall congregate for the purpose of dancing or—now, listen closely—performing any lewd acts. They seem to think that Solon and Big Ears Wanda might of been doin' somethin' lewd and unspeakable," he said as he raised his eyebrows mockingly. He turned toward Luke Short and pointed his finger. "Ordinance Number 81 states that you cannot have a pi-ano player, Luke. No singers, neither."

Clayton thanked the men for their friendship, and he and Solon left. They were no sooner outside the Long Branch when Solon, who had been silent, shouted out.

"By damn! If I never see Dodge City again, I'll be happy! I can go to the next world, and not look back!" He started waving his hands as he talked. "I mean, I'm in there, mindin' my own business. You know that, Clayton? Then, this young Texan pissant pulls down on me and shoots!" He shook his head and held up two fingers. "I was this close to bein' a dead man! Do you know why I cut him, Clayton?" he asked. Without waiting for an answer, he said, "I didn't want to hurt that boy! Why, I could see that fight comin'. I had my pocketknife in my fist, and I was just waitin' for the right time, when I could give him a clip on the chin. You ever hit a man with a pocketknife in your hand? You can knock a stud bull down to the size of a heifer! Remember ol' Baldy Barker, in Fort Worth? Remember when I knocked him out, cold as a Colorado mornin'?" He started nodding his head. "I had my fist curled around my pocketknife that time, too."

Solon was talking so hard, he missed it when Clayton stepped into Henry Sturm's Liquor Store. He took several steps past the door, then had to turn around and go back.

"I could use a drink," he said as he stepped inside.

"Ain't buyin' no whiskey," Clayton said. "I promised to buy Tracy a raspberry soda pop."

"A what?" Solon asked.

"A soda pop. Ever had one?"

"Not to my recollection. It's that sweet stuff, ain't it?" Solon said.

Clayton asked, "Well, what flavor do you want?"

Solon looked forlornly at the bottles of whiskey. He licked his lips. His brow wrinkled. He slowly pulled his eyes from the bottles and studied the question a moment. "I sure don't want no raspberry," he said.

Henry Sturm said, "Well, we got ginger ale, strawberry, lemon, and vaniller."

Solon glanced once more at the whiskey, "Well shoot, I'll try lemon."

Clayton bought two raspberries for himself and Tracy. They took their soda pop and went to Ham Bell's Livery Stable, where they paid fifty cents boarding fee and saddled up Solon's horse.

Solon had his bottle of lemon soda pop open before they were out of town. He took a big drink, then made a face and spit. "My gawd, it's awful, Clayton!" he gasped. "Why, it's sweet as honey." He took another little drink. This time, he swallowed and rubbed his tongue around the inside of his mouth. "Tastes like somebody squeezed a lemon and dumped a bunch of sugar and syrup in it." He continued to cuss the soda pop all the way to Tracy's, but he managed to drink it all. He held up his empty bottle. "We can use this when we get the house built," he said. "Hell, a man could put water in it, or put it up on a shelf for people to look at." He put the bottle in his saddlebag.

Clayton became gloomy when Solon mentioned building the house. He'd already been angry at himself for spending so much money during their stay in Dodge City. He reckoned the only hope he had was selling half of his beeves to Kirby Wiggins. Maybe it was good that Solon had been ordered out of town, he thought. It was best to leave while he still had at least some pocket change.

But Clayton was having a hard time pulling himself away from Tracy. He was enjoying her company and the regular-as-clockwork frolicking. He wished Solon wasn't with him right now. It would have been nice to be with Tracy one more time before he left.

When they reached Tracy's place, he told Solon, "You go on in and talk to Tracy. She was mighty concerned about you. I want to give the horses a good feed and waterin'." He led the horses around back.

Inside, Tracy hugged Solon and took his arm. "I'm so glad to see you," she said. "I've been nearly sick with worry over you. Shorty Gillis was here this mornin'." She motioned toward the table. "Sit down and let me get you some coffee. Shorty told me all about it. He said Clayton came down hard on Dave Mathers." She set his cup on the table and filled it. "Solon, you look after Clayton, now," she said sternly. "That Dave Mathers is a dangerous man."

Solon snorted at the idea. "Clayton don't need any lookin' after! I'd be more worried for Mysterious Dave Mathers than I would for Clayton."

There was a nice aroma in the house. Tracy sat down with her own cup of coffee. "I'm fryin' a chicken," she explained. "It'll be ready shortly." She paused and sipped her coffee. "Where is Clayton? I thought he rode in with you."

"He's takin' care of the horses. We're leavin', ya know."

Tracy pulled back, the hurt showing on her face. "You're not serious?" she said. "Why, Clayton said just this mornin' that you-all were gonna stay a few more days."

Solon rubbed his hands over his eyes and looked sheepish. "Well, that part's my fault, Tracy," he said. "That derned Marshal Bridges said I have to leave town right away, if'n I don't want to stand trial. You shoulda seen it!" he said, suddenly excited. "Wyatt Earp and Bat Masterson come and got me out of jail! They took me over to the Long Branch, and you know who was in there? Doc Holliday, and Luke Short, and Billy Petillion, and Frank McClain. They all come to town to help ol' Luke Short out of a tight spot. I couldn't believe my eyes!"

"I've heard about those men, sorry to say," Tracy said.

"Most of 'em have earned their reputations with their guns. I swear, men are all alike!"

The mention of these men's names brought back memories of Pug. Tracy hadn't gotten used to the fact, but out here in this God-forsaken country, a man was more thought of for how he handled himself in a fight than for any other accomplishment. It still surprised her that she had fallen for Clayton, and at their very first meeting. She had felt an instant spark for him, in spite of the fact that she'd known about him and his reputation as a gunhand, even before Solon had introduced them. She had always deplored tough men and their violent ways. Even the mention of Wyatt Earp, about whom she heard nothing but praise—in fact, Shorty Gillis had once told her that Earp would rather walk around a fight than join it—brought a feeling of sadness to her.

Somehow, though, Clayton was different, in a way Tracy didn't understand. He made her feel safe, and she knew that he was a good man. She reached over and took Solon's hand.

"Maybe I'm an awful foolish woman, Solon, but I've developed some very strong feelings for Clayton. I can't help it. Please," she said, "tell me more about him. There's so much I don't know."

Solon stared at her for several seconds. "Well," he said slowly, "he don't say a lot. Kinda keeps to himself, ya might say. But, I don't have a better friend in the world than Clayton Crist. Why he puts up with me, I don't know." He stopped and his shoulders drooped. "Look here, Tracy, honey. I ain't never talked about Clayton behind his back. Never. But I think the world of you, and I guess you have a right to know about him." He grimaced. "I believe he might just be the saddest man I've ever known."

Tracy frowned. "What do you mean, the saddest man?"

Solon didn't like talking about Clayton in this manner. He knew he had a tendency to ramble on and on and say things he shouldn't, but it seemed the more he rambled, the more there was to say. He couldn't help himself. Most men made fun of the fact, but Clayton never had. In fact, no one had ever been a more loyal friend than Clayton, even during the times when Solon drank too much and made a fool of himself. Clayton had always been there for him.

Pug O'Brien had been a good man, too, and had married a good woman. Solon gave Tracy's hand a squeeze. She had always accepted Solon for what he was, without question.

"Well, Tracy," he sighed, "like I said, you've got a right to know. I guess you could say Clayton is generous to a fault. Hell, he's like me, in that he'll never keep a dime in his pocket. Always doin' for others." He smiled. "You know, he should've had young'uns. I always see a tenderness in him when he's around young'uns."

Solon could see her eyes softening. A pleasant look returned to her face.

He went on in a serious tone. "I've heard him scream out in the night, like a little kid," he said, leaning forward for emphasis and squinting his eyes, "and I mean pretty dern regular. Though Clayton's never told me about the war, I've run across fellers that served with him. I heard tell that there wasn't a better fighter in the whole Rebel army. Why shoot fire! Ol' Grant ran for president, and got elected, 'cause he was on the winnin' side. Maybe if the South would've won, things would've been different for Clayton. I just don't know." He paused a moment, then added, "One thing's for sure. Somethin' died inside of Clayton durin' that war."

Solon felt guilty for going on about such personal matters, but he couldn't stop. He had seen the romance that was starting up between Tracy and Clayton, and he didn't want to see her get hurt. He nodded sadly. "Yes, I think he's got a lot of demons inside him, and I don't think there's a person livin' that can get deep enough inside the man to drive 'em away. Clayton certainly don't know how to do it. He won't even talk about it."

"Then why would he want to take up a gun after the war?" Tracy said, her face gloomy again. "I read about him once, in Chicago, and I've heard there's no one better than Clayton Crist in a gunfight." She gave a sad smile. "I remember when you told me what folks call him. 'The

Gunny.' At the time, I thought it sounded so silly. But everybody talks about him and how many men he's killed. Has there really been that many, Solon?''

''I wish I could say no,'' Solon said. ''You take Wyatt Earp and Bat Masterson, and that hot-headed little Luke Short, and that loco Doc Holliday. Why, if a fight had erupted in there between them and Clayton, Clayton would've shot every one of 'em! And that ain't braggin'. There's none better under pressure. He can kill easier and more efficient than anyone I ever saw.'' Solon stopped and saw the hurt in her eyes. ''Tracy honey, Clayton's the best I ever saw at two things. Killin' and catchin' women.'' He took in a deep breath. ''The trouble is, I think they're both his biggest demons. Hell, everybody talks about his killin' and''—he squinted one eye nearly shut—''he can catch women easier'n I can catch fish. I think that might be where the sadness comes from. I think Clayton's been lookin' for love all his life, but for some crazy reason, he seems to run from it.''

Solon watched Tracy's pretty face and tried to read her innermost thoughts. Over the years, he'd gotten so used to Clayton and his way with the ladies, he'd stopped paying much attention. There'd been few if any places where some lady hadn't fallen all over herself to get close to Clayton, and surprisingly, Clayton seemed to be easily smitten, himself. When it came time to ride, though, he'd leave, always quietly and in a thoughtfulness that could last several days. He and Solon had been in Dodge City for over a week, and Solon knew well what was happening. Clayton could extract a lady from her drawers more quickly than anyone he'd ever seen. But Tracy was special, and Solon held her in deep respect.

''You've fallen for him hard, haven't you?''

Tracy swallowed. She felt a deep aching inside. She had already lost Clayton. Solon's words verified it. Barely above a whisper, she said, ''Does it show that much?''

Solon raised his eyebrows and nodded.

''What am I gonna do, Solon?''

''I wish I could tell ya.''

Tracy nodded and bit her bottom lip. ''I told him I could

love him, but who did I think I was kiddin'?" She stood up and started to walk back and forth, clutching her coffee cup in her hands. "I've missed Pug so much, and I've been lonely for so long," she went on. "At first, I thought I was just turning to Clayton for comfort. But I was wrong." She stopped and sat down again, looking guilty and miserable at the same time. "Please don't hate me, Solon, but I think I love Clayton as much as I loved Pug!"

Solon awkwardly reached up and gently squeezed her chin. "I could never hate you, Tracy. I wish Clayton were a different sort. I really do."

"So, that's that," Tracy said. She blinked back the tears that welled up in her eyes.

Just then, the door opened, and Clayton stepped inside. Tracy got up and turned her back at the stove. She was rubbing her eyes.

"Well, I guess Solon told you," Clayton said. "We gotta be goin'."

Solon jumped to his feet, knocking the chair over. "I gotta take care of somethin' outside," he said.

Clayton nodded. "Thanks."

Tracy turned around to look at him. Her eyes were red. "I guess you'll be goin' to Ness City?" she asked.

Clayton nodded. "Yeah, it's Ness County to most folks, but they've got a little town there now. I should have six or seven beeves, and I figure if I sell off three of 'em, we'll be able to buy those pigs and some lumber and get started," he said unnecessarily.

"Well, there's no need to rush off. Surely, you have time for a bite to eat?" Tracy said. She started to walk past him to the larder, but he caught her by the elbow.

Clayton saw the hurt in her eyes, and he wanted to make her understand. He wanted to understand, himself.

"Look," he said, "there's nothing there. No comforts. It's just a dugout in the ground, if it hasn't caved in, that is. You've got everything that creeps and crawls, runnin' through your food and your clothes. It's no place for a woman."

She shrugged away from him. "You don't have to make

excuses, Clayton. We were good for each other for a short time. Let's just leave it at that.''

Clayton took hold of her shoulders and pulled her mouth to his. She kissed him back, and they both felt the same passion come over them.

''You said you could love me,'' Clayton whispered. ''I could love you, too.'' He breathed into her hair. ''Maybe I can come back and get you, when the house is done and the place is ready. Will you wait for me?''

Tracy was shaking. She nodded. ''I'll wait.''

Clayton could hardly pull himself atop his horse. He didn't want to leave. He wanted to stay right there in that little house with the picket fence, to go to bed that night with Tracy lying on his shoulder, her breath soft against his neck and her fragrance filling his nostrils.

He needed that comfort.

19

CHICKAMAUGA HAD been the victory that the South so desperately needed. It should have been a glorious time, and among the soldiers it was. They celebrated for days.

If any other general besides Braxton Bragg had been in charge, it might have been the turning point in the war. Bragg, however, remained obstinate to the end, choosing not to pursue Rosecrans and the Federal army. Instead, his idea was to cut off the Federal lines and starve them, rather than cutting out their hearts. He ordered the erection of permanent lines of earthworks on Missionary Ridge and Lookout Mountain. Bragg's intention was to give his army time to regroup and catch their breath. All the while, though, the Federals were fortifying, too, in Chattanooga.

Rosecrans's army was not admitting defeat. His chief of engineers, General Saint Clair Morton, soon laid waste to the town of Chattanooga. Homes were turned into blockhouses. Breastworks were stretched all along the river, above and below the city. Even the final resting place for the dead, the Citizen's Graveyards, were turned into rifle pits. The Federal army was preparing itself to turn defeat into victory.

As Bragg held the railroad line from Bridgeport to Chattanooga, with the hope of starving the Federals into submission, the resourceful Rosecrans brought in wagon trains of supplies across the Cumberland Mountains. In the meantime, Bragg was managing to starve out the citizens of Chattanooga, as well. Forced out of their homes, they huddled about on the streets, victims to the fall rains that had started. Their bellies cried out for food. Little children died of hunger and exposure, clinging to their mothers' breasts.

Clayton's bitterness toward the war and General Bragg, himself, had nearly reached its peak. He had to turn a deaf ear when his messmates began discussing politics and the war. Nothing made any sense anymore, and that made him angry.

He had come to the decision some time ago that this was Mr. Lincoln's war. It wasn't about slavery, really. In fact, in the beginning, very little had even been said about slavery. That had been Mr. Lincoln's doing. He needed votes, so he'd turned the big issue into slavery, working on people's sympathies and emotions.

So, Clayton wondered, exactly why was he fighting this war? Slavery was as foreign to him as was dining in Paris. No one in Beartooth Flats had ever owned a slave, and many had never even seen one. They were just poor dirt farmers who spent every spring and summer worrying about how to put back food and supplies for the winter months.

Clayton knew better than to voice such thoughts to his messmates. Once, though, he entered into a discussion over slavery with a corporal from Columbia named Sammy Vestal. When Clayton honestly voiced his opinion that no man should own another, Vestal grew hostile and declared Clayton to be a Yankee sympathizer. A fight ensued, during which Clayton bit off the top of Vestal's left ear.

He was sent to Colonel Hume Feild. Feild was largely understanding of Clayton's position. He tried to explain to him the issue of states' rights, and cautioned Clayton to be careful about making such remarks. In confidence, Feild also admitted that he, too, questioned the rights of one man to own another. Slavery was on the way out, he said, when the war started, and it was just a matter of time. He did, however, wholeheartedly believe that each state should have the right to self-govern.

"If the Federals don't believe in slavery, so be it," Feild said, "but they have no right to tell the good people of Tennessee, or Georgia, or Mississippi how to live their lives! Why, if I were president of the Confederacy," he went on, "I'd release all the slaves. Let 'em go live with the Yankees.

Let the Yankees feed and take care of 'em! Slavery's an issue that we never should have gotten involved with in the
first place. Morally, I would agree with you, Clayton. It's
wrong for a man to own another man. But I can understand
why our fathers and their fathers used them. The South's not
like the North. We never had the manpower or the industry.
I guess slaves were just deemed a necessity. But, to tell you
the truth, we would have been miles and miles ahead if our
country had never established slavery in the first place. And
that's including the North!'' He added emphatically.
''Sometimes, I wish I could find the first man that brought
them over here, dig him up, and hang him!''

Colonel Feild grew reflective. ''You know, Crist, I'm
afraid the South will forever be tarnished over this slave
issue if we lose the war. It's already hurt us abroad. I think
some European nations would've given us support, even
military support, if it hadn't been for the slave issue.
There's an arrogance that runs rampant in the North that
doesn't set well in other parts of the world. But,'' he said
in a resigned voice, ''this slave business is liable to hang
around our necks for generations to come.''

Clayton left Colonel Feild's tent with the same distaste
for this war as when he'd gone in, but he felt better justified
in his thinking. He liked Hume Feild. Feild was a decent
man and a fine leader—a rarity, in Clayton's opinion.

He wished he could say the same of the generals. Besides
Frank Cheatham, the only other Southern generals worth their
salt were Generals Pat Cleburne and Nathan Bedford Forrest.
These were men that Clayton would willingly follow, for he
knew that they fought as gallantly as the privates, laying it all
on the line. The other generals were nothing more than pomp
and circumstance who sent innocent boys to their deaths
while they stood back and watched.

As Braxton Bragg's trump card was to starve out the
Federal army, he succeeded in starving out his own men as
well. Those who were supposed to have faith in his
leadership were now living on one-third rations. Food was
cooked behind the lines and brought forward every three
days. The men scarfed it down, but it hardly satisfied their
ravenous hunger. Three long days would pass before more

rations were brought. For a conquering army, the Confederates themselves looked as broken and filthy as they had at any point during the war. Their bodies were thin and undernourished. They took to eating everything that crept or crawled in the north Georgia wilderness. Starved horses and mules lay dead on both sides.

It was during the standoff that the president of the Confederacy, Jefferson Davis, arrived. He rode in among the soldiers, saddened by what he saw. The men looked up to him and called out for food for their empty bellies and clothing to cover their weary bodies.

President Davis stopped and gave a speech. He admonished the men to remain patriotic. Their cause, he said, was every bit as important as the one they had upheld during the Revolutionary War. They must regain Chattanooga. They must continue to present a vigorous, united, and persistent effort. They would win this war, the president said. Soon, the fields of Tennessee would once again be green, and the army of the South would again be able to eat their fill.

As the men of the South cheered, long and loud, at President Jefferson Davis's promises, Clayton stood quietly in their midst, unmoving. He didn't hear the shouting and the applause. His eyes were fixed on some unseen object, as his mind studied the lack of substance in Davis's words.

How could this weakened, half-starved army ever make the fields of Tennessee green again? Clayton could almost visualize the entire state burning, its soil poisoned with the rancor of death. He had a fleeting thought of pulling up his rifle and shooting the president. Maybe then the army would disperse and give up this lost cause. Maybe some of these boys who stood there, cheering, could go home to their families and live again. Was defeat a more bitter harvest than no harvest at all? Clayton looked throughout the crowd. He wondered how many of these faces would be alive thirty, sixty, or ninety days from now.

Nearly one month after the South's victory in the Chickamauga Valley, General Bragg still sat on his plans. On October 16, General Thomas replaced Rosecrans as commander of the Army of the Cumberland and began to turn the beaten Federals back into a proud, fighting army. On October 23, General Grant, now the commander of the military division of the Mississippi, arrived at Chattanooga. He quickly began to open up a river road to Bridgeport to get supplies through.

On November 1, Bragg sent General Longstreet's corps to fight Burnside in Knoxville, along with the cavalry under General Wheeler, and the artillery under General Alexander. Bragg could not afford to lose Longstreet's seasoned army, and it threatened to be a costly move for the Confederacy and Jefferson Davis's idea of seeing fields of green once again in Tennessee.

General Bragg's starvation plan took a complete turnabout when General Thomas attacked and took Bragg's outpost line at Orchard's Knob, only a mile in front of the Southern army on Missionary Ridge. The next day, General Sherman crossed the river and attacked the north end of Missionary Ridge. General Hooker attacked Lookout Mountain.

Cleburne managed to turn back Sherman's attack, but Hooker was making progress. The Confederates were climbing up Lookout Mountain with the Federals in hard pursuit. On November 25, Hooker's army raised the stars and stripes over the summit of Lookout Mountain. By now, the three Federal armies had come together, devastating everything in their sight. The outnumbered Confederates threw the Federals back, time after time, but anyone with an eye could see the inevitable.

Five Confederate batteries fired grape and canister shots at the advancing enemy, spewing death and destruction on the attacking army. The rifle pits fired hail and brimstone at the Federals, but still they came.

Clayton surveyed the ground in front of him. It was littered like a prone forest with the bodies of dead and dying Yankees, yet there seemed to be no end to the numbers of Northern soldiers, as their columns marched forward.

Clayton was reloading when he noticed the silence around him. Below, the Yankee fire continued. He looked around and realized then that he was the only one left alive on the little ridge. His dead mates covered the ground like a thick growth of vegetation, bodies twisted and mangled, hanging over limbs and among the rocks. Below, the Yankee artillery kept shooting up Missionary Ridge. Clayton could almost hear the men's laughter through the booming of artillery and the crack of musketry, like friends at a wild turkey shoot.

Clayton climbed up higher and grabbed two of his dead companions' rifles. One had been fired. He took careful aim with the other and dropped a man in blue at a distance of sixty yards. Then, he climbed farther. He couldn't find a man in gray that wasn't dead or badly wounded. He stopped again to fire his own rifle and noticed that the sixty yards had been cut down to half that distance as the Federals advanced.

Clayton made it to a rock that jutted out like a big buck tooth, and took refuge behind it. From this point, he could see what was left of his own army, retreating and running for their lives. Some had thrown down their guns so they could run faster.

Clayton was soon overtaken by two Yankees. He killed the first with his pistol, and was grappling hand to hand with the second. The Yankee was bigger and stronger. He manhandled Clayton, throwing him to the ground while Clayton held on to his shirt for dear life. They struggled, until in desperation, Clayton grabbed the Yankee behind the head and, with all his strength, pulled him forward. He sank his teeth into the Yankee's nose as hard as he could, biting down deep into the flesh. The Yankee tried to wrench away, and Clayton thought his teeth might be pulled from his head, but he held on.

The Yankee's scream was deafening. His blood ran onto Clayton's face, into his mouth, and down his chin and neck. Around them, Yankees were running past to the top of the mountain, ignoring their struggle.

Clayton worked his left arm around the Yankee's neck and fumbled with his right hand until he had his bowie knife grasped firmly in his fist. Finally, he plunged it into the Yankee, pushing with all his might, then working the knife back and forth. The Yankee thrashed and jerked violently, but Clayton held on to him until he was dead.

When he was sure the Yankee had breathed his last, Clayton lay there, letting the deadweight of the Yankee rest upon him. He tried to quietly cough out the flesh and blood that filled his mouth, making it hard to breathe.

This was the safest place for him to be. He lay there, underneath the dead Yankee, with his heart pounding so loud, he was sure that one of the passing Yankees would hear it and stop to kill him.

He lay there for what seemed like several hours, playing 'possum under the dead Yankee and barely able to breathe through the thick blood that still covered his mouth.

When it seemed peaceful, Clayton crawled out from under the body, retrieved his rifle, and crawled in among some trees to wait for darkness.

Just before dusk, he heard someone beating a single drum. It was only a few yards away, and approaching. He strained his eyes to see.

Suddenly, like a deer stepping out of a thicket, a young Yankee drummer boy appeared before him. Their eyes spotted one another at the same instant, the boy keeping a steady beat on the drum, and Clayton with his finger steady on the trigger of his rifle. Fear splashed across the little drummer boy's face as he recognized the enemy, and the drumming stopped.

"How old are you, boy?" Clayton asked.

"Twelve."

"This ain't no place for you. You oughta be home with your mama and papa. What are you doin' out here alone?"

The boy's hand slowly went to his head. He removed his cap. "I don't really remember," he said. There was a bloody bump at the hairline on the right side of his head.

"A minié ball grazed me. I guess it knocked me out." He stopped and tilted his head slightly. "Are you gonna kill me?"

Clayton grimaced and shook his head. "No boy, I'm not gonna kill you. Git along now, and don't be beatin' that drum out here by yourself. The next feller you run across might not be as generous."

The boy replaced his cap and started up the mountain. He was nearly past Clayton when he turned and said, "I'm from Ohio. Where are you from, Johnny Reb?"

"I'm from Tennessee."

"Do you think this war's about over?"

"I hope so."

"Yeah, me too."

When it was dark enough for cover, Clayton left the shelter of the trees and went looking for his army. He had no idea how he managed to stay alive, for every warm body he passed by was that of a Federal. It took a long series of twists and detours, and he nearly gave up hope before he found his regiment.

The First Tennessee was drawing rations. Colonel Feild spotted Clayton right away.

"Get somethin' to eat, Crist. We're the rear guard. We must move fast," he said.

Thus, the First Tennessee retreated, and Clayton lived to fight another day. He found no comfort or happiness in the fact. Missionary Ridge had killed something inside of Clayton. Something that would never live again.

When they arrived at Chickamauga Station, they were ordered to stay there and burn the town and all the provisions that had been gathered there in Bragg's efforts to starve out the Yankees.

There wasn't a soldier in the Tennessee army that didn't curse Bragg, as the hungry men watched everything go up in flames. There was bacon, molasses, huge piles of corn, crackers, potatoes, and barrel after barrel of flour. Clayton, like all the others, filled up empty corn sacks with as much as he could carry. He ate crackers by the mouthful and consumed ears of corn, filling his shrunken belly until it was comfortably miserable.

There was enough to feed and replenish the entire Tennessee Army, to strengthen and comfort the men who'd been living on rations of one meal every three days. Clayton looked upon the destruction, and he knew what he had suspected all along.

Not only was his own army outmanned, outprovisioned, and outarmed. They were outgeneraled, too. So far, it had been a give-and-take war, with neither side showing any clear-cut edge. But, as Clayton stood there and breathed in the ashes of what had been Chickamauga Station, he knew that an army that would starve its own and then lay such waste as this was an army that could not win.

20

ON DECEMBER 16, 1863, orders came down that General Joseph E. Johnston was to take over command of the Army of Tennessee from Lieutenant General Hardee, who had temporarily taken over when Braxton Bragg resigned. Members of the First Tennessee were pleased with Bragg's resignation. Bragg had become extremely unpopular, not only with the foot soldiers, but with the officers that served under him as well. He could barely pass by his own troops, that they didn't greet him with some type of catcall. Bragg had a favorite saying, "Here's my soldiers," and the men had taken to responding in unison, "Here's your mule!" Clayton heard the chants, "Bully for Bragg!" and "He's hell on retreat," so often, he stopped paying attention to their meaning.

Whereas Bragg had never been a soldier's commander, General Johnston became a favorite leader. He immediately set about to reshape the Army of Tennessee, ordering much-needed supplies, provisions, and new clothing. He rationed whiskey and tobacco, and began issuing the men something they hadn't had in a long time: furloughs. Under Bragg's command, it had been almost impossible to obtain a leave, but Johnston used them to set up incentives. One was based upon how well a soldier performed in the field. It became a common joke among the men in Clayton's company that he could easily get the rest of the war off.

Bragg had been accused of killing off more of his own soldiers than of the enemy. Many men were executed upon his order. General Johnston was just as bully as Bragg on issuing executions as punishment, and for that reason, it was indeed ironic that he was able to lift the morale of the Tennessee Army higher than at any other point in the war.

By now, Clayton had gone through another bleak and lonely Christmas. He'd lost all feelings for the war and its participants, and his hopes for a good outcome were gone. He couldn't have cared less about the hullabaloo that surrounded Johnston's officially taking over the Tennessee Army on December 27. He couldn't foresee Johnston as being any different from Bragg or the other generals. As far as he was concerned, he hadn't had any use for Bragg, and he wouldn't have any use for Johnston, either. Johnston, he decided, was just another deadly puppet for President Davis, sent to wear field glasses and sit on a ridge, watching the good and the young die below him.

One of the first items on General Johnston's agenda was to call meetings with the staff and members of the army. Clayton had just come in off picket, when Colonel Feild informed him that he was to meet with their new commander.

Clayton looked puzzled. "I don't understand," he said. He confronted the colonel, eye to eye. "This isn't about a promotion to lieutenant, is it?"

Colonel Feild was one of the few people of rank whom Clayton respected. After Lieutenant Rice, whom Clayton considered to be a true friend, Colonel Feild seemed to be the most genuine of the men in leadership. In return, Feild held a special fondness for Clayton.

"I wish you wouldn't feel that way, Crist," Feild said sincerely. "You should deem it an honor that your name has been held in such high esteem for promotion. Why, your fellow soldiers believe that you would make a fine officer. Nevertheless, to answer your question, I have no idea what the general wants. I do know that he's trying to get a feel for his new command and the men under him."

General Joseph Eggleston Johnston had been born in

Longwood, Virginia, on February 3, 1809, to a family of above-average means. He had been in the same graduating class at West Point with General Lee. Previously, he had served in both the Florida and Mexican wars and was considered by some to be the smartest officer in the entire Confederate Army. He had worked himself up through the ranks, distinguishing himself at every level.

Johnston did not take his new position lightly. The Army of Tennessee was in need of a man such as himself. He immediately set out to turn things around, if that were at all possible.

Even at the beginning of this war, he had held no illusions about the South's chances. Besides being far less populated than the North, the Confederacy lacked the financial support needed to win such a war. The armies of the South had fought hard, and at one point, Johnston had even thought the war might be won solely by the men's sheer courage and determination.

Now, it was the beginning of a new year. General Johnston sat in his tent in Dalton, Georgia, and wondered what 1864 had in store for the beleaguered Confederate Army. Bragg had been wrong in not pursuing Rosecrans after Chickamauga. Now, Grant had the upper hand. He owned the waterways and shipping lanes. Bragg had left an army of officers that doubted not only themselves, but their commanders as well. That would never do, and Johnston knew it.

Time was running out on the South. Johnston knew that his only chance to win this war was to make his army believe in themselves again. They had to know that they could prevail against all odds. He called meetings with the officers and the men who had been singled out for distinction. He gave them encouragement and, he hoped, the guidance that would reassure them into once again believing in their commanding general.

Seated in his tent, Johnston again looked down at the name on the list he held in his hand. He had heard many reports about Corporal Clayton Crist, a man who had distinguished himself in every campaign and conflict. Johnston's pulse raced. He had to see for himself what this

Clayton Crist was like. He wanted to talk to the man who they claimed had a guardian angel with him in battle. Reports stated that Crist had killed a brigade of Yankees—some even said a *regiment* of Yankees—since the war had started. Never had Johnston heard such talk about one soldier. He wanted to find out more, to determine why a man with such credentials on the battlefield was not commanding troops. He drew in his breath as he saw Colonel Feild approaching his tent. He stood up and tilted his head sideways, trying to peer at the soldier who was walking behind the colonel.

"Come in," he said.

Johnston had expected to see a man who was larger than life, tough and aggressive in attitude. What appeared before him took him completely by surprise. Clayton Crist was an average-sized, undernourished corporal with piercing blue eyes and tender features. His clothing was filthy and torn. His hands were small and delicate, even though the knuckles were caked with grime and the fingernails black. He moved with a gracefulness, his body seeming loose and natural. He looked very young, and he was strikingly handsome. Johnston pictured him in full uniform, fancily dressed with a saber hanging at his side. He would cut a dashing figure, he thought.

But there was no fear in the corporal's eyes, nor was there any of the innocence of youth remaining. Johnston studied them a moment. He pondered the effects of war and how it had stolen a part of this man's life from him. Then he motioned Clayton to a chair, and they both sat down.

"Let's see," he began, referring to his list. "You were at Shiloh, Perryville, Murfreesboro, Chickamauga, and Missionary Ridge. Your name was placed on the Roll of Honor at Murfreesboro and Chickamauga. It says here that, had there been a Roll of Honor at Shiloh and Perryville, your name would've been added there, as well." He paused and looked up at Clayton, his eyes serious. "Tell me, if you will, Crist. What is it about you that has caused you to distinguish yourself so? Is it anger? Are you angry when you go into battle? Or are you just tougher than the rest?"

He didn't appear to expect an answer, so Clayton sat quietly as Johnston paused a moment to gaze off in thought. "You see," he went on, "I've always wondered what makes some men fight, while others run. For the life of me, I cannot discern what makes one man distinguish himself from others. And you, I must admit, are the most intriguing of all." He tapped the paper against his hand. "According to this report, you have displayed heroism at every campaign in which you participated. In that regard, Corporal Crist, you are unique. So many times, I've seen men who rally in one effort, but fall behind in the next. They are unable to maintain that high level of courage at every battle." He shook his balding head and tapped his index finger against his bottom lip. His face was one of puzzlement. "But you've done it at every turn. Why?"

Clayton shifted about nervously. He had heard that Johnston was a dandy, and he certainly wasn't disappointing. He was exactly what Clayton would have expected a commander to be, distinguished in his fine dress, beard, and mustache. In a small way, he reminded Clayton of General Lee, except with a bit more polish. He knew the general wanted a sincere answer, but none came to mind. Finally, he shrugged. "I don't know what to say, sir. I'm afraid you're asking a question that I can't answer."

Johnston studied him for several seconds. "Ever since the day I reached Dalton, I have heard your name mentioned, over and over. It is the consensus that you should be a lieutenant. Hell, some have said that you should be promoted to colonel or general! I hear the same opinions about you expressed by all. Time and again, you have said that you don't wish to take the added responsibility, yet in battle, you always do!" He thoughtfully tapped his lip again. "I'm not going to insist that you take the promotion, Crist. I could, but I have decided that you must have a good reason for declining. If anything, I would like to persuade you to change your mind. It's not just a matter of bestowing a new title. We *need* men like you, more than any other time in this war. We need good leaders." He frowned, as if reflecting on something that disturbed him. "What are your thoughts on the state of the war, Corporal?"

Clayton fidgeted again in his chair. He rubbed his sweaty hands together and took in a breath. "I'm afraid you don't want to hear my thoughts, General Johnston," he said.

Johnston waved his arm amiably. "Oh, but I do! And please, by all means, understand that I will not judge you for your frankness! A man with your record would never be judged harshly. The battlefield, and the battlefield alone, is where I will base my opinions. So please, speak freely."

Clayton cleared his throat. He didn't want to be here, and he certainly didn't want to speak his innermost thoughts. After all, they belonged to him, and him alone. And hadn't he done his duty on the battlefield? That was where his obligations should end. Still, sitting across from the general, Clayton knew that this man would not be easily put off. He felt a sudden anger rise up inside, almost out of nowhere.

"Well, sir, if you really want to know the truth, I'll be as frank and honest as I can," he said tensely. "I'm sick of this war. I'm sick of steppin' over piles of bodies, of seein' boys I've known all my life lyin' there with their heads shot off. I'm tired of watchin' men bein' pulled off the field with their legs and arms missin'. And what's it all for? So generals and presidents can feel glorified with what they call a victory?"

The general was sitting very still, staring at Clayton without expression. Clayton didn't know what the general was feeling, but he didn't care. He leaned forward.

"And Mister Lincoln," he said, almost spitting out the words. "Just who does he think he is? Why, he's nothing more than a bloodthirsty politician! He doesn't care a thing about the coloreds. His only concern is getting himself votes. I heard he was angry after Gettysburg, because Meade didn't pursue Lee and destroy the Army of Virginia. Well, I wasn't at Gettysburg, sir, but I was at Perryville." He thought then about Jolene, and a bitterness filled his voice. "The trouble with Mister Lincoln is, he didn't see the *blood*. He didn't see the hurt in those men's eyes, or hear 'em cryin' out whilst they died. He hasn't seen nothin'. Nor has Mister Davis. Neither one of 'em has had to experience the sorrowful sounds on the battlefields. I doubt they've ever been inside the surgeons' tents and heard the screamin' of boys havin' their arms and legs sawed off, while some sweaty, smelly stranger holds 'em down. Boys that should've been home with their poor worried mamas.''

Clayton stopped and remembered briefly his own boyhood romance with war. His visions of fighting for one's country had been gentle, almost sterile. No blood, or horror, or fear. No walking up to find one's best friend lying there, his eyes staring up in death.

"And all the executions! Why?" He held his hands up as his voice rose. "If anybody has to be executed, why not the generals, instead of the privates! I mean, a private gets executed for runnin' away from the fightin', but why not Bragg? Is he any less guilty for not goin' after Rosecrans's ass after Chickamauga? Think of all the fine boys that'll die because Bragg didn't have the sense or courage or maybe both to do what should've been done! Isn't that just as wrong, sir? You generals lose your command when you make a mistake. The private soldiers lose their lives!" Clayton pounded his fist gently against his leg. "No sir"— he shook his head—"I don't believe I want to lead nobody nowhere. Not in this war. I just don't believe in it anymore."

An eerie silence followed. General Johnston felt the heat rise from his neck and spread up to his face. He felt stunned by Clayton's words, as if he'd been attacked personally. He didn't know what he'd expected from this fighting man about whom he'd heard so much, but it certainly wasn't this. Soldiering had been Johnston's life. He had served his country to the best of his ability, yet this man was making him feel guilty. His nostrils flared and his jaw twitched as he bit down hard.

Slowly, he said, "I guess war is not to be understood. There are powers higher than you and I who make the decisions. I've not always been comfortable with war, and I certainly would gladly open up all the graves and return the men to life, if I could. But what you have said sounds terribly close to treason." He again tapped the paper in his hand and shook his head. "But, I would find it most difficult to use that word in connection with a man so brave on the battlefield as yourself. Corporal Crist, whether you like it or not, there's always war. There have been wars in the past, and there will be war in the future. Men are conquerors, and there will always be freedoms to fight for. The fact that we are able to sit here today, on this very ground, is because others shed their blood before us, at another time and another place. It wasn't that long ago, when our young country took up arms against the Crown for our own freedom. Now, as Americans, we find ourselves defining another freedom, all over again. Tomorrow, and in the future, there will be issues, and other wars to resolve them.''

The general thoughtfully tapped his fingernails against his teeth. He seemed disappointed when he spoke.

''Perhaps they're wrong about you, Corporal. Maybe you aren't of leadership ability.'' He took in a deep breath and blew it out. ''Perhaps you're just an enigma, after all.''

He stood up and walked to the opening of the tent. There were several seconds of silence.

Clayton's dander was still up. He spoke, but more softly, ''Back home in Beartooth Flats, they had to give up every man who could carry a weapon.'' He looked at the general's back. ''I'm all that's left, sir. They're all gone, but me! And for what? For slavery? For states' rights? Who's gonna do the plowin', sir?''

Johnston frowned and turned around. He put his hand to his ear. ''Pardon me?''

''The plowin', sir. The only males left back home in Beartooth Flats are little boys and old men. Who's gonna work the fields? Who's gonna be there for the womenfolk at night? Have Mister Lincoln and Mister Davis thought about that? The poor womenfolk,'' Clayton said, barely above a whisper. ''Their lives were tough enough to begin with, before this war took their men away.''

Their eyes met. Clayton said, ''Sir, have you thought about who's gonna do the plowin'?''

21

WINTER QUARTERS in Dalton, Georgia, became a camp of rejuvenation. President Davis had made it clear that he wanted the morale of the Army of Tennessee revived to a point as high as it had once been. He wanted to see the rebirth of a fighting machine, stronger and more committed to victory than ever. Even though Davis didn't like General Johnston much on a personal note, he realized that Johnston was the best man for the job. For his part, Johnston wasn't about to disappoint him or anybody. His camp became like a training camp for new recruits just starting out.

During this period, the Federals also changed commanders. General Grant was given his fourth star, becoming the first general since George Washington of the Colonial army to be so honored. Grant then would move on to Washington as commander-in-chief. His old command was handed to General Sherman. This gave Sherman three separate armies to use at his discretion: General Thomas and the Army of the Cumberland; General Schofield and the Army of Ohio; and General McPherson and the Army of the Tennessee.

Discipline became the order of the day. The men received proper training and direction and encouragement. Johnston began to reach his goal. At the surface, he did have a happier army. This was quite a feat, considering that most of the Army of Tennessee, and in fact all of the Army of the South, could see their cause tumbling.

Talk among the men in camp was of a different nature

than it had been one or two years earlier. Words like "states' rights" and "slavery" were rarely even heard anymore, let alone debated. Before Johnston's command, most of the soldiers had felt ready to quit, to lay down their arms and take their medicine. Johnston had changed that, or at least had been given the credit. It might truly have been the food in their bellies and the new clothes on their backs that cheered their basic nature, but to an inexperienced eye, Johnston appeared to have brought back a fortified, happy army.

Clayton went through the motions. He drilled with the rest and walked picket with the rest, but became more and more distant with those around him. He was finished with friendships and developing feelings for anyone who might end up dead the next day. And he certainly didn't want to know any more names of family, friends, or hometowns. He was through with that kind of pain. Detached and void of emotion, he watched the slow transformation of the Army of Tennessee into a camp filled with refreshed spirits and energy. His spirits should have been lifted, too, but Clayton wondered if he even had any spirit left, at all. If he did, it was locked away too deep inside.

To the north, Sherman made no secret of his plans to capture Atlanta, the town that boasted four railroads and manufactured virtually every product used in the South. Slowly, he began making his move, sending the Army of the Cumberland into the center and using his other armies to flank the rear.

Clayton wasn't surprised with Johnston's countermove retreat. Johnston wasn't so much different from Bragg, after all, he thought. Clayton lay awake at night and thought about what he considered the futility of it all. What nonsense must run rampant in the minds of the Southern generals! The army did indeed look healthier and better clothed on the outside, but what Johnston had truly built was nothing more than a hollow shell. The executions still went on, if anything, at a faster rate than under Bragg's orders.

It was there, at Dalton, that Clayton grew tired of the South. He was finished with hearing about gentleman cavaliers and such terms as "Pride of the South." The meanings had somehow changed.

In May, Sherman began his trek to seize Atlanta at Ring-gold Gap, where the Western and Atlantic Railroad ran. This line was extremely important to both sides. Hard fighting broke out there, and both armies moved southward. They fought at Tunnel Hill and at Rocky Face Ridge, a wall of quartz that stood nearly eight hundred feet tall.

The battle proved to be a difficult one for Sherman, since the South put up a hell of a stand. Every stone, every tree, held a Confederate behind it.

Clayton had settled into a spot between a boulder and a rock wall. His vantage point was good. He could see out, yet remain hidden with a place to steady his rifle.

For once, the defensive tactics of the Confederates seemed to be working. There at Rocky Face Ridge, they cut the Yankees down like twigs in a hurricane.

It was Monday, May 9, a fine Georgia morning. What had started out as a skirmish had turned into hard fighting. Winning this battle was almost a gimme to Clayton. Always before, he'd done his fighting out in the open, charging hard to the front. Now, though, he sat safely in his haven, like a marksman at a turkey shoot. It almost amused him, casually taking his time as he picked off the Federals, one by one.

When the Federals finally stopped coming, Clayton stood up and looked below, making sure there was nobody sneaking up close. He'd rolled a cigarette and lit up, noticing his hands were black with gunpowder from firing so many rounds. Suddenly, he felt a sickening pass through his body. It knocked him backward and slammed him against the quartz slab. He felt the air rush from his lungs, as his head struck the rock. He thought he might lose consciousness, but managed to pull himself out of it.

Everything was silent for several seconds. He knew he'd caught a bullet, but he wasn't sure where. At first, he felt no pain, but then a pain rose up in his left breast.

Clayton put his hand under his shirt and felt. There was no blood, only pain at the touch. Then, his hand touched the Testament, the book given to him by General Robert E. Lee. He pulled the Testament out and stared. A ball had gone through the front and lodged itself in amongst the pages, almost to the back cover.

Clayton sat there a moment. Then, he began to chuckle, starting softly at first, then bursting into loud laughter. He looked upward.

"I've debated you, Lord! My, how I've debated you!" The laughter died as tears began to roll down his cheeks. He kissed the Book. "You've heard all of Mama's prayers, ain't you? Well, I thank you."

That evening, Clayton couldn't get his mind off the miracle of what had happened. He held the Testament in his hands, frequently opening it to gaze at the minié ball lodged within. For some time, he'd carried the Book in his knapsack, pulling it out from time to time to thumb through the pages. The trouble was, though, he seldom got around to actually reading it. Following Perryville, he'd stuck it under his shirt, and had carried it next to his breast ever since. He'd never again opened it, but he did touch it before each battle and again at the close.

When he awoke the next morning, Clayton was so sore he could barely lift his left arm. Every breath sent pain through his body. When he took off his shirt, he saw the black-and-purple bruise that covered the left side of his chest, stretching all the way to under his arm. From the way his back hurt, he assumed it was black-and-blue, too. Again, he looked at the Testament and kissed it. He also thought about his mother. Coming so close to death, he realized that only through her diligent prayers had the Maker seen fit to spare his life—either that, or it wasn't his time yet.

When he began his move on Atlanta, Sherman had nearly one hundred thousand troops at his disposal. In response, Johnston started moving his army from one spot to another, traveling by night. Each morning, the troops woke up to renewed fighting. The pattern continued for what seemed like forever. Sherman moved forward, while Johnston kept retreating farther south. On May 12, Sherman's army passed through Snake Creek Gap, near Resaca. Johnston evacuated Dalton that night and positioned his army in front of Sherman's. The next day, General Polk arrived from Mississippi.

It seemed almost as if the entire world was ablaze with the fighting sounds of war. At Tilton, close to Dalton, and at Resaca, the armies constantly realigned themselves. The battles raged on for several days at Lay's Ferry, on the Oostenaula River, south of Resaca. In the middle of May, Johnston pulled out of Resaca in the darkness of night. Upon leaving, his army burned the railroad bridge. They headed toward Adairsville and Calhoun. At the former, Clayton was nicked by a minié in his left shoulder.

Two days later, Johnston ordered another withdrawal during the night, sending two corps to Cassville, and one to Kingston. Sherman was right behind both. Fighting broke out in the two areas, with only Hardee being able to hold position. Once again, Johnston retreated in the night and moved his army around Allatoona Pass to be near the Chattanooga-Atlanta Railroad.

The Confederates were run ragged. It seemed as if all they had done was fight and retreat, grabbing what little rations they could while on the run or in battle. Clayton's weight began to drop, along with his sagging spirits.

Late in May, Johnston's army had located at New Hope Church. They had been trying to get in front of Sherman's army and now, just barely twenty-five miles north of Atlanta, Johnston felt his army had finally gotten into the right position. Hardee was situated on the left, Polk was in the center and Hood commanded on the right. Sherman's counterposition had General Schofield on the left, Thomas in the center, and McPherson on the right.

Through a vicious, drenching thunderstorm, Sherman attacked. Johnston's rejuvenated army fought with everything they had and kept turning the Federals back. Once again, Clayton escaped death, as a minié ball split open his scalp, causing only superficial damage.

When the fighting ceased, the Confederates had stopped Sherman in his tracks, but casualties were high. The next day, it started up again, and with a new fervor. The war had taken on a frenetic pace, with continuous entrenchments and flanking movements, and renewed fighting every day. Oftentimes, the enemies would be located within yards of each other, but invisible to the eye in the thick Georgia countryside.

At New Hope Church, the Confederates inflicted heavy casualties on the Federals, yet the victory meant little to Clayton and men like him. He had long since lost the ability to differentiate between defeat and victory. Defeat was when a man got killed or severely wounded. Victory was when you lay in your bedroll with a splitting headache, sweat covering your body and your belly aching from hunger. Victory was when you longed to be home with your family, but knew you would fight another day, instead.

May passed and June arrived, with Yankee General Stonemen capturing Allatoona Pass. The railroad ran through the pass, and it was a major coup for Sherman's army. Once again, in a driving rainstorm, Johnston responded by moving his army in the night from New Hope Church outside of Atlanta, northward along the Lost, Pine, and Brush mountains.

The wet weather had become a daily feature. The men's provisions were soaked clear through. Mold grew openly on trees, tents, and even the men's clothing. Clayton paid it little mind. Misery had become a way of life, as natural as breathing, and there didn't appear to be any relief in sight. He'd quit thinking about it, along with most things that occur in a man's daily musings.

It was mid-June before the rains stopped, and a terrible loss came to the Confederate Army. General Johnston was in conference, standing high atop Pine Mountain with Generals Hardee and Polk. They were watching Sherman's army sending lines toward the Confederate works. Suddenly, an artillery shell struck General Polk dead center, passing through his chest and opening up a hole big enough to see through. The man that the South had lovingly referred to as "Bishop Polk" was dead in the blink of an eye.

It was a sad day, indeed, all throughout the Southern army. Even Clayton, who had little regard for generals, felt a sadness. That night, he prayed about it, long and hard. He asked questions and sparred with God. "Why Polk?"

he asked over and over. Why had God allowed a man who was ordained in His word to die such a dramatic death? Polk had been standing far above the fighting, in a place that was usually safe for the commanding generals to observe.

Clayton thought about the story of Jesus and the two thieves on Calvary. Anytime he read the Bible, he remembered the stories his mother had told him as a boy. There had always been a great significance placed on each and every story—a lesson to be learned. The general's death, he decided, was a message from God that this war should be brought to an end.

When Clayton awoke the next morning, it was business as usual. Nothing had changed. The fighting continued, just as if the general had never existed, and mourning for "Bishop Polk" was set aside. Clayton offered up a prayer that someone would heed the sign that had been sent. He prayed for strength, and patience, then went on about the job of staying alive.

Johnston moved his army to Mud Creek, then two days later, moved them again and formed a semicircle close to Marietta. On Monday, June 27, Sherman hit them hard, but Johnston's defensive line was ready. What had previously been two months of skirmishes turned into a day of heavy casualties. Johnston's army was too well entrenched behind their breastworks. They picked off the Federals like boys gone squirrel hunting. During that day, the Federals lost two thousand men.

That night, the Confederates rejoiced. Clayton sat by himself, silently smoking a pipe he'd taken from a dead Yankee. He'd seen the Yankee, holding the pipe in his teeth as he made his charge. Clayton had watched the Yankee fall, and as darkness approached, he'd worked his way back to where the dead soldier lay. Sure enough, the pipe was still there, along with some good smoking tobacco in the soldier's knapsack.

Now, as he sat there enjoying the fine tobacco, Clayton listened to his comrades celebrate the day and felt little regard for any of them. It did occur to him that he might be wrong in his feelings, or lack of them. Maybe he should also rejoice in their moment of having the high hand, but he couldn't.

July's heat rolled in. Johnston evacuated Kennesaw Mountain during the night and formed another line along Nickajack Creek. Now, Sherman's troops were closer to Atlanta than Johnston's were. Again, Johnston moved during the night, situating his army along the Chattahoochee River.

Word was spreading through the Army of Tennessee that President Davis was unhappy with Johnston for his defensive tactics. Clayton heard the talk like everyone else, and it angered him. He, too, had cursed the Southern generals for their retreating tactics, but he'd actually grown to admire Johnston. His countermovements, though they had prolonged the war, made sense. Under the same circumstances, Clayton thought, Sherman would have easily overtaken any other general.

Sherman sent General Schofield's army across the Chattahoochee to a location near the mouth of Soap Creek, and ordered McPherson on a feinting move at Turner's Ferry. Once again, Johnston moved his army in the night, back across the river.

On July 13, General Bragg arrived at Atlanta, where he was roundly booed by the Tennessee Army. Four days later, President Davis replaced General Johnston with General John Bell Hood.

Immediately, Hood began to take the offensive. He failed miserably, but blamed General Hardee, saying Hardee's men hadn't fought hard enough.

Three days into Hood's command, General Sherman now controlled nearly half the perimeter around Atlanta. Hood, still angry with Hardee, sent Hardee's corps on a fifteen-mile forced march to attack McPherson's army between Atlanta and Decatur. When the sun arose on July 22, Hardee's troops were like the walking dead, following the long march through the stifling heat with no sleep. Clayton couldn't remember a harder fight than on that day. His rifle grew so hot, it gave him blisters on his hands. But the men bravely went through the motions, the sky above them like a giant fire. General Cleburne did his best to lead by ex-

ample that day. Again, he distinguished himself among the
men of the Tennessee Army, and it was a big victory over
the Federals, as General McPherson was shot dead during
the battle.

That evening, Clayton fell to the ground amongst the
dead and dying and ate his rations. His eyes were accustomed to the thick blood that gelled and turned black and
seemed to be everywhere. He was so tired, a Yankee could
have walked up and shot him, and Clayton wouldn't have
moved. His knees were shaking. He couldn't relax. Around
him, he noticed a silence. Gone were the sounds of celebration, even after such a solid victory.

Sherman laid siege to Atlanta the following week, and
all railroad lines leading to and from the city were cut off.

From where Clayton sat, he could see buildings burning
in the city. The sight made him sick. It all made him sick.
He was ready to go home. Maybe Lee and Grant or Sherman and Hood didn't know it, but this damn war was over.

Clayton knew that the day's victory meant nothing. This
war was useless and meaningless. A deep repulsion came
over him. He hated Lincoln, but more than that, he hated
Sherman. He had read papers with stories about Sherman's
plans to teach the people of the South a lesson that they
would never forget. They'd never forget, all right, Clayton
thought. They'd never forget how Sherman had laid waste
to everything his army had come across. From Chattanooga
to Atlanta, he had burned crops and destroyed livestock,
homes and churches. He had ruined the lives of innocent
people.

This wasn't a war about right or wrong. It was a war
between politicians and their ideals. What gave Lincoln and
Sherman the right, Clayton asked, over and over?

He couldn't stop thinking of Beartooth Flats. What if the
Federals had come along and burned down his mama's
farm, killed her stock? What had happened to her, and
Wendelin and little Joshua? The worry was more than he
could stand. It left him with a helpless rage. The killing on
the battlefields was one thing, but taking the war into the
homes of those left behind was terribly wrong.

The more Clayton had read about Sherman and his arrogance, the angrier he'd become. Who was he to teach the people of the South a lesson about anything? He touched his Bible with his fingertips and thought of Rocky Face Ridge. He would gladly give his life for the chance to kill this man General Sherman.

As he sat there, watching the destruction of Atlanta, Clayton thought about the past month and the hundreds of people and families who lived in places he'd never heard of before. Mothers carrying dirty-faced children, with more young'uns holding on to their skirts. Old men and women who had worked hard and watched their own children grow into adulthood. Aunts and uncles, cousins and good friends, all watching as their barns and houses burned to the ground or their cattle lay slaughtered. Having to cook and care for the very soldiers who had destroyed their lives. Clayton forevermore would remember names like Tunnel Hill, Buzzard Roost, Resaca, Calhoun, Adairsville, Cassville, Kingston, Burnt Hickory, Cass Station, Dallas, New Hope Church, Pumpkin Vine Creek, Mount Zion Church, Allatoona, Acworth, Raccoon Bottom, Lost Mountain, Roswell, Noonday Creek, Golgotha Church, Mud Creek, Noyes' Creek, Powder Springs, Lattimer's Mills, Nickajack Creek, Ruff's Mills, and Vining Station. There was also Pace's Ferry, Turner's Ferry, Howell's Ferry, Isham's Ford, Peachtree Creek, and Buckhead. Small, insignificant little places and towns. If he survived this war, Clayton would remember, even though others might forget. They were imprinted on his memory forever.

He would remember Lois Shealy, the woman he'd accidentally come across at a little spring one day. She sat beside the water in her tattered dress, nursing a little baby boy. She cried out when she saw him.

"They killed my six layin' hens!" was all she said.

Clayton offered her a biscuit from his knapsack. He'd been saving it for his own hungry belly.

She got up and took his hand. Wordlessly, she led him through the thick underbrush to a small cabin in the clearing. A pile of rubble and ashes lay where a barn had once stood. Smoke still drifted upward.

Inside the cabin, Lois revealed a cellar door, hidden un-

der a rug. She lit a lamp and led Clayton down the stairs
to a full supply of corn, and turnips and other vegetables.
Silently, she gave the baby to Clayton and prepared a meal.
Clayton could hardly take his eyes from the dirty-faced
little boy. He was as somber as an old man. Clayton thought
about Joshua.

That evening, he ate until he thought his stomach would
pop. They sat outside until the sun went down. When the
little boy, whose name was Kimsy, fell asleep, Lois put
him to bed, then came to stand before Clayton on the small
porch.

Lois was small, probably ninety pounds at best and under
five feet tall, with skinny arms and legs. She wasn't pretty,
but she had nice eyes that were kind. She looked at him
sadly, then unceremoniously pulled off her tattered dress.
Silently, she led Clayton to her bed and helped him undress.
Afterward, she cried against his shoulder.

When Clayton left Lois's small house, his knapsack was
filled with corn and potatoes and turnips. He thanked her
and waved good-bye while she stood on her porch and
wept.

Outside of telling him her name and the baby's, Clayton
couldn't remember Lois saying more than a dozen words
to him. Once, he'd started to ask about Kimsy's father, but
he hadn't.

It didn't matter.

22

THEY HAD left Dodge City, and were five miles north of town, when Solon couldn't hold back any longer.

"Clayton," he began, "you know I've never meddled in your affairs."

Clayton looked ahead. "That's right, you haven't, and I appreciate that fact," he said.

Solon ignored the wary tone in Clayton's voice, and went on, "I've always believed that what a man does, and who he does it with, is his own affair. I never could stand to be around a meddler. Don't believe in it. That Shorty Gillis is a meddler. Hang around him long enough, and he'll be tryin' to stick his nose in everything you do." He took off his hat, and rubbed his sweaty face on his sleeve. "I don't like to say it, but the truth is, you left that poor Tracy in an awful hurt." He put his hat back on his head and waited, as if he expected an explanation.

Clayton pulled rein on the roan and stopped. He studied Solon's words a moment. "I think you might be exaggeratin'," he said.

"Naw, I ain't exaggeratin'. She loves ya, Clayton. She told me so."

Clayton was bothered by Solon's words, but he didn't want Solon to know it. He frowned. "I don't know that I appreciate you havin' a conversation with Tracy about somethin' so personal." His voice was hard.

"Now, Clayton, that ain't no reason to get surly. Tracy's almost like family to me."

"I ain't surly," Clayton said. He didn't enjoy being angry at Solon, but he hated being reminded about Tracy O'Brien even more. He was trying hard not to think about her. She hadn't left his thoughts for even a minute, and he surely didn't need Solon or anybody else interfering.

Tracy would be a nice punctuation to his life. There was no doubt in his mind. If he could just get that house built in Ness City, then he'd have a fitting place for a woman. He'd been trying to get the house built for several years, but until now, there hadn't been any urgency about it. Something inside Clayton had changed. He'd never felt this old and hollowed-out before. He yearned to settle down, to have a life that was predictable and secure in its comforts. Sometimes at night, when he could pull his thoughts together, he would envision himself, there on his land. His house was all built and finished, with smoke rising from the chimney. From his front porch, he could see the beeves grazing in the pasture. Out past the barn, he could see a pen full of hogs. There was a fruit orchard and a vegetable plot and, always in his thoughts, he saw a woman tending a garden filled with flowers. The vision of the woman was the clearest in every detail, down to the way she tied the knot in her apron. He saw the bonnet she wore, the color of her dress, and the curve of her body. The only detail he couldn't see was the woman's face. Clayton was almost certain, though, who she was. The way she stood, the way her dress moved over the slender body. It was Jolene. He wanted to see all of her, and he tried to force her face into his thoughts, but the face always faded from sight. The harder he tried, the dimmer the picture became. Nothing, it seemed, would ever come about in Clayton's grand scheme of things.

"Well, Solon, not that it's any of your business, but just what could I ever do for Tracy?" he asked. "What could I offer any woman? I couldn't expect her to live in that hole in the ground. And before you say anything, I couldn't move into her house there in Dodge City. It wouldn't look right. She'd always be a scorned woman. In truth, I have nothing to offer. 'Sides, I ain't felt so good for a while now. Not that I mean to complain."

"Now, you're readin' what I said all wrong," Solon said. "I was just talkin' about the way she felt, is all. Still,

I haveta say that none of your excuses hold any water, Clayton. We can get that house built in no time.'' He took off his hat and rubbed his head. ''You know what I think, Clayton? You can get mad at me for sayin' this, but I think poor ol' Tracy fell in love with you, while all she was to you was just a pleasin' night. Like I said, you might get mad, but that's what I think.'' He shrugged. ''Probably ain't none of my business.''

Clayton felt annoyed, but he'd lost too much energy to get full-blown angry. ''That's right,'' he said. ''It ain't none of your business. But for your information, you got that pleasure business all wrong. I could be real happy with a woman like Tracy. I could settle down and never look at another female. But hell, I'm a good fifteen years older than her. Don't you think she might deserve something better? Did you ever think about that?''

Solon had taken out his handkerchief and was trying to rub off the sweat stain on his hat. ''Why, hell, Clayton! What difference does age make? It sure didn't seem to matter to Tracy, I can tell you that! You done somethin' that left a big impression on that girl! Age? Horseshit!'' He said the word bitterly. ''I'm older than you are, Clayton, and I know from experience that it don't matter to a woman how many years you been alive. It's how you're livin' that counts. Do you remember Alan Pickney? Hell, he was twenty-three years older than Carolyn George when they got married. I don't know a happier couple.''

Clayton shook his head, ''That argument don't hold water. Alan Pickney's been dead for almost four years. The last I heard, Carolyn had a new husband.''

''Well, they were happy,'' Solon said stubbornly.

''What you've gotta understand, Solon, is that when Tracy's my age, I'll be an old man. What if we had young'uns? Before long, she'd be left to raise 'em all by herself.''

Solon nodded his head. ''I suppose you're right,'' he said.

''Dern right, I am.''

They grew silent, each in deep thought. Clayton had won the argument, but it had left him rattled. He had never

known Solon to poke his nose in his business before—not
that the man didn't have opinions—but Solon had actually
talked to Tracy. He knew her feelings firsthand.

Staying atop his horse was getting more painful by the
hour. Clayton had started feeling good in Dodge City. His
eyesight had improved, and he'd lost his terrible thirst.
Now, his legs were back to aching, and he was sweating
something awful. He'd begun to suffer from a bad indiges-
tion the night before, after his second helping of Tracy's
pot roast. That morning, he'd awakened feeling stiff.

Whatever was wrong, Clayton knew that he had to keep
going, or else he soon wouldn't feel like doing anything at
all. He decided that they would put off making camp and
wait until late that night. The idea didn't set well with Solon, but Clayton didn't care.

Later, he fell asleep immediately and dreamed about his
mama. When he awoke the next morning, she still lay
heavy on his mind.

He'd been in Brownsville, Texas, the day he received
word that Flossie had taken ill. By the time he reached
Beartooth Flats, his mama was already dead and buried next
to his papa. Clayton still carried a load of guilt that he
hadn't been there to take care of her. He missed her
something awful. In the back of his mind, he'd had a desire
to go back someday to live on the old homeplace.

Wendelin had married a lawyer by the name of Jake Gris-
ham and moved to Columbia. After their mama died, Joshua
had gone to live with her. It was hard for Clayton to imagine
that his baby brother would be twenty-one next month. He'd
been only fourteen the last time Clayton had seen him.

Clayton was anxious to get to Ness City and to the letters
that would be waiting for him. Through the earlier years, poor
Wendelin had never given up hope that Clayton would return
home. She still wrote him often, keeping him updated on her
life and Joshua's. She and Jake had a nice home in Columbia,
she said, and it was doubtful if she would ever return to Beartooth Flats, even if something were to happen to her husband.
She had grown accustomed to city life, as had Joshua. Their
younger brother had no interest in farming. He'd gone to work
for Mr. Goss in his dry goods store, and was quite happy there.

Mr. Goss had lost his only son, Marion, at Murfreesboro. Wendelin wrote that Mr. Goss had no other living relatives, and he treated Joshua like the son he had lost. If Joshua stayed with him, he would someday inherit the store. "Joshua, really runs the store now," she had written. "You would be very proud of him." She told Clayton that the homestead was his if he wanted. "It's good, rich farm country," she wrote. "It'll grow anything."

Clayton often did get a longing to go back home. Sometimes, that fishing hole would appear in his mind, so real, he could feel the water cooling his body and the mud squishing between his toes. But that was where his dream ended and the bad memories began. There were too many ghosts from the past. Clayton knew he could never walk the valleys and hollows again. He couldn't face the old folks and serve as a reminder that he had come home, a survivor of a war so cruel to have stolen their sons away from them.

As they drew nearer to Ness City, Clayton reflected on how amusing it was that he had ended up in Kansas. About eight years previously, he'd been working down in the Cherokee Outlet with a cowboy friend named Winnie Thomas. Winnie had kept Clayton entertained with stories about his family up in Ness County. He'd told how a body could graze beeves thirteen months of the year there, and how good the land was for raising crops. The stories had been so fascinating, Clayton had finally accepted Winnie's invitation to go visit.

Kansas, Clayton discovered, was hot and windy, and not at all the way Winnie had described it. But the grazing was good, and there was plenty of wide-open space. Clayton liked the people there, even if they were mostly Yankees. They, in turn, accepted Clayton with no questions asked, and friendships were made. It wasn't long before he had land of his own and was quite fond of the place.

The county was steadily growing. When Clayton had first arrived, there'd been only around two hundred people in the area. The last census had been taken in '80, and it showed more than three thousand inhabitants. Ness City, itself, became a townsite and, after a heated election, was named county seat in the winter of '78. Clarinda was located in the center of Ness County and seemed to be the logical choice, but

Clarinda had trouble obtaining water. To the east of Ness City, the town of Parris vied for the county seat location. Citizens of Schohare, lying five miles east, wanted the county seat to be there, arguing that it was the oldest city in the county. Lastly, a mile south, the town of Sidney entered the race.

An election was held in June, 1880. Clayton was amused by all the politicking that went on before the winner was declared. He couldn't have cared less where the county seat was located, but he enjoyed the daily visitors at his door who stopped by to campaign for his vote.

In the end, Ness City came out the winner with 390 votes. Sidney, the closest rival, received 260 votes. Parris, whose name was changed to Waterport just prior, ended up with 50 votes, and Clarinda, formerly the front-runner, came in last with only 14 votes. There had been court battles ever since, and arguments on every street corner. Clayton steered clear of the controversy, but Solon never failed to express his own opinion. Once, he got into such a heated argument with the sheriff, Gilmore Kinney, they nearly had a fight, and Clayton had to separate them.

As Clayton thought back on Beartooth Flats and his family, he felt a nostalgia for the lush green countryside, the rippling river waters, and the memories of playing in the creeks. He missed the abundant hunting and fishing. Sometimes, he even thought about Abigail Beecher and her smooth white skin.

But his new roots were in Ness City and all of the Ness County, so distant in geographics from his beautiful homeland in Tennessee. It was the people that really mattered, though, and Clayton felt a genuine fondness for his Kansas neighbors. He'd be quite content to live out his days there, raising beeves and hogs, and listening to Solon's endless stories. The only thing missing would be a woman's touch at night, a soft, comforting soul to drive away the demons at night when he woke up scared and confused.

Just like life's fisherman, he'd let another one get away. Clayton had to fight the urge to ride back to Dodge City and get Tracy O'Brien. He didn't want to wait. He needed so badly to have her with him, to share his dreams and chase away life's demons.

23

GENERAL HOOD was a pitiful-looking sight, his poor body a remnant of what it had once been. Early in the war his left arm had been so badly damaged that it was useless. He carried it tied up against his body. Then, at Chickamauga, he had lost his right leg. Still, he held to his command, riding strapped atop his horse. His troops wondered openly about his abilities to lead them. Somehow, they couldn't separate bodily injuries from mental alertness. He was taking laudanum for his constant pain, and it was no secret that some thought this diminished his capacity for thinking clearly.

In Clayton's opinion, it really didn't matter. He wondered if God, Himself, could successfully lead the Southern forces. The cause was lost, plain as day. Poor General Hood, he thought. was just a symbol of the hopelessness of the entire Confederate Army and the South in general.

Unlike Johnston and others before him, General Hood refused to spar with Clayton over accepting a promotion. Matter-of-factly, he ordered the deed done. Cool as a cucumber, he said, "We have no officers left in your company. The men need a leader, and to a man, they voted for you. I might add," he said without expression, "that you received two votes for general."

With that, Clayton was promoted to brevet lieutenant. General Hood performed a brief ceremony, strapped to his horse, and then departed.

Clayton saw his first action as an officer at Jonesboro. It

was August 31, 1864. He had promised himself that his
new rank would not change anything; he was soon forced
to take on the responsibility of the men. For the first time,
he had to think about how they were fighting. He had to
think for them. He watched the men of his company respond to his leadership. They fought tirelessly, and he
couldn't help being a bit proud of those under him.

The same could not be said for most of the beleaguered
Army of Tennessee. Some outfits were even refusing to
attack Federal breastworks, hiding like little children who'd
been beaten one too many times.

That night, the two armies were so close to each other,
the men were drinking water from the same stream and
taking wood from the same fences to build their fires.

Clayton was on his knees, bent over the water and drinking from his cupped hands, when a Union corporal approached, quietly, like a cat in the night. They saw each
other at the same time, not more than a dozen feet apart.

"Mind if I have a drink, Johnny Reb?" the corporal
asked.

"Take all you want," Clayton said.

They sat on the bank of the stream, Rebel on one side,
Yankee on the other, and exchanged war stories. They
talked about their homes, and agreed that they both were
praying that the war would end soon.

"You got a wife or sweetheart waiting at home?" the
corporal asked.

Clayton thought about Jolene, but shook his head.

"I've got a wife, two sons, and a daughter," the corporal
said. He paused reflectively. "I've been in the blamed war
since the beginning," he said. "To tell you the truth, I
never expected to live this long. I've been wounded three
times." He stopped, reached into the stream, and splashed
a handful of water on his face. "Don't mean to get all
sentimental," he went on, his voice shaky, "but I'm ready
for this thing to be over. I miss my family so much. I've
even thought about running off a few times. I'm afraid if
this thing don't end soon, I might just do that."

They sat there a while longer, bitter enemies by day, but
now just two human beings sharing the same thoughts and

emotions about this thing called war. The next day, their two armies met up in battle. Clayton was grateful that he didn't see the corporal again.

On September 7, General Sherman sent General Hood a message that read, ''I have deemed it to be in the interest of the United States that the citizens now residing in Atlanta should remove themselves. Those who prefer may go South and the rest North.''

The message was the most disturbing of the war. Once again, Sherman's brutality had reared itself. Soon, the roads were crowded with families moving southward: old men who could barely walk; women wearing expressions as blank as the sky on a dark night; children and little babies whose cries filled the countryside. They left in twos and fours. They left carrying the elderly, sick, and disfigured. Possessions that had a taken a lifetime to procure were either packed and carried laboriously on horse, mule, a buggy, or on their backs, or they were left in the home to ruin. Now, their precious homes would most assuredly be occupied by a hated army. Almost blinded by the injustice, they stared at the road in front of them as they walked, their eyes lowered and spirits broken. Where they were going was anybody's guess.

The sight of the refugees killed the soldiers' spirits, as much as any canister shot or shell. A broken army was broken even deeper. The men themselves had suffered from near-starvation and disease. They'd walked barefoot over rocky ground and slept out in the freezing rain without shelter. They'd been eaten up by mosquitoes and gone for days without fresh water. They'd endured every hardship in man's imagination and sacrificed their own lives, but nothing was as cruel a blow as watching the people whom they protected suffer.

This war had gone on too long, Clayton thought. It had to end. Often, he pondered the idea of seeking out General Sherman and killing him. He knew in his heart that, had he not been forced to take his promotion, he would have made that attempt on Sherman's life. Now, though, he had a company of men and a responsibility that he could not shirk.

Hood moved his army into quarters at Palmetto, Georgia. Then they headed toward Tennessee, back through areas where they had fought before. They stopped in Dalton, where, like so many other places, they flew the stars and stripes. Clayton was taken by the irony of it.

Heading northward into Tennessee, they moved until Columbia was in sight. For four days in late November, they skirmished against the Federals. Clayton felt strange, knowing that he was only miles from Beartooth Flats. It was so close, he was sure his mama could hear the thunder of the cannons. He prayed that she wouldn't know he was there.

It was the first time that Clayton didn't fight like a man possessed, but then, neither did the two armies. Most of the time was spent with the two sides trying to outflank each other. The casualty count was mercifully low. As his army left the area, Clayton took a lingering look at the Duck River. A range of emotions swept through him as he saw his mama's face in the rippling waters. He saw Wendelin, standing on their front porch. He remembered Joshua's firm little body, wriggling on his knee, and the feel of the fishing line in his hand, and the sight of Abigail Beecher's curvy body.

Then his vision became clouded with the images of fire and smoke, flames singeing hair, burning hot against the cold winter air. He saw the barn burning, and Mama's garden in ruin. Joshua cried against his mama's shoulder as they watched their house being enveloped in flames. Clayton wanted to turn back, to leave the army and this senseless war behind and hurry to his family. He wanted to chase away the fires and hold them in his arms until all was safe. But, instead, he ordered his troops onward and left farm and family behind.

On November 30, Hood's army was at Franklin. That afternoon, the earth split open as war commenced. Fire and brimstone spewed outward. The devil came out amid the flames and hell covered the earth. Clayton fought with his men. He ran and charged and defended with a blind detachment. Once, he paused and reached inside his shirt to remove his Testament. His finger lingered a second on the minié ball. Around him, a million shots and shells scarred the earth and all of its inhabitants.

"And I saw when the Lamb opened one of the seals, and I heard, as it were the noise of thunder, one of the four beasts saying, 'Come and see.' And I saw, and behold a white horse, and he that sat on him had a bow and a crown was given unto him. And he went forth conquering, and to conquer."

The fighting that day was more brutal and bloody than all the others put together. Clayton was no longer affected by the visions of death that were everywhere. By the time darkness hit, the bodies were fallen one atop another, and still the deadly fire continued to rain down on all of God's creation. The musketry fire was wicked as the bullets whizzed by, making terrible thuds as they ripped into human flesh. Clayton felt sickened.

"And when he had opened the second seal, I heard the second beast say, 'Come and see.' And there went out another horse that was red. And power was given to him that sat thereon to take peace from the earth and that they should kill one another. And there was given unto him a great sword."

In the darkness of night, through the thunder and lightning of the cannons, man's sins were brought forth like some macabre Shakespearean play. The shell would burst, sending sparks and flames, and bodies were blown into the devil's theatre. Arms and heads landed to the left, legs to the right. Steadily, consistently, the Tennessee Army charged the beastly, deadly breastworks. Men who just weeks before had cowered behind bushes and fences and rocks, now suddenly hurled themselves into death's open arms, as if some evil force was sending them forward against an impossible enemy. They ran barefoot, across ground as cold as ice beneath their numb feet. They ran directly into the enemy fire and had their limbs shot off. Tops of their heads were blown into the faces and breasts of their campmates behind them. Still, they charged forward, like an army possessed.

"And when he had opened the third seal, I heard the third beast say, 'Come and see.' And I beheld and lo a black horse; and he that sat on him had a pair of balances in his hand. And I heard a voice in the midst of the four beasts say, a measure of wheat for a penny, and three measures of barley for a penny; and see thou hurt not the oil and the wine.''

Clayton continued to fight like a man on a death mission. He was detached from himself, given into the moment when a man turns his life over to destiny. When he reached the breastworks, the bodies were stacked so high, he had to walk right over them. He crossed that line and stepped in, amongst the devil and all of his archangels.

''And when he had opened the fourth seal, I heard the voice of the fourth beast say, 'Come and see.' And I looked, and behold a pale horse. And his name that sat on him was Death, and Hell followed with him. And power was given unto them over the fourth part of the earth, to kill with sword, and with hunger, and with death, and with the beasts of the earth.''

The next morning, the dead lay everywhere, stacked like sacks of potatoes, bodies twisted and limbs gone. Their spirits had joined the spirits of others, and the devil had returned to his hiding place. For one afternoon and night, he had unleashed all of hell, and now, there in the morning sun, his display of evil and destruction was in full spectacle.

''And when he had opened the fifth seal, I saw under the altar the souls of them that were slain for the word of God, and for the testimony which they held: And they cried with a loud voice, saying 'How long, O Lord, holy and true, dost thou not judge and avenge our blood on them that dwell on the earth? And white robes were given unto every one of them: And it was said unto them, that they should rest yet for a little season, until their fellow servants also and their brethren, that should be killed as they were, should be fulfilled.''

Six generals had been lost. Clayton stood atop the breastworks, next to General Pat Cleburne's dead horse. He took off his hat and cupped it to his breast. He had admired the general for his tenacity and bravery, and it grieved him to look at Cleburne's twisted and torn body. There wasn't an area from his head to his toe that hadn't taken a bullet. There'd been almost fifty hits in all.

General Adams and his horse were also there on the breastworks, both cold dead. General Cranbury and General Carter had been mangled to death. General Strahl had died with his horse during the night of hell. General Gist, a noble fighter, his hand full of saber, had given everything on the breastworks.

For the first time during the war, tears ran openly down Clayton's face, and he didn't try to hide them. Sometime during the night, a ball had passed through his forearm, ripping off a piece of meat. Another had nicked the top of his ear. His cartridge box had been hit, and there was a hole in his cap. Clayton couldn't even remember being hit. It surprised him to wake up after a short nap and be notified that he'd been shot. His eyes again fell upon the dead and wounded.

"And I beheld when he had opened the sixth seal, and, lo, there was a great earthquake; and the sun became black as sackcloth of hair, and the moon became as blood; and the stars of heaven fell unto the earth, even as a fig tree casteth her untimely figs, when she is shaken of a mighty wind. And the heaven departed as a scroll when it is rolled together; and every mountain and island were moved out of their places. And the kings of the earth, and the great men, and the rich men, and the chief captains, and mighty men, and every bondman, and every free man, hid themselves in the dens and in the rocks of the mountains. And said to the mountains and rocks, Fall on us, and hide us from the face of him that sitteth on the throne, and from the wrath of the Lamb: for the great day of his wrath is come; and who shall be able to stand?"

Six thousand two hundred and fifty men had been killed and wounded at Franklin. It surely had been a night of hell, as a beaten army made a last great thrust.

Clayton's face was wet with tears. He squeezed the Testament in both hands, put it to his lips, and breathed against the cover. He looked up into the heavens, trying hard to see his father, Burgess, and Andy. He looked for the cool water of the fishing hole, but all he saw was blackness.

He spoke aloud, "And when he had opened the seventh seal? What then, Lord? Is it all over now? Are you comin' for us? Is the moon gonna turn to blood, and the rivers? I seen the water at Chickamauga, Lord. Seen it turn red. I heard the voices and the thunderin' and lightnin' last night and felt the earthquake."

Suddenly, Clayton stopped talking. It was out of his hands, and the burden was now lifted from his shoulders. The fear left his body, and he accepted God's will. He held the Testament to his breast.

"Send the angels, Lord. Send all your angels."

That afternoon, General Hood promoted Clayton to brevet colonel. Little was said by either man. Thoughts and emotions had been taken care of during the night of hell.

The army moved toward Nashville and faced wicked wind and snow. No one alive could remember a colder time. Hood gathered up what was left of his army and tried to convince them that victory was at their fingertips, but no one would believe him. The men held no anger toward the once-great general. There was only sadness for the man who was so handicapped that he could barely remain strapped atop his mount.

Again, he led the disheveled army into two days' battle at Nashville. But, as gallant and brave as they had been just two weeks before at Franklin, his army panicked. Entire companies and regiments threw down their weapons and ran. Hundreds let themselves be captured. Only a few stood their ground and fought to hold Franklin's Pike. At the end, the casualties were mercifully low, but that was mostly due to a defeated army that didn't wish to fight anymore.

It had all begun on that hot day in July of '61, catching a train at Nashville with a passel of other eager young men. Clayton had been a mere boy that summer, full of enthusiasm to hurry and join the fray. Now, three and a half years later, Clayton knew himself to be a different person. He had become a man, a beaten and tired man, surrounded by others who, like himself, wanted to go home and forget that there had ever been a war.

Nashville had always held a special allure. To folks who

lived in places like Beartooth Flats, it was almost like the capital of the world, full of excitement and refined. But now it belonged to the Federals. All of the South had been taken from them. Clayton wondered if it would ever be the same. Would the names of Andrew Jackson, Davy Crockett, and others still be held in esteem as they once had been?

The winter of '64–'65 was the coldest anyone could remember. Now, the death bells rang as men succumbed to the cruel, bitter elements, as much as to the musketry.

On January 13, the honorable General John Bell Hood resigned as commander of the Army of Tennessee. To the south, Sherman continued to burn, pillage, and destroy everything in his path as he marched toward the sea. The Army of Tennessee went through the daily motions of life, trying to survive. Desertions were commonplace, and death from exposure was an everyday affair.

The men went through that coldest of winters. Their minds were void of anything but staying alive. Talk of the war and its meaning were now completely diminished. January came and went, as did February and March, with every man clinging to precious life and the dimmest of hopes.

April 15 was a sunny Saturday morning. President Lincoln, a man who some said was as good and pure as a morning dove, was cursed by others as being as evil as the devil for imposing his own values on the nation. Whichever viewpoint one held, Lincoln was a leader that both sides had turned to at one time or another. That morning, the nation lost their commander-in-chief. Lincoln died at seven twenty-two.

Clayton took the news without emotion. How ironic, he thought. Even Lincoln hadn't survived his own war. The president wasn't really any different from any of God's other creations. Clayton wondered if the death would bring an end to all the carnage. He wondered if the country would ever mend itself into one nation again.

The following Monday, General Johnston, whom President Davis had removed from command, was back in the saddle again. He promptly met with General Sherman at Durham Station, North Carolina, to discuss surrender.

Eleven days later, at Greensboro, Johnston surrendered the Army of Tennessee.

Clayton had never felt more grateful. Nearly thirty-three hundred had served in his regiment during the war, and only sixty-five were still alive to be paroled that day. Clayton thanked God. He kissed the Testament that he still carried, the minié ball still embedded in the pages. He prayed that the Almighty would accept all the souls of those who could no longer breathe in the clean morning air.

General Grant approved the terms of surrender, and it was finally over. The Confederates were to leave all their weapons and public property at Greensboro. They would each take a pledge not to take up arms again. Officers were allowed to keep their sidearms and their private horses, along with any baggage they might have. Most important, they were allowed to return to their homes. The Federal army even provided transportation to some.

Clayton had been given a chestnut mare following his promotion. Even though the mare did not belong to him, he was allowed to take the horse as his own. He departed Greensboro and headed toward Kentucky.

His heart still lay heavy with thoughts of Jolene. He prayed over and over that he would find her alive and well and waiting for him in Perryville. He would ask for her hand in marriage, and then he would take her home to Mama.

24

CLAYTON HEADED toward Asheville. Before he went north to Perryville, he stopped off in Knoxville to see a man and a woman. Their son, Isaac Danforth, had been lost on the breastworks at Franklin, and beforehand, he'd given Clayton a few personal items to take to his parents.

Clayton pulled the letter out of his pocket and turned it over in his hand. The names were written in a fine, clear hand. Isaac had been a good soldier. He had fought in many major battles, but for some unknown reason, he'd felt it necessary to make the arrangement with Clayton on the day before they fought at Franklin.

The Danforths were gracious folks, and most grateful for Clayton's kindness. They offered to let him stay with them a while, but he declined. As he rode away from the Danforth place, the sky seemed to open up and turn brighter. A great burden had been lifted from him, and he breathed in the fresh air around him. He couldn't remember ever having this sensation in life before. It was like being at death's door with a dreadful illness and suddenly getting word that everything was going to be all right.

Clayton had always appreciated nature's beauty, but he'd never noticed all the fine details before. Everything was enhanced—the vastness of the mountains, the sun's rays reflecting off the clouds, the freshness of the air, and the serenity. Chickamauga had been a beautiful place. He'd seen many beautiful places, but none held him in awe like this.

He felt a keen urgency to get to Perryville, and at the same time he dreaded the thought of finding out that Jolene was dead. It occurred to Clayton that she might not even remember him. After all, it had been a long time, and maybe their time together hadn't meant as much to her as it had to him. He tried to hold a positive thought.

High in the mountains in eastern Tennessee, Clayton found himself at a little farm. He was hungry and tired, so he decided to stop. He rode up to the large cabin and was greeted by an older lady. He got down from his mare and looked up at her.

"Hello, ma'am. My name is Clayton Crist, from Beartooth Flats. That's close to the Duck River, by Columbia." He remembered to remove his hat. "You see, I was with the First Tennessee." His voice dropped and he lowered his eyes a bit. "We just surrendered our army at Greensboro." Clayton shifted his feet and swallowed back his pride. "I was wonderin' if you could spare a bite to eat. I haven't had a thing all day."

She was handsome, he thought, and rather large. She looked nearly as tall as he was, and though she wasn't fat, she was thick and somewhat broad-shouldered. Her hair was piled on top of her head, and he could tell that it was straight and black when let down. Wisps of gray were scattered here and there. He guessed her to be about the age of his own mother, who was in her forties.

The big woman smiled gently, and that softened her size. Her face became even prettier. "My, my," she said. "You still got a fer piece to go. I got an aunt and two sisters that live this side of Columbia." She pointed to the corner of the steps. "Step on over to the water in that pail and refresh yourself. I'll take care of your horse."

"I'm much obliged to ya," Clayton said, "but I can unsaddle my own horse."

"Nonsense." She walked down the steps and took the reins. "Do as I say. Get yourself a drink, and I'll fix you somethin' to eat."

She led his horse to the barn. When she came back, Clayton was sitting, drinking the sweet well water. She bent over and studied his clothing. "My late husband was a

colonel,'' she said. ''Perhaps you ran across him. Asa
Tankersley? He died at Murfreesboro.''

Clayton shook his head slowly. ''I'm real sorry, I can't
place him.'' He felt bad that he hadn't known this woman's
husband, and he wondered to himself if the misery of war
would ever fade away.

Mrs. Tankersley took him through the house to a back
porch. ''I'll heat some water up. You could use a bath,''
she said matter-of-factly. She left a moment and returned
with some clothing. ''These'll be a little big, but you can
wear 'em while I wash up your things.''

Her gesture made Clayton think of Jolene and how she
had bathed him and washed his clothes. A good sensation
came over him. He felt relaxed as he stepped into the tub
of hot water.

Clayton languished in the water until it cooled. His hands
and feet were wrinkled when he got out and put on the
fresh-smelling clothing. Colonel Tankersley had been a tall
man. The shirt felt snug around the shoulders and waist,
but he had to roll the pant legs up.

The food was wonderful. He ate potatoes, thick slices of
fried bacon, corn bread, and good buttermilk. Clayton
crumbled the corn bread into the buttermilk. He hadn't
tasted anything so good since he'd left home.

Mrs. Tankersley watched silently, her tired eyes smiling
at him as he ate hungrily. She didn't speak or try to disturb
him, but waited until he'd spooned out the last bit of corn
bread and buttermilk.

''Were you in the army long? You look so young,'' she
commented.

''Yes ma'am. I joined almost four years ago.''

Mrs. Tankersley shook her head sadly. ''This war
should've never been fought,'' she said. ''So many good
boys lost forever! I declare, I don't know if the South will
ever recover.'' She looked around her well-kept kitchen.
''This was our dream house. Mister Tankersley was a banker
in Knoxville for many years. We'd always talked about
moving to the country. Asa always said he wanted to get so
far away from folks, he wouldn't have to hear their complainin'.'' She smiled in remembrance. ''Well, one day, we

up and moved to this spot. You should've seen it back then! You wouldn't believe it, from the way it looks today. I declare, there were trees as far as you could see! Asa and our sons, Robert and Peck, worked hard to clear the place out and build this fine home. We moved in two years before the war. Asa and the boys kept on working, right up to the time they were called to duty." She paused reflectively, her bottom lip quivering. "Now, they're all gone. I sit here all by myself with Mister Tankersley's dream."

Clayton wished he knew some comforting words to say to her, but nothing seemed sufficient. After all, he was alive, and he'd soon be home to fill his mama's waiting arms. It made him feel guilty, sitting there with Mrs. Tankersley and her grief. She, like so many other mothers, would have to live out her days in loneliness for her family.

Mrs. Tankersley forced a smile. "I'm sure you don't want to hear about my problems. Tell me somethin' about yourself. Are you married?"

"No, ma'am, but I am on my way to Kentucky. I'm gonna ask a girl to be my wife."

"Splendid," Mrs. Tankersley said. "My sons both had sweethearts." Once again the reflective mood came over her. "Childhood sweethearts, they were—girls they'd met back in Knoxville. I've had friends write me letters and ask me to move back there, but I just don't think I can face anyone right now. I surely couldn't face those young ladies. It would be too painful." She nodded sadly at Clayton. "You be sure and have a houseful of little ones. They'll bring you great joy in life." Sniffing, she got up to clear the table.

The next morning, Clayton set about fixing some things around the farm. He had noticed a broken fence, and the roof of the chicken house was missing a board. He worked up a good-sized sweat, while Mrs. Tankersley worried over him, repeating that he should stop and relax for a spell. But, it felt good. Clayton worked all that day, stopping only to eat.

Clayton's stay stretched into two days, then three, and pretty soon he had been with Mrs. Tankersley for a week and a half. He had mended everything that could possibly be mended. Even her garden was expanded, with enough food to carry her through the winter. Mrs. Tankersley was exceedingly pleased to have him around. Clayton began to put on weight from her generous meals, and she had mended his uniform. It seemed to be a healing period for her as well as for him, but then there came the day when he had no more reason to stay on. He was needed by his own family back in Beartooth Flats.

And maybe Jolene needed him, too. Clayton realized the chances were that he wouldn't find her. Maybe that was why he'd hesitated on his trip and settled in so easily to the comforts of life on Mrs. Tankersley's farm.

On the day he left, Mrs. Tankersley cried like a mama who's saying good-bye to her own son. A woman he'd known for such a short time was laying a heavy load of guilt on Clayton's heart. He already carried a fondness for her that was more than strange. There had been moments of vulnerability between them, when both of their needs had become thick as smoke. She had insisted on rubbing ointment on his tender feet, which still held sores from the miles of walking, sometimes without shoes. On the third evening, her hands had moved from his feet upward, caressing the calves of his legs. They had both grown silent, nervously staring at each other. At the first sight of her, Clayton had been reminded of his mother, but the signs of age had softened. The gray in her hair had gone from his eyes. The fine lines on her face had smoothed away. The curves of her body and the beauty of her face dominated his thoughts. Age didn't seem to exist. Clayton had felt a stirring inside, and he could see a familiar look in her eyes. Finally, they had both said good-night and slipped off to their own rooms.

Now, as Clayton departed, he was glad he hadn't crossed that line with such a dear woman as this. He could leave with no regrets, and she wouldn't have to suffer from the shame of acting on her own weakness.

When Clayton reached Perryville, darkness was approaching. He stopped by the Chaplin River and made camp for the night. Many emotions ran through him over the thought of being so close to Jolene. He tried not to dwell on the negative side, hoping beyond hope that she had survived. He would get as good a night's sleep as possible, then ride to her farm the next morning.

Clayton woke from a nightmare just before dawn. He'd been dreaming about the redheaded Yankee that he'd killed with his bayonet. In the dream, the Yankee was half skeleton and half flesh, in a decomposing state. His face was nothing but bone, but the eyes were crystal clear and filled with pain. His bright hair had grown long and tangled. Clayton could almost smell the rotting flesh. Everywhere he went, the dead Yankee followed close behind, reaching out as if asking Clayton to take back the bayonet thrust and give him back his life. The dream scene changed to the Yankee's family, peering down into his grave, wailing and moaning. Then, the Yankee rose up. He turned toward Clayton and began to run at him, wielding a huge bayonet that was twice the normal size. Clayton felt the bayonet being thrust into his own body, and then he was lying in his own bed, with the half-rotted body of the Yankee lying beside him.

When Clayton awoke, he sat up and pulled his blanket around him. He felt so cold and scared, he'd have given everything he owned for daylight suddenly to appear. He sat there and waited for the sun to show itself. He was afraid to look around him, for fear the dead Yankee would come out of the shadows.

When morning did come, Clayton's fears had subsided, but he felt gloomy. He got up and made water, then washed himself in the cold water of the Chaplin River, trying to wash off the gloom, as well.

He gazed out over Perryville in the daylight. Memories began to rush over him. He saw the faces of his fallen campmates and remembered the terrible battle, as vividly as if it had been yesterday. As he prepared to mount the mare, he thought he could feel the faint trembling of the earth beneath his feet from the artillery shells.

He set out for Jolene's farm, and immediately the doubts set in. Maybe he was wrong in coming back, and foolish for thinking that she had survived. Besides, did he really deserve to have Jolene as his life's mate? He cursed himself

again for not staying there long ago, searching through all
the rubble until he had found her.

He rode through the middle of town, noticing the men,
women, and children with their solemn faces and despon-
dent stares. Until now, it had never occurred to Clayton to
buy new clothing, and he still wore his clean, but tattered,
Confederate uniform. He felt sure that his passing through
town was calling up sad memories for the inhabitants.

He was nearly at the end of the main street, when he
noticed that the people had fallen in behind him and were
following. He pulled rein on the horse, and the crowd encircled him. At first, he thought he might have ridden into
the middle of a hornet's nest full of angry citizens.

A small woman, her face wrinkled beyond her years,
stepped forward and spoke in a voice that was so soft and
resigned, Clayton had to strain to hear.

"Is the war over?"

Clayton nodded. "Yes'm, I think it's mostly over. General Lee surrendered the Army of Northern Virginia on
April 9, I think it was, and General Johnston surrendered
the Army of Tennessee on April 26. That was my army—
the Tennessee," he added. He looked around at their grim
faces. "Didn't you know?"

A man next to the little woman said, "We've heard rumors. The paper in Lexington had a story about General
Lee and General Johnston, but it said there was still some
fightin' goin' on in spots." He walked up closer and put
his hand on the horse's neck. "Are you sayin' it's over
everywhere? Has the fightin' stopped?"

"A man told me yesterday that General Taylor surrendered his army in Alabama. Yes, sir, I think it's over,"
Clayton said.

A tall, erect man with piercing eyes pointed his finger
knowingly. "You were here, weren't ya? In October of
'62."

"Yes, I was here."

A few more questions were asked, but most were too
specific for Clayton to answer. Eventually, the crowd
thinned, then disappeared altogether. The dispirited town
members left to go back to rebuilding their lives.

Clayton rode on up the hill toward Jolene's farm. Reminders of the battle, fought two and a half years before, could still be seen. At the edge of town, two artillery pieces sat in a man's front yard. One had taken a hit and was broken, the other one looked ready to fire its deadly load. When Clayton got close enough, he could see that Jolene's house had been mostly torn down, and a new one had been erected, closer to the barn. It didn't seem to be as large or as fancy as the other.

There didn't appear to be anyone home at first. Clayton rode up and stopped, then noticed a man step out of the barn. He looked warily at Clayton a moment, then walked a little closer.

"Is there anything I can help you with?"

Clayton didn't know where to begin. He looked around, and his eyes fell on the foundation of the old house. A portion of the chimney was still standing where the fireplace had been. "I was here," he said simply, "during the war."

The man just nodded, his face unchanged.

Clayton didn't see the woman appear in the doorway. She surprised him when she spoke.

"You're Clayton Crist, aren't ya?"

He whirled around to see her. As she stepped out into the light of day, he noticed that her eyes were teary.

"Oh, Harry! It's him!" The tears rolled from the rims of her eyes and down her cheek. "Please, get down from your horse."

The woman hugged Clayton tightly, then pulled back to look at him, her hands still clutching his arms.

"You're as handsome as Jolene said you were. Please, come into the house." She called back to the man. "Take care of Clayton's horse, will you, Papa? And get some ham from the smokehouse."

Inside, there were no signs of Jolene, but Clayton was sure that she must have survived. How else would they have known about him? Clayton searched his mind to recall the names of Jolene's guardians. "You're Aunt Esther, aren't you?"

The woman smiled. "Jolene told you about me and Papa?"

Clayton nodded. His eyes scanned the room. "Where is Jolene?"

Esther cocked her head to one side, and her eyes welled up again. "You were all she could talk about. She prayed for you every night. That girl waited and waited. But you didn't come back." She sank into a chair at the table.

Clayton couldn't help reaching out and touching her gently on the shoulder. She looked up at him. "She thought you were dead."

She looked so bereaved, Clayton felt his voice rise in panic. "What are you saying? What happened to her?" he asked.

"She lives in Lexington, but you mustn't go there. Clayton, she's married." Esther took Clayton's hand and directed him to a chair. She reached out and touched the fine features of his face.

"Jolene loved you very much. Papa tried to tell her that it was only infatuation that she felt—that a lot of women met fellas in the war and thought they were in love without really knowing the young men." She shook her head. "But Papa was wrong. I know. We met during the Mexican War. Papa was a soldier, and I fell in love with him the first time I saw him." She looked at the hurt in Clayton's eyes, and lifted his hand to her cheek. "She loved you, indeed. My, I can still see her face light up when she spoke of you. But the waiting and not knowing became such a terrible burden. Why didn't you write her a letter, son? It would have meant the world to her. She's only been married for three months."

"What's his name?" Clayton asked.

"Enoch Ritter. Owns a gristmill. He's a good man. He'll provide well for her. I know she'll be happy with him, in time."

Clayton nodded. His brain felt like it had been struck by lightning. Of all the times he'd driven himself half-crazy, wondering if Jolene was dead or alive, he'd never once considered the idea that she might find somebody else.

During the war, Clayton had felt a change going on inside himself. A lot of life's innocence was gone, and he found it hard to care about things the way he once had. He'd grown cynical and bitter. A part of him was even overgrown with indifference. He didn't like the fact, but at least he'd been able to hold on to one constant. He'd still loved Jolene. Now, that one promise was broken, too.

Clayton was at a loss. Life had taken a sharp knife and cut out his heart, then thrown it into some dark, bottomless hole.

Esther invited him to stay and eat with them, but Clayton only wanted to get away from there. He felt like a little boy who needed to hide somewhere and cry, unseen. The urgency ran through him like floodwater. His emotions were a levee and the waters were about to burst through.

Esther understood, but she did want Clayton to stay. After all, Jolene was like her own daughter, and she had loved this young man—this Clayton Crist. And Esther could see why. He was surely the most handsome man she'd ever seen. Her heart went out to him.

"Please, just stay long enough for me to fry up some ham. I'd like to send somethin' along with you," she said, fighting to hold back the trembling in her voice.

Clayton said good-bye after breakfast. Esther handed up a sack of leftover ham and biscuits, and stepped back to watch him leave, her handkerchief pressed against her face. There was little for either of them to say.

Clayton turned the mare to the south and headed back toward Tennessee. When he was sure he was well out of sight, he began to cry. He wished he'd died, right there at Perryville. He would be quite happy to be lying there right now, under the battle-scarred landscape, with Kentucky grass growing above and the soft wind blowing the memories away.

25

CLAYTON AND Solon could smell bacon frying long before they rode up on Wilbur DeShazo.

"I wonder what Wilbur's doin' out here?" Solon said curiously. "I seen him in Dodge last week. He was at the Lady Gay, drinkin' their cheapest rotgut. Lots of it, too. I swear, Clayton, if you'd seen ol' Wilbur, you'd of sworn he was tryin' to chase away some demon."

Clayton had noticed Wilbur DeShazo on occasion while they were in Dodge City, but he'd never had the chance to have a visit with him. Clayton liked Wilbur. They'd crossed paths many times over the years since the war, and had shared some enjoyable times.

"Well, I'll be derned," Wilbur said when they rode up. "It seems like I just left you fellers back in town." He got up and dug around in one of several sacks. "Let me put on some extra bacon and taters. You might as well eat with me. I'll be pleased for the company."

Solon sniffed the air. "That's mighty kind of ya, Wilbur. Where in the world are you headin' to?"

"Ness County, I reckon," Wilbur said slowly. He didn't look any too happy.

"No foolin'?" Solon said. "Why, that's where we're headin', too! Not that it's any of my business, but what draws you there?"

A melancholy came over Wilbur. He added more bacon to the frying pan, then sliced potatoes into another pan that was sputtering with grease. Barely loud enough to hear, he said, "I'm gonna git married."

"Married!" Solon repeated loudly. "A man that's been a bachelor as long as you have, Wilbur? What in the world for? Why, you oughta know better! By damn! You know that Judson Benny, don't ya?"

Wilbur nodded.

"Hell's fire! I heard tell he just got married, himself! Why, Judson's got to be fifty, maybe even fifty-five! And now you! Lord, what's comin' over everybody?"

The more Solon talked, the more forlorn Wilbur looked. He stared into the fire, deep in thought, and even managed to cut his finger while he sliced potatoes.

Clayton took pity on Wilbur for having to play host to Solon when he brought along so many worries.

"Ah, leave him alone, Solon. A man's got a right to marry if he wants to," he said. Right now, Clayton envied Wilbur DeShazo and men like him who enjoyed having a warm-bodied woman to curl up with at night. Men who came home to a hot supper and maybe even the aroma of a fresh-baked pie, sitting on the windowsill to cool. Clayton imagined how nice it would be to wake up from a nightmare and have someone there to comfort him. No, he thought, there wasn't anything wrong with Wilbur getting married.

Somehow, the idea made Clayton sad. Wilbur DeShazo was taking on a wife, and that meant a home—maybe children, church, social activities, and the like.

But Clayton hadn't produced a darn thing in life. If anything, he'd done the opposite. He'd sucked out all he could get and put back nothing. As he grew older, he'd taken to noticing other men with families, how they doted over their children and bragged about their bumper crops. They had accomplished something through themselves and their families.

Clayton asked himself what he had to show for his life. There was nothing, except for the memory of the horror in men's eyes as they left this world for the next. The thought nearly sickened him. He often lay awake at night and thought about the hereafter. There surely wasn't any way that he could see of making it to Heaven's gate. His mother's voice rang in his memory. She'd reminded him almost daily of the commandment, "Thou shall not kill." Clayton had never figured out how he could fear God, and still justify taking a life. For a long time, it had hurt him deeply to know that he would never see those streets paved in gold, and up until the last year or so, he'd worried over the fact. Nowadays, things were easier to just accept for what they were.

Clayton watched Wilbur and wished it could be him who sat there, frying up bacon and potatoes and talking about going somewhere to get married. Ever since the day he'd met Jolene, he'd developed a longing to be settled down with a family.

But, he asked himself, how could he expect a woman to live with a man like him—someone whose life represented only death? Suddenly, he felt like leaving Wilbur's presence. He wanted to run away from the reminders of what his life could have been. It felt like someone was driving a stake into his body and letting the blood of life run out.

"Maybe we oughta skedaddle," he said.

Solon looked at Clayton and squinted his eyes in disbelief. "Why shucks! What for? Wilbur's gone to all the trouble of puttin' on bacon and taters for us."

"That's so," Wilbur agreed. "Please stay, Clayton. I can't eat this food all by myself. 'Sides, I like the company. I ain't gonna be a free man for long, ya know." He forced a smile. "I mean, this may be my last time together with a couple other free men."

Clayton moved off by himself and sat down, while Solon and Wilbur's constant chatter went on like a distant mirage. It was there, but it wasn't. Clayton shut out their voices and pondered over his life, until Wilbur offered him up a plate of food.

The food made him feel a little better, once it filled and warmed his stomach. In a more sociable mood, he said to Wilbur, "You don't seem all too happy about this marryin' business."

Wilbur swallowed and shrugged. "Oh, I am, really. I

guess when you've been a free man all your life, it takes a bit of gettin' used to.''

"But why are you hitchin' up now?" Solon said. "Just when you got your own ways of doin' things all lined out. Hell, I've been a bachelor all my life, and I sure ain't lookin' for some woman to lay a deed on my life. Why, I reckon a body would be answerin' all the way to his grave, once that deed was filed!''

Wilbur shrugged and nodded, "I can't say as I don't agree with you, Solon," he said in his slow drawl. "But you know, I've done seen the elephant. Shoot fire, I've done seen it in Dodge City, Hays City, and Ellsworth. Back years ago, I seen it in Abilene. I guess I done seen all the elephant I wanta see.''

"Yeah, I seen the elephant, too," Solon said. "And I think I'd like to see it again when I want to.''

Wilbur got that faraway look in his eyes again. "Oh, it ain't the same anymore, boys. Nothin' is. Shoot fire, I used to hunt buffalo just west of Dodge City, back before the herds came up from Texas. I seen that town go from nothin' more than a hole in the ground to Sin City. For my money, I think it'll go back to bein' another two-bit town. The days of the herds are over. Shoot fire, you can't even find buffalo anymore. We kilt 'em all off like a bunch o' idiots.''

Solon agreed. "Ain't nothin' I miss more than the sight of those beautiful animals scattered out as far as the eye can see. To tell the truth, I always figured they'd be here forever. There were so dang many of 'em. Seems hard to believe they've all been kilt. Yep, I guess you're right, Wilbur. Things are a-changin'. But hell, we don't need buffalo for meat anymore. We got lots of Texas beeves.''

Wilbur said, "I wouldn't count on that if I were you. Them farmers in Kansas are busy passin' laws to get all the Texas cattle out of the state, claimin' they brought in Texas Fever. Shoot fire, it ain't never been proved to me that longhorns bring in Texas Fever. I'll tell you what, boys," he added, pointing his fork in the air with a piece of bacon dangling from it, "I've been cowboyin' off and on ever since I was a half-growed man. I've ridden all the trails and crossed the range more times than I care to recall.

Shoot fire, I've lived through stampedes and lightnin' storms and crossed ragin' rivers! My my! I've lost half a dozen friends in those dang rivers. I ain't ashamed to say it, but it used to scare the daylights outa me, thinkin' about drownin', myself.'' He looked at Solon and Clayton for emphasis, and maybe a little sympathy. ''But all that don't seem to make any difference. It's all changed out here.''

Wilbur DeShazo was one of the few men alive who could hold a one-sided conversation as well as Solon. Clayton had always held a fascination with watching the two of them talk. One would be waiting like a frog that's poised to jump on a june bug for the other to stop for a breath. Once Wilbur paused, Solon saw his opportunity.

''You're right, Wilbur,'' he nodded heartily, ''things sure aren't like they used to be. Some of that's for the good, but most of it just makes me sick. Take the temperance league. Why, them ninnies will throw a fence around the state of Kansas if nobody stops 'em! Hell, you'd think folks could figure that out! As for Dodge City dryin' up, though, I don't really believe that'll ever happen, Wilbur. Why, it's the wildest, fastest town I ever seen! What do you think, Clayton? Will Dodge ever dry up?''

''Beats the life out of me. Once all the cowboys quit comin', I suppose it might could happen,'' Clayton said.

''I don't believe so,'' Solon repeated. ''Hell, we still got Fort Dodge, and they got the railroad! As long as they got soldiers and railroaders, they're gonna have a red-light district. Naw''—he shook his head—''nothin's gonna dry that up. And Shorty Gillis tells me he's got more business than he can handle.'' Solon stopped long enough to take a big bite of potatoes, then started to choke.

''Hell, them taters are hot,'' he exclaimed. ''Seems like I've et so dang many taters, I swear I might start sproutin' any day! My pappy use to tell me a story about a man who got a bean stuck up his nose. He woke up one morning, and beans were growin' right out of his face. That story used to scare the dickens out of me when I was a little boy. I still think about it, every time I eat taters.''

Solon stopped and looked at Wilbur, who was eating and

didn't appear to be paying much attention. "You never said who you was gonna marry," he said.

"Huh?" Wilbur looked up.

"Your bride. What's her name?"

"Cornelia Howard."

Solon scratched his stubble and mumbled her name. "I can't recall the woman," he said. "Where'd you meet her at, Wilbur?"

"I met her four or five years ago in Wichita. We been writin' to each other ever since. Her father just died six months ago. Left her some land on Walnut Creek. She's been beggin' me to come up. Said she couldn't work the place by herself. Shoot fire, boys. Like I say, I done seen the elephant, and I've done all the red-lightin' to last a lifetime. It's time to settle down," he said with some finality. "See that poke over yonder by my saddle? It's got my marryin' clothes in it. Fifty dollars' worth at Wright and Beverley. Got new boots, too." Once again, he grew melancholy. "Yessir, it's time for me to settle down. 'Sides, Kansas is gonna turn into nothin' but farmin' country before long. I use to hate that idea, but as I get older, I don't mind so much."

The next morning, they wished Wilbur good luck with his marriage and said good-bye. Wilbur sat by his campfire and waved to them glumly, apparently in no hurry to get to Ness County.

When they rode onto Clayton's land, it was early afternoon.

"Why, hell, Clayton, the place looks better than I remember," Solon commented. "Ol' Frusher took pretty good care of things."

"He always does," Clayton said. They rode up to the dugout. There were new patches of sod on the roof. Inside, Clayton lit a lamp and saw where Martin Frusher had put in some new rough poles to replace the old rafters. He'd packed in willow and brush to keep the dirt from falling through on everything.

They settled in for their first night in the dugout with a pot of coffee over the campfire and a supper of Wilbur's leftover bacon and potatoes. While they were eating, Solon was about to warm up with one of his many long conversations, when Clayton suddenly froze.

"Don't move, Solon."

Solon sat still, with only his eyes moving back and forth in his head. Then, he saw the rattlesnake, sliding right up next to his boot. He let go a holler and jumped to his feet, and the snake began to rattle. Quick as a cat, Clayton shot the snake in its striking pose.

Solon sat slowly back down. His face had turned a shade paler. "We need to build that house, Clayton," he said. "After all, it's apt to get cold and damp this winter, and I don't mind tellin' you that this old body of mind can't stand the cold like it used to."

Clayton nodded. "First thing."

The next morning, they began clearing a spot for the house on a little rise northwest of the dugout. Clayton had always carried the best of intentions of building a home, but this time, his feelings were different. It almost seemed like fate was telling him he had one chance left, and he was not going to take it lightly.

He'd originally planned on putting up a large one-room affair, but something made him change his mind. Clayton refused to even consider that it might have been Tracy's suggestions that steered his decision. Nevertheless, he decided to go all out with a couple of separate sleeping rooms, a kitchen, and a big parlor. Solon thought it was a silly idea.

"Why, all we need is a place to sleep and eat where the cold can't get in. Or the snakes," he added.

"You know what your problem is, Solon?" Clayton said. "You've got a bunkhouse mentality! Don't you know, this is gonna be a real home. What if we have guests come by? What if those guests are females? Why, you wouldn't wanta have us all out here in the same room, sleepin' together, would you? No sir! We're gonna build us a fine, proper house."

Solon started to say more, but stopped himself and gave Clayton a curious look.

They were still clearing off the little rise, when Martin Frusher rode up.

"I heard you come back," he said as they all shook hands. "How does everything look to you?" He surveyed the place with a proud look.

"Looks just fine. You've done nicely," Clayton said. "It's hard to believe I've been away for almost a year and a half. Seen Kirby Wiggins lately? He's still around, ain't he?"

"Oh, sure. Kirby's still runnin' his beeves. Are you figurin' on sellin' your cattle?"

"Three or four head, anyway, if I still got that many."

Martin Frusher smiled. "Oh, you got that many, all right. You got nine head now, Clayton. Had two calves in the spring."

Clayton frowned. "I don't see how that's possible, since I ain't got no bulls."

"No, but I do, and I been grazin' my cows with yours. I decided it was kinda silly, my usin' part of your pasture and not hardly payin' you nothin'. It seemed like it was only right, so I turned Herman out with your cattle. Herman took to those heifers with great joy!"

"What do I owe ya?" Clayton asked.

"Not a thing. Herman enjoyed the experience."

Solon laughed.

"Course," Martin Frusher went on, "we're lucky to have any cattle at all. Been a rough year. I won't ever forget January 18. That day, there come the awfulest blizzard that's ever hit these parts. I lost a couple of beeves in it, myself. The old people said they never seen a storm that bad. Folks got trapped inside for weeks. Then, this past summer, the damned grasshoppers hit. Like to ate everything up. I guess it was the worst grasshopper year since '74. They say back then, in '74, they came in by the millions. Blackened the sky. The old people thought it was surely Judgment Day come to pass! A big dark wall, pressin' down from up above." He paused and shook with the thought. "I never seen it, myself, you understand. But they say them grasshoppers was a foot deep on the ground, and spread out as far as the eye could see."

Solon looked doubtful over Martin Frusher's claims. "You're kiddin'. Why, I've seen a bad case o' grasshoppers before, but none that were a foot deep!''

Martin Frusher was undaunted by Solon's skepticism.
''I'm tellin' you what I heard, told to me by folks that
wouldn't lie. They say back in '74, them damn grasshoppers stripped everything that grew. When they finished
here, they flew back up in the sky and landed somewhere
else. They damn near eat Kansas up. They even stripped
the trees of their bark. That's what they say!'' He nodded
his head confidently. ''But, I been thinkin' about it, and
you know what I decided?'' He looked first at Clayton, then
at Solon. ''I think these grasshoppers we had this year were
the great-grandchildren of the ones that came in '74. You
know what else? They say those things lay eggs and eat
the clothes off your back.''

''Grasshoppers don't eat the clothes off your back,'' Solon said. ''Moths do, but not grasshoppers. Moths'll lay
eggs on your clothin' and in your hair. That's why I always
run a comb through my hair, once a day. Hell, don't nobody
know what might lay eggs up there! It stands to reason it
would make a nice layin' bed.''

''Well, I'm just tellin' you what the old people told me,''
Martin Frusher said adamantly. ''They claim those grasshoppers eat right through their clothes.''

That night, Solon had the worst time getting to sleep.
Finally, he asked Clayton what he thought of the subject.
''Do you reckon ol' Frusher is right?''

'' 'Bout what?''

''Grasshoppers. I mean, do you reckon they could eat the
clothin' right off your back?

''I ain't never heard of it, but I guess if there was enough
of 'em, they could. Why? You ain't worried about grasshoppers eatin' the clothes off your back, are ya?'' Clayton
yawned.

''Not as much as I'm worried about them damned rattle-
snakes,'' Solon said.

The next day, Clayton sold his five oldest cows to Kirby
Wiggins, then he and Solon went to buy lumber and six
pigs. Martin Frusher continued to stop by every day, all but
shucking his own chores. He had a fascination with Clayton

and went out of his way to be helpful and friendly, pitching in with the house-building effort.

One day, Wilbur DeShazo rode up and invited Clayton and Solon to his wedding, which they accepted. A week later, that feeling of doom came over Clayton once again as he sat in Union Church, listening to the Reverend Daniel Bondurant expound on the sanctities of marriage. As he stood at the altar, Wilbur looked stiff, and his neck was wet. He seemed about to faint any minute, and when he repeated his vows, he could barely be understood for the shake in his voice.

Yet, Clayton would have traded places with Wilbur in a heartbeat. It was only a dream, but he wished he could take back all the killings. He wished he could be the kind of man that a woman deserved in a husband. But, you couldn't erase the past, and dwelling on such things only led to disappointment. After the wedding, when they left High-point Township and headed home, he was in as low a mood as he'd ever been.

Solon, glad on his part that Wilbur was the one who'd gotten himself hoodwinked into matrimony, was in a fine frame of mind. He was just about to embark on one of his long-running commentaries, when Clayton spoke up and asked didn't he ever keep his mouth shut? Shocked, Solon fell silent, and Clayton had to apologize for making Solon take the blame for his own regrets.

The days stretched into weeks and the weeks into months. As the time passed, Clayton began to realize that this time, things really were different. He had beeves grazing in the fields, the hogs were already growing in number, and even though it was as bare as a poor man's church, Clayton at last had a home.

It took him a much longer time, but one morning, as he was headed out to feed the hogs, he stopped at the door and unbuckled his gun belt. Slowly, he hung his pistol and belt on a nail. He stared at it for some time before he went on outside, but from that day, he resisted the urge to reach for his sidearm and strap it back on. At first, it felt like a part of him was missing. Constantly, he found himself reaching for his side to touch his Colt, as he had done so many times before. In time, though, the urge lessened, and he stopped missing the weight of the pistol against his leg.

On the first day he went into town without his gun, he felt as nervous as a cat. He worried over being recognized and challenged. After all, he had a reputation.

But folks appeared friendly and accepting. They smiled and exchanged courtesies, and even invited him to church suppers and the like.

Clayton Crist was becoming just another Kansas farmer.

⚞ 26 ⚟

AFTER THE war, Clayton had assumed that his life would go back to normal, once he returned home. But Beartooth Flats wasn't the same anymore. Things had changed, just as they had in the rest of the country.

The people were still friendly enough, but there was no gaiety among them. Clayton noticed the weariness in their walk and the faraway, empty stares in their eyes.

There was a deep sadness in his mother. Flossie was tearful and happy to have her son safely back home, but Clayton knew she was deeply grieved over the loss of her husband. She seemed to have accepted a life of loneliness and made no attempts at socializing. She had aged so, lines now dominated her once-pretty face, and her hair had turned gray. Gone forever was the spark in her eyes. Clayton wanted to remind her that she could possibly marry another, but that was something he could never say to her.

Wendelin was transformed into adulthood and had taken a job in Columbia to help out the family. At eighteen, she looked nothing like the little sister Clayton remembered from his furlough two and a half years before. Now, she was a full-grown woman with a burden of responsibility on her shoulders. She acted older than her years. There seemed to be a sadness lurking inside Wendelin, as well.

The entire community of Beartooth Flats was covered with a veil of sadness. Gone were the days of laughter and lightheartedness among the people. Even Happy Lyta's store, where Clayton used to sit on the pickle barrel and listen to the men tell stories, was a somber place, with folks coming in and doing their business and then silently waving good-bye. The pickle barrel had been moved into a corner, and no one stayed to chat. Happy Lyta, himself, no longer lived up to the nickname he'd earned early in life. He'd become an old man in the war's duration and now seemed like an elderly stranger.

The biggest tragedy of all could be found among the families of Clayton's fallen messmates. The menfolk went about their duties in the fields like ghosts. The women paused in their washings to wipe at their eyes. Even the children's play was subdued. There lurked a terrible quiet in their homes. Clayton thought about the distant battle-fields. Each of these folks had had a part of themselves die out there, too, along with their beloved sons.

And Clayton still carried his own tragedies in his heart. Nighttime was the hardest. He could barely lay down his head that the nightmares didn't start. He got to where he dreaded seeing the sun go down. He threw his energies into working the farm, from sunup to sunset, hoping to escape his own memories and become too exhausted to dream.

Soon, his body began to respond to the hard labor. He became strong and healthy again. The sun tanned his skin, but the dreams never faded. As healthy as he was on the outside, there still remained a deep hurt and a painful emptiness. Not an hour went by that he didn't think of Jolene. Her Aunt Esther had been right, he told himself again and again. He should have written her. Then maybe she'd be with him right now, to share his life and help him fill up the emptiness. She could have helped him chase away the nightmares.

Clayton had been home a little over a month, when Abigail Beecher came to visit. He was out chopping trees to clear out a bigger garden area, when he looked up and saw her riding in.

Abigail was dressed all in yellow, with a big flouncy skirt and a matching bonnet. She tossed aside her lace parasol and ran to him with her arms outstretched.

Clayton didn't mean to, but he awkwardly stepped back-ward as her arms encircled his neck. It surprised him that he did it. He'd thought about Abigail many times since his return home. He'd thought about her, in fact, every time he passed the fishing hole.

Abigail didn't seem to notice his reaction—or if she did, it didn't seem to dampen her spirits any.

"Clayton Crist!" she cried. "Let me have a look at you!" She stepped back and let her excited eyes fall over him. "I swear, you're even more handsome than I remember! Haven't you got a little kiss for me?" She moved close again and rubbed his neck with her gloved hand.

"I don't reckon I should be goin' around kissin' a married woman," Clayton said, trying to suppress the sensuous feeling that swam through his body.

"Oh, drat! Why, we've known each other all of our lives. I figure you can surely kiss me if you want to." She moved her arms up around his neck and pulled his face to hers.

Reluctantly, Clayton gave her a peck on the cheek.

"I swear, Clayton! You can do better than that, now." Abigail puckered her lips. "Here, kiss my mouth."

Clayton tried to look around with her arms still locked around his neck. "Somebody's gonna see us, Abigail. This just ain't right, with you bein' married," he protested.

"Don't be silly! I want a hello kiss, and I'm not gonna let go of you 'til I get one!" Abigail giggled, the sound coming from deep in her throat. More softly she said, "I swear it."

Clayton gave a quick glance to make sure his mother wasn't in sight, then leaned forward and quickly kissed her lips. "There, are you happy?"

"I guess that will do for now," Abigail said. For all the sadness that seemed to fill the hollows of Beartooth Flats, Abigail was as bubbly and enthusiastic as ever, and still completely wrapped up in her own affairs. Clayton couldn't deny the fact that she had grown from a pretty girl into a beautiful woman.

"So," she said, "I suppose your mama told you about my gettin' married. Well, I truly am a married woman. I am now Mrs. Silas Bowden." She raised her eyes to his and tilted her head.

Clayton couldn't understand why, but he felt a touch of

anger that she'd gotten married. "Did you marry one of old man Bowden's boys?" he frowned.

"Well, I declare! Silas never had no *boys*! When his wife, Pearl, died three years ago. I went to work for him. But shush! Let's don't talk about that!"

Abigail suddenly dropped to the ground. She took off her bonnet and playfully tossed it at Clayton. "Come, sit down and talk to me. I declare, I haven't had anyone interestin' to talk to in a long time."

Clayton sat down cross-legged in front of her. He couldn't hide the shock on his face.

"You mean, you married old man Bowden?" he grimaced. His mother had told him that Abigail had gotten married the summer before and moved off to be with her husband in Columbia, but she hadn't mentioned who the groom was. Silas Bowden was the richest man in the county, but he had to be close to eighty years old. Clayton just stared at her.

Abigail's foot began to twitch back and forth. "I did," she stated flatly, "and there ain't no use in your sittin' there, thinkin' there's somethin' wrong. He needed me."

Clayton said dryly, "I guess you needed him too, huh?"

"Oh drat! Can't we talk about somethin' else?" Abigail pouted. Then she smiled. "You know, I read in the Columbia newspaper that they made you a colonel! Just think of that! Our own Clayton Crist, a colonel! Everybody in Columbia talks about you. I declare, you're a regular *hero!*" Her foot had stopped shaking. She reached over with the toe of her shoe and playfully rubbed it up and down Clayton's leg. "Have you been to the fishin' hole with anybody?" she teased.

"I'd like to know who that would be," Clayton said. "The girls I growed up with have all left. Barbara Perky lives in Nashville, and Sandra Nixon moved with her family to Alabama. 'Course, you know that already."

"I suspect you're right," she said. "There weren't very many girls our age. Oh," she sighed. "I just get so almighty sad when I come back here. I hardly ever do, you know. All the boys are dead. Sometimes, I go to bed and just bawl. I mean it. I cry my heart out. Poor Andy and

Burgess! Sometimes I wonder how I'll go on with my life, knowin' I'll never see them again. I thought many times that I might not ever see you again either, Clayton.'' Abigail looked like a sad puppy dog. ''I declare, I would've waited, surely I would have. But I was so afraid you'd never come home. And what's a girl to do? My father's in such poor health, he can barely work the farm.'' She looked off thoughtfully. ''Silas has been a godsend. He's taken a lot of burden off my family, Clayton. He surely has.''

Clayton was somewhat taken aback by the sincerity in her tone. ''Oh, you don't need to apologize for anything. I guess we've all had to deal with life our own way.''

The puppy dog look disappeared, and Abigail's eyes regained their sparkle. ''Oh, let's don't talk of such serious things! Let's go to the fishin' hole! I declare, it's so hot, the water would feel cool and refreshin'!''

Clayton shook his head. ''I don't think that would be a very good idea. If anyone saw us, it would get folks to talkin'.''

''Oh, drat! Let 'em talk. They already do. People can be so hateful. My sister, Miriam, says folks think I married Silas for his money.''

''Well, didn't you?'' Clayton asked matter-of-factly.

''Why, I declare, Clayton! I can't believe you'd say such a thing!''

''Why else would you marry an old grandpa like that?''

''Don't be difficult, Clayton. Come on, I'll race you to the fishin' hole.'' She got up.

''I'm not goin' to the fishing hole with you, Abigail. You're a married woman,'' Clayton said, even though his response was somewhat weaker. Abigail was more beautiful than ever, and his memory of her body was still pleasantly fresh.

''Bein' married don't stop a body from livin'.'' She took his hand and pulled him up. ''Come on, let's go.''

Clayton shook his head back and forth slowly. Barely audibly, he said, ''I just can't.''

Abigail would have none of that. ''Well, I'll just go without you, then. People will talk about that, too! 'Sides, who's gonna see us, outside of your mama? There ain't a soul within a mile or two." She left her horse grazing, and started running in the direction of the fishing hole, giggling and throwing her bonnet up in the air. Clayton ran after her, a small panic rising up inside him.

"Please, hold it down!" he pleaded. "Mama's gonna hear!"

"I declare, you're right."

Abigail stopped and took hold of his hand, pulling him along. As soon as they got to the water's edge, she stripped down to her bare skin and tested the water, dipping in a toe. Goose bumps rose on her body.

"Water's nice and cold. It'll feel great!"

Clayton stood there, feeling like a little boy back in Happy Lyta's store, staring at all the tempting candy sticks. Abigail surely had been sculpted by the Master. She had dimples when she smiled and beautiful white teeth. Her body was smooth, lean, and curvaceous. Everything was perfectly proportioned, down to her feet. She had strong, muscular legs. Her hands were veined like a man's, but they were definitely womanly. Clayton didn't know why he hadn't fallen in love with her. With the exception of Jolene, she was surely the most beautiful girl he knew.

Then in the middle of his thoughts, he saw her run out knee-deep into the water. She playfully cupped water in her hands and threw it at him.

"Come on! You'll love it. You aren't shy, are ya?"

She waded on out, until the water came to the bottom of her breasts. Clayton watched them, fascinated, as they bobbed up and down with their dark red tips, the areolae pulling up tight.

He couldn't help himself. Clayton started unbuttoning his shirt, then pulled off his clothes.

He swam out toward Abigail. She ducked under the water and disappeared. When she didn't resurface, Clayton called out to her.

"Abigail, don't play games."

Clayton called out again, this time louder.

"Abigail!"

Just then, he felt her arms around his body. She slid up next to him and came to the surface. She pulled her mouth

to his and kissed him deeply. Her hands ran up and down
his back, caressing his buttocks.

"Oh, Clayton," she whispered in his ear, "I've waited
so long for this minute! Truly I have."

After that, meeting Abigail at the fishing hole became as
regular as clockwork. She appeared every Monday, using
the excuse to her husband that she was going to see her
family. Instead, she rode straight to Clayton's. At first,
Clayton was torn by guilt, but his loneliness and lust won
out over honor, and he got to where he looked forward to
Mondays.

For over two years, they continued their Monday ren-
dezvous, and life otherwise went on as normal. Clayton's
mother became aware of their goings-on and voiced her
deep disapproval, but she, too, grew accepting over time.

Then, on New Year's Day of '68, Silas Bowden died in
his sleep. Abigail carried on as if his death was the most
tragic thing that had ever happened, but she still didn't miss
her secret Mondays with Clayton, even with Silas not yet
cold in the ground.

In the public eye, Abigail was the mournful widow
dressed in black. And, left with Silas Bowden's considerable estate, she became the wealthiest person in the county.
She set her sights on Clayton right away and talked him
into visiting at her mansion.

"This can all be yours," she said, showing him the vast
lands that went with the beautiful home. "We'd have more
farmland than twenty families could work."

It was clear that she had fallen in love with Clayton, but
it was unfortunately a one-sided love. Not that Clayton
hadn't been tempted. Abigail was beautiful, and nice in her
own way. He considered the things he could buy for his
mama with the instant wealth, and the comforts of living
in such a fine home.

But the truth was, he wasn't in love with Abigail in an
everlasting way. He was in lust, and he knew it. Frolicking
with her had been the most pleasurable thing he'd ever
experienced, and he felt almost addicted to the delights of
her perfect body. At the same time, though, he'd also felt
repulsed at the both of them and their wrongful weakness.

He had never blamed Abigail completely for cheating on her husband, but he knew he could never trust her. He had known for a long time that Abigail's greatest love was for herself.

Abigail persisted for a while, but when Clayton finally made it clear that he wasn't going to marry her, she accepted the fact with bitterness. She stopped meeting him at the fishing hole, and soon was seen being courted by Lem Scoggins. Before the frost was gone from Silas Bowden's grave, they were married.

Clayton saw her only once more, at the Beartooth Church Homecoming Dinner. Abigail and Lem had ridden up in the fanciest carriage, and they were both dressed like some royal couple. Lem behaved like a servant, feverish to satisfy her every whim. After the church service, while the families picnicked on the grounds, Clayton and Abigail ended up alone at the dessert table.

Clayton still held a fondness for Abigail, and harbored no resentments, but his mama had told him about the rumors and suspicions that had gone on about the two of them. He wanted to speak, but felt it more respectful to act distant.

His silence only enraged the passionate Abigail. After several attempts at conversation, she began to shout.

"Lem! Come here!" she called. "He insulted me! Now, I demand that you defend my honor!"

Everyone stood in stunned silence. Even the children, who'd been running around the tables and filling the hollow with their loud voices, grew silent and stared at Abigail and Clayton.

Clayton looked at Abigail's red face. She was like a volcano, bubbling before eruption, but in her eyes there was hurt and pain.

"Why are you doing this?" he said softly.

This seemed to anger Abigail even more. She grabbed Lem by the coat sleeve, and pushed him toward Clayton. "Are you going to defend my honor or not?" she said.

"Please, darlin'! This is not the place. Everybody's lookin'," Lem said weakly.

Clayton had known Lem since childhood. He was three

years older than Clayton, and was known to be a sissy. Back when the war had first started, Lem had told everyone that the army had turned him down. Clayton had heard that Lem, in truth, had never even tried to join, and he'd somehow managed to avoid the war entirely. Clayton couldn't begrudge Lem for not fighting. After all, he was alive and breathing in the fine Tennessee air, wasn't he? Instead, Clayton felt sorry for the likes of Lem Scoggins. Abigail was likely to get him hurt someday, if she didn't eat him alive, herself. Clayton watched Lem sweat, and his bottom lip quiver, and quickly left the church picnic among the folks' stares and murmurs.

After that day, Clayton knew he couldn't live in Beartooth Flats any longer. Like nature calling the geese from the frozen north to the warm fields of the south, he started feeling something pulling him away. He couldn't stand to see the empty faces, and know that he was a reminder of sons lost. He couldn't stand to see Lem Scoggins sweat and degrade himself over Abigail's silliness.

It pained him, thinking about leaving his mother. The guilt was almost more than he could stand, but the pain of staying was even worse. He just couldn't go on dying inside. He had to find whatever it was that would make him whole again.

Maybe he could come back, he thought. Maybe someday, he would find out that he'd been wrong. Maybe time would heal. Whatever the case, like the geese, he had to go.

27

CLAYTON HAD no idea where he was going when he left Beartooth Flats, or what lay ahead. He just went west.

Beartooth Flats had somehow failed to give a true representation of the scars that the war had left. In Clayton's hamlet, the defeat lay in the loss of all the young men. The land, itself, was untouched. The community remained as it had always been: a place where poor farmers grew their food, raised their livestock, and struggled to get through life.

But other communities had been hard-hit. Clayton was disturbed by what he saw as he traveled. Anywhere the Federals had set foot, there was destruction. Stores were closed up and buildings boarded shut. Once-wealthy land-owners mourned the devastation of their fertile fields, gone to weed with the lack of money for seed or stock to graze the land. Beautiful land had been laid waste, the fine homes burned to the ground. The South had been ripped apart, as if someone had taken a giant knife and cut into its heart. So many were having to start all over again. Clayton wondered resentfully what the North looked like. Probably business as usual, he guessed, as if there'd never been a terrible war—as if time had just marched forward.

There'd been a few reports of Yankees seen wandering around Beartooth Flats. They were mostly deserters who were afraid to return home. They usually came into town in pairs, scavenging for food. The people tried to ignore them for the most part as unwelcome visitors. Then, in June of '64, two of them broke into a home where Elsie Paine was sleeping—she who was still mourning the death of her husband at Chickamauga. The men raped Elsie and left her for dead. When a neighbor, Old Man Sapp, heard about what had happened to the poor widow, he single-handedly hunted down the two men and shot them both dead. Many of the deserters left Beartooth Flats after that and headed elsewhere. Elsie recovered, but she refused to ever step outside of her house again. Old Man Sapp was seen taking her food from time to time, and tending to what chores needed to be done around her place.

Clayton stopped at a farm east of Union City, located in Obion County in northwest Tennessee, to inquire about a meal. The Box family welcomed him like an old friend and insisted he stay the night. After supper, a neighbor rode up, and Clayton was surprised to see that it was Hume Feild. They had a warm reunion, and Hume Feild invited Clayton to spend a few days at his home there in Union City.

It was good being with the colonel again, under much more pleasant circumstances. Clayton was surprised at Hume Feild's gentle and quiet way; he'd been such a strong fighter and leader of men for the Tennessee Army. Hume had been a fair and caring man, but never lacking in discipline. Clayton couldn't recall a more honorable soldier for the South.

Hume Feild was glad to see Clayton and appeared to be without bitterness over the outcome of the war. Little was said about what they had gone through on the battlefield. Instead, Hume took pleasure in showing off his gardens and flowers to Clayton. His only concern now was to rebuild and get on with life. He was genuinely interested in Clayton's future as well, asking him repeatedly what his plans were.

"Why don't you settle down here?" he asked. "Union City's a wonderful place, and we're gonna recover just fine. This would be a good place to get married and raise your children. There's lots to do. Besides, we need more good men." He added, "There's lots of pretty young women. You could take your pick!"

Clayton felt tempted. Union City did appear to offer opportunity, but he could still feel that urge to roam. He needed time to think things through and see what else life might have to offer. Nothing that Hume Feild or anyone else had to say could satisfy that need.

Hume Feild introduced him to Dudley Bickerstaff, a big, friendly man who owned a ranch along the Navasota River in Limestone County, Texas. Bickerstaff was originally from Obion County, and had returned to care for his dying mama. Whereas Hume Feild had been trying to sell Clayton on the idea of settling there in Union City, Bickerstaff quickly spurred an interest in Clayton for Texas.

The three men were seated on Hume Feild's front porch, talking. Bickerstaff was to return to Texas the next day. He looked out over the Tennessee countryside, stretched out his long frame and sighed.

"Sure wish you could see Texas," he said. "You fellas don't know what you're missin'! Land as far as the eye can see! A man can almost get lost on his own place."

"I've always had a desire to see it," Clayton said.

Bickerstaff had noticed the interest in Clayton's eyes when he'd told his stories about Texas. "Well," he said slowly, to let the words sink in, "I'm gonna take a herd of longhorns to Baxter Springs, Kansas, come the first of June. I can always use a good hand."

Clayton stirred in his chair. The offer excited him. During the war, he'd heard many stories about Texas, and there wasn't a boy in all of Tennessee who hadn't heard about Davy Crockett and the Alamo. He couldn't think of any reasons not to accept.

"Mr. Bickerstaff, I'd be mighty pleased to go with ya."

Hume Feild spoke up. "Doggone you, Dudley!" he said. "I'd like to keep Clayton around here!" He turned to Clayton. "I hope you realize that if you ever go off to Texas, you'll never come back! Why, I reckon Texas is made up mostly of Tennesseans already!"

They said their good-byes the next day. Clayton made an attempt to convince Hume Feild to join them, but he only shook his head. "I got all I need here," he said as he waved from his porch.

Clayton enjoyed the trip to Texas with Dudley Bicker-

staff, who proved to be a most-entertaining fellow. Back in
the forties, he'd left his native Tennessee to head for Texas,
and he regaled Clayton with stories about the "Republic of
Texas," as he called it.

Limestone County was longhorn country. Clayton had
never seen so many beeves in all of his life. He remarked
to Bickerstaff that the starving Confederate Army surely
could have used some of those beeves. Bickerstaff replied
that Texas had become overrun with cattle during the war.

"Guess they had their minds elsewhere. Forgot all about
us," he commented.

Bickerstaff's ranch was so large, Clayton wondered how
many days it would take to cross it by horse. Finally, they
rode up to the main house and on a short way to the bunkhouse. There were several men standing outside by the corral.

Clayton was introduced around.

"Boys, I'd like you to meet Clayton Crist. He's from
Tennessee, and that in itself speaks well for him. You boys
introduce yourselves."

A baby-faced man stepped forward. "I'm Jamie Wilson.
My daddy's from Nashville." They shook hands.

Another man stared at Clayton a moment before he
spoke. His eyes were cool and appraising. "Solon Johnson,
and I ain't from Tennessee," he said sourly.

"Pay no attention to Solon," Bickerstaff said. "His bark
is worse than his bite. He's always unpleasant to green
hands."

"That's all right. Talk all you want, Mr. Bickerstaff, but
you ain't the one has to break these new calves in," Solon
Johnson said. He climbed up on the fence and spit. Clayton
let his eyes roll past him to the next man.

"I'm Nipsy Gray, and I'm glad to make your acquaintance. I'm from Alabama. Did you fight in the war?" he
asked directly.

Clayton nodded. "First Tennessee."

Nipsy Gray laughed. He grabbed Clayton's hand again
and shook it vigorously. "Shiloh. It was the First Tennessee
that spelled us. Was you there?"

"I was."

"Hot damn! I can already tell you're a good man. You hear that, Solon? He was with the First Tennessee."

Solon nodded but didn't appear to be any more impressed.

A Mexican man walked up. "I am Arturo Baca," he said, nodding his head, then stepped back.

"Baca, there, says he don't speak nothin' but Mescan, but don't let him fool you. He understands English, all right," Bickerstaff said. "He's been with me for five years."

An older, heavy man stepped forward last. "My name's Tilly Sparks," he said in a gravelly voice. "You do your job, stay out of the way, keep your area clean in the bunkhouse, and wash your ass once a week, and we'll get along just fine."

"I'll try to remember all that," Clayton said honestly.

After the introductions, Bickerstaff ordered the men back to work. They were still in the process of rounding up calves to brand. Bickerstaff assigned Jamie Wilson the job of breaking Clayton in, then headed off to the big house. Within half an hour, Clayton noticed Bickerstaff was back among the men, working just as hard as his hands.

Jamie Wilson had sandy-colored hair and a stocky build. His arms were well muscled and darkened by the sun. He gave Clayton a serious nod, and together they rode out.

"You been workin' for Bickerstaff long?" Clayton asked.

"Ever since I could ride," Jamie said. "Ain't worked for nobody else. Learned it all from him."

"Must treat you good, then."

"He's a fair man. You respect him, he respects you back," Jamie said. "Sometimes he lets us go into town and pays for everything."

They rode out about a mile, where they found two calves in some brush by the river.

"I sure hope you know how to handle a rope," Jamie commented. " 'Cause these two are gonna be wild as jackrabbits, I guarantee. What we gotta do," he went on, "is get a rope on 'em and take 'em back to that pen where we're puttin' all the calves in. Mr. Bickerstaff wants to take

a herd to Kansas in June, and we gotta get 'em all branded.
We woulda had all this done, except you can't brand the
calves 'til after March. We've already got the brand on
everything else.''

Clayton watched him swing his rope and lasso one of
the two calves. He took out his own rope and made several
attempts before he was able to snag the other calf.

"Not too bad for a green hand," Jamie Wilson laughed.

"It ain't as easy as I thought," Clayton admitted.

Working on the ranch became a pleasurable time for
Clayton; in fact, he'd never done anything in the line of
work that pleased him more than working for Dudley Bickerstaff. He liked the solitude, and it didn't take him long
before he could ride and rope with the rest of them. He
even enjoyed life in the bunkhouse among the other men,
though it did remind him of a little bit of his messmates in
the war. Back then, Clayton had drawn inside himself, and
he'd never let anybody get too close. Even now that the
war was over, Clayton still found it hard to enter into any
of their conversations. Outside of Jamie Wilson, none of
the other men said much of anything to him. Clayton
bunked next to Jamie, and that suited him just fine. Jamie
respected the fact that Clayton didn't say much, and the
others just flat didn't care.

It was clear that Solon Johnson and Tilly Sparks were
the bunkhouse lawyers. Most topics centered around the
two of them. Both were highly opinionated and voracious
talkers. The other men joined in their conversations once
in a while, but when they did talk, it was mostly to kick
up their heels and tell stories about themselves.

In late May, Bickerstaff sent Solon Johnson down the
river to hire on two or three more hands. There were right
at two thousand longhorns ready to move, and Bickerstaff
needed at least ten men for the job. Two days later, Solon
returned with two brothers, Cyrus and Rufus Keuchel, and
a half-breed by the name of Black Eye Lamerton. Black
Eye's mother had been a southern Cheyenne from the Territory. His father was a trader, and he was also rumored to
be a horse thief who would steal the horses in Texas and
take them to the Nation to sell or trade. Bickerstaff wasn't

too pleased at the latter acquisition. He'd known Black Eye's father and had no use for him or his offspring. The younger Lamerton was known to have a foul temper, and there'd been innuendo that he'd been involved in some cattle rustling of his own. The Keuchel brothers were from a family of means, and their father had sent them out, Solon said, to gain some genuine work experience. They were riding nice mounts and were very well armed, but they were both young and green.

Bickerstaff looked at them and just shook his head.

"Well, you hired 'em, Solon. You'd better make sure they can handle themselves on the trail. It's a fer piece to Baxter Springs."

"They'll do fine," Solon Johnson said stubbornly. "I'll see to it."

The three new men found their places in the bunkhouse and were treated with the same silent disregard as Clayton. The Keuchels seemed too intimidated to utter a word to anybody, and Black Eye Lamerton just kept his mouth shut and glared.

One day, Dudley Bickerstaff called Clayton to the big house. He took him into a fine room with a large oak desk and a deep leather chair and closed the door.

"Come here, Crist."

Bickerstaff opened a gun cabinet. He tossed Clayton a pistol and gun belt.

"That rifle of yours is fine," he said, "and Jamie tells me you're mighty accurate with it, but out here you need a six-shooter. There'll be times when you're better suited with a sidearm. This is an Army Colt .44 caliber. It's quicker." He handed Clayton two boxes of shells. "Run a box through it and get used to how it feels and shoots. Keep the other box for the trip north."

Clayton was surprised at Bickerstaff's gesture, but he was even more surprised at how familiar the gun felt in his hand, like an old friend.

Bickerstaff watched how Clayton handled the gun, and how he rubbed the smooth metal with his fingers. He nodded to himself.

"Much obliged," Clayton said sincerely. He eagerly

went off to do some practice shooting, and thereafter took special care of the Colt, keeping it clean and clear from anyone else's hands.

Getting ready to move the cattle to Baxter Springs wasn't such an easy task, but looking forward to the drive ahead put some excitement back into Clayton's life—something that had pretty much been missing since the war. The men used packhorses to carry all their equipment, which consisted mainly of several iron skillets. They took along an oven to cook their bread in and three big coffeepots, along with cups, tin plates, knives, and forks. For beans, they packed flour, soda, salt, coffee, and plenty of bacon. Each man carried a bedroll and extra clothing. The Keuchel brothers seemed to have a hard time with the fact that they traveled so light. They had to leave behind such items as their books and toiletries to have enough room for an extra pair of pants and a shirt.

28

BICKERSTAFF LED the two thousand longhorns out. It was early on a bright, clear morning. From the beginning, travel went slow, as the land had buffalo grass as far as the eye could see. They allowed the longhorns to linger and graze on the grass as much as they could, hoping to flesh out some of the old longhorns whose ribs showed.

The longhorns bellowed and bawled, while the men sang lullabies and whistled softly. Clayton had never felt happier, as his ears took in the sounds of the drive. He and Jamie Wilson had enjoyable conversations over the cattle as they rode, and at night he rested hard until his turn to take watch.

On the third day, Dudley Bickerstaff decided that the job of cook was an assignment that took a top priority. Earlier, it had been decided that every man would take his turn at preparing the meal, but after Jamie Wilson had burned the biscuits, fried the bacon to a crisp, and made weak coffee, the men became so irritable they were thinking about stringing Jamie up. After listening to them gripe and bellow for two days, Bickerstaff finally reconsidered.

He'd been keeping a close watch on Tilly Sparks. Once, Clayton overheard him say to Solon Johnson, "Tilly's put on so much weight, he can barely stay in the saddle. I'm a-feared one of them longhorns might cut him good."

Tilly did, indeed, look uncomfortable in the saddle. He could ride well enough, but he just wasn't much good at working cattle anymore. It was funny, Clayton thought. All along, he'd looked at Tilly, Solon Johnson, and Arturo Baca as the best hands in the outfit, but now he noticed otherwise. He'd heard about how a man could grow old almost overnight, but he'd never really understood, until now. Maybe, he thought, that was what had happened to Tilly. Maybe he'd just aged, all of a sudden. It made him feel a little sad for Tilly Sparks.

Tilly raised seven kinds of hell when Bickerstaff named him the one and only cook for the duration of the drive. He was also to take care of the horses.

If Tilly had, indeed, grown old overnight, it surely didn't show itself in his tirade. His big face grew red, and he looked as mean as a rattlesnake.

"I ain't no cook!" he protested. "I'm a cowhand, and a damned good one, too. I ain't gonna be lookin' over no packhorses and doin' women's work!"

He acted as ferocious as a mad dog, but Bickerstaff paid him no mind. Finally, after much yelling and complaining, Tilly cooked supper, and he did so from that day on. Surprisingly enough, the meals improved greatly, as Tilly had a fine imagination.

The skies to the north began to darken, and for days before they reached the Trinity River, storm clouds threatened. Off in the distance at night, they could see streaks of lightning reaching down toward the earth. When they got to the Trinity, it was swollen up to its banks.

The men were apprehensive. For the last two evenings, camp discussions had centered on the bad weather to the north. How would the cattle react to the loud thunderbolts and lightning flashes of a bad storm? The word "stampede" had circulated through the men so often, it was the uppermost thought in their minds.

All of the men, with the exception of Clayton and the Keuchel brothers, knew firsthand about stampedes, so they were all thankful when the bad weather stayed to the north and passed right by. But the Trinity, with its banks so swollen, brought on a new problem. Where they hadn't had to ride through any weather, it was plain there had been plenty of rains ahead to fill up the river and make it dangerous to cross. Bickerstaff looked the situation over.

"Well boys, we might as well graze them right here, until the water goes down," he said. "Give them clouds up ahead a chance to move on out."

They waited two days for the river to lower, while the men caught up on some sleep. There was still plenty of grass for grazing, so the cattle stayed close.

On the second night, Clayton sat next to Rufus, eating supper. At seventeen, Rufus Keuchel was away from his home for the first time in his life. Both he and his older brother, Cyrus, who was nineteen, did their best to talk and act like the other men, but their inexperience in life showed through. Clayton often watched the Keuchels and thought about his own early years in the war. Back then, he remembered the false bravado in all the new soldiers, and he now saw the same strugglings in Rufus. Sweat was beaded up on Rufus's face, and his eyes couldn't hide the fear as he studied the currents in the river. Clayton knew the feeling. He knew that Rufus's mouth was like cotton, and that his heart was pounding.

"Are you a good swimmer?" Rufus asked in a hushed tone. His hand shook as he lifted his plate.

"I reckon so. Good as anybody else. Can't you swim?" Clayton asked.

"Some." Rufus stabbed at a piece of bacon with his fork, then pushed it around on the bottom of his plate. His eyes were still focused on the river. "That current's pretty bad. I heard Solon say we're gonna start movin' 'em across tomorrow mornin'." His eyes shifted around wildly. Clayton saw the worry in them. He'd seen it many times before.

"Oh, it ain't no different from other rivers," he said. "Your horse'll take care of ya. Just don't lose contact with 'im. If you lose your seat, hang on to his tail or your saddle or whatever you can get your hands on."

Rufus nodded. "Just let the horse do the work, huh? That makes sense." He added hopefully, "We've done all right so far, haven't we?" His spirits seemed to pick up a little, and a touch of bravado returned to his voice.

Clayton's eyes rested on the Trinity River. The water was moving at a steady pace, but not too bad, he thought. "Sure. You'll be all right," he said.

But, as they watched the water for a while longer, Rufus grew gloomy again, picturing himself and Cyrus being sucked downward into that angry river, grabbing and clutching for their horses, while the rest of the men crossed on over without even noticing.

Clayton gave up trying to be convincing and made a mental note to keep his eye on Rufus the next day.

Right after breakfast the next morning, Arturo Baca went out ahead, and they began leading the longhorns into the river. At first, everything went smoothly, but then a few of the cattle started milling about. Soon, several were going around and around in circles. As the circle grew in number, the cattle got packed in tighter and tighter, to where those in the middle were in danger of being crushed. Alarmed, Arturo Baca rode in amongst the beeves and was trying desperately to break them up. He had his right hand full of rope as he slapped at the milling longhorns.

Dudley Bickerstaff saw what Arturo Baca's intentions were and tried to stop him.

"Arturo, no! Get out of there!" he hollered. "Get out of there, right now!"

But his warning came too late. The longhorns were turning faster, and Arturo's horse started to panic. It reared up and managed to get its front legs across the back of one of the longhorns. Caught up in the swirl, the horse gave a shrill whinny. Its eyes rolled wildly in its head as it tried to kick itself free of the longhorn's back and the tightening circle of cattle.

Arturo yelled out once, just as he lost his seat and disappeared. The other men rode in from all sides, firing their six-shooters and shouting at the crazy cattle.

They worked from the outside inward, diverting the herd away from the circle layer by layer. It took an hour to get everything settled down, but by that time, Arturo Baca was lost, and at least twenty head of cattle had drowned.

As everyone worked to keep things calm and in order, Bickerstaff sent Black Eye Lamerton downstream to look for Arturo Baca. Clayton was overseeing one end of the herd, when something like a premonition made him turn to the water. Just then, a cry rang out.

Rufus had ridden upstream into the river to fetch a stray, and had suddenly lost his seat. He was kicking and splashing wildly in the water, clutching on to his struggling horse's reins. His head bobbed desperately in and out of the water like a cork.

It almost seemed like a dream. Clayton wondered if this wasn't something that had already happened, and he was reliving it in his sleep. Maybe it was just Rufus's fears coming to life. Whatever, Clayton felt a strange feeling of time stopping.

He shook off his ponderings when he saw Rufus go under again. "I'm comin'!" he hollered. "Just try and relax!" He could see the panic that gripped Rufus when his head popped up, and he knew his words were in vain. He tried to turn his mare into the current, but his own horse was wanting to swim on across to the other bank. He yanked hard on the reins, cutting the mare's mouth.

Just then, Rufus lost hold of his horse and quickly got swept away from the animal. Clayton tried to grab him as he floated by, but he managed only to tear Rufus's shirtsleeve. Clayton dived into the water after Rufus, but when he came up, Rufus was nowhere in sight. Clayton dived back into the water, trying to judge where Rufus might be, but he couldn't see anything. The water had become murky from the rains and the milling of the two thousand longhorns, and there was no visibility at all. Clayton resurfaced and looked around him. His heart pounded wildly in his chest as each second ticked by. Again, he went back under and was barely submerged, when a piece of floating wood struck him in the back of the head.

Clayton saw stars and nearly blacked out, but then something struck him on the knee. His instincts drew his hands downward, and he felt Rufus's leg.

Rufus was upside down, and he was kicking wildly. Clayton fought hard to pull him closer, but one of Rufus's kicks caught him in the chest and he fell back, letting go. Clayton's lungs were already screaming for air, but he dived farther into the blackness, reaching out his arms, hoping again for the touch of Rufus's struggling body.

Just when he thought he'd lost the fight, he felt

something hit his hand. One of Rufus's kicks had caught his finger. Clayton reached out and groped wildly, until he found Rufus's leg and took hold of it again. Rufus gave one last kick, then the leg went still.

With his right arm cradled around the leg, Clayton pulled at the water with his left, straining for what he hoped was the surface. He had no idea how deep he was, or in what direction he was swimming, and he was starting to take in some of the muddy water. Down there, in the darkness, something deep inside told Clayton that he and Rufus were going to die. He tried pushing harder, but he was done for. There was no fight left. His lungs were about to explode. He accepted his fate, and was beginning to let it all go, when suddenly his face felt the warm summer sun. His head shot out of the water, and he began to cough and choke, as his lungs filled with the sweet morning air.

He felt the rope sting his face, but it didn't really register at first. It was only when the rope cinched tighter underneath his left arm, that he realized someone had lassoed him. He didn't know it was Solon Johnson, until he had been pulled up on the bank.

Solon was looking down at him.

"You all right?"

"I think so. I'm obliged to ya," Clayton said.

Solon nodded silently.

Beside Clayton, Rufus Keuchel was lying on the river's bank, his leg still across Clayton's right arm. His face had turned blue. His brother, Cyrus, who had watched frozen in fear during Clayton's rescue effort, sat holding his brother's hand and crying out.

"Poor Mommy!" he kept wailing, over and over. "She was scared for us to go! She knew this would happen! Why did you send us out here, Father? Wake up, Brother! Oh please, wake up!" He looked at Solon. "He'll be all right, won't he?"

Solon shrugged helplessly. Lines of concern wrinkled his brow. He turned his back and looked at Dudley Bickerstaff for some sort of answer.

Water poured from Rufus's mouth. Suddenly, he began to cough. He threw up and coughed more violently. He got to his hands and knees and tried to crawl a way, but couldn't for having to stop, cough, and puke some more. It surprised everyone, for they'd been most certain he had drowned. In fact, Black Eye Lamerton even said as much.

"Leave him to the wolves and the coyotes," he said.

"I believe I'll make those decisions," Dudley Bickerstaff said, irritated.

Black Eye Lamerton just shrugged at Bickerstaff's words.

"Don't mean nothin' to me," he said. "But it's a damn waste of time to sit here and worry over him."

"If you don't like it, just ride on," Solon Johnson said irritably. "I hired you for Mr. Bickerstaff. I reckon I can let you go."

Black Eye Lamerton's jaw twitched. He rested his hand on the handle of his Colt. "I might kill you someday. Your mouth's as big as the Trinity," he said. His menacing eyes bored into Solon's, and the sinister grin was inviting Solon to give him a reason to back up his words. Solon only stared back.

"I'll stay with Rufus, if need be," Clayton offered. Rufus had managed to sit up and was still coughing hard.

"We're all gonna stay," Bickerstaff said. "And we're gonna stop the arguin' right now. We've already lost Baca." He put his hand on Cyrus Keuchel's shoulder. "We'll stay with your brother," he nodded. "Don't you worry none."

Cyrus Keuchel looked at Black Eye Lamerton, but he couldn't hold his gaze very long. He wanted to stand up for his brother, Rufus, in the worst way, but he was in genuine fear of Black Eye Lamerton.

"Let it go, Cyrus," Bickerstaff said. "He didn't mean anything personal. It's just his way." He knew he didn't sound any more convincing than he felt. He, himself, was far from comfortable with the likes of Black Eye.

By that afternoon, Rufus was alert. He amazed everyone by insisting that he was ready and fit for travel. All that day and into the night, he coughed and carried on so much, he began to complain that his ribs hurt. His breathing was heavy and labored. Cyrus worried over him like a mama would, while some of the other men appeared annoyed at the goings-on. When Cyrus asked Tilly Sparks to make up a soup for his brother, Tilly looked like he'd been asked to wrangle the moon.

Dudley Bickerstaff was of a mind to send the two boys home. The trail, he knew, wasn't for everyone. It took a certain breed—a certain toughness—to handle the long hours, the stampedes and river crossings. It took men who weren't afraid to face off against Indians and such. And, even though the Keuchel boys had worked hard at presenting themselves as tough and hardy, he knew it wasn't so. Still, as much as he would have liked to send them back, it would have left him too shorthanded.

A ten-man crew had been cutting it close with two thousand head of cattle. At first, he'd considered fourteen or fifteen hands, and then that number had been whittled down to a dozen. Bickerstaff now regretted the day he'd listened to Leslie Brown, a neighboring rancher who had boasted that he could do the job with eight to ten men.

He never should have let Brown talk him into such a small number, Bickerstaff thought. After all, what did Leslie Brown care that he was now seriously shorthanded?

And Arturo, Bickerstaff thought sadly. Arturo Baca had arguably been his best all-around man. Now, he was gone. They hadn't even found his body.

Dudley Bickerstaff's chest burned as he drank Tilly Sparks's muddy coffee. It was a long way to Baxter Springs, and the rumors he'd heard about Black Eye Lamerton were coming all too true. That would not make things any easier.

There would be no rest that night. Bickerstaff ordered Cyrus Keuchel off night watch to get some sleep. He'd take night herd himself.

29

THEY CROSSED the Red River at Saddler's Bend and took the Cloud Trail north. The longhorns were fattening up along the way, feeding on the thick buffalo grass. Dudley Bickerstaff had originally wanted to move the cattle as quickly as possible, but the grazing was so good, he got less and less in a hurry and set a slow pace. He tended to the cattle more like a herder, letting them graze long and often. This was good for the beeves, but it caused the men's tempers to grow even shorter, as they waited idly through the long delays.

Somehow, the men managed to get along peacefully enough, but it was becoming more and more apparent that hiring Black Eye Lamerton had been a big mistake. He and Solon Johnson had almost come to blows on more than one occasion and had to be separated. Black Eye enjoyed keeping the men stirred up with his rude comments and wild stories. He'd managed to get about half of them good and scared, telling tales about the Cheyenne warriors. The Keuchel brothers were so badly spooked, they'd lost sleep for worrying about being attacked in their bedrolls. They both slept holding their weapons, and Dudley Bickerstaff was sure that one of them would end up shooting either himself or one of the other men. He tried to reassure them that the stories were purely fictional and warned Black Eye to quit scaring the boys, but Black Eye only laughed.

It was a good, clear night. They had bedded the herd down in a valley that sat in a chain of mountains, and the air felt warm but pleasant. They ate supper, and as they sat around the fire, the talk centered on what the men planned to do with their pay, once they had the beeves delivered. No sooner had Jamie Wilson opened his mouth to speak, when Black Eye Lamerton cut in.

"Ain't no use in dreamin', boys," he said. "The Cheyenne warriors will most likely attack us any day now." He grinned. "They come like giants, with their long legs hangin' so low from their ponies' backs, their moccasins split the prairie grass and kick up dust. The ponies, they seem to have six legs instead of four."

"They ain't no such thing as giants," Jamie Wilson said, annoyed at being interrupted. "I run across some Cheyenne once." He paused and looked at the others. "Come to think of it, though, they *was* tall. But they weren't no giants," he directed at Black Eye.

"You probably saw the little ones," Black Eye said in his deep voice. "But the most of them, they are giants, I tell you." He looked around at each of the men and narrowed his eyes. "The warriors will come with ropes attached to their bodies. On the end of the ropes, they have spikes. They drive the spikes into the ground to hold them there, so they can't run away. They have to fight until they die. It was against the blue coats, when all but a few of the giant warriors had been killed, that they used the spikes and fought to the death, rather than be captured." He looked over the fire at the other men, each one in turn. "'Course, against pissants like you, they will not need their ropes. They will come in so many numbers, you will all be dead before you have wakened from your slumber."

"Do we have to sit here and listen to this bullshit?" Solon said.

Black Eye's laugh echoed into the mountains. "Pissant! They will kill you first." He nodded at the Keuchel brothers. "They will take pups like you and tie you up. Then they will cut your hands and arms off and let you stumble around with the bones sticking out. Their dogs will yelp and try to lick at the blood that drips from your bodies."

"That's enough!" Dudley Bickerstaff said. "It's about time you go and relieve Nipsy Gray."

Black Eye left, his deep laughter still filling the air.

"Somebody oughta kill that son of a bitch," Solon said.

"That there's a fact," Tilly Sparks agreed. "But, the trouble is, a man might get himself killed tryin' to do it. You boys know I ain't afraid of much, but that damn half-breed gives me the creeps."

"You men stop listenin' to such talk," Bickerstaff said. "This ain't Cheyenne country. They're located northwest of here. We're in the land of the Chickasaw now, and their neighbors to the east, the Choctaw. Shucks, both the Chickasaws and Choctaws fought for the Confederacy, boys! Clayton and Nipsy Gray both fought for the South, and most all of us are Southerners. So we're all pretty much on the same side! Outside of maybe beggin' for some food, I doubt we'll have any trouble with 'em." He paused and pointed to the west. "Now, out that way, it's another story. There's Comanche out there, and Kiowa and Apache, too. I'm not sayin' we shouldn't be cautious and keep an eye out for any kind of trouble, but don't be sittin' around, worryin' about no Indian trouble."

"You don't think them Choctaw or Chickaway are gonna give us no trouble, Mister Bickerstaff?" Jamie Wilson asked.

"I don't think so," Bickerstaff said. "I've heard tell they'll sometimes show a force, when all they want is a few head of beeves for their bellies."

Solon spoke up irritably. "You can stop all this Injun talk anytime you want to," he said. "I don't know a tame one from a wild one, personally."

Tilly Sparks said, "I can't tell a Comanch from a Choctaw. If you ask me, they all came from the same pecker a thousand years ago."

This struck Solon as funny. "That's good, Tilly. Real good."

In the Nations, the buffalo grass was tall and plentiful. The longhorns were allowed to graze at leisure as often as possible, and they fattened up nicely. Dudley Bickerstaff was pleased, but he worried to himself that it was becoming easier to herd the cattle than to separate the men.

More and more often, Indians started coming by to beg. Most traveled in small bands and could have been easily dissuaded, but Bickerstaff didn't want any trouble. He gener-

ously cut out a head of beef, and sometimes two, to give to the
hungry Indians. Halfway through the Nations, he gave more
than a half dozen head to a large band. The Indians seemed
pleased, and a few offered pottery or skins for trade.

They had entered the lands of the Creek Nation, when a
small band approached. Dudley Bickerstaff, Solon, Black
Eye, and Clayton rode out to meet them.

One of the Indians spoke broken English.

"I am Lefthand," he said. "My people hunger."

Bickerstaff nodded. "All right. We'll give your people
some meat. Clayton, pick out a couple of fat ones."

"No!" Lefthand said. He pointed to a group of twenty-
five or so longhorns, standing off by themselves, and waved
his hand in a circle. "My people hunger!"

"By damn, he wants a whole herd of 'em!" Solon said.

Bickerstaff shook his head. "I can't give you that
many," he tried to explain.

The Indian again waved his hand.

"I'll give you two, or I might see three, but that's all,"
Bickerstaff said flatly.

Lefthand glared at him a moment, then he showed his
teeth. "I come back," he said. "I make your cattle run."

Bickerstaff turned to the men, but he was mainly talking
to Solon. "What should we do?" he asked. "We don't
need him stampeding the herd, but we can't give him
twenty-five beeves neither."

"Beats the life outa me," Solon said. "We could run
him and his friends off, I reckon." He turned to Black Eye
Lamerton. "What do you think? I suspect you know Injuns
more than us."

Black Eye stared at Lefthand and the five others that
were with him. Finally, he said, "He is bluffing. I will talk
with him."

Black Eye rode up to Lefthand and grinned at him. Then,
without so much as a word, he pulled his Colt and shot Lefthand dead. The other five Indians, startled, turned their ponies
and lit out, but not before Black Eye shot another one in the
back of the head. He fired twice more, but missed.

There was silence. Clayton stared hard at Black Eye Lamerton. He had seen men like him during the war—men

who were crazy killers. He had listened to Solon and Tilly's discussions about Black Eye. They were both of the opinion that Black Eye was mostly bluff. But Clayton now knew that they were wrong.

His hand rubbed his own Colt. He had the urge to pull down on Black Eye Lamerton, and he had no doubt that, if he were trail boss, he would shoot him right on the spot. It wouldn't be long before Black Eye turned on all of them. That was plain.

Bickerstaff regained his speech. "What did you go and do that for? You're likely to have the whole blamed Indian Nations after us now." His words were intended to sound harsh, but his voice was so shaky, it lacked conviction.

Black Eye gave a cold, silent look to Bickerstaff as he reloaded his Colt. He turned his horse and rode back through the middle of the three, causing Solon to have to turn his horse out of the way. Then, his cold eyes found Clayton's, and they held. Neither man blinked. Black Eye silently rode on by.

That night, none of the men were allowed to sleep. Bickerstaff put them all on the night herd. They stayed alert, watching for the return of avenging Indians, but nothing happened. The next night was the same, and the following night.

There was no sign of any Indians, at all. In fact, it was the first time since they'd been in the Nations that there were no visible signs of them. An eerie quiet settled over the land, and the men grew even more fidgety and wary.

The lack of sleep was having an effect on the men, too. Tempers grew shorter, and even the Keuchel brothers had to be separated over a disagreement at supper. That same night, Tilly Sparks hit Jamie Wilson with a frying pan, splitting Jamie's eyebrow open and causing a nasty black eye. The swelling went all the way up to his hairline. Even his nose was pushed to the right.

Bickerstaff tried his best to control the men and their tempers, but it was a futile effort. Life on the trail was hard on good days, but it was nearly impossible with no sleep and the tension of worrying over Indians.

On the third night, lightning flashes began to appear in the northern sky. The longhorns felt the charge in the air and grew so restless, all the range singing in the world wasn't going to soothe them down. Ordinarily, they were all bedded down by ten o'clock, but tonight they would not be calmed. They kept moving around, bellowing into the night, as the lightning and storms moved closer.

When the rain came, it came in buckets. Big, fat drops by the millions made little popping noises as they struck the earth down below. Thunderclaps shook the earth. The cattle were bumping into each other in a panic, and all at once, the two thousand longhorns stampeded.

Clayton had heard talk about stampedes, and he'd tried to think a thousand times what he would do. Now that the dreaded moment had arrived, he could only chase after the herd. He felt small and insignificant. His eyes caught the flashes of gunfire as Bickerstaff and the others tried to stop the raging longhorns. The rain, the cattle's beating hooves, and the booming thunder were so loud, they smothered the sounds of the shooting.

The longhorns raced on as the rain came down harder and lightning lit up the world. Clayton rode hard to keep up, trying to steer his horse well enough away from the crazed cattle. All at once, light flashed, and two balls of fire appeared on the mare's ears. Clayton felt a tingling go through his body. Then, he saw the fire light up the tips of the cattle's horns. Strips of fire ran down their backs. Clayton wanted to rub his eyes. He thought surely this was a nightmare, and he would wake up any minute. Another bolt of lightning cracked, and four thousand balls of fire continued their dance over the horns of the beeves.

It was during one of the great flashes of light that Clayton noticed something off to his left. He turned to look, and just as the earth went dark again, he saw. Suddenly, a cold fear swept over him.

There were at least fifty Indians, riding toward the herd at an angle. Clayton heard a tremendous roar as flames and sparks spewed from a tree. He looked to see if the Indians were closer. There were five or six, not ten yards away. Clayton jerked hard on the mare's reins and almost lost his seat as she reared up on her back legs. The sky flashed again, and the Indians were right on top of him.

Clayton fired his pistol at one, but no sooner had he squeezed the trigger, when the sky turned black again. He cursed, and was waiting for another lightning flash to see, when a deep pain shot through his shoulder and ran all the way down to his feet. He had to grab the mare's neck with his right arm to keep from falling.

A horrific pain overwhelmed him. He felt sick to his stomach. When the night lit up again, he saw blood on his shoulder. He also saw the Indians, riding up toward the stampeding longhorns.

Clayton gave spur to the mare, but then dizziness hit him like another thunderclap, and he had to pull rein. He knew he was going to pass out. The pain pounded in his shoulder and spread to his chest, to where he had to struggle to catch his breath. Desperately, he turned his head upward and let the rain beat upon his face. He saw the heavy drops glistening in the final lightning bolt, and then he felt a blessed relief, as darkness spread over him.

The next thing Clayton knew, the sun was a bright melon, hanging high in the sky. He could see it through his eyelids and feel the warmth on his skin. All the senses and feelings in his body were centered on his shoulder, which hurt something awful There was a tugging on his arm. He opened his eyes and tried to see the face above him against the bright light.

"Lay still," Bickerstaff said. "One of 'em got his damned hatchet in your shoulder. I'm dressing it the best I can." He turned his head to call over his shoulder. "You got that grease ready, Tilly?"

Clayton had never felt such pain in his life. He'd suffered a couple of horrendous toothaches before, but this was far more painful than the worst toothache. This time, the abscess sat right in the middle of his shoulder. He realized that Bickerstaff was sewing up the wound, and each time he gave a tug, it felt like Clayton was hooked to a mule that was trying to pull his arm off.

"You're lucky," Bickerstaff was saying. "You got a nasty gash, here. It looks like the hatchet cut into the meat, then bounced off the bone." He wiped sweat from his brow. "You're going to be sore for a while, but I think you'll be just fine." He smiled at Clayton, but he looked a little dazed, himself. "You're lucky," he repeated. "Jamie Wilson's missing. We lost him during the stampede."

The herd was scattered over several miles, and Clayton was allowed to convalesce during the three days it took them to round up the stock. On the second morning, Nipsy Gray found Jamie's body, lying in a washout with two arrows in his back. He had been scalped, his throat slashed, and his body badly mutilated. The Indians had even cut off his genitals.

Bickerstaff took the news hard. He felt a deep responsibility for the men he had hired. He felt sorry for Jamie's mama and papa. It suddenly occurred to him that he didn't even know if Jamie had any brothers or sisters. He didn't recall ever hearing Jamie talk about his family. Bickerstaff was ashamed that he didn't know such things.

It was also discovered that over forty head of cattle were missing. *A hell of a price*, Bickerstaff thought. He said as much to Black Eye Lamerton, and added in no uncertain terms that, if Black Eye had any more ideas of using his six-shooter, he could leave right then and there. For once, Black Eye remained silent.

All of the men attended the burying. Dudley Bickerstaff read a verse from his Testament, then Jamie Wilson was laid in a shallow hole and covered with a pile of rocks. Clayton made a cross of tree limbs and propped it up as best he could. Solon also said a few words, mentioning that Jamie had been a top hand, and so was the epitaph spoken of Jamie Wilson's time on earth.

After that, sleep was scarce among the men—nearly as scarce as it had been after Black Eye killed Lefthand. There were grumblings that Black Eye Lamerton was causing more trouble than just a loss of sleep, and many of the men wished he'd take a notion to leave. Clayton had half expected Black Eye to get bored with the day-to-day routine of following the slow, cumbersome longhorns, but so far, he'd shown no intentions of doing anything else.

There was no more trouble with Indians, but there were several more encounters. Bickerstaff continued with his generosity, cutting out a head or two of beef for anyone who stopped to ask. The longhorns continued to graze on the rich buffalo grass, and even stampeded one more time. All in all, though, the remainder of the drive was uneventful, and on the day they rode into Baxter Springs, the cattle were fat and the men were ready for some socializing.

As they approached Baxter Springs, cattle buyers rode out to meet the herd. Bickerstaff immediately struck a deal and sold the entire herd for eighteen dollars a head. Once in town, he gave every man seventy-five dollars, then bought them all new clothing, picked up their hotel tabs, and even paid the fines to get Nipsy Gray and Tilly Sparks out of jail for their part in tearing up a saloon.

Once back on civilized ground in Baxter Springs, Cyrus and Rufus Keuchel gave Bickerstaff notice that they were going to stay in town and seek employment. The hard trip north had been too much for them. Rufus still suffered nightmares about crossing the rivers, and Cyrus was scared to death of the idea of riding through the Nations again.

Tilly Sparks took a job cooking at the hotel. Even though he'd hated how the men had cursed his lack of culinary genius, Tilly now considered himself a fine cook.

Black Eye Lamerton took his money and disappeared without a word.

Bickerstaff called Solon, Nipsy, and Clayton together. They were seated in the saloon. It was late afternoon, and the place was mostly empty. Bickerstaff ordered a bottle of whiskey and four glasses.

"Well, boys, looks like we're all that's left, and it's just as well. Tilly was getting too blamed fat for the trail and handling stock. And those dang brothers weren't never cut out for this line of work." His face grew serious. "And, if I never see that Black Eye Lamerton again, it'll be fine by me." He shook his head and poured a round.

Solon agreed. "He's a snake, all right. I say good riddance. I'm sorry I ever hired him in the first place."

"Makes a man wonder," Nipsy said philosophically. "How does a man like that go on livin', when nice boys like Jamie Wilson have to end up dead?" He gulped down his whiskey.

"Same reason why I ain't never found a potful of money,

and never will," Solon commented. "It's fate. We all got a destiny. Some of 'em's good, and some ain't."

"Well boys, speaking of money," Bickerstaff said, "the payoff for the herd was considerable. I can't possibly carry that much gold and silver by myself. There's thirty dollars in it for each of you, if you'll help me carry it back to Texas."

"Sounds good to me," Clayton said.

"I ain't heard no better offers," Solon shrugged. "Texas sounds like as good a place as any to be."

Nipsy Gray nodded. "Same here."

They left the next day and rode hard, not willing to waste any time hauling the money across the long, lonely stretch of land. A sizable rainshower passed over, and the weather turned hot and muggy.

Two mornings after leaving Baxter Springs, they were in camp, drinking coffee. Solon was recalling the first time he'd ever worked with cattle. Dudley Bickerstaff sat next to him, listening, while Nipsy Gray packed everything away from breakfast. Clayton was off from the others, saddling up the horses, when Black Eye Lamerton rode in.

Solon stopped talking in mid-sentence and stared. Bickerstaff appeared to be nervous. Nipsy Gray, who had just dumped out the coffee grounds, dropped the pot and took a step backward.

Black Eye laughed. "You act like you have just seen a ghost," he said. He gestured toward the pot. "I sure could use some of that coffee."

Bickerstaff cleared his throat. "What are you doing here?" he asked.

"You don't sound very glad to see me. I thought we were all friends," Black Eye said casually. He got down from his horse and walked over to where Bickerstaff sat. "I am going to Texas, just like you." He took the coffee cup from Bickerstaff's hand and drained it, then tossed the cup on the ground. He smacked his lips. "Of course, I will take your money with me," he added, turning his steely gaze on Dudley Bickerstaff.

Solon's face was a raging shade of red. "Now, you see here," he said slowly. "Maybe you ain't done your arithmetic. If'n you had, you'd see that there's four of us here,

and only one of you. You may of got away with that smart
mouth of your'n before, but we ain't trailin' cattle now."

"Why you pissant! I'll kill you first."

Clayton appeared then from among the horses. He
walked up to within a dozen steps of Black Eye and
stopped. "I don't think so," he said.

Black Eye turned toward Clayton, and a small laugh
rumbled in his chest. "You are all the mouthiest bunch of
pissants I ever saw." Quick as a hiccup, his Colt filled his
hand, and his big finger squeezed the trigger.

In his haste, he missed. Black Eye squeezed again, but
the Colt misfired.

Clayton was slow on the draw, but his aim was sure. He
fired one shot that struck Black Eye deep in the chest, then
ran forward and stuck the barrel of his Colt just inches from
Black Eye's forehead. Before the big, bad man fell, Clayton
added a .44 slug to his brain.

Solon spilled his coffee in his lap. Dudley Bickerstaff let
go a holler and fell backward off the dead tree he'd been
sitting on. Nipsy Gray just stood frozen in one spot. He
stared, wide-eyed, at Clayton with his mouth open.

Slowly, Solon stood up and walked over to where Black
Eye lay. He squatted down and inspected the body, almost
as if he couldn't believe Black Eye was dead. When he
straightened up again, he narrowed his eyes and nodded his
head at Clayton.

"By damn! I ain't never seen nothin' like that in my life,"
he said. He held out his hand. "Let me shake your hand."

"That was purely somethin'," Nipsy Gray agreed. He
slapped Clayton on the back and grinned like a boy.

Bickerstaff took out his handkerchief and wiped the layer
of sweat off his face. He took in several deep breaths. "I'm
much obliged to you, Clayton," he said. Not for the money,
but for my life." He also shook Clayton's hand. His voice
was still shaking when he said, "Gentlemen, I reckon it's
time to go."

They rode south toward Texas, leaving Black Eye Lamerton for the coyotes and buzzards.

⚔ 30 ⚔

THEY MADE it back to Texas in mid-September. Clayton, Solon, and Nipsy decided to stay on with Dudley Bickerstaff for a spell. They got on nicely. Bickerstaff had taken an early liking to Clayton, and the killing of Black Eye Lamerton had lifted Clayton to an even higher esteem in Bickerstaff's eyes.

Solon Johnson had once regarded Clayton with a critical eye, but over time he'd grown a respect for Clayton's abilities. He viewed the hiring of Black Eye as a noticeable mistake, and Clayton's handling of the matter had spared Solon a considerable amount of embarrassment. They'd barely reached Texas, when he was talking to Clayton about practicing with his Colt.

"You'd better learn how to get that dern pistol out of the holster quicker," he said often. "That is, if'n you expect to uphold the reputation you've made for yourself."

Clayton paid little attention when Solon made the remark, but Solon talked about it so much, Clayton finally gave in. The two began going to the river each night to fire at floating objects or any bottles they could get hold of. More than anything, though, Solon wanted Clayton to slicken his draw.

Clayton was a natural with his pistol. They practiced together the same amount of time, but Solon never could overcome feeling awkward with his gun. To Clayton, it was second nature.

Solon insisted on continuing their daily practice by the

water, and by winter, Clayton got so good, his hand was a blur to the onlooker. He could be standing, completely relaxed, and, in a blink of an eye, fill his hand with his Colt. Even more impressive was his accuracy. Pretty soon, Clayton had the ability to draw and hit a bottle, dead center, before Solon's hand had barely gripped the handle of his own Colt.

The short stay they'd intended with Bickerstaff lasted until the summer of '69. It was early June, and they'd just finished branding all the new calves, when they made the acquaintance of Miles Duncan.

He rode onto Bickerstaff's place one morning, asking for Clayton. He'd heard of Clayton's shooting exploits, he explained, and was interested in hiring his talents.

"I'm a buffalo hunter, by trade," Duncan said. "Gotta hire me two outfits, each with a shooter, a cook, and two skinners. We'll be headin' up north to the Plains, west of Fort Dodge, to do some huntin'. What I need is another good shooter, and I hear you're good." He stood there, waiting, as if he expected Clayton to be grateful and excited over the offer.

Solon spoke up. "We're a pair. You hire him, you hire me, too."

Miles Duncan looked Solon over, then nodded. "All right," he said. "I'll take you on. Skinner or cook. Take your pick."

Solon grimaced. "I ain't no cook, so I guess you got yourself a skinner."

Miles Duncan gave them each twenty dollars and told them to wait for him in Fort Dodge. He'd be there as soon as he could, after he'd gone on south to hire some more men.

Dudley Bickerstaff begged Clayton and Solon not to leave. He talked until he was blue in the face, trying to convince them to stay. He even took Clayton aside and promised that he might someday deed the ranch over to him. His wife, Martha, had died shortly after their marriage, and he'd lived a lonely life, although he did occasionally like to sport the ladies at the canteen up the river.

"I never had any children of my own," he told Clayton.

"Why, I guess I've sorta come to consider you like a son. You're a good one, Clayton. You've got a good heart. You're honest and a hard worker. And you know I'll never forget what you did for me with Black Eye. I'm not one to take such things lightly." He looked slightly embarrassed, but added, "You'd have a happy life here. I'd make sure of it."

Clayton felt flattered, but he didn't take the offer seriously. He'd enjoyed working for Bickerstaff, but deep inside, he felt the wanderlust coming back, strong as ever.

"I'm forever obliged," he said. "But me and Solon, we have to go on. I truly can't say why."

Bickerstaff nodded sadly. "I suppose I can. I was young once, myself. You go, but remember that you're always welcome here."

"I'll be back sometime. I promise," Clayton said.

And those were their parting words. The next day, Clayton and Solon left for Fort Dodge.

It was late July and hot as hell when Miles Duncan finally showed up. He outfitted Clayton with a .50 caliber Sharps rifle, then introduced Clayton and Solon to the rest of their crew, along with the members of a second outfit.

The other skinner was a tall man named Digger Anderson. Duncan introduced him as an experienced hand. Digger and Solon eyed each other carefully before they shook hands. Georgie McDowell was the cook. He seemed friendly, but had little to say in the way of pleasantries. He was fat, which Solon later pointed out to Clayton was a good sign.

"Shows they don't mind eatin' their own cookin'," he said. "Looks like Georgie don't mind, a-tall."

They were briefly introduced to the members of the other outfit. Jeremiah Foster glared at them suspiciously through a head and faceful of dark brown hair. He was a skinner and a behemoth, standing over six-four. The rest of the outfit seemed somewhat intimidated by his presence.

They immediately set out west to where the buffalo herds roamed. The hunting was good, and Clayton could kill between seventy-five and a hundred each day. Solon and Digger Anderson worked hard, with Digger showing Solon the quickest way to do the job. They'd split and loosen the skin from the legs and head, then attach ropes to the hides and use a horse to strip the hide free. The carcass was left, wherever it had been shot. Back at camp, the hides were spread out and staked down with pegs, so they could scrape off the remaining flesh and then let the hide dry. The hides were folded and packed into wagons to be hauled into Buf-falo City.

Skinning a buffalo was a time-consuming job, and the most Solon and Digger could manage a day was about fifty. After a couple of weeks, they were so far behind, the wait-ing carcasses began to swell and rot in the hot sun. Soon, they were complaining about having to skin the rotted car-casses. They offered to leave several of the dead animals behind, but Miles Duncan would not hear of it.

"I'll not leave a single hide to waste," he said firmly. "You'll have to work faster, is all. If you can't do the job, I'll find some that will."

He and Solon argued violently, but Miles Duncan was a stubborn man, and Solon needed the work.

Clayton tried to help by slowing down on his killing. This seemed to ease the situation for a while, but Clayton and Solon both were quickly growing tired of their work.

Clayton enjoyed the shooting sport at first, but it soon made him uncomfortable. The big Sharps kept his shoulder bruised and sore, and the smell of gunpowder was all over him. He even tasted it in his food at night.

And the killing of the animals. It seemed senseless and wasteful to leave the carcasses of those huge beasts behind to desecrate the land. He was reminded of the war. Those buffalo were a lot like soldiers, he thought. As one was shot and dropped to its knees, another would simply jump over it and continue with its grazing. One by one, they met their death, as if death meant nothing.

And the stench was everywhere, filling his nostrils day and night. Again, Clayton was reminded of the war. It was a smell so familiar, yet one that he'd never grown used to.

At first, he'd enjoyed the taste of buffalo. Georgie Mc-Dowell made a hump roast that was delicious, but evening after evening of hump roast soon got tiresome. Georgie

switched to cooking the tongues, and the men found that
more to their liking for a while. After that, Georgie took to
flip-flopping the menu. Hump roast one night, tongue the
next. There was little else to vary the meals, except for liver
or steak on occasion.

"You'd think Georgie could come up with a little more
imagination," Solon grumbled to Clayton one night. "I'd
go out and kill us a few rabbits, if'n I had the time, but
I'm too busy skinnin' all day. Why couldn't Georgie do a
little huntin', once in a while. I seen plenty of rabbits out
here."

It was a lonely and tiresome existence, and even though
Clayton and Solon cared nothing about the life, they really
had nowhere else to go. Since neither one could come up
with any other ideas, they stayed with Miles Duncan for
almost a year and a half.

Solon later remarked that they could thank Jeremiah Foster for finally giving them a reason to move on, but Clayton
had to kill him first.

Foster had never been friendly, and kept mostly to himself except to argue. It was one night, when the men had
stopped off at Fort Dodge for supplies. They were in Sut-
ler's Store, just browsing around, when Foster was overheard outside. He'd been at the saloon, and was in a
drunken rage against two soldiers. A fight started.

Clayton and Solon ran outside, but before anyone could
stop him, Foster had killed the two soldiers with his big
knife.

"My lord!" Solon shouted. "Jeremiah!" He held up his
hands and started to walk toward him.

Foster was crouched low over the bodies, his chest heaving and his eyes wild. He stared at Solon, then started to
growl.

"I'd stay back, Solon," Clayton warned. "He ain't right
in the head."

"Git," Foster said to Solon in a guttural voice. "You
git away from me, or I'll skin your damned hide."

Solon tried to calm him. Nervously, he said, "All right,
Jeremiah. Just relax. It's over."

Suddenly, Foster lunged at him. He raised his knife and

towered over Solon like a mad bear. His teeth showed and an angry cry rose up from deep within him.

Clayton's Colt rang out. Once, twice. Both bullets struck dead center in Foster's chest. Slowly, his arm fell, and he hovered a moment before he finally went down.

The next day, Clayton and Solon took their leave of the hide business. Miles Duncan was sorry to see them go. Jeremiah Foster had needed killing, he said, and no one would hold it against them.

But Clayton and Solon had found the excuse they needed. They decided to leave Miles Duncan to his buffalo killings and head back to Texas. Both had saved all their money. Maybe, as Solon put it, Dudley Bickerstaff would still think highly enough of them to see fit to help them get started in their own business.

Miles Duncan surprised them by asking if he could travel south with them. "I'm gettin' old enough to enjoy my comforts in life," he told them. "Winter's too harsh for me up here. Think I'll head back to Texas before the snows come 'n find me another crew for next spring."

The three left by horseback the next morning. Georgie decided to spend the winter at Fort Dodge.

They rode most of the day at a leisurely pace, none of the men in any hurry to end the peacefulness of their ride together. Miles Duncan had achieved a sizable profit from his hides, and Clayton and Solon were just grateful to be out of the business.

That night, they were camped in a small bluff, when they heard riders approach. Solon fetched his gun and holster. Clayton still had his Colt strapped on. He held his hand close to his side.

There were three of them. Rance Lovett, Carl Foster, and his brother, Israel, were skinners for a nearby outfit. They were also Jeremiah Foster's cousins. They rode right up to the camp and stopped within the light of the fire.

"We're here to see the low-down bastard that killed our cousin," Rance Lovett said.

"I guess that'd be me," Clayton said.

"Wait a minute," Miles Duncan said. "How did you find us?"

"Rode to your camp. That damned cook refused to tell us where you was at, so I shot the sumbitch in his leg. Funny thing, he suddenly remembered that you-all was headed for Texas." Rance Lovett laughed. He lifted his rifle and drew a bead on Clayton.

Miles Duncan spoke up again. "Clayton killed Foster, all right, but he had no choice. Foster was drunk. He'd just killed two men with his knife, and was about to attack an innocent man."

"Don't matter to me what you think," Rance said. "He got no business killin' one o' my kin."

"I'll not have you comin' in here, threatenin' us," Miles Duncan said.

No sooner had he spoken, when Israel Foster's gun went off, striking Miles Duncan in the throat. Duncan stared at him a moment, then went down.

Clayton's Colt exploded, and five shots later, the three cousins lay dead on the plains. Solon had drawn his pistol, but by the time he shot Rance Lovett, the man was already dead.

He stared at the cousins and their riderless horses, then at Miles Duncan. "My lord," was all he could say.

The next day, they buried Duncan in a nice spot with buffalo grass all around. Lovett's and the Foster brothers' bodies were left to fend for themselves.

They rode all day, then made camp in a small thicket of sandhill sage. Little had been said between them, and as they lay down in their bedrolls, taking what little comfort the sagebrush gave them from the chilly wind, Solon spoke up.

"You know, ever since I left my parents and took to livin' on my own, I've seen a lot of killin's and such." He paused and looked into the brush, as if he was replaying the events in his life, then went on, "But you know, I ain't never seen nobody like you. There's somethin' special about how you handle yourself and that Colt o' yours. I've always been a studier of life, and you may not believe this, but I can just look at a feller and tell you exactly what he's gonna say next. I can size up a rough sort in a heartbeat, and I rarely miss on what he's like on the inside. But you," he said thoughtfully, "you're a mystery to me."

"How's that?" Clayton yawned.

"Well, you're a nice enough sort. Cordial and friendly in a quiet way. You seem confident and warm to the ladies. But underneath . . ." he stopped.

He didn't add that he'd noticed a coldness in Clayton. An anger that was more than just dangerous. It was almost deadly.

"Underneath what?" Clayton mumbled, almost asleep.

Solon let the subject drop. He lay there, shivering, deep into the night. He couldn't go to sleep for having so many thoughts. The north wind was howling, and cold. He wished he could put the thoughts behind him, or turn them into a blanket so he wouldn't feel so damn cold.

But the truth was, he couldn't keep from trying to figure out a man like Clayton. Many a night, Clayton had called out in his sleep. It was always too garbled to understand, but Solon could hear the fear in Clayton's voice and the restless way he slept. Solon looked over at the dark silhouette that lay a few feet away. What made Clayton Crist so humane on the outside, yet so deadly a killer on the inside? Solon had never really feared anyone before, not even that smart-ass, Black Eye Lamerton. He'd respected Black Eye enough to not want trouble, and his confrontations with the man did make him a little edgy. But, when push came to shove, Solon hadn't really feared the man. As he lay there, thinking and losing sleep, he had to admit to himself that he liked Clayton, but that he was a man you didn't cross.

31

AT THE Navasota River, they ran into Nipsy Gray.

"Well, I'll be damned. I thought Texas had seen the last of you two. What are you-all doin' back here?" Nipsy said.

"Came back down to talk to Bickerstaff," Solon said. "I assume you're still workin' for him?"

Nipsy nodded. "Sure enough. You fellers are a sight for sore eyes. To tell the truth, I never expected to see either one of you again. Bickerstaff's run onto some tough times, but he'll be glad to see the likes of you boys. Come on," he gestured, "I'll ride the rest of the way with ya."

At the ranch, Dudley Bickerstaff was tickled to see the two and invited them to the house. Inside, they sat down at the table, and he poured coffee.

"Tell me about the skinnin' business," he said. "Was Duncan a fair man to ya?"

"Fair enough," Clayton said. "But he's dead. Got himself killed in a shoot-out with some bereaved family members."

"That's a shame," Bickerstaff said. "I didn't know him well, but we were never enemies. 'Cept for when he came and took you two off," he added.

"Nipsy said you been havin' some hard times," Solon said, sipping his coffee.

Bickerstaff nodded sadly, and explained how he'd made some bad business decisions. "I had to sell off some of the ranch to Leslie Brown to help pay off a few debts," he said.

"But, when we left, you had the best operation in these

parts," Solon pointed out. "You was so full of money, you was stuffin' your pillows with it."

Bickerstaff nodded again. "I'm a good one, all right. Good at makin' money, but good at losin' it, too."

Both Clayton and Solon knew about Bickerstaff's love for gambling. He was a hardworking man with the few vices, but the man had been known to bet on anything.

"How'd you lose it?" Solon asked anyway. "Gamblin'?"

"Mostly," Bickerstaff admitted. "I guess you fellers are lookin' for work. I'm afraid I'm not in a good position to do any hirin'."

"Don't worry about nothin'," Clayton said. "We've got some money. We thought we'd like to maybe buy a few beeves to sell. But looky here, I'll be glad to throw in what money I got, if it'll help things."

"Same goes for me," Solon added.

"Boys, I couldn't let you do that. But I'll tell you what I will do," Bickerstaff said, his spirits picking up considerably. "If you boys want to invest in cattle, I'll let you graze them here on my place. Won't cost you a dime. In return, you can work for me for, let's say, half wages."

Clayton and Solon looked at each other. Clayton knew what Solon was thinking. He'd been around the man long enough to tell when he was excited.

"Mr. Bickerstaff, that's generous," Clayton said. "I guess we'd be fools not to take you up on it. But, we surely wouldn't want to take advantage of you."

"I'm surprised at you, Clayton! You're a Tennessee boy!" Bickerstaff said. "How in the world would you be takin' advantage of me? 'Sides, I'll only be payin' you half what you're worth. If anybody's takin' advantage, it'd be me!"

Bickerstaff got up from the table to fetch the coffeepot from the cookstove. His hand was shaking as he poured. "Look here, boys," he said earnestly. "Let's cut through all the bull. I need hands. Nipsy's the only steady one I got. I can't afford nobody else. You stay on, and I'll even sell you boys the beeves at a fair price."

Before the day was out, Clayton and Solon found themselves the owners of sixty head of longhorns. Bickerstaff had sold them the beeves for nine dollars a head. They decided that, come next summer, they'd gather up their small herd, plus any new calves, and take them to Kansas, along with anything Bickerstaff might want to sell. It was a deal that would help everybody, they all agreed.

The men worked hard on the ranch, and by the middle of May, they, along with Bickerstaff, had almost four hundred longhorns ready to move to the Kansas market.

Clayton and Solon were making their plans to head the cattle up north, when Dudley Bickerstaff died suddenly in his sleep. It was Nipsy Gray who found him, lying peacefully in his bed. There was no family to be contacted, so Nipsy made the burial arrangements. Other than that, he told Clayton and Solon, there was little he could do but stay on until the place was sold.

Clayton and Solon cut out forty-eight head, plus twenty-three calves, as their own. But, the day after Bickerstaff was laid to rest, Leslie Brown rode onto the place with the law and a piece of paper.

"What I got here is a document, signed by Dudley Bickerstaff," Brown said, holding up the paper: "It says right here that upon his death, all his property and belongings go to me."

"Let me see that!" Nipsy said. He grabbed the document and looked it over. "Where in the hell did you get this?"

"Oh, it's all legal and bindin'," Brown said. "Bickerstaff owed me quite a tidy sum, what with his gamblin' debts and all. Now he's dead, and all his land and the cattle on it are mine."

"The hell you say!" Solon shouted.

Clayton said, "We paid Bickerstaff for forty-eight head. We got 'em over there in that pen, along with twenty-three calves." He motioned with his head. "You can take the rest."

"Fine," Leslie Brown said, "but you'd better have a bill of sale."

Solon nearly exploded. "The only bill o' sale we got is what we know!" he said. "We paid Bickerstaff for them beeves, fair and square. We shook hands on it." He looked at the sheriff, Newton Baker, to reinforce his statement. Sheriff Baker just shrugged.

"Ain't nothin' I can do for you boys. You'll have to work that out with Judge Edmondson. The only thing I can do is seize everythin'. The judge'll have to work out the details," Baker said.

Dudley Bickerstaff's method of dealing had left Clayton and Solon in the cold. He had sold them the cattle on a handshake, and neither Clayton nor Solon had felt any doubt as to his sincerity or honesty. Leslie Brown, though, was a meticulous sort and a bookkeeper who had kept his records.

Bickerstaff had originally owed Brown $11,000. After deeding over part of the ranch and adding some cash money, he'd paid the debt down to $2,800. He had agreed to pay the rest by July of '72, or forfeit everything. Bickerstaff had not intended to die, for he'd also signed a clause that, in case of his death on or before said date, everything would go to Leslie Brown.

Gentleman's agreement notwithstanding, Clayton and Solon had no argument in the matter. Even Sheriff Newton Baker said he felt sorry for them, and people in the town offered their condolences. Several pointed out the fact that they had warned Dudley about his careless ways in dealing with folks.

In court, Judge Chester Edmondson made the comment that it was a paper that Bickerstaff should never have signed. The judge sternly admonished Leslie Brown for being what he termed "greedy and self-serving," but he had no choice but to rule in Leslie Brown's favor.

Clayton and Solon returned to the ranch a last time for their personal belongings and found Leslie Brown waiting, with two men armed with Winchesters.

"I don't want no trouble from you two," Brown warned. "Just get your stuff and leave peacefully."

"That's right," one of the men with him said. "Either of you bastards got any ideas, think again. I'll tell you right now, I don't need much of a reason to shoot your asses." He raised and pointed his Winchester at them.

Solon's face got red as a beet. "Why, you low-down son of a bitch! Don't you threaten me!"

The man's angry eyes flashed. He squeezed the trigger. The bullet missed Solon's head by inches.

Somewhere in the hereafter, the man with the Winchester who had a foul tongue and an eager shooting finger was now keenly aware that Clayton Crist needed less of a reason than he did. The man had barely pulled the trigger, when Clayton shot him dead.

Clayton emptied the .44 Caliber Army Colt, the one that Dudley Bickerstaff had given him. All three men dropped where they stood. When they weren't dead enough, Clayton pulled his own Winchester from its scabbard and shot them again. Their bodies jumped, then lay still as their blood sullied the earth.

Clayton bent over the bodies and rifled through their pockets. He came up with $37 and gave twenty to Solon. Then, they got their belongings from the bunkhouse and left.

They were almost to the river when Nipsy Gray caught up with them. His face was an ashy white.

"I seen the whole thing," he said, "and if you want, I'll surely cover for you boys, if'n I'm asked. I doubt whether they'd believe me, though." Nipsy fumbled with his hat. "Hell, if you want to know the truth, I don't wanta stay. Things are likely to get a little tight around here. I'd like to ride with you boys for a spell, if'n you don't mind."

The three rode west all the way to New Mexico Territory, where Clayton and Nipsy found jobs on a ranch, while Solon went to work for a boot and saddle maker.

Nipsy Gray lasted almost a week, before he decided to head back to Alabama. He missed his family, he said, and the traveling life was too much. In truth, Nipsy was worn out from having to look over his shoulder for posses and such. He'd spent days worrying and nights awake, wondering when the Texas law was going to ride up with guns blazing.

Nipsy had seen enough. He'd been through a war and worked his way across the South to Texas and now New Mexico. All he wanted to do, he told them, was go home to Alabama, away from all the killing and reminders of such. He was ready to become a farmer, just like his daddy, and his daddy's daddy.

Clayton and Solon wished him well. The last they saw of Nipsy Gray, he was riding at a hard lope for Alabama.

32

CLAYTON AND Solon had pretty much settled into life as a pair of Ness City, Kansas, farmers. It was plain and "simple to the point of being boring," as Solon put it. They had gotten their house built in a fairly short time, and though they hadn't yet furnished it with more than a couple of beds and a few chairs, it was comfortable, with a nice porch.

They worked their land and tended to their cattle, and to break the monotony, they occasionally slipped into town.

But there was a problem that neither had reckoned with. There were no single females to speak of. On a couple of occasions, a widow lady named Nola Smith had invited Clayton to attend the church picnics, but she had nearly driven him crazy with her endless talking. Nola could hold up a man's ear even better than Solon Johnson, and Solon had the ability to wear him out.

The few other available females weren't much more than schoolgirls, in Clayton's opinion. He felt old just listening to their giggling and carrying on.

Throughout the winter, he'd thought a lot about Tracy O'Brien. It pained him that he'd done so poorly in life. He should have a wife and young'uns to enjoy, like other men. He yearned for the company of a woman. Solon had tried to talk him into going to Hayes City several times, but he knew what Solon had in mind. These days, though, Clayton was starting to think the company of a sporting woman might not be such a bad idea.

They were seated outside. It was a Sunday, and the weather was clear as glass. Solon stretched and yawned.

"You know," he said, "I hear tell folks don't sleep good when they get older. Been hearin' that all my life. Remember that Tilly Sparks? He used to go on and on about that very thing. By damn, I think he was right. I tossed and turned all night." He yawned again. "I think I'm gonna ride over to Beelerville and see Elmer and Maudie Mc-Nutt's new baby."

"Oh?" Clayton said, surprised. Elmer and Maudie were friends who had also moved up from Texas. Before he and Maudie were married, Elmer had worked for a spell on Bickerstaff's place. "Last time I seen Maudie, she looked like she was carryin' a watermelon. Bet she had a big ole boy."

"Nope. Had a girl. Named her Rhonda Elizabeth." Solon slapped his belly. "You wanta come go with me?"

"Just as well."

Rhonda Elizabeth McNutt was a healthy, ten-pound baby with fat cherubic cheeks and a little wisp of blond hair at the top of her forehead. Solon took to her right away, and played with the baby like a grandfather. Watching the two of them together reminded Clayton of his own grandpa. Even though he'd died when Clayton was seven, Clayton still remembered sitting at the old man's feet, listening to him tell stories.

Maudie was setting the table for supper. She had talked them into spending the night, instead of making the long ride back home. Clayton watched the way she moved around the room, fussing with the plates and hurrying back and forth to the stove. It was a nice feeling, and it gave him a yearning inside to have the domesticity of a woman in his home.

They were just sitting down to eat when a visitor stopped by. He stepped inside the house and removed his hat.

"Excuse me for the interruption, ma'am," he said to Maudie. "But my name is Darnell Hill. Come from Dighton, and I'm lookin' to hire me a stage driver. I thought your husband might know of someone who might be interested."

"Stage driver?" Solon spoke up. He was still seated with

the baby on his lap. "Where are you gonna run a stage to?"

Darnell Hill said, "I'm wantin' to have a stage service that runs right through here. Through Beelerville. Eventually, I'd like to run it on through Ness City, and to Bazine, and farther. Are you interested?"

"What kind of pay are you talkin' about?"

"Well, if I can find the right man, I thought I'd start him off at thirty-six dollars a month, plus meals." Darnell Hill's eyes scanned over Solon. "It wouldn't be easy work, you know. Probably best suited for a young man."

Solon started nodding his head. "A young man," he repeated. He stood up and handed Rhonda Elizabeth to her mother. "That's the trouble with this world! I'll tell you right now, if you want to see your stage all torn up, and your team of horses ruined, go git you a young'un! You just better be able to replace 'em ever few months!" He started pointing his finger as his temper heated up. "And this stage of yours. Are you figurin' on runnin' it on time? I'll bet you ain't considered that," he added smugly.

Darnell Hill looked buffaloed. When Solon paused for a breath, he spoke up in a hurry.

"Now, hold on a minute!" he said. "I don't believe I caught your name, sir."

"Solon Johnson." Solon stood up and reached for Darnell Hill's hand. "I remember a man in Texas, name of Benny Jurgenson," he said, glancing at Clayton. "You remember Benny, don't ya? Went out and hired a bunch of boys. Ha! His business didn't last more'n eight or nine months!"

"Mister Johnson!" Darnell Hill said. "I never said nothin' about hirin' no boys! Are you interested in applyin' for the job?"

"Well," Solon paused with his mouth hanging open, "not really, but I can dern sure do it."

Darnell Hill, who had originally stopped by with the intention of talking with Elmer McNutt about his knowledge of possible drivers, happily accepted Maudie's invitation to supper. He wasn't as good a conversationalist as Solon, but he could hold his own, and they enjoyed a lively conversation over the meal. Elmer managed to work in a few recommendations for stage drivers between topics, but the rest of the group mostly just listened.

After supper, Clayton was sitting by the open front door, watching several black birds foraging their evening meal. He was hoping to see a jackrabbit or a 'possum. Life on the farm had finally taught him to appreciate such things.

Maudie came up beside him. "Have you ever held a baby?" she smiled at him.

Clayton nodded. "But it's been a spell." He thought back over the years, to his furlough, when he'd come home from the war and first held his new baby brother. It made him feel a little sad, sitting there in the McNutts' doorway with the spring breeze hitting his face. All those years had passed, and he was just now learning to stop and notice the simple pleasures of life. Like holding a baby.

"Well, now's the time to refresh your memory." She plopped Rhonda Elizabeth in his lap. "Hold her for a spell, if you would. As you can see, the others are all wound up in their talk."

Clayton took his eyes from the bouncing black birds outside and peered inside to the table, where Solon and Darnell Hill were back on the subject of stage lines and such. Elmer, though not engaged verbally, was all ears.

Maudie could see that Clayton was nervous with a baby in his arms. "Thanks. Now, I can get my dishes done." She reached down and gently tucked the blanket around the baby's neck. "You'll not break her, I promise," she said, then gently rubbed her finger over the baby's lips. "Who's got you?" she teased softly.

Clayton stared down at the tiny creature on his lap. The baby's eyes were a deep blue. They didn't seem to focus on any one thing. Her eyes reminded him of a new puppy, wide and unknowing. Maudie continued to talk to the baby in her adult voice, as if the baby could understand. Clayton doubted if she could. It troubled him that he knew so little about such things. He also felt big and dirty, sitting there holding such a precious thing.

Did Maudie know about his past, he wondered? Would she let him hold her baby—her most prized possession—

if she knew about his bloodstained hands? He tried to feel
relaxed and normal with the child. She felt good in his
arms, with her own good smell and feel. It vaguely did
remind him of holding his little brother, Joshua. It had been
so many long years ago. Clayton wished Maudie would go
on about her business and leave him there, alone with little
Rhonda Elizabeth. He couldn't help worrying that, if she
stood there long enough, she might notice all the bad in
him and take her precious baby back.

Maudie suddenly turned away and went back to her work
in the kitchen. Clayton smiled down at the baby. His fingers
quivered as he pulled back her blanket to get a better view
of her entire face. She was so little and helpless. Clayton
closed his eyes for a few seconds and pretended she was
his. He pulled the baby closer and rubbed her soft cheek
with his nose. His nostrils breathed in her scent. Then the
baby smiled at him, and Clayton knew that being alive
counted for something special.

All too soon, the evening passed, and they turned in for
the night. Alone in his bed, Clayton lay awake, recounting
his life, as he had so many nights before. He thought back
to Virginia during the war.

It had all started there, in that miserable rain. The sight
of the Union soldiers' blood was as red and as real in his
memory as if it had happened yesterday. He felt lonely,
like a human whose redeeming graces have been dried out
and wasted. He took Maudie's quilt and rolled it up, then
cradled it against him. He pretended it was his wife, sleeping next to him, and that his children lay in the next room.
Sleep finally came sometime later, and so did the nightmares.

He was dreaming that he was in a black pit. There was
light at the top, but he couldn't reach it. He was standing
ankle-deep in a pool of water, and there were snakes swimming all around.

In his dream, Clayton tried to climb the walls of the pit,
but they were slick, and there was nothing to grab hold of.
The more he tried, the deeper the hole became, and the
farther away the light seemed. Then, the snakes started
slithering up his body, winding up and around his legs. As

he struggled to shake them off, they tightened around him, sliding upward through his hair. They were choking him, pinning his arms to his sides and squeezing the life out of him.

Just as he started to scream, the baby's cry brought him awake. Clayton's heart was thudding. He opened his eyes and looked at the room around him, getting his bearings. Then he remembered where he was.

Maudie was making noise in the kitchen. He could tell by the sounds that she was making coffee. The baby was still crying. Clayton felt grateful to the little thing for waking him from his dream.

Solon was snoring lightly. No baby was going to rob him of any sleep, Clayton thought.

He lay back for a moment, enjoying the pleasant feel of being in Maudie and Elmer McNutt's home. There was pale light beginning to shine through the yellow curtains on the windows. Maudie's homemade quilt and hand-stitched pillowcases were strewn across the bed. Family pictures hung on the walls, and Maudie had embroidered a little sign that read "God Bless Our Home." It was a nice house, he thought, made better by her presence. He remembered back, some twelve years before, to that earthen jail in Limestone County, Texas.

In June of '72, Clayton had quit his job in New Mexico. He'd tried to convince Solon to leave, but Solon had become excited about his new career at the Boot and Saddle Shop. Not only that, he had taken to drinking heavily, and he'd lost his ambition to move to anyplace new. So, he and Clayton had parted ways.

Clayton had headed back toward Texas, in hopes of eventually making it back to Beartooth Flats. He met a man in Waco who offered him a temporary job, and it was there that he was arrested.

The four lawmen came from Limestone County, and the charges against Clayton were for the killing of Leslie Brown, Elijah Simmons, and Joey Crouch. Clayton would get his trial, they told him, but in the meantime, his new home would be courtesy of the county.

The jail was nothing more than a big hole in the ground, covered with logs. It was damp and cold, and rainwater collected in stagnant puddles. After one series of heavy thunderstorms, Clayton spent two weeks in knee-deep water. He almost caught his death of cold. Buckets were used for lowering down food and for sending up nature's call. Clayton found he had no other choice but to urinate right where he stood. There was no bed or chair, and the hole stank something awful. Piles of old feces were scattered about where some hadn't waited for the bucket.

Eleven months went by. Sores formed and festered all over Clayton's body. His clothes became tattered and worn. In the wintertime, he nearly froze. In the summertime, he could barely breathe the air. His weight dropped, and his spirits along with it. Once again, he was in the First Tennessee, only this time, he was alone. There were no battles with guns to be fought, and Clayton was not the hero, and survival was every bit as hard. He worked hard at keeping himself sane, recalling conversations he'd had and people he'd known. He tried to remember Bible verses, but it had been so long since he'd read the Good Book, he could only think of a few.

Then one day, Sheriff Newton Baker came to set him free. As Clayton emerged from the hellhole, he noticed that it was spring. Things were starting to green up and bud out. He noticed things he'd never noticed before, like how good the air felt to breathe. At first, the light hurt his eyes, but he was too full of wanting to see everything around him to care.

The sheriff was accompanied by Judge Chester Edmondson. The judge had ordered Clayton's release, and had come to explain the matter. They had been preparing for Clayton's trial, he said, when it was discovered that there was a sizable reward on the head of Joey Crouch for the murder of two men. Elijah Simmons had also been wanted on several counts of robbery and horse theft.

Judge Edmondson stated many times that he held no tolerance for what Clayton had done, but after receiving the news about Crouch and Simmons, he felt more inclined to believe Clayton's story that he had killed the three in defending himself.

With no further ceremony, Clayton retrieved his mare and other belongings, and Sheriff Baker fetched him a bar of soap. Clayton rode straight into the Navasota River, where he stripped off his clothes and scrubbed himself nearly raw.

He crawled out of the water and sat for a while on the grassy bank. He looked down at his clothes. They were rotted, and smelled like the bottom of a privy. He grimaced at them and decided to count his money. When he was arrested, he'd had sixty-three dollars, but now there was only eight dollars among his belongings. He surely needed to buy new clothes, he thought. Then, he remembered seeing a woman out hanging clothes to dry behind a house he'd passed on the way to the river. They were men's clothes. He bundled up his rotted clothes and tossed them into the river, then mounted up and rode naked to the house.

The clothes on the line were dry, and he couldn't see anyone around. Clayton pulled off a pair of men's pants and a shirt and tried them on. They were big, and they hung loose on his half-starved body. He managed to roll up the sleeves and the pant legs to where he could walk, and was reaching for a pair of socks, when the woman appeared. Clayton started to run for the mare, but the woman only snickered and put her hand over her mouth.

"Just what do you think you're up to, pray tell?" she said, and laughed.

Clayton stopped and looked at her. She was young and fairly pretty, and the friendly way she spoke took away his fear.

"I have some money in my saddlebag," he said. "I could give you a couple of dollars for the clothes."

"You certainly do need the clothes, I reckon," she commented.

"Yes'm, I do."

The woman was walking toward him, barefoot and wearing a thin cotton dress. She had a round face with chubby cheeks and a dimple etched in one side. The rest of her body was slender. But it was the mischievous look in her eyes that drew his attention.

"I don't want your money," she said. "These clothes belong to my stepdaddy, and you can take all of 'em if you want to. They don't mean nothin' to me."

Clayton felt fascinated at the sight of a woman. It had been so long since he'd been close to one, he couldn't stop staring at her.

"You shouldn't talk about family like that," he said.

She shrugged and walked over to the line, running her fingertips over a shirt that hung there.

"He ain't no family of mine," she said. "Anytime my mama ain't around, he tries to have his way with me." An angry look passed over her face.

Clayton suddenly thought about what she was saying. His eyes shot to the house.

"Oh, don't worry none. Ain't nobody home but me." She pulled the shirt down off the clothesline and held it out to him. "Here, put this on. It'll look better than that old thing." She started to grin at him again. "I watched you ride up, you know." She pointed to the window. "See that little hole in the curtain? I was peekin'." She giggled. "I must say, it ain't every day a handsome man like you rides up, dressed the way he was born."

Clayton took off the shirt and stood there a moment. He couldn't take his eyes off her. He wanted to say something, but the sight of her struck him speechless. He let the shirt fall to the ground and drifted his eyes over her body, down to her legs and bare feet.

He stood there, bare-chested. She was still holding the other shirt out to him, but he didn't want to put it on. Not yet, anyway. He wanted to make small talk, become familiar with her, but he couldn't find the right words. He could feel the familiar stirring going on inside him, so strong he couldn't control it. More on instinct than anything else, he stepped closer to her, so close he could smell the fragrance of her body.

She let him reach up and feel her hair. As he rubbed the soft strands between his fingers, he noticed the goose bumps on her arms. When he lowered his head to kiss her, the giggling had stopped, and she spoke in a nervous voice.

"You don't even know my name," she said.

Clayton covered her mouth with his. He pulled her tight against his body. His blood seemed to quicken and run faster through his veins. It had been so long, Clayton had somehow forgotten the sensation that a woman's touch could bring. Her lips pressed back, hard against his, and he began to explore her body with his hands.

The girl pushed hard against his chest and looked up at him. Her eyes were glassy. She licked her full red lips and took in a deep breath. "I don't even know you," she gasped.

But Clayton only put his hand behind her neck and kissed her again. She struggled weakly against him for a moment, but then gave in.

"Come on," she said in a raspy voice. She grabbed his hand and pulled him toward the doorway. The house was dark, and Clayton, who had been in the bright sun, couldn't see a thing at first. He followed her blindly to the bedroom, where he lifted the thin cotton dress over her shoulders.

She was naked underneath. He kissed her slender body.

"Please," she said, barely above a whisper, "please, tell me your name."

Clayton heard her plea, but the words didn't register. The long months of isolation in the dark, wet cell had left him starved and selfish. He couldn't get enough of her womanly scent and her baby-soft, moist skin. It made him powerless to stop and consider anything but his want. But she wanted him, too, and before she could offer any more protest, they were having each other.

Afterward, she lay with her head on his shoulder. A long time passed, and Clayton thought she'd fallen asleep, when he felt the warmth of her tears. He kissed her forehead. "Why are you cryin'?" he asked.

She didn't answer at first. She was still crying, and Clayton realized she didn't want him to see her. Finally, he heard her say softly, "We should've at least knew each other's name."

He couldn't think of anything to say.

She suddenly sat up. "I mean, I didn't mind bein' with ya," she said. "I wanted to."

Clayton tried hard to think of something fitting to say to her. He felt bad for being so inconsiderate, but nothing came to mind. He lay there, feeling like a kid who's disappointed his mama. He wished he knew more about making a woman happy, more than just the act of pleasure. They surely were a hard bunch to figure out. All full of passion one minute, crying the next.

She touched his cheek and ran her fingernail over his skin. "I'm sorry to carry on so. But I wanted to know your name. It just seemed right. My name's Laura."

Clayton wanted to answer, but all he could do was swallow hard. What in the world had he done? He felt like an animal that had been locked away until it went crazy. He had violated her for his own selfish needs, and now she was all hurt and crying. He wondered if she felt guilty, too, over what was clearly all his fault.

Suddenly, Jolene and Flossie entered his thoughts. What would they think, if they could see him in this strange house, with this poor woman? Clayton thought he must have lost part of his mind in that jail hole.

Laura broke into these thoughts, "Are you gonna tell me your name, or do you plan to just get on your horse and ride off?" Her voice was shaky.

Clayton had to swallow again. He didn't really want to leave his name behind, but then, his wants didn't seem to matter as much as they once had. He owed it to her to know who she'd slept with.

"My name's Clayton Crist," he said meekly.

"Clayton Crist." She nodded, apparently satisfied. "I ain't never heard that name before. Knew a man named Clay once. Clay Philpot." She smiled sadly. "I wonder if his real name was Clayton."

33

CLAYTON HAD fallen asleep. He felt comfortable with Laura lying against his shoulder. There was enough brisk-ness in the air that it tossed back the curtain and felt re-freshing on his naked shoulders. He wrapped one of his legs around Laura's. In her sleep, she responded, and they coiled around each other like contented snakes.

He needed this. The cold, damp hole of a jail had opened up many scars—not just the ones on his body, but all those that Clayton had tried to bury from the war.

What he needed was a good hard sleep, but he was drift-ing in and out, waking every now and then to soak in this sudden turn of good fortune.

He'd been dozing for a while, when he suddenly came awake. Something wasn't quite right. He wondered for a minute if he was dreaming. But when he opened one eye, he saw the walls of Laura's bedroom, just as he remem-bered. Her hair was still soft against his shoulder. His eye settled on the curtain that was blowing in the breeze. Slowly, he closed the eye, and then both eyes opened wide.

There was someone on the other side of the room. He could feel the presence. He wanted to flip over and see, but Laura's weight was too heavy to allow any sudden movement.

Clayton's mind raced over a hundred things at once. The things Laura had said about her stepfather made him imag-ine a big shotgun waving in his face, then blowing his body into oblivion. He couldn't wait for whoever was in the room to make a move. He yanked his head to the left, and there, in the semidarkness, he saw the outline of two men.

"I told you he was here," one of them said.

"By damn, boy! Ol' Jess'll cut that thing off if he catches ya!" the other said to Clayton.

"People don't do that sort of thing around here," the first man said.

Clayton had heard those voices before. He groggily searched his mind while he stared helplessly at the dark figures. Then, the second man moved around to the foot of the bed and yanked back the covers. Laura's naked backside was revealed. "Ummm," he said.

The first man spoke up, and then Clayton recognized it to be Judge Chester Edmondson's voice. "Get away from her, Newton, and behave yourself!"

Clayton stared at the judge as Sheriff Newton Baker moved back to the side of the bed. He blinked his eyes, trying to get them focused in the dimly lit room. Where had he left his Colt, he wondered? He couldn't shoot a judge or a sheriff, but he had no desire to go back to that hole in the ground, either. At least he could bluff his way out, if he had his pistol.

Laura started to squirm, then woke up. When she saw the two men, she pulled the covers over her front.

"W-what are you doin' here?" she stammered, her voice still full of sleep.

Newton Baker leaned over her. "Why, you little tramp!" he said. "If'n your pa comes and catches you, he'll womp your ass real good."

Laura looked surprised, then her face came alive. She started to scream at him. "Newton Baker, you bastard! What are you comin' into my bedroom for?"

"Just settle yourself down, little girl! 'Less you want me to tell your pa what I seen here," the sheriff said.

Laura got so angry, she climbed to her knees, letting the blanket fall. She faced off with Sheriff Baker and went on at the top of her voice.

"Just what are you gonna tell him? While you're doin' all your fine talkin', are you gonna tell him how you always come around, pawin' all over me? Are you gonna tell him that, Sheriff?" Her anger was boiling up into her face, which was a dark red. Her eyes were getting teary. "Yeah, that's right," she added. "Be sure and tell him about yourself while you're at it." Hot tears started rolling down her cheeks. "This ain't none of your damn business, Newton Baker! So you just git out of my house!"

Judge Edmondson put his hand on the sheriff's shoulder. "That's enough," he said. "We didn't come here for this."

At the sound of the judge's voice, Laura slumped back down on the bed and pulled the quilt around her. She stared up at him, suddenly subdued. "What do you want, then?" she asked softly.

"We came to talk to Crist," the judge said.

Sheriff Newton Baker kicked the bed with his boot. "That's right! You heard the judge, Crist! Come on out of that bed and git your clothes on!"

Clayton sat up and reached slowly for his clothes. A cold feeling had stolen over him. He looked across the room at his Colt. It was lying on the bureau. "Am I under arrest?" he asked.

Judge Edmondson shook his head. "No. You haven't done nothin'. We just wanta talk to ya, is all."

Clayton threw on the clothes he'd stolen off the line. He'd turned to walk past the judge, when he heard a loud slap. Sheriff Baker was rubbing his face.

"Don't you ever touch me again!" Laura hollered. She was standing with the quilt wrapped around her, glaring at the sheriff.

Once they got outside, Judge Edmondson instructed Clayton to get his horse. "We're gonna ride back to the river and do some talkin'," he said. "It's nothin' to be all worried about."

But, Clayton *was* nervous. Riding between the two men, he ran several scenarios through his mind. Were they just tricking him into going someplace where they could arrest him again? He surely didn't fancy killing a sheriff or a judge, but the idea of returning to that sorry jail in the ground made him sick. The putrid smell still lingered in his nostrils. Even after he'd bathed in the river, the odor seemed to cling to his body. But then, he thought, if they *were* going to arrest him, why not just do it at Laura's house?

When they reached the bank of the river, they all three dismounted. Judge Edmondson motioned for Clayton to sit down on the ground, and he followed suit. Sheriff Baker looked at them a moment, then sat down, too, pulling on his hat. Both men seemed anxious and nervous.

The judge rolled a cigarette and offered it to Clayton, then rolled a fixin' for himself and the sheriff. They sat there, smoking, for a couple of minutes. Clayton watched them fidget and look back and forth at each other. Like two worried young'uns, he thought. Finally, he took the initiative.

"Looky here," he said. "I can see that you've got somethin' on your mind, and I'd just as soon get it over with." He paused and looked the judge in the eye.

Sheriff Baker's body moved as if he was going to speak, but Judge Edmondson grabbed his arm. "Better let me handle this, Newton," he said. A sudden weariness came over the judge, and deep lines formed on his face. He reminded Clayton of a man who's just been bereaved of a close family member.

"You see, Crist, after the war, some of the men around here took it upon themselves to protect folks." He nodded reflectively. "And rightly so." He took a big pull on his smoke, and his eyes widened. "It weren't just around here, either. Why, counties all over Texas and the South felt a strong need for 'em. You may of heard of these men. Some call 'em White Caps. I heard down in Georgia and Alabama they call themselves the Ku Klux Klan."

Sheriff Baker looked impatient. He was itching to talk. When the judge paused, he said, "What Chester's tryin' to say is—"

The judge nudged Newton Baker in the arm again. "What I was sayin'," he said in a raised voice, "is that there was a great need for this organization in the South, *at first.* But there ain't a need anymore." His face took on that deep, worried look again. "Things just got too far out of hand."

Clayton was starting to feel impatient, himself. "I understand what you're sayin', but what does all this have to do with me?'' he asked.

Judge Edmondson started to answer, but stopped. Looking away, he said, ''You go on now, Newton. Tell 'im.''

Sheriff Newton Baker jumped to his feet, full of his own importance.

''I'll tell you what it's got to do with you!'' he said. ''It's that gun of your'n! It ain't no secret that you're a mankiller, and we got a couple of men we'd like you to kill.''

Judge Edmondson held up a hand. ''Now, hold on right there!'' he said. ''Newton can be a bit too blunt at times,'' he explained, giving the sheriff a hard look. He rubbed his fingers on his gnawing stomach and grimaced. ''You see, Crist,'' he began, ''here in Limestone County, things have always been peaceful. After the war, we didn't have much trouble at all, and the White Caps that lived here were just ordinary citizens. I belonged to them, myself.'' He nodded thoughtfully. ''Things would've stayed just the same, and everything would've been all right, if'n those other White Caps hadn't come in from other places. Why, they weren't nothin' but a bunch of common thugs!''

He paused, and sat there silent for so long, Clayton started nodding to get him on with his point. Finally, the judge sighed.

''Well, three or four years ago, just about the time our band was ready to break up, a couple White Caps showed up from McLennan County. They've tried to keep things all stirred up, when there ain't a need anymore. Names are Slab Kirkland and Alva DeKock.'' He shook his head. ''These are bad men, Crist, them and their cohorts. They ain't in it to help nobody but themselves. Hell, if you want to know the truth, they're just outlaws. Nothin' more.''

There was a sadness in the judge's manner. Clayton remembered back to the war. General Johnston had seemed to have a sadness about him, almost as if he'd taken on the burden of all the deaths of the men under his command. He wondered if Judge Edmondson somehow blamed himself for the way the White Caps had turned out.

He said, ''Yeah, I've run across some of those White Cap fellers, myself. And I can sympathize with what you're sayin'. But what you're wantin' is to have these two men killed!" He stared at the two men. "You may be judge and sheriff of these parts, and I've done plenty of things I'm ashamed of, but I ain't never murdered nobody!"

Newton Baker said, "Oh, it ain't *murder*, exactly."

"What would you call it?" Clayton asked. He desperately wished he had taken his bath at the creek and ridden on, without stopping for clothes at Laura's. Then again, he knew he'd been followed ever since he'd left jail. He should have given spur to the mare, he thought, and ridden hard. They surely couldn't have caught him.

"We're not asking you to murder nobody," Judge Edmondson repeated. "Newton, here, sometimes gets excited and overreacts. What we're askin' you to do is run them out of this part of the country. We'd hire you on, sort of like a deputy, to help us with the task."

Clayton studied the situation. Sheriff Baker was full of excitement over the prospects of what could happen. The judge, though, clearly had little stomach for what he was asking.

"You call these men outlaws. Why don't you just arrest them?" Clayton asked.

Newton's face reddened. He stared down at his boots.

Judge Edmondson said, "With all due respect to Sheriff Baker, here, it's not that simple. These men ride at night. They have left their mark by burnin' down farms and killin' innocent people. They're ruthless and mean to the core. I'm afraid if the sheriff tried to arrest 'em, he'd most likely get himself killed."

After a long silence, Clayton said, "Well, how am I supposed to do this, and not get myself branded a murderer?"

This time when Newton answered, he was not interrupted by the judge. It was apparent that he had been rehearsed on what to say. "It'll not be murder," he said. "You'll get your opportunity. Those sons of bitches will give you just cause."

Clayton stared at the two men and they stared silently back. He knew that he was in no position to refuse their "offer." If he did, he'd most likely find himself under arrest, and right back down inside that hole.

They could read the thoughts that were running through his mind. The judge began to nod his head.

"You start today," he said.

34

CLAYTON WAS never given a badge, but in the days and the weeks that followed, he rarely left Sheriff Newton Baker's side, or the judge's either. Judge Edmondson ran his affairs from a small log cabin that doubled as the sheriff's office.

As for Slab Kirkland and Alva DeKock, Clayton saw them his first day on the job, and most days thereafter. When he made it known that he'd just as soon confront them and get the killing over with, he was reminded that he was to wait until it could be done all "legal and proper," in so many words. The appropriate moment would come soon enough, the sheriff told him. Kirkland and DeKock, he added, occasionally went on drinking spells at Paterno's Canteen and sometimes liked to shoot up the place before they were finished. Clayton remembered, during those eleven months in the hole, when he'd heard gunfire at night. Now he knew why.

Sheriff Newton Baker was a bachelor, and he didn't partake of many vices. He did, however, enjoy his drink. Rarely an evening went by that he didn't stop in Paterno's, a large, crude building with a dirt floor, where locals played cards and drank their spirits.

Clayton hadn't cared much for the sheriff at first, but as the days and nights passed, he came to realize he'd been wrong in his first impressions. Newton Baker really wasn't such a bad fellow, Clayton thought. For the most part, he was a quiet studier of people. And, he was a creature of habit.

For one thing, Newton's drinking pattern never varied. He would have one drink, then two, and sometime during the third, he would begin to relax and become talkative. Clayton soon learned that Newton was a storyteller with a limited number of stories to tell. On into the fourth drink, Newton would retell the same stories, over and over. Most involved women, and many were recountings of his life as as a boy, working for his father in Virginia. They were the stories of a lonely man, Clayton realized.

Vito Paterno had first immigrated to New York, then eventually settled in Texas several moves later. He ran his canteen with a stern eye, measuring the drinks out to the last drop. He also kept sporting ladies.

There was a small room in the back of the canteen that held two beds and a table with a pitcher of water, a bowl, and a small lamp. The little room had been hastily built for its one purpose, and in the daytime, the light shone through the cracks in the logs. There was usually only one sporting lady at one time, Newton told Clayton, but occasionally there had been up to four working in the one room. Most all of them were Mexicans in their mid-teens to early twenties, who came looking to earn money for their families. Paterno hired them, but not for any charitable reasons.

It was in that drafty little room that Sheriff Newton Baker played out his dreams. Night after night, he'd sit there and drink his four drinks, swirling the whiskey around in his glass as he told the same stories, over and over, about his ways with the women. Once or twice a week, he'd stop, give Clayton a crooked grin, and disappear into the little room with one of the Mexican whores.

Clayton didn't begrudge the man his drinking and boring stories. He felt a little sorry for Newton. Being a lawman was a lonely enough lot in life, but the sheriff didn't even seem to enjoy being with himself.

One Friday night, Newton was on his fourth drink, and was relating his fifth story about a woman he'd met in St. Louis.

"She was a beauty, Crist," he said, swirling the amber liquid in his glass. "Had blond hair and curls that draped down over her shoulders. Sweetest thing in all of Mis-

souri.'' He stopped and let his eyes drift to the back of the
canteen, to the door of the little room.

Clayton saw the desire rise in Newton's eyes, just as Slab
Kirkland and Alva DeKock walked in with three companions. Four men who'd been playing cards quickly dispersed
their game and left. Vito Paterno looked upset at the loss
of business, but he managed to put on a practiced smile for
Kirkland and DeKock and the others as he set a fresh bottle
of spirits on the counter.

Soon, the rest of the canteen had cleared out. Newton
Baker's story about the blond-haired woman was forgotten.
Clayton saw the fear that clouded the lustful eyes. His stare
was nervously fixed on the men at the bar.

The men were rowdy and full of themselves and gave
the impression that they were there for the night. One of
the companions immediately headed for the little room in
back. No sooner had he entered, when a short, chubby Mexican girl who looked no more than fourteen ran out barefoot. She was laughing. The man stuck his head out after
her.

''Unless one of you wants her for yourself, keep her fat
little ass occupied! I don't cotton to havin' spectators!''

Alva DeKock grabbed the barefoot young whore by the
wrist and, with a bottle of whiskey in the other hand,
dragged her back into the room.

Vito Paterno was now all smiles. He'd forgotten about
the four card players and their small drinking habits. These
men meant real money, and his cut from the Mexican
whore was more than appeasing.

Clayton looked back and forth from the goings-on to the
sheriff's face. He knew that Newton's lust was strong and
he was bothered by what he saw, but Newton was too
scared to go anywhere near that little room.

The evening wore on. Clayton expected all hell to break
loose, but it never did. Kirkland and DeKock were well
aware of the sheriff's presence, but there was no threat felt
in the fact. The outlaws were loud and braggadocious. All
except Slab Kirkland took a turn at the Mexican whores.
Several times, the door to the canteen opened, but when

the customers saw who occupied the room, they quickly downed their drinks and left.

Newton passed his drink limit that night. As he tossed down his sixth, then his seventh, then his eighth, he grew drunker and quieter. Gone were his stories about his exploits with blond hair that draped past white shoulders. He was beaten. Sadness was his ally, and Clayton knew it was because the sheriff was scared.

The drink also numbed any sense of pride the sheriff might have clung to. As he sat there, staring first at the bottom of his glass and then at the whores' door, he began to weep. Embarrassed for him, Clayton got up from the table.

"Come on," he said softly. "Let's go."

When Newton offered no answer, Clayton took him by the arm and helped him to the door. He didn't realize how drunk the sheriff really was. Newton wrapped his arm around Clayton's neck and clung to him. They made it to the door, when Alva DeKock walked over with Newton's hat.

"You forgot this, Sheriff," he said, and pulled the hat down hard over Newton's ears.

The others laughed hard, and Clayton had to bite his tongue hard to keep from answering. His hand itched for the .44 that hung at his side. But, as angry as he felt, and as much as he'd grown to trust Newton Baker and Judge Edmondson, he knew he had to wait for the right circumstances to deal with Slab Kirkland and Alva DeKock.

He managed to get the sheriff back to the office and to his bunk, but Newton wouldn't lie down. When Clayton did get him to sit down, Newton started to bawl like a little boy.

"Y-you think I'm a stinkin', sorry excuse for a lawman, don't ya?" he said.

Clayton gave up trying to make Newton lie down. He sat down in the chair behind the sheriff's desk and sucked in a deep breath. Newton was in a talkative mood again. A drunken talkative mood.

"I don't think that, at all," Clayton said.

Newton was trying to rub something off his face. Whatever it was he couldn't seem to find it, because he kept rubbing. "Well, I ain't no good. A good lawman would do his job." He looked up at Clayton through bloodshot eyes. His nose was running. "What I am is what you see right here. Nothin' more. I don't even have a family, nor nothin' else. That gal in St. Louis with the blond hair? Her name was Marianna. She was beautiful, all right, but I lied about the rest." His shoulders shook as he started crying again. He reached up with his sleeve and wiped the snot and tears away. "I lied. I never had her. I used to go look at her and hear her sing. Sh-she never even gave me the time of day."

Clayton had suspected all along that Newton's stories about women were just that—stories. Still, he didn't begrudge the man for having them. A lot of men did. Clayton thought it was a harmless thing that men did to make themselves feel better.

"What do you think about a man that would lie about such things?" Newton said.

Clayton shrugged. "I don't think nothin' about it, Newton. We all talk foolishly, I guess."

"Not you. You're a mankiller. You don't have to brag," Newton insisted. He looked across the room. "There's a bottle in the judge's desk. Get it for me, would you, Crist?"

"Aw, you don't need nothin' more to drink," Clayton said.

"Yes, I do. You see, I'm a fake and a phony. Everything I do is a lie. All I can rightly do is spend my money on Mexican whores and whiskey. I wouldn't never hire me as a lawman or anything else." He got up and started to stumble toward the judge's desk.

"Sit down," Clayton said, "I'll get it."

He fetched the whiskey bottle and sat down on the bunk. Newton drank in big gulps from the judge's bottle. It nearly took his breath away. He held the bottle against his chest and let the fire melt down. "You see, Crist, I'm a phony lawman, and you're a mankiller." He took another drink and looked down at the bottle in his hand. "That danged ol' Judge Chester Edmondson, he's a lot smarter than us. He don't drink none of Paterno's cheap shit. He gits this in Waco from a whiskey peddler. Judge has got money, you know. You and me'll never have a damned thing.'' He drank again. "I was purely scared tonight," he went on. "Thought that when the time came, we'd argue with 'em. But I could no more have stood up to them bastards tonight than I could fly." He held the whiskey up to the light and swayed as he tried to look through the contents.

"I don't always drink the judge's whiskey, you understand. Sometimes, I have to pour some of Paterno's stuff in here so the judge don't miss it and suspect I been in it. It wouldn't be good," he said, "for a coward lawman to be drinkin' the judge's good whiskey." He gave a harsh laugh.

"Come on, Sheriff," Clayton said. "Don't be so hard on yourself."

"That's easy for you to say. You weren't like a scared jackrabbit." Newton nodded his head and waved the bottle at Clayton. "You didn't look scared, at all, but I was." Tears started rolling down his cheeks. "Y-you know what the plan was? The plan was for me to piss those fellers off, so you, the mankiller, could shoot 'em. But I was t-t-too scared to do even that." He leaned forward and laid his head on Clayton's chest. "All I got is me, and I didn't want to die."

Clayton hesitated, then awkwardly patted Newton on the back. "Don't worry none, Newton. Ain't nobody gonna know about nothin'," he said.

Newton pulled his face up to where it was just inches from Clayton's. "Maybe not," he said. "But *I* know."

⚞ 35 ⚟

AFTER THAT night, Sheriff Newton Baker seemed to have lost whatever small amount of happiness in life that he'd once had. His favorite stories were all but forgotten, and for several days, he sulked around like a whipped puppy and complained about life's disappointments.

He even managed to avoid Paterno's for almost a week, although that proved too much punishment, even for the depressed sheriff. On Saturday night, he asked Clayton if he'd like to go get a drink. Clayton was glad to see him coming around to his old self.

There was a good crowd at Paterno's. Two card games were in progress, and several men stood at the bar. The little room at the back was busy. Paterno had taken on a new whore named Maria. She was tall and dark-skinned, with straight black hair. As the evening wore on, Clayton watched and counted as she made seven different trips to the back room. Viola, the whore Clayton remembered from a week ago, had made three trips with customers. Carmella, the chubby little whore, had not made a sale. Clayton felt sorry for her, as he watched her work the crowd. Her young eyes flitted back and forth over the men, smiling invitingly at them, but the most they would do was tease her, pulling her on their laps to squeeze her rolls of flesh. Clayton noticed the pain that crossed her young face. There was an innocence in her eyes, too. He didn't know why, but he suddenly wished he had the money to buy her away from Paterno. He'd send her back home to her family where she belonged. Then she wouldn't have to suffer like this. She could go about the business of being a girl again.

Through the evening, Clayton kept one eye on the goings-on between the whores and their little room, while the other eye held a watch on Newton Baker. The sheriff was still not his usual boisterous self. He sat quietly, drinking his whiskey, almost as if he was ashamed to be sitting there among people. Clayton knew he was watching Carmella closely, even though he appeared to be concentrating on his whiskey glass.

It grew late. The card games broke up, and most of the customers went home. The men that Clayton had been expecting hadn't shown up at the canteen. Newton looked over at Carmella, then up at Clayton.

"I think I'll go with Carmella," he said, looking back at the young whore. "I could pick one of the other two, but they both made good money tonight. She ain't made a dime," he added, as if to justify himself.

He got up and moseyed over to Carmella. Her eyes danced shyly back and forth from the floor to his face as he talked to her. Then she nodded, almost sadly. Awkwardly, the sheriff took hold of her chubby hand and led her to the little room. At the door, he spoke inside to Maria to hurry with her last customer, then pulled Carmella in behind him.

After that night, Newton quickly settled back into his regular routine at Paterno's. After his four drinks, he would disappear into the back room with Carmella. Clayton was glad he wasn't still sulking around and feeling sorry for himself, but he knew that the sheriff was far from being a happy man. He'd lost much of what he saw as his respectability, and most of his own self-regard. Clayton reckoned Sheriff Newton Baker was about the most miserable human being he'd ever known.

It surprised Clayton when, a few weeks later, Baker sat down next to him and asked, "What do you think about me marrying Carmella?"

Clayton couldn't answer right away. He knew that Newton was pleading for his approval. "Well," he said slowly, "if you're wantin' my opinion, for whatever it's worth, I think you two need each other."

Newton looked so confused, Clayton stopped himself. "Ah hell, Newton," he said. "I'm a bad one to give advice about anything, 'specially when it comes to females. I do know one thing for sure. Carmella ain't meant for that kind of work. She'll get her life eaten away in this canteen. So," he lifted his glass and offered a toast, "here's to you and Carmella."

Newton grinned and lifted his glass.

Vito Paterno was not so enthusiastic. He pitched a fit when Newton told him of his intentions of marrying Carmella, but he couldn't argue Newton down.

"Look," he tried to reason, "this is my business, you understand? You can't just take away my women! Give me fifty dollars, and then you can marry her."

This made Newton angry. "Have you lost your mind?" he said hotly. "I ain't payin' nobody no fifty dollars to git married!"

"I ain't lost nothin'," Paterno insisted, "and I ain't figurin' on losin' nothin', either." He grabbed up a white rag and bitterly slung it over his shoulder. "I invest money in these ladies for your convenience and pleasure, and I figure I got at least fifty dollars invested in that one!"

Neither man would budge, and the argument went on for days. At first, Clayton thought Paterno was just funning with Newton for amusement, but the canteen owner was dead serious about collecting his fifty dollars. Several times, the two nearly came to blows and had to be separated.

After one particular hard argument between the two, Newton finally walked away from the bar and sat down at a table. He seemed tired, and somewhat confused. Clayton knew that look. He'd seen it many times, on the faces of bereaved families. Right now, Sheriff Newton Baker had the looks of a man who had pretty much given up on ever finding happiness in life.

Newton gazed sadly at Clayton. "What do you think I oughta do?" he asked. "Would you give the son of a bitch fifty dollars if you were me?"

"I wish you wouldn't ask me that question, Newton,"

Clayton said. He picked up Newton's tobacco and rolled a fixin' while he thought the matter over. He hated giving advice to anybody, but Newton looked so upset, he knew he had to offer up something. "Well," he said, choosing his words carefully, "I guess Paterno's lookin' at the situation through business eyes. He don't really mean nothin' . . ." He let his words fade off. He wasn't sounding very sure, himself. "Ah hell, Newton. I don't know what to tell you. I guess it's a river you'll have to swim yourself."

Clayton felt a pang of guilt. In truth, he thought Paterno's request was crazy, but he had known plenty of other men who thought they owned their whores. Some did, in fact. They'd make payment and get a bill of sale, much as a man would do when buying a horse. Clayton had his doubts that the sale would hold up in a court; after all, the coloreds were all free, and if that was the case, he was sure whores would be considered free, too.

Newton just nodded to himself and said nothing more about it. The next day, he got up early and walked to the canteen, carrying his Winchester. Inside, he walked past Paterno to the little back room and fetched Carmella.

"What in hell do you think you're doin'?" Paterno said.

Newton stopped at the door and turned around to face him. "Now, don't you try nothin' crazy, Paterno. I wouldn't want to have to hurt you," he warned, but his words lacked any conviction. His jaw twitched nervously.

Paterno stood red-faced. His angry glare was turned more toward Carmella than Newton. She almost seemed to wither under his look. Finally, Paterno gave a low grunt.

"Aw, go on and take her! She wasn't worth a piece of shit to begin with! Weren't but a few that would have her. She only cost me money. I'm surprised you'd want her, Newton. But then, you never did have any good taste or sense."

Newton's neck swelled up like a bullfrog's. Sweat beaded up on his forehead. He said, "Just who do you think you are, anyway, talkin' about Carmella that way? Maybe you've forgotten, but I'm the law around here." He'd been holding the Winchester in the crook of his arm, but now he waved it in Paterno's direction.

Paterno grunted again. "Yeah, you're the law, all right. What a good joke that is! You're the law," he paused, his eyes narrow and mean, "only because Chester Edmondson allows you to be. Now, take your fat whore and get out of here. I'm tired of lookin' at both of you."

Newton's finger wrapped around the trigger. He wanted so badly to pull it back and fire. He wanted to blast away the superior, disgusted look in Paterno's eyes—to shut his mouth for good.

But he couldn't. Suddenly tired, he dropped the rifle to his side and took Carmella by the hand. He said weakly, "I'd shoot you if there was another canteen, but there ain't."

Once he had Carmella outside in the fresh, Texas air, he had no idea what he was going to do with her. He certainly hadn't planned on this happening, he thought. Carmella was watching him through the slits of fat around her eyes. The sudden exposure to the sun made her face seem even fleshier. Newton suddenly felt weak all over. He took a trembly step toward the jail, then stopped and grabbed Carmella by the arm. Quickly, he steered her toward his horse.

He needed to get out of town, and fast. He needed to go someplace where he could be alone with Carmella and think. They mounted up and headed for the river.

They stopped at a little sandbar where he liked to fish. It was a place few folks knew about, and far away from any of the main trails in the area.

Newton had fallen in love before. There'd been several women who'd caught his fancy, and he'd watched them from a ways off and had romantic dreams in his bed at night. He'd never gotten up the nerve to actually tell a female how he felt about her, much less say he loved her. They had all just come and gone out of his life, without ever knowing the feelings in his heart.

Carmella was different. Newton had felt a kinship with her, ever since she'd arrived at Paterno's place. She had an innocence and kindness about her that the other girls didn't have. She was young and still fresh, and that had seemed to give him a comfort. Newton had been her very first customer and, he later learned, the very first man she'd ever lain with. She had been nervous and awkward, but her anxiousness to please him appealed to Newton. He had later boasted to others about the rise he'd brought out of her, but in fact, he'd been patient and tender. There was something in her cherubic cheeks and dark, trusting eyes that reminded him of himself.

There in that drafty little room, watching Carmella remove her clothes for the first time before a man, and nervously trying to cover her breasts, Newton Baker had been reminded of the pain of his own youth. He thought back to the day he and the other boys had gone swimming, and how George Strunk had made fun of his privates. How all the other boys had laughed and called him "fatty" and "stupid." He remembered being so big on the outside, yet feeling so tiny on the inside. He had never felt like he measured up to the others. And he'd never gone swimming again.

Now, as he sat there on the sandbar, wondering if he had made a mistake, he looked at Carmella and saw that mirror again. He reached for Carmella and took her in his arms. He would be a good husband, he thought. He would never say bad things to her or make jokes about her fat.

What was wrong with a man getting married, anyway, he wondered? Of course, he knew, everyone would surely always point to the fact that he had married a whore. He briefly entertained the thought of trying to convince them that she wasn't really a whore, at all. After all, she'd never had any customers to speak of, besides himself. But that would never work. Even he didn't feel all that convinced. Besides, this was a small town, and everybody knew the whores, almost by name. The menfolk were so keen on the subject, they found out the particulars on the women within a couple days of their arrival. And hadn't Carmella offered herself up, anyway? The women in the area had never approved of Paterno or his canteen in the first place. Two years before, a bunch of women had shown up early one Sunday evening after camp meeting, carrying torches. Their intention had been to burn the place down. Newton had been sent to break up their gathering and send them home.

At first, he'd laughed at the sight of all those women, waving their torches in the air and talking in their shrill voices. He'd never considered women equal to men in very many things. But these were angry women, and they meant business. In the end, they'd nearly scared him to death with the half-crazed looks in their eyes and the way they stood up to him. He'd been eternally grateful when they had finally laid down their torches and left. No, he thought, the women of Limestone County would never cotton to a man marrying a whore, and a Mexican whore at that. He didn't really need the women's approval, he supposed, but it surely would have been nice to have a regular marriage. Since he was small, Newton had always believed that he would someday marry, and that he and his family would join the church and be a part of the community. The womenfolk would never accept Carmella as one of their own.

And the men. The thought caused Newton's stomach to churn. They would out-and-out make fun of him. He'd never have a peaceful day, that someone wouldn't make a comment or two. He thought back to a man he'd known in St. Louis. Blake Hargrove had married a retired sporting lady, and she had never been referred to as anything but "the whore that Hargrove married." Newton glanced at Carmella's young face. She surely didn't deserve such treatment, and he wasn't sure that he did, either.

They stayed there on the sandbar into the night. Newton fetched his blanket, and they lay under it. Carmella quickly fell asleep in his arms. Her full young body felt soothing and comfortable to him.

Newton was just about to nod, himself, when he heard a rider. He jumped up naked and began to move toward his guns, cursing himself for leaving his Winchester and pistol so far away. The rider spoke.

"That you, Newton?"

Newton was glad it was dark, so Clayton couldn't see his nakedness. He went back to where Carmella was still snoring lightly and put on his britches. Clayton rode in closer, but respectfully stayed atop his horse.

"How in the world did you find me?" Newton asked.

Clayton said, "I saw you leave and figured you'd come here. Is everything all right?"

Newton couldn't help reaching over to touch Carmella's thigh. He rubbed it gently. It embarrassed him that Clayton had found him there, but he wasn't angry. Clayton Crist was a competent sort—one you didn't fool easily. It suddenly occurred to Newton that he felt comfortable in Clayton's presence. If Newton should ever have a friend, he reckoned, it might be someone like Clayton Crist.

"Yeah, I'm all right. Carmella's fine, too," he said. "What brings you out here?"

Clayton said, "You know that old man, Keg Drayton? Somebody beat the hell out of him and dumped him in front of the office."

"Is Mister Drayton gonna be all right?" Newton asked.

"I think so, but he's an old man."

A chill went through Newton's body. Keg Drayton had come to the office several times in the last couple of weeks, complaining about Slab Kirkland and Alva DeKock. They'd been after him to buy his place, and Drayton didn't want to sell.

"It was them that done it," he said. "Kirkland and DeKock. They've bought up several ranches in the area. Nobody's ever really accused 'em of doin' anything illegal, except Mister Drayton." He left Carmella and stood up. He'd started to make a fire, but hadn't ever gotten it started. Suddenly, he felt cold. He went about lighting it.

"I should've listened to Mister Drayton," he went on. "He was a-feared of 'em. Tried to tell me." Newton grew irritable. "Why ain't you killed those fellers yet? Ain't you supposed to be a mankiller? Ain't that what we're payin' you for?"

"I was of the understanding that they had to start somethin', so it would be legal," Clayton said defensively. "They ain't started nothin' yet."

Newton knew his anger was misplaced. The news of what had happened to Keg Drayton—after he'd told Drayton time and time again that the man's fears were unfounded—tore at his insides. He couldn't stand the thought of facing him. Even with the mankiller at his side,

Newton was just plain afraid to face all that waited for him in town.

He fumbled with starting the fire, and his eyes rested on Carmella. If he'd had any sense at all, he'd have taken her and headed straight for St. Louis. He had a sister there, and he knew that Annalea would know just what to do.

Without pulling his eyes from Carmella, he said, "Does Judge Edmondson know about this?"

"He does. He told me to come and find you. Ain't no use in messin' with that fire. We gotta get back right away."

Newton nodded. He felt so foolish. He wished Clayton would just go away and leave him be. Then, he could disappear with Carmella. Back in St. Louis, folks were more tolerant of Mexicans, and nobody would know she was a whore.

Clayton didn't leave, though, and soon they were all headed back to town. Carmella had barely awakened when he helped her get atop the horse. She had fallen back into deep slumber. Newton could feel her heavy breathing against his back. Her chubby arms held him tightly.

When they reached Newton's office, a light was burning inside. Judge Edmondson's horse was tied out front. Newton felt slightly nauseous. Now, he knew he had made a mistake, taking Carmella. He glanced longingly down the street at Paterno's Canteen. It was dark and still as a statue.

Clayton sensed Newton's dilemma. He said, "Don't worry about Carmella. Everything will be all right. Here, let me give you a hand with her."

They'd no sooner got Carmella inside, when she slid down against the wall and went right back to sleep. Judge Edmondson and Keg Drayton eyed her curiously. Newton wanted to find a hole to crawl into. He wanted to scream and holler that she'd begged to go with him, that he'd only wanted to save her and get her away from Paterno's. Instead, he said nothing. He just dropped his eyes to the floor. Mercifully, neither the judge nor Keg Drayton pursued the matter.

"We've got problems, Sheriff," Judge Edmondson finally said. He pointed to Drayton's face. "It looks like Kirkland and DeKock made Keg an offer, and they wouldn't take 'no' for an answer." He walked to his desk and sat down. His eyes were bloodshot, and there was a tic in his left eye. "This was their doin'." He looked pityingly at Drayton, who sat in Newton's chair. His right eye was swollen shut. There was a big gash on his chin, compliments of Alva DeKock's boot. Drayton was having trouble breathing, where they had stomped and kicked his ribs.

Newton had a hard time keeping his eyes on Keg Drayton's face. Dried blood was caked on his snow-white hair. He looked so old and weak sitting there, Newton expected he might die right then and there. He found it a mystery how such an old man could take such a beating and stay alive. Newton stole a glance at Carmella. She'd begun to snore, lying there against the wall.

How could he have been so stupid, he thought? He had always been one to occasionally do something irrational, but never had he gone this far. He was sure to be ridiculed for the rest of his life. He struggled to pull his thoughts away from Carmella, and concentrate on being the sheriff.

He had never been a particularly brave man, but right at this moment, with Carmella sleeping on the floor and his own feelings so low, he had to scrape down deep in his inner being for any ounce of courage or decency that might be left.

All his years, Newton had been so scared of dying, it had affected his enjoyment of living. Now, at this very moment, it occurred to him that death might be the answer to all his problems. After all, if he got killed, maybe nobody would care anymore that he'd run off with one of Paterno's Mexican whores.

"Mister Drayton," he said, "I have to admit to you that I've been wrong." He looked at the Judge. "We were wrong, Chester. We were wrong to put up with this for so long. It's time we did something. I'm goin' after Kirkland and DeKock right now." He turned and headed toward the door.

Judge Edmondson spoke up in a loud voice. "Now, don't go off half-cocked and get yourself shot up! They'll kill you! You understand that, don't you?"

Newton nodded. "Yeah, Chester. They're killers. I understand that. But maybe if I'd done somethin' about it three years ago, then Mister Drayton wouldn't be sittin' here all beat-up, and maybe our cemetery wouldn't be so full.''

"Well, can't you at least wait until mornin'?" the judge asked. He pointed at Clayton. "And take him with you?"

Newton felt a trembling in his legs. His stomach fluttered. It was hard not to feel completely scared, through and through. He could hardly believe the fact that he'd gone this far, when not five minutes before, he would have bet anything on earth that he'd never set foot anywhere near Slab Kirkland and Alva DeKock.

Once again, his eyes fell on Carmella. He'd made a terrible mistake in being so hasty about running off with her. Was he doing it again?

Whether it was courage or foolishness that had moved him, Newton knew he was liable to lose his nerve if he waited any longer. Still, he was just as apt to stumble around and shoot himself in the dark if he didn't. Finally, he walked over and sat down.

"I guess we can wait 'til daylight," he said.

⋈ 36 ⋈

AT EIGHT o'clock the next morning, the Texas landscape was already bracing itself for a heavy dose of sun. Newton sat in his chair and watched it rise like a ripe melon in the sky. He felt tired and sleepy, and the decision he'd made in the dark of night just hours before seemed vague and far away.

He got up to splash some cold water on his face, careful not to make any noise. Judge Edmondson and Keg Drayton had gone home to sleep. Carmella was still lying up against the wall, snoring. On the other side of the room, Clayton was stretched out with his face buried under one arm. Newton looked down at his own blankets that lay unused on the floor. He wished he could've caught at least a couple hours' sleep, but he hadn't had a wink.

It had been a miserable few hours, spent mostly in his chair, thinking back over his life. Newton felt depressed. There'd been no high spots in his life, unless one counted his frequent trips to the whores' rooms. But that wasn't a prideful thing that made a man feel good about himself.

Newton wished he could have made a better sheriff, but he'd known all along that this job was too big for him. He should've gone to St. Louis, he thought, the first time he noticed that the judge was so afraid of Kirkland and DeKock. Like everything else he'd done in his stinking life, though, he'd hung on until it was too late.

Newton stood in the middle of the room and made his decision to run. There really weren't many details to consider, he realized. Outside of a couple of shirts and another pair of britches, he was wearing everything he owned in life. His hand reached into his pocket and pulled out its contents. There was a small knife and twenty-one dollars. It was all the money he had, but it would have to do.

His stomach growled, and Newton realized how hungry he was. Ellen Stanford would be coming any minute with breakfast. Maybe he should wait and eat first, he thought. But then, Carmella and Clayton would wake up. No, he had to go now and think about his empty stomach later.

Carefully, he tiptoed toward the door, holding his breath. He had just got it open, when a voice from behind stopped him in his tracks.

"What time is it?" Clayton said. He sat up and rubbed his hands through his hair, squinting up at Newton.

Newton had an urge to pee his britches. He'd been a bed-wetter as a boy, and he could still remember the mixture of shame and pleasure that crossed over him as he lay there half-asleep in the warm wetness, knowing what he was doing but unable to stop himself. He turned in the doorway and felt his bladder aching so bad, he almost let it go.

"It's a couple minutes past eight," he said sadly.

"Well, what's your plan? Wanta eat breakfast, then head out to Kirkland's place?"

Newton nodded. He wanted to pull himself on out through the door, but he couldn't. His legs felt heavy as he walked back inside the room. "That's my plan," he said.

After breakfast, they saddled their horses while Carmella stood in the doorway with her plate and ate the last of the food that Ellen Stanford had brought.

Clayton carefully checked his .44 and his Winchester rifle. Newton left his own .44 in its holster. He was sure he'd never be able to pull it out in time, anyway. His hands were already quivering. He kept imagining a picture of himself facing up to Kirkland and DeKock. He was reaching for his gun, but his hand was shaking so bad, he dropped it to the ground. Newton could see himself lying there on the ground, gunned down by Kirkland and DeKock.

Newton took the big .10 gauge shotgun down from the wall. Maybe, he thought, he could get his finger to pull its trigger fast enough. That was his only chance, he knew.

Both Kirkland and DeKock lived on what had once been Harry Tatum's place, three miles from town. Riding alongside Clayton, Newton suddenly started to pray. His mother had preached to him endlessly about being a religious person, but her words had never taken a very strong hold on Newton. Over the years, he'd thought about praying on occasion, especially after gambling or visiting a whore. His mother had preached hardest about the evils of both, and Newton figured that running with fallen women and gambling your money must carry more sin weight than anything else. Still, he'd never entered a card game or climbed into a whore's bed thinking about God. It was just as he'd start to enjoy himself when those disturbing thoughts would start. Often, he'd carry the thoughts with him for days afterward, and hell's fire would get hot. But eventually, he always went back. Newton had done a fine job of avoiding religion, and he'd pretty much accepted the fact that he was surely going to burn forever.

Now, as he rode those three miles to see Kirkland and DeKock, he desperately tried to recall every word that his mother had said on the subject. He prayed so hard, he began to mumble out loud. Once, Clayton looked over and asked him to repeat what he'd said, so Newton had to remind himself to do his praying more quietly.

As they neared the ranch house, he put a quick finish to his last request to his Maker. Alva DeKock was sitting in his underwear, leaned back in a chair, whittling. Newton noticed right away that he had his Colt strapped on over his long johns. He wondered if DeKock slept that way. That would be a hell of a way to live, he thought, always looking over your shoulder and sleeping with one eye open. Not to mention uncomfortable.

Newton and Clayton looked over the rest of the place. Down by the corral, Bert Blackman was shoeing a horse. Newton had always considered Bert harmless and never feared him much, but now he saw that Bert, too, had his pistol strapped on.

Newton altogether missed noticing Slab Kirkland, until Kirkland had walked up at an angle right behind him, along with Robert Cleary. Cleary was a local boy who came from a good home, but he'd hooked up with Kirkland and DeKock and was now earning himself a reputation for lawlessness.

"Well, well. What brings you boys out here so early?" Kirkland said.

Newton nearly dropped his shotgun as he swung around to face Kirkland. He tried to think of something challenging to say, but there was no strength of courage inside him. His heart pounded in his chest. He just knew that they could all see that he was weak with fear. He avoided meeting Slab Kirkland's eyes, but he noticed the relaxed smile on Kirkland's face as the man walked slowly between the two horses. Newton nearly cried out when Kirkland reached out and patted him on the leg.

On the porch, Alva DeKock kept whittling, but his eyes were stuck on Clayton. Clayton stared back harder. Neither man's gaze wavered.

Bert Blackman had left his horse and was walking toward them, tying his Colt to his leg as he came. Newton started to pray again. He'd been crazy to take this job, he thought, and he'd been crazy to come here.

"Well, Newton, you surely didn't ride all the way out here with that shotgun to ask for a cup of coffee, did ya?" Kirkland asked. He crossed his arms and his body rocked gently back and forth. His smile was gone, and he had his jaw set.

Newton glanced forlornly at Clayton, but Clayton was closely watching Alva DeKock and the others. He tried to swallow, but his throat was so dry, the swallow stuck.

"Mister Drayton—" he started, then stopped.

"What about Drayton?" Kirkland said shortly.

With one final plea to Jesus, Newton took in a shaky breath, then said, "That was wrong what you did to him. Real wrong."

"What *I* did? What did I do to Keg?"

"You beat and stomped Keg Drayton," Newton said.

"Now, just let me get this right," Kirkland said, grinning again. "You rode all the way out here to accuse me of hurting Keg Drayton? Why, I'm surprised at you, Newton!

You know that Keg's a drinker. Maybe he got drunk and fell off'n his horse. You ever think about that?''

Newton nodded slightly and gave a small shrug. "M-maybe. I don't know," he stammered. He was so flustered, he forgot that he hadn't come alone.

As he watched Kirkland, an anger had started rising up inside Clayton like he hadn't felt since the war. There was something about Kirkland and DeKock that reminded him of the arrogance of so many of the Federals. It took him back to those days on the battlefield, days when he'd been carried along by an anger that was deep and dangerous. It was a feeling that he couldn't put words to, but he felt it now. Death was near. When he spoke, his strong voice surprised Newton and Kirkland both.

"Looky here. Why don't we just forget the niceties?" Clayton said. "Newton, here, has come to arrest you boys. Your free days are over."

Newton jumped. He felt astonished by what Clayton had said. For a moment, he lost his fear and became a spectator to what was unfolding. He looked at Kirkland, then at Clayton, then back to Kirkland. He'd known a lot of mean men, and he'd seen more fights than his mind could remember, but without a doubt, Clayton Crist was of a different breed entirely. His words had sounded so deliberate and cold, they'd sent a chill running through Newton, like a cold gust of wind in the wintertime. Newton searched Slab Kirkland's face to see if he, too, had felt that coldness. He had no doubt that no one had ever spoken that way to Kirkland and lived to tell it. Kirkland's expression didn't change much, but Newton could see that he'd been caught off guard by Clayton's challenging words.

But Slab Kirkland didn't stay surprised for long. His face turned red, and his bottom lip began to quiver in anger. "Newton ain't gonna arrest nobody," he said. "Not here, anyway." He unfolded his arms and let them hang at his sides, letting his fingers tap against the holster that held the deadly Colt.

Alva DeKock had stopped whittling. He gave a push with his shoulders, intending to tilt the chair forward, but instead the back legs of the chair slid out, dumping DeKock

onto the seat of his britches. He yelped as he made a grab
to catch himself and managed to cut his hand on his knife.

Newton was already so jittery, the sudden movement by
DeKock sent him into a spasm. His big finger, already
poised on the front trigger of the .10 gauge, squeezed involuntarily. The shotgun exploded.

Robert Cleary began to wail. Most of his right foot had
been blown away by the .10 gauge. He hollered so loud,
Slab Kirkland got unnerved. He jumped about a foot off
the ground and, yelling like a man who's stepped on a
snake, he reached awkwardly for his Colt. Before he could
clear the gun from its holster, another shot rang out.

The .44 slug from Clayton's Colt struck Kirkland
squarely in the Adam's apple. He died with angry eyes,
still staring in disbelief at Newton and his smoking shotgun.

Clayton sent two more shots at Alva DeKock. One bullet
splintered the bottom of his chair, but the other struck
DeKock, shattering his pelvis. DeKock managed to find his
own gun with his bloody hand and got three wild shots off,
before Clayton ended his reign of terror with a heavy slug
through the top of his heart.

Bert Blackman was slow getting his pistol in his hand,
but he struck Newton once in the side and was aiming
again, when Clayton's last .44 cut him through the temple.
Blackman felt nothing. He stumbled backward, then tried
to walk forward a step before he went down.

Robert Cleary was rolling around on the porch with his
arms wrapped around his right knee. What was left of his
foot dangled in the air, dripping blood and flesh. Clayton
would have killed him, but his Colt was empty, and by the
time he pulled his Winchester from its scabbard, the driving
force that had come alive once again inside him had subsided.

Newton was inspecting the wound in his side. The bullet
had entered just below his bottom rib, and he'd never been
through such pain in his life. It felt like some big force was
blowing hot air inside him.

"Do you think I'm gonna die?" he asked Clayton.

Clayton really had no idea. The thread of life was mostly
a mystery to him. He'd seen men get shot to pieces at

Shiloh and Franklin and Perryville, and live to tell about it. On the other hand, there'd been men who looked like they'd barely been scratched in battle, but had keeled over dead while they were talking in mid-sentence.

As it happened, Newton did survive. He did much of his convalescing in the canteen. Vito Paterno hailed Newton like a conquering hero, expressing great relief at the news that Kirkland and DeKock were dead. He would miss taking their money, but having such new peace of mind was well worth the loss of income.

Each night, Newton enjoyed his newfound notoriety, regaling the men in the canteen with the story of how he and Clayton had ended the reign of terror. Before long, any lost business that Paterno might have suffered was made up for, as one by one the men who had stopped coming to his canteen two or three years earlier started returning.

The women baked pies for Newton and brought him their favorite dishes. Soon after, he and Carmella were married. The wedding was attended by almost everyone in the area, and not once did Newton hear anyone refer to Carmella as a whore.

For the first time in his life, Newton was enjoying himself. But sheriffing was no longer his calling. He wasn't really sure if he'd ever been meant to wear a badge. He knew he would never forget the gut-wrenching fear that he'd experienced that morning. Even though the others bragged about how brave he'd been, confronting the likes of Kirkland and DeKock and firing the shot that had ripped off Robert Cleary's foot, Newton knew the truth. To himself, he faced it head-on and acknowledged the fact that he was lucky for having fired an accidental shot in the right direction, and for having someone with him on that morning who was more than an equal to Kirkland and DeKock.

Newton was eternally grateful to Clayton. Clayton had saved his life and, in a miraculous way, turned his life around. Clayton was a quiet man and a peaceful drinker, but when coaxed, he never failed to tell of how Newton had taken the first shot and fought the men with a great show of bravery.

Newton no longer called Clayton a mankiller. Now, he

referred to Clayton as "the Gunny, the best I've ever seen." The other men in the canteen liked the nickname, and it wasn't long before the word spread. All throughout Limestone County, whenever anyone spoke about that eventful morning, Clayton Crist was referred to as "the Gunny."

As soon as he was able to travel, Newton turned in his badge to Judge Edmondson, and he and Carmella set off for St. Louis to live close to his sister.

For Clayton, there soon didn't appear to be anything to keep him in Limestone County anymore. He was offered Newton's old job, but he didn't want it. He'd grown stale here. He needed to scratch the old familiar itch.

On the day he got wind of a job in Brownsville, he turned his mare in that direction.

37

BEVERLY TOWNSEND had lost her husband to consumption. On the day of his funeral, she announced that, instead of moving back to Ohio where her family all lived, she was going to stay and run the Townsend farm by herself. The place lay between Ness City and Beelerville, and was a sizable piece of land, but Beverly Townsend had sizable ambitions.

It was on the way to Elmer and Maudie McNutt's house one day that Solon decided to stop by Beverly Townsend's place and ask to water his horse. They had never properly met each other, but Beverly knew enough about Solon Johnson to welcome him inside.

He stayed for nearly two hours, holed up in Beverly's kitchen, enjoying her stories. It was a refreshing experience for Solon. Being a voracious talker, himself, he had sometimes felt lonesome living with Clayton, who didn't have a whole lot to say. Beverly, though, had plenty of comments on everything, and even though she talked her share, she was a pretty decent listener, too. Before long, she was addressing the fact that Solon was still a bachelor. Solon didn't seem to mind the innuendo, and over the next few weeks, he'd started finding more and more excuses to visit Elmer and Maudie, with frequent stops at Beverly's farm. Sometimes, Clayton made the trip with him. He never said a word, but busied himself with making small repairs on Beverly's farm while she and Solon drank coffee and talked.

It was early spring. The winds and rain were at their peak, and Clayton was stuck inside with a bad cold. Solon was fretting about the house, worried. He had picked up some cloth at the mercantile in Ness City for Beverly a few days before, and he'd promised that he would take it to her.

"Why, you can't be goin' out in weather like this. Looks like a bad storm comin' in. Don't you think she'd understand?" Clayton said.

Solon shook his head. "I just couldn't live with myself if I didn't take that cloth to her," he said. He peered out at the dark sky. "Don't look that bad," he said weakly.

As the wind blew and the clouds grew even darker in the northern sky, Solon saddled up his horse, Doolittle, and set out. He'd barely gone a mile, when he started to regret his decision. The wind was chilly and cutting, and tiny drops of sleet starting coming down, stinging his face. Halfway to Beverly's, he could hear the ground crunching under Doolittle's feet.

By the time he reached Beverly's farm, a spring blizzard was in full swing. Solon was so cold, his feet and hands were numb. The sleet had blistered his face.

At the door, Beverly admonished him for being so foolish to get out in such weather, but Solon could see that the admonishment was only on the surface. Her eyes sparkled as she pulled him inside.

"Get in here and sit next to the fire," she said. "I'm telling you, if I live to be a hundred, I'll never understand men. You're all like children, you know."

Solon didn't like it when she scolded him, but it still didn't lessen the fact that he was drawn to her. He'd argued with himself about it, but he couldn't help the fact that Beverly could pretty much say what she liked. He enjoyed her company regardless. He moved close to the fireplace and reached for the heat, trying to ignore her carrying on about men.

Beverly's demeanor soon changed, anyway. She pulled off his wet coat and boots and fussed over him, rubbing his hands and feet until there was feeling in them again, and pouring him cups of hot coffee. As she sat next to him, he noticed the concern on her face, her cheeks aglow from the light of fire.

By midafternoon, The sleet had turned to hard snow, and the wind was already forming large drifts.

"I guess you're here for the night," Beverly said, her voice pleased. "I've got beans cooking in that pot on the stove, and I'll make us a big pan of corn bread." She stared at him a moment. "You could stand a woman's cooking, you know. I'll swear, I never understood you living with Clayton. You're both such handsome men." She got down on her knees in front of Solon. "Here, let me get some more of those wet clothes off."

Solon wanted to protest, but Beverly didn't leave much room for protesting in life. It was times like these that Solon sometimes thought she might have driven her husband to an early grave. But then, she would walk off in a female way, or make a certain movement, and Solon would forget about such thoughts. She was a handsome woman; there was no denying it. Solon was pleased that Clayton didn't seem to have any inclination toward her. He wasn't a dandy with the ladies like Clayton, and it was true that most of the women he'd lain with were whores, but he was comfortable enough with a female to make a forward move if he wanted. It was strange, he thought, that he'd never approached Beverly. He'd often sat and thought about her, holding her and undressing her in his mind, but he'd never gone beyond those thoughts.

The fact was, Solon was afraid of making any overtures with Beverly. He was afraid he might not walk away a single man. There were those women who posed a clear danger in that regard, and Beverly was one of them.

Right now, the thought of spending the night in her home was having a terrible effect on his thinking. A part of him was excited and full of hope, but a bigger part of him was scared silly. Solon was still thinking on both sides of things, when Beverly put the food on the table.

"Come to the table and eat, Solon. You could use some warm food to go with all that coffee." She smiled.

Solon hadn't really felt all that hungry, but once he started on Beverly's beans, he felt sure the pot didn't hold enough to ease his hunger. They were surely the tastiest beans he had ever eaten. They were spicy, with delicious pieces of pork. He wondered where she'd gotten the meat. He hadn't seen any hogs around the place. He made a note in his mind to bring her a pig the next time he came. That way, she might feel obligated to cook him beans again.

After three big bowls, Solon's hunger was completely gone. He'd eaten to the point of feeling miserable. He leaned back from the table and looked down at his belly. It stuck out, hard as a rock.

"Those were the best beans, I ever et," he said sincerely.

Beverly smiled tenderly and said, "Well I'm glad you liked 'em. I cook like this all the time, you know. It saddens me not to have a man to cook for." Her smile was replaced by a more serious look. "Who does your cooking?"

Solon hated to think about such things at this very moment, with his belly so full, even though he did plan to have another big bowl later in the evening.

"I do, mostly," he said. He thought about the tasty pork in Beverly's beans, and suddenly felt sorry for himself and Clayton for having to eat his cooking. He'd never been able to get meat to taste right. His steaks were always tough, and his attempts at beans were mostly disastrous. He could never get the beans cooked tender, and they were mostly tasteless. Solon was afraid of salt. There was a fine line when dealing with salt. If he put a little in, he couldn't taste it. When he got more generous, he seemed to ruin the taste.

"Why don't we just get married," Beverly said, all of a sudden. "This farm's too much for me to handle by myself. Besides that, it gets lonely out here."

Solon's thoughts crashed to a halt and he stared at her. *Maybe she's kidding*, he thought. Beverly surely had a healthy teasing side to her. But, as he looked into her eyes, he knew this was not a funning matter.

He said earnestly, "Oh, I wouldn't know nothin' about bein' a good husband, Beverly. I guess I've been a bachelor too long. I'm real set in my ways. We'd more'n likely be buttin' heads most of the time."

"You aren't the only man set in his ways," Beverly said. "I reckon I could learn to live with you." She laughed. "I never met a man in my life that wasn't more trouble than he was worth. But''—she paused, looking away reflectively—''that's just one of the evils of life.'' She turned her attention back to Solon and smiled at him. ''Why haven't you ever tried to get forward with me?''

Solon was surprised at her question. ''Why, I'd never be disrespectful to you, Beverly.''

''No one would ever accuse you of that, Solon. But, don't you find me attractive?''

Solon had never thought Beverly was pretty, exactly, but she was a handsome woman who carried herself with a graceful air. The more he'd come to know her, though, the more attractive she'd become to him. And she'd entered his thoughts more and more lately. Now, as he sat there across from her, she did seem pretty to him. He didn't want to answer her question, but he knew he had to, for Beverly was not the type that would let something lie. He tried to study her delicate features, but her sparkling eyes kept drawing him in. He felt intimidated.

''I guess I do,'' he said finally.

Beverly took his hand and placed it between hers. ''I swear! If you men don't beat everything! My late husband, Herb, was a slow starter, just like you. I literally had to walk him down the aisle.'' She looked off again in thought. ''I wondered about our wedding night, while we were standing there in that church back in Ohio.'' She smiled again and lifted her eyes. ''But, everything turned out just fine! She leaned forward and kissed his hand, then gently squeezed his fingers. ''I'll bet you're a lot like Herb.''

Solon pulled his hand away. ''I can't believe you'd say somethin' like that!'' He shuddered. ''I feel funny, anyway, sittin' here in the late Mister Townsend's home.'' Suddenly he shifted his weight and started to stand up. ''I'll bet this was his chair.''

''Don't be silly,'' Beverly said pushing him back down, ''chairs don't belong to anybody!'' She frowned at him. ''Maybe I was wrong about you. You and Clayton aren't . . . funny, are you?''

''What do you mean?''

"Well, there's something unnatural about two grown men living with each other."

It came to Solon at once what Beverly meant. His face grew red as anger welled up inside him. "Are you crazy? I can't believe you even think such a thing as that!" he said.

"Now, don't get your dander up," Beverly said. "It's just that Clayton Crist is the handsomest man in all these parts, and you aren't bad, yourself. It's unusual for two such nice-looking men to be living together, alone. That's all."

Solon wondered if other people had pondered the same thing. His anger turned to self-defense, and he felt a tinge of embarrassment. "There ain't nothin' funny about it, at all. It's a business arrangement. Why, Clayton's been with more women than you could shake a stick at, I reckon."

"Is that so?" Beverly offered. "What about you, Solon?"

Solon thought he would just as soon go back to talking about beans and such, but he knew that was a futile wish. "I don't know that it's anybody's business, but I'm a healthy man," he said.

"Why haven't you ever had yourself a wife then?" Beverly asked. Her tender smile had returned, and Solon felt nervous again.

"Like I told you," he said, almost in desperation, "I'm set in my ways. I wouldn't want some female to come along and change me."

Mercifully, Beverly let the subject drop, but she continued to smile at him.

That evening, Solon had another big bowl of beans. He scraped up the last bite and wiped the bowl with a piece of corn bread, then sat back with his coffee.

"That surely is the tastiest pork I've ever eaten," he said.

Beverly said, "It is? Why that's pretty good, considering that it's not pork at all. It's 'possum. Dang thing was hanging around the barn a couple of nights ago, and now he's in my bean pot."

Solon was surprised. He had eaten 'possum before, but he'd never cared much for it. Back in Kentucky, and in

Indiana and Missouri, he'd eaten his share of groundhogs and found them to be pleasing, but 'possums tended to be covered with fat and carried a greasy taste.

They turned in early, Beverly leading him into the extra bedroom and smiling at him as she closed the door. Solon was just drifting off to sleep, when he felt the bed jiggle. At first, he thought he was dreaming, but then the bed moved again, and just as he opened his eyes, Beverly crawled under the covers with him. She wrapped them both up like a mother wrapping a baby to keep it warm. She slid her legs over his. "I'm cold," she said in a low voice.

Solon turned onto his back, and Beverly moved with him, draping herself over half his body. He started to protest, but he didn't.

Beverly was naked, and she quickly started to tug at his underwear. Soon, Solon was in the same state of undress. She nuzzled her head against the crook of his neck and whispered again how cold she was and how warm he felt next to her. Her cold feet rubbed against his.

Solon's manhood came to life. She'd gone too far to stop now, he decided, and he turned toward her.

Beverly moaned when Solon's hand caressed her backside. Her bottom felt cold.

"That feels good," she said. "I get so cold at night, since Herb's been gone."

Silently, Solon pulled her toward him, then tried to push her onto her back.

"Don't," she said. "Not yet, anyway. I want to get warm first. You feel so good lying here next to me."

Solon eased back onto his back and let her wrap herself around his body. He was getting warmer, and it didn't help that she was so insistent. He tried thinking about anything that would pop into his mind, wanting to slow down the throbbing sensation. He thought back to his school days, and when that didn't work, he thought about the trail drives he'd made from Texas to Kansas. The more he thought, the closer he came to losing control. He went to biting on his lip, concentrating on the pain, and that seemed to help a bit.

Finally, Beverly must have gotten warm enough. She

crawled quickly on top of him and began to move. Solon had to hold on, as the bed squeaked and banged against the wall. He quit biting his lip and thinking about trail drives and gave in to the most pleasurable feeling he'd ever known. His release came quickly, but Beverly wasn't finished. If anything, her motions grew faster. The bed started scooting out from the wall, and Solon could hear the legs scraping across the floor. He let go of his grip of her hips and reached up to grab hold of the brass headboard. Down below, he shrank, but Beverly continued. Solon was sure she was going to injure him. She grabbed his hair and pulled hard. Just as he started to cry out, her movements slowed, then stopped, and she fell over him.

They went to sleep that way.

38

CLAYTON AND Jolene were standing in the middle of a dark street. Clayton took hold of her hand, and together they began to run toward a hotel that sat less than a block away. The wind swirled and rustled around them, and the harder they pushed against it, the farther away the hotel became.

Then, Clayton found himself inside the hotel lobby. From the dim light of a single lamp, he saw a figure walking toward him, raising an arm. As he watched, helpless, the glint of steel flashed, and the knife's blade came at him in a downward arc. It sliced through the air and neatly entered his back, but he felt no pain. He felt nothing.

A lightning bolt sent an icy blue light across the room, followed by huge thunderclaps that shook the earth around him. Lightning struck again, only this time, it was there in the room with him. Clayton looked down at his feet and saw drops of bright red splashing onto the floor. He reached back and felt his gaping wound. His hand came away cupped with blood.

In a panic, Clayton called out Jolene's name and turned to grab her, to protect her from the knife, but she was gone. Just then, another flash of lightning lit up the room, and he saw Abigail Beecher standing at the foot of a long staircase.

Abigail was naked, smiling, and motioning for him to come to her. "The water's fine," her lips moved.

Clayton stumbled forward, reaching out for Abigail's hand, straining for the warmth of her pretty face and naked body, but he couldn't reach her. She was still calling out for him, when the room went black and quiet.

The silence was broken by footsteps, faint at first, then growing louder and louder. Shackled by fear, Clayton stood rooted in one spot, unable to move, his eyes wide and searching the darkness. The footsteps came nearer, until he could sense that they were all around him, boots pounding on the hardwood lobby floor. When the lightning again cracked, the room came afire with a light so bright, Clayton had to shield his eyes.

Now, he was standing in a room of doors. In each door there stood a man holding a knife. Goose bumps covered Clayton's entire body as he recognized some of the men. They were men from his past, he realized. They were men he had killed.

All at once, they stepped from the doorways. The terrible light bounced off the knives they held poised in their hands. They walked slowly toward him, in an ever-tightening circle. Clayton tried to move, but he was frozen in place. Desperate, he closed his eyes and waited.

All around he felt their presence, their bodies moving in close. He could hear their ragged breathing.

A pair of arms encircled him and held him tight. Clayton felt himself being pulled and tugged. His arms were pinned to his sides. He gave in and let himself be carried off.

But they became gentle arms, soft and familiar. Clayton sank gratefully into them, and then his nostrils were filled with the scent of Tracy O'Brien's hair, as it tickled against his face.

"We have to hurry," Tracy said. Together, they moved blindly to the staircase and ran up the steps. At the top, Tracy pointed to a door. "Solon went in there," she said and pushed him inside.

A man stood over a table. Clayton recognized the surgeon from Chickamauga. He motioned for Clayton to gather up the bandages. When Clayton blinked, the room became bright with light. Everywhere, bloodstained cloths had been scattered over the floor and furniture. Clayton didn't want to touch them.

Smiling, the surgeon handed him a clean bandage that

was white as snow. Clayton took it gratefully. He sat down
and put the cloth to his face.

A horrible odor assaulted his nostrils. Clayton knew this
smell. It was the smell of death and rotted flesh. He pulled
the cloth away from his face, and before his eyes, a trail
of dark red began to soak through it. The blood gushed
forth, running over his hands and down his arms.

He dropped the cloth and ran from the room, frantically
trying to wipe the sticky blood onto his clothes. At the top
of the stairs, he stopped and looked down to see Tracy
sitting there on the lobby floor, holding Solon's head in her
lap. There wasn't a single part of him that hadn't been
slashed. Solon's face wore a smile, as if he had given in to
death and already crossed over that river.

The lightning and thunder rocked the earth again and
completely devoured everything. Clayton shut his eyes and
waited for it to subside.

Then he was back in the room of doors. He was standing
in the middle, and the men marked by death were with him.

They formed a ring around him, grins stuck on their de-
cayed faces in some sort of macabre pleasure. At once, as
if on cue, they all began to walk toward him, but this time,
the gleaming metal of their knives was already dripping
with someone's blood.

Clayton wanted to run, but a hand grabbed hold of his
leg. He looked down and saw a woman wearing a long
white gown. Her hair was so pure a white, it nearly blinded
him with its pearly glow. It ran all the way down to the
middle of her back. She was clasping his ankle and making
a low moaning sound as the men drew nearer to them both.
Just before the room went black, the woman looked up at
Clayton. It was his mother, and her face was a thousand
years old.

Clayton awoke. It was still dark. He raised up and looked
all around, taking several seconds to realize where he was.
The nightmares had always bothered him, but this was the
worst he had ever experienced. He was scared half to death.

He lay back down and pulled the blanket as tightly
around him as he could. He shivered and prayed for the
morning light to come and chase away his fears. Time

wasn't in a hurry, though, and neither was his memory willing to forget the nightmare. Clayton lay there and cursed Solon for being gone.

As Clayton tried to calm himself, he pondered the fact that he was getting older. Parts of his body would ache for days. It seemed like he would wake up one morning hurting in his ribs. That pain might last for a week, then go away and move to a knee, then to his neck, and so on. Now, as he lay on his porch, thinking about the nightmare and the fact that he was getting older, his eyeballs felt like a wind had blown sand into them. He needed more sleep. On the rare nights that he didn't have nightmares, he could manage to sleep into the morning, but he'd still get up so stiff and sore, he was sure there was something seriously wrong with him. It often took most of the day before he felt like himself again.

Along with the nightmares and physical complaints, Clayton had to admit that he was lonely—more lonely than ever before. In the past, he'd enjoyed his solitude and privacy, but nowadays, it seemed like a part of him was walled off and sealed away to rot and die. The feeling had gotten worse since the day of the snowstorm, when Solon had announced he was going to visit Elmer and Maudie and had stopped off at Beverly Townsend's place. That trip had stretched into four days, and ever since that first visit two months ago, Solon had been away more than he was at home. Over the years, there had been spells when Clayton hadn't seen Solon for a year or two. He'd never missed him that much.

But all that had changed. Some days, Clayton wondered if the loneliness wasn't going to just eat him up. Maybe it was something Martin Frusher had said. Frusher had told Clayton that the gossip was out that Solon was courting the Widow Townsend pretty heavily. Speculation had it that a wedding might be near. Whatever the reason, Clayton knew he felt miserable.

The north wind was dependable and kept things cool on the Kansas prairie. Even with the discomfort, Clayton had started sleeping on the porch. With Solon gone, the inside of the house made him feel boxed in and trapped. Clayton had slept out under the stars enough that he didn't really miss the softness of the bed. What he did miss was having someone else around.

Clayton studied the nightmare some more. It pained him that all he had to show for his existence on this earth was the killing of men. Every time he closed his eyes, it seemed like death appeared. His mind kept going back to the faces of the men with the knives. Then, even though he had never met them, he could imagine the faces of their families twisted with grief. He wished he could take it all back. He would give anything if he had never been a part of death. Often, he wished he had died during the war.

He had never understood what made him different from other men. He had never understood why they died and he lived. He recalled the remarks his mother had made about how he had a special purpose in life. She had told him that no one knew what God had in mind. Surely, though, a merciful God would not give a man a skill at taking others' lives! Clayton guessed he had asked himself the question "why?" at least a million times.

Clayton was talking to God and praying for answers, when he dozed back off to a restful, dreamless sleep. It was daylight when he awoke.

He scooted up and leaned against the house. His fear was gone. He looked off and tried to study the nightmare he'd had. This dream seemed more important than the others. Maybe God had sent it to him with a puzzle attached, so he could learn something from it.

Try as he might, though, he couldn't divine any great wisdom from the experience. As the morning Kansas sun lifted higher over the horizon, the dream began to break apart and disappear from his mind's eye.

Clayton rubbed his hands on the exposed parts of his body. His flesh felt as cold as a dead man's. He pondered that thought. There had been death everywhere he'd been in life, throughout the war and after. He thought back on his time spent in Limestone County, Texas. He could've been happy there, he thought, living and ranching with Solon on Dudley Bickerstaff's place. He wished that Dudley Bickerstaff were still alive.

Pangs of guilt washed over Clayton. There he sat in Ness County, Kansas, alive and feeling sorry for himself, while such a good man as Dudley Bickerstaff had been called before his time to meet the Maker.

Clayton's memory lingered a little while longer on Limestone County. He didn't care to relive any bad occurrences, but his musings settled briefly on Slab Kirkland and Alva DeKock. Then he wondered about Newton and Carmella. He hoped they were still happily together in St. Louis.

Brownsville. Even the name gave Clayton a sick feeling in his stomach. Clayton had always felt that he might have somehow overcome the condition that the war had left him in. He might even have lived through the killings of Kirkland and DeKock and become a normal, hardworking citizen with a nice piece of land, a wife, and children and a respectable place in the community. Maybe he could have done all that, if it hadn't been for Brownsville.

It was there that he had first hired out his gun. He'd arrived at the town hopeful of starting a new life, but the word about him had already spread. From the very first day, that was all anybody had ever wanted from him.

Clayton yearned for a cup of coffee, but he was too miserable and stiff to get up and make it. The coldness reminded him of Colorado. He and Solon had almost settled there. The summers had been cool and pleasant. It was a beautiful, peaceful place, and, for a short while, Clayton had thought he would be free to find another means of support. But word soon followed. In fact, it was there in Colorado that a writer from Philadelphia had begun a series of stories about the West. One which was titled "The Gunny" soon appeared in newspapers all across the area. After that, if there was ever going to be any peace in Clayton's life, it wasn't going to occur in Colorado.

Besides the notoriety, as pleasant and enjoyable as the Colorado summers had been, the winters had been bitterly cold. Eventually, both Clayton and Solon had decided that Colorado was too frigid for their taste, and they headed back to the warmer climes.

A movement in the distance broke into Clayton's thoughts. He could see a rider approaching. He wondered who was coming out this way so early in the morning, then he recognized who it was.

Solon's face was long as he tied Doolittle to the post. "You sleepin' on the porch again?" he asked.

Clayton paid no attention to the inquiry. "It's awful early in the morning for you to be ridin' up. Where've you been?"

Solon knew that Clayton was aware that he was staying at Beverly Townsend's, but this was the first time he openly acknowledged it. "Been to Beverly's," he said.

"My Lord, that's a good fifteen, sixteen miles from here! You must've left in the middle of the night," Clayton commented.

"I don't reckon you got any coffee made," Solon said as he walked past Clayton and went into the house. He didn't come back out until the coffee was done. Clayton had gotten up and relieved himself and fed the stock. Still cold and miserable, he was grateful for the cup that Solon handed him.

Back on the porch, they sat together and drank their coffee in silence. Solon refilled their cups.

Clayton yawned and stretched. His body was still tired. He tried hard to make a better effort at being more talkative. "You never did say why you came back here so early in the mornin'."

Solon blew on his hot coffee. "Beverly wants to get married," he said bluntly. He took a sip. "Cussed women. They come along and think they gotta change a man's life."

Clayton felt envious and not a bit sorry for him. "I guess there's worse things that could happen to a man," he said simply. Again, the nightmare entered his thoughts, and he remembered waking up cold and alone. He would be more than grateful to have a woman to wake up with, he thought.

"Maybe so," Solon said. He took several leisurely sips of the coffee, as his mind thoughtfully considered the recent events of his life. "Know what she told me last night? She said I've gotta make an honest woman out of her, or else quit comin' around." His face wrinkled. "That really makes me mad. So once she was good and asleep, I left."

He looked unhappily at Clayton. "But now I ain't so sure. All the way back here, I kept thinkin' about Matthew Albright."

"What in the world were you thinkin' about Albright for?" Clayton asked, unable to see the connection.

"Well, he courted the Widow McCorvey for damn near two years. She finally gave up waitin' on Matthew and married Basil Woods." Solon shook his head sadly. "Ol' Matthew was never the same after that. Finally one day, he sat down at the foot of an oak tree and shot his brains out."

Clayton frowned. "He did? I thought he got robbed and shot. I heard tell he had Rollie Cranepool's payroll with him when he got killed."

"Nope. He did it himself. I worked with Matthew for almost a year down near San Angelo. All he could talk about was how Mary McCorvey had thrown him aside for Basil Woods. I'm tellin' ya, it tore Matt up somethin' awful." Solon nodded. "I guarantee he killed himself. Besides that, they never did ever look for anybody that might of robbed him and killed him. He shot himself, all right."

"Well, whether he did or he didn't, what's that got to do with you?" Clayton leaned forward and squinted his eyes. "You wouldn't ever kill yourself, would ya?"

Solon gave Clayton a disgusted look. "Hell no! Where'd you get such a fool idea?" He shook his head back and forth. "That's about the craziest thing I ever heard you say."

Clayton smiled. "I was just funnin', but I still don't see the connection."

"Well, the connection is that Mary drove poor Matthew crazy. I never thought I would say this," Solon went on, "but I've gotten kinda used to Beverly—more so than with any female I've been around." He paused a moment and looked ashamed. "Do ya think it would be foolish for me to marry her?"

"No, Solon, I don't think it would be foolish at all."

"I sure wish I felt that way," Solon said earnestly. "Clayton, it's about to eat me alive! I guess the joke's on me. All the times I've spent makin' fun of other men, and now I'm about to do the same fool thing." He looked quizzically at Clayton. "Do you ever get to thinkin' we're just plain old? I think about that a lot. Maybe I'm gettin' old and crazy."

Neither man spoke for a long time. Clayton's thoughts returned to his nightmare. He had a sudden longing to see his mother. He'd give anything if she was still alive. It made him angry that he hadn't gone back home more. Life had gotten away from him. It seemed like the months and years were nothing more than a blur in his memory. It was an odd thing, he thought. Lately, he'd grown more and more forgetful about daily things. He would plan to do some small job, then forget all about it in the space of an afternoon. On the long-term events, though, his memory was as fresh as if they had occurred the day before. Rarely a day went by that something from the war didn't cross his mind, and he thought often about his mother. The older he got, the more he missed her. It filled him with guilt to think that he hadn't been a better son. He wished he could go back and make amends, but that was only a futile dream.

Clayton studied Solon and wondered if he had similar thoughts. Life was slowly running out on him, too, and even though he enjoyed Solon's company, he surely didn't want to see his friend grow old and die all alone. He couldn't allow himself to be selfish, even though loneliness was eating away at him. He needed to let Solon know that it was all right by him for Solon to get married, even if it wasn't.

"Well," Clayton said, "I think you oughta marry Beverly. Settle down with her. That's my opinion, and I suspect it's what you're wantin' to hear."

Solon gave him a half grin. "You don't think I'm crazy?"

"No, you're not crazy. You might be if you let somethin' like her get away from ya. Look at us, Solon. What do we have to show for bein' alive?"

Solon thought it was queer, hearing Clayton talk that way. It had never been Clayton's nature to be so philosophical. Maybe he was just feeling sorry and didn't want to hurt Solon's feelings. "Well, I wouldn't quite agree with that," Solon said. "We got a nice house here, and some

stock. In a couple more years, I think we'll be sittin'
pretty."

"No," Clayton interrupted. "What we got is a house
with no furniture, except for a couple of beds and a cookstove. Hell, our table ain't nothin' but a whiskey barrel with
two slabs of wood on top! I tell you, the world's passin'
us by, Solon. Ain't ya thought about that?"

"Well, I reckon it's always suited me," Solon said, "and
I thought it suited you, too."

"Looky here," Clayton said. "I ain't complainin', but
there's got to be more to life than this. I ain't speakin' for
you, but for me, I ain't done much more than exist in life.
It just ain't normal."

Solon was surprised. In all the years he had known Clayton, he had never heard him talk this way. He had been the
one who had complained about the complexities of life.
Maybe Clayton had decided he didn't want him around any
more. It would be like Clayton to not want to hurt his
feelings.

"Sounds like you're tryin' to get rid of me," Solon said,
somewhat dejectedly.

Clayton shook his head. "That ain't it. That ain't it at
all. It's just the plain truth of the matter." He got up and
walked to the edge of the porch. Staring out at the vast
Kansas prairie, he went on. "Maybe I've been thinkin' too
much lately. Being around real people, here in Ness
County, makes a body do that, I suppose." He turned
around. "Solon, I'll tell you exactly what I think. If it were
me, I'd marry Beverly. I'd help her with her crops. She's
got a nice place. You could run several head of beeves, and
you know what? On Saturdays, I'd take her into town to
see folks and go shopping, and it wouldn't hurt to visit a
church on Sundays. I'd settle down and grow old with her.
Yes sir, that's what I would do."

Solon could hardly get over his shock. It wasn't Clayton's words so much, nor the meaning of what he'd said.
It was the fact that Clayton had said them. It gave him a
lot to think about.

He stayed there on the porch all morning and most of
the afternoon, dozing on and off. He didn't mention Bev-

erly again that day or the next, but his thoughts were still on her and the things that Clayton had said. Over and over, he tried to examine the situation. Part of him did want to marry her, of that he was sure. She was the finest cook he'd ever encountered, and she wasn't stingy with her frolicking. He even admired the fact that she liked to sit and drink with him. Beverly didn't tolerate daytime drinking, not even a little nip. In the evenings, though, when the table was cleared and the dishes were put away, she would take out the bottle and match him, drink for drink. The conversation never seemed to run out, and Solon liked that. He also liked the way she made him laugh.

In the end, he finally decided that, whether it was love or convenience, it really didn't matter. Beverly Townsend was the best thing that had ever happened to him.

39

SOLON KNEW what lay in his heart, but he couldn't quite get up the nerve he needed to act on it. He didn't bring up Beverly's name for days. In fact, he refused to talk about anything at all. He walked around with his head down, tending to his chores halfheartedly. One day, he and Clayton were splitting logs, and Solon nearly had a bad accident. The ax caught his leg, tearing through his britches and slicing through the skin. The wound was minor, but the accident unnerved Clayton.

That was when Clayton finally decided to quit minding his own business. "Go and see Beverly," he told Solon.

That seemed to open the gate of conversation. Solon turned to Clayton with the look of a man drowning in misery. He started to talk and carried on for hours, recounting Beverly's ultimatum about their getting married.

"I just ain't sure I wanta get married for everlastin'," he worried. "I like bein' single too much."

"Looks to me like bein' single is makin' you miserable," Clayton commented.

Solon nodded unhappily. "I just don't know what to do," he mumbled.

"Why don't you go see her?" Clayton suggested. "Talk to Beverly and see how you feel then."

The next day, Solon was up early. He saddled up Doolittle and took off just after breakfast. He didn't return until long past sundown. The next day, he went back. And the next. Soon, he was back to spending four out of five days at Beverly's. He seemed happy again, but something was clearly troubling him. He was his usual talkative self, but he didn't have much to say where Beverly and marriage were concerned.

Clayton refused to pry. For him, life had become dry and meaningless. Nothing differentiated one day from the next, and the time passed slowly.

He'd been a failure at life, and he knew it. Chores were now routine, to be done over and over again with no noticeable end in sight. He was totally alone, not happy, but not feeling enough to be sad, either. Eventually, he stopped shaving. His appetite went away, and the potbelly he'd acquired began to shrink. One day, he glanced into the mirror, and was stunned to see the sprigs of white scattered amongst his beard. Then he noticed the graying at his temples. He stood there, confused. Had time just totally gotten away from him? And where was Solon? How long had he been away this time? Was it a month? Weeks? Or only a few days? He really couldn't remember. He felt afraid.

The greatest fear in his life had always been growing old all alone. His eyes grew red and a lump formed in his throat. It was happening, right before his eyes. Looking closer into the mirror, he studied his features. He was still a decent-looking sort, underneath all the stubble. His body was toned and muscular from hard work. It was the vacant look in his eyes that bothered him the most.

Quickly, Clayton dressed and saddled up his horse. He headed into Ness City with no purpose, other than that he wanted to be in civilization. Never one to idle the time away, he nevertheless found himself walking to the barbershop. He got himself a shave and a haircut, then stayed around to talk to the men who congregated there. He found himself enjoying their company, listening to their stories and speculation about upcoming crops and elections. He learned that there was a new schoolteacher in town. Ollie Knowles, the barber, was an amiable sort and a knowledgeable speaker on many subjects. Clayton felt accepted by Ollie and the others.

In return, Ollie was excited to have such a famous man sitting in his chair. He couldn't help mentioning several times what a pleasure it was to have "the Gunny" right there, in his shop. Before, Clayton had always bristled when anyone mentioned the name or referred to his past. Now, he only smiled at Ollie.

When Clayton finally left Ollie Knowles's barbershop, he stopped by the bakery and bought some bread. Joshua Milburn, the owner of the bakery, pushed Clayton's money back to him.

"What's this?" Clayton said warily.

Joshua Milburn smiled. "You're a new customer. First loaf of bread is on me. I hope you'll be comin' back." He gave Clayton a toothy grin. "You'd be Clayton Crist, wouldn't ya? Well, welcome to Ness City. I know you've lived here for a spell." His voice dropped. "Off and on, anyway. But I hear you're gonna stay this time. Heard you built a house. That's just fine."

Clayton shook Joshua Milburn's hand, thanked him, then took his loaf of bread and went outside. He looked up and down Kansas Avenue. Suddenly, he felt a strong desire to be a part of this town and its people.

He shopped around for a while and bought a few items, and when there was nothing else to do in town, he rode back home. He felt a little bit alive again, and much less lonely.

That evening, after supper, Clayton went to his room and pulled a trunk out of the corner. It had been his mother's trunk. He hadn't opened it in years, but had used it to sit on. Inside, he felt for a small cloth bundle and untied it. There, inside, were his life's memories. He stared down at his daddy's pocket watch, and an old tintype of his mother. He rubbed his fingers lightly over both, then picked up the Testament.

The minié ball was still buried among its pages. Clayton started when a big, wet tear splashed on the Testament. He picked up the book and rubbed it up against his shirt to wipe away the water, then tucked it into his shirt pocket. Right now, he needed his faith. He needed to touch the Testament, feel it close by.

He picked up the .44 Colt that Dudley Bickerstaff had given to him years ago. He didn't know why he'd kept it.

It was tainted with the blood of so many others. He'd carried it until the day he'd bought the .45 that now hung on a nail on the wall—the gun he'd had customized for killing. Clayton could almost see all the faces of the men that he'd faced behind the .45's short barrel.

Two mornings later, Clayton was up early, feeding the hogs, when he looked up and saw a buggy coming his way. He watched it hopefully. Maybe it was someone he'd talked to in town the other day.

It was two women. What in the world would they be doing riding out to his place? Absently, Clayton touched the Testament. They must be from the church down the road, he thought. Sometimes, folks from the church would stop and invite him and Solon to come worship with them. They had never accepted the offer, but this time, Clayton thought he might.

The buggy pulled up in front of the house, and Clayton walked over to meet the women. They were both wearing hats, and their faces were covered in netting to protect them from the dust of travel.

It wasn't until Clayton had reached the wagon, and the woman turned to him, that he felt a tremendous shock of recognition.

Tracy O'Brien smiled down at him as his mouth opened. He felt so guilty, he didn't know what to say. He had promised to go back for her, but he hadn't. He hadn't even visited or written. Several times he'd considered inviting her to come, but that had also gone undone. Still, all throughout the lonely days and horrible nights, he had thought of her. His legs felt weak as he stared at her, speechless.

"You've lost weight, Clayton," Tracy said softly.

A big knot had formed in Clayton's throat, almost choking him. He reached up and took her hand to help her down. She put her hands on his shoulders and left them there, staring up into his eyes. "Aren't you gonna say anything?" she asked, her smile faltering.

"Tracy—" he began, but his eyes grew moist and he had to stop.

She turned to the other woman. "This here's Wanda Brackhage," she said.

Clayton glanced up at the woman who still sat in the carriage. He mumbled, "Nice to meet you."

Tracy leaned close to him, as if to kiss him on the cheek. "Wanda Brackhage," she whispered, "as in Big Ears Wanda." She wore a delicious smile when she pulled back to see Clayton's reaction.

Wanda climbed down from the carriage and reached behind the seat to gently lift out a small bundle. She brought it to Clayton and Tracy.

It was a basket with a white blanket inside. Wanda pulled back a corner, and Clayton glimpsed a tiny head.

Tracy took the bundle out of the basket and gave a knowing look to Wanda Brackhage. Wanda nodded, then walked past them to the porch and went inside the house.

Tracy pulled the blanket back farther. The baby was sleeping. Its little hands were curled in front of its face.

Clayton took a step backward, not knowing what to think. He'd been overwhelmed at the sight of Tracy. Seeing a baby gave him a terrible start.

Tracy held the tiny infant up to Clayton. "Here, hold her."

Awkwardly, Clayton took the baby in his arms. She felt so small. He thought of Maudie's baby, Rhonda Elizabeth. She had been so much bigger than the one he now held in his arms. Curiously, he looked closer at the small delicate eyes and the round mouth. Her skin looked so soft. She had a shock of dark hair.

"Her name's Fonda Alice, but I call her Alice."

Clayton looked sharply at Tracy. "She's yours?"

"Yes."

The news hit him with a jolt. At first, he felt anger. Someone had come along and taken advantage of her loneliness, left her with child. But, he reasoned, didn't the fault lie with him? He had left her behind with promises to return—promises he hadn't kept. He no longer held any claims to her. He bit down hard, causing his jaw to twitch. It took most of his strength and courage to simply nod his head.

"She's a beautiful baby," he said stiffly. "I'm real happy for ya."

"Oh, Clayton!" Tracy cried. "She's our baby."

She studied his face, searching for his reaction. Her own face turned red. "I know I should've told you," she began. "I started to come when I first learned that I was gonna have a baby, but I didn't think you would want to see me."

Clayton stared down silently at the little girl, biting his lip, taking deep breaths. Tracy's voice began to tremble.

"Please, Clayton—"

He shifted the bundle into the crook of his left arm, then reached out with his right and pulled Tracy close. He hugged her tightly against him.

"Then, you're not angry?" Tracy whispered.

"Why would I be angry?" Clayton said. He couldn't stop looking at his daughter.

Tracy pulled away from him. "She's wonderful, Clayton. She's a good baby."

"You should have told me."

"I know. I hope you'll forgive me. I hope you can find it in your heart to love her."

Clayton felt no doubts about that. There was a strange new sensation inside him, a feeling so powerful it was almost frightening. He gently rubbed the soft little cheek and noticed that his hand was quivering. The big lump returned to his throat, so big that when he tried to swallow, it hurt.

That morning, Tracy and Wanda killed a hen, then busied themselves preparing the midday meal. Clayton let the women do the work, happily occupying himself with getting acquainted with little Alice. He had held her all day, only begrudgingly giving her up when Tracy had to feed her or change her soiled clothing. Never in his life had he experienced such a sense of closeness and belonging. He knew he had never wanted anything as much as he wanted Alice. And he'd had no idea that anything could feel so wonderful.

They had just sat down to eat, when Wanda inquired about Solon.

"Where's that Solon Johnson at these days? I thought he was up here with you," she said casually.

Clayton stared at his plate. He hadn't given any thought to Solon all day. It hadn't even registered with him that Wanda would be there to see Solon. He tried to pretend he hadn't heard, but Wanda persisted.

"I talked to Shorty Gillis last week, and Shorty said somebody told him that Solon is still livin' up here." There was a more direct tone to Wanda's voice.

Clayton didn't figure Wanda had a claim on Solon. After all, they hadn't seen each other in a long time. Still, there was something that looked wrong about Solon's being at Beverly Townsend's place. He thought hard. He knew he couldn't lie, and Wanda deserved a fair answer.

He finally looked up to meet Wanda's stare. "Yeah," he said, "Solon's still here. Right. now, he's at Elmer and Maudie McNutt's house. Took a sow and half a dozen pigs over there this mornin'." He reached up and flicked a drop of sweat that had collected under his eye. "It's a fer piece. I doubt he'll be back tonight. Of course, If he knew you were here, my goodness." He stopped, looked nervously down at his plate, then shook his head back and forth. "My goodness," he repeated, "he'd sure be here if he knew you'd come. He's gonna be sorry he missed ya, and that's a fact." He looked apprehensively at Tracy.

Tracy smiled brightly. "Well, he'll be back tomorrow, won't he?"

Clayton's eyes blinked rapidly. He nodded, "I suspect you're right. He'll be back tomorrow." He paused, "That is, if he doesn't have to stop to do something in town."

Tracy's eyes bore into his. "He is coming back, isn't he?"

"Oh sure! He'll be back, he'll be back. Why, he's got hogs out there. Solon likes to mess with the hogs. Me, I think they're a nuisance." He reached up and wiped off more of the sweat that was rapidly covering his face. "Solon likes messin' with those hogs, and that's a fact," he added, his voice trailing off.

"Cut through the bull, Clayton," Wanda said sharply. "Where's Solon at? If he's not around, just say so. If he's with some whore, you can say that, too. I'm not proud. After all," she added, "that's how I met him."

Clayton's eyes widened at Wanda's directness. "Oh no! That ain't the case, a-tall!"

Wanda fell silent. She picked at her food a while, then pushed her plate away and went outside.

After the meal, Clayton rode into town to get some coal oil. He had guests, and it wouldn't do to have a dark house that evening. More important, there was a baby in the house, and babies needed tending to.

He gave the mare a spur. He felt light in the saddle, and alive. He breathed in the Kansas air. For the first time in so long, he didn't feel lonely or scared. He was going to town to buy coal oil, and he would buy some extra blankets, and some much-needed supplies for the house.

40

SOLON WAS gathering eggs in the henhouse and thinking about Beverly. He had bounced back and forth at least a dozen times, between proposing marriage, and hightailing it as far away from her as he could. It was no use, though. The struggle was virtually over. He wanted to be with her, stronger than anything. Still, the idea frightened the hell out of him.

The clucking hens were irritated by the intrusion of his hand into their nests, but they quickly settled back down as he moved on. They reminded him of little mirror images of himself. He could envision himself with wings and covered in feathers. He was brown—a rust brown—and fat. His face was dominated by a large beak under two beady, cowardly eyes. He stood there, fascinated and repulsed by the idea, holding an egg in one hand, and a basket in the other. He surely didn't want his life to be that way, henpecked and tied down. He'd spent the better part of his own life criticizing other men for getting themselves hitched. Why, marriage would turn a man into a big, fat old chicken, he'd often joked. A man with a wife would never again rule over his own life. He shook his head and wanted to kick himself. Here he was now, closer than he'd ever been to tying the knot, himself. He ought to jump in amongst the chickens right now and claim himself a nest, he thought.

Besides his own concerns, Solon couldn't help but worry about Clayton. In the past, Clayton had never seemed to mind being alone. As of late, though, he'd taken to falling quiet whenever Solon mentioned leaving the farm for a few days. And he seemed especially appreciative when Solon came back home. It had often bothered Solon to think that he'd been more of a burden than anything else to Clayton over the years. Clayton had never offered very many words of encouragement or pleasure over Solon's company. But all that had changed. Clayton was more talkative these days, and his face seemed to light up whenever Solon was around. While Solon was somewhat flattered by the fact, he also hoped it didn't mean his old friend was falling into a low state of mind.

Off in the distance, Beverly called his name. He put the egg in the basket and quickly gathered the rest of them. With one last forlorn look at the hens, he stepped outside.

"I declare, I thought you'd wandered off," Beverly said. "We've got a lot to do today."

When he looked at her, any doubts that Solon had just been having flew from his mind. She was smiling at him, and he found himself smiling back. Thoughts of the big brown hen slipped to the back of his mind. He felt hungry for some of Beverly's cooking. Maybe after they ate, they would have time to squeeze in a quick frolic before they left.

"Did you saddle the horses?" Beverly asked.

Solon looked around, as if in some magical way, he would see the horses saddled and ready to go. He finally said, "I thought I'd do that after we eat."

Beverly produced a sandwich from a bundle she was carrying. "Here," she said. "Eat this. It's a long ride, and the sooner we get started, the better."

Solon's hunger faded when he looked at the sandwich. He'd been thinking more in terms of hot biscuits with cow's butter and a bowl of stew, or some of her wonderful beans. But he ate the sandwich, anyway. He also knew better than to pursue the idea of a quick frolic.

He had to admit the sandwich was good, and by the time he'd taken a second bite, he wasn't thinking about biscuits and cow's butter anymore. The frolicking was still on his mind, though, and he hurried to get everything ready. As

he was walking back toward the house, Beverly stepped
outside in her fancy bonnet, carrying a bag. He cursed under his breath.

"I was just thinkin'," he said. "You don't have to go.
I could go tell him myself."

"I don't mind," Beverly said. "Besides, I don't trust
that you'll have the nerve to tell him."

Solon started to take exception to the comment, but he
knew that she was right. He'd rehearsed over and over in
his mind just how he could tell Clayton that he and Beverly
were going to get married right away. Oh, they'd discussed
the possibilities a time or two, and Clayton had offered his
own opinions on the subject of marriage, but that had pretty
much used up any nerve Solon had on the subject.

As they headed out through the gate, Solon felt a strange
tingling sensation. This was really it, he thought. Beverly
would have no trouble at all telling Clayton about their
immediate plans. He nervously pulled his hat down hard
on his head, as once again he visualized the fat brown hen,
sitting on the nest.

They stopped in Ness City to sell the eggs. Solon noticed
the people's stares. He thought every eye in Ness City must
be on him and Beverly. He mentioned it to her.

"Well, I declare! They can look all they want, as far as
I'm concerned. We'll be married soon, and then they can
find somebody else to look at!" With that, Beverly climbed
atop her horse and gave the townfolks a big smile. They
waved in return, and Solon pulled his hat down even
tighter, wondering if he looked like some kind of possession, riding next to her.

Clayton had visitors. Solon could see at least three figures, sitting on the porch, as they rode in. He felt a little
curious when he noticed that the guests were women. Who
could they be? Probably callers from the church, he
thought. That was all he needed. Beverly certainly wouldn't
be shy about making their announcement in front of them.
They might as well walk through town and tell everybody.

They drew closer, and Solon felt his skin start to crawl.
He was sweating. Nervously, he reached up and rubbed his

neck. It felt raw under his collar. The people had turned and were watching him and Beverly.

When he was close enough to see, Solon almost swallowed his tongue. There on the porch, fanning herself, sat Big Ears Wanda. Solon had the urge to jerk his horse back around and give it spur. He glanced over at Beverly who, up until now, had been silent.

"Who are those ladies, Solon?" she asked, her voice serious and full of questions.

"I can't rightly say," Solon mumbled. He scarcely noticed Tracy sitting there with a bundle in her arms. He felt totally miserable as he stared at Big Ears Wanda. A big smile had broken out across her face, and it brought back memories of things that Solon now wished had never happened. What was she doing here? What would she say to Beverly? He looked hard at Clayton, hoping for some kind of miracle help. Clayton only shrugged slightly.

All at once, Beverly pulled her horse in front of Solon and turned around to face him. "Is there something you need to tell me?" she asked.

"I-I don't know what that would be," Solon stammered. Once again, he envisioned that fat brown hen, but this time the hen was roasting over a blazing fire. He could almost feel the heat.

He looked back at Big Ears Wanda, and their eyes met. There was still a smile on her lips, but her eyes were full of uncertainty. She could see his fear. Wanda had always been able to read him like a book, Solon thought. His mind played back over their encounters. There had been several—as many as he could afford, but he could recall every one. He remembered her laughter and bawdy talk. She had given him so much pleasure, if he'd been a man of wealth, he would have spent a fortune on her and never once complained.

Sitting there before Beverly's demanding eyes, Solon thought back. He remembered the sensation that had always gripped him when he left Wanda's room. The instant he'd stepped into the night, her sensuous feel had begun to crawl all over him. He'd longed for her and dug desperately in his pockets, searching for enough money to return to her.

Some nights, he'd been lucky, and he'd partaken of her pleasures a second time. It had always been hard for Solon to have a second release, but that hadn't seemed to bother her, at all. She'd been interested only in pleasing him. Before Beverly, Solon reckoned, Big Ears Wanda had made frolicking feel better than anyone else.

Solon pulled his gaze from Wanda and glanced nervously at Beverly, who sat staring holes through him. With no other choice in sight, he nudged Doolittle on past her.

They dismounted and stepped onto the porch. Clayton made the introductions.

"Ladies, this here's Beverly Townsend." He hesitated before he finally said, "Beverly, I'd like you to meet Tracy O'Brien, and this is uh . . . uh . . . Wanda Brackhage."

Solon said, "You remember me tellin' you about Tracy, don't ya?"

"Yes, I do recall you mentioning Tracy," Beverly said. She smiled broadly, but Solon could see that it wasn't a happy smile. There were a lot of questions behind it. "But I don't believe you've ever spoken of a Wanda Brackhage."

If Solon had been chewing tobacco, he would have swallowed it. He could feel the heat rising from his raw, sweaty neck to his face, as he coughed nervously and tried to speak.

Slowly and with deliberate ease, Big Ears Wanda stood up from her chair. She smiled pleasantly and looked at Beverly. "Well, that's probably because I've never met Mr. Johnson."

Solon was never more grateful for anything in his life. He nodded his head in agreement. "That's right," he said. "We've never met. He tipped his hat. "Nice to make your acquaintance, er—Wanda, is it?"

Clayton's voice interrupted and cut through the tension. "Solon, Tracy's brought us a surprise. She's got a baby girl. Her name's Fonda Alice." He walked over and picked up the child. His voice caught as he added, "Sh-she's mine, Solon. She's my little girl."

"Yours?" Solon said. He stared down at the baby, then at Tracy and Clayton. Suddenly all of his worries faded from importance. "Well, I'll be damned. Who would've believed it?"

Beverly elbowed him in the ribs. "You shouldn't use such language in front of a little one," she said.

Solon's mental picture of the fat brown hen flashed again, and he turned and glared at Beverly. "I wish you wouldn't do that," he said. "That baby is too little to understand what I'm sayin'. Just ask Tracy."

"I reckon I'm grown up enough to know it ain't right to be talkin' like that!" Beverly said stubbornly.

Clayton interrupted again. "Would you folks like some coffee?" he asked. "Can't guarantee it's as good as you women make."

"I'll make it for you," Wanda volunteered, happy for the diversion. She followed Clayton and the baby inside.

Beverly was true to her word, and that evening over supper, she announced her and Solon's impending marriage. It would be held right away, she said, and she couldn't be happier.

Solon wanted to crawl into a hole, but instead he just sat there, staring at his plate with his head nodding up and down. His neck was burning again, and the food seemed to stick in his throat. For the rest of the evening, conversation was lost on him.

Occasionally, he stole a quick glance at Wanda. She was still attractive to him, but that old stirring wasn't there anymore. In fact, there was no stirring in him at all—not for Wanda or for any other woman. Not even for Beverly. That had never happened to Solon before. He'd rarely ever even seen an attractive woman, that his mind didn't consider what she'd be like in a compromising situation. But now, they could all strut before him naked as when they'd entered this world, and he was sure he wouldn't be the least bit aroused. It was a frightening realization, and Solon couldn't help wondering if he had made a mistake in agreeing to marry Beverly. Maybe he should have never come to Ness City. Maybe he should have avoided the state of Kansas entirely and stayed the hell in Texas.

After supper, the women doted over the baby, then set about cleaning the house. Solon gratefully accepted Clayton's suggestion that they take care of the stock.

They were silent all the way to the hog pen. Once there, Solon let out a sigh. "Well," he said, "now I know what a bull feels like when he gets his nuts cut off. That's exactly how I felt tonight. Like a steer." He reached down and felt his crotch. "I still got mine, but it don't feel like it."

"I was hoping you wouldn't show up," Clayton said.

Solon's voice rose. "Doggone it! Why didn't you come and warn me?"

Clayton looked surprised and a little defensive. "I never had the chance," he said. "Besides, you couldn't have hidden out very long. That Wanda asks more questions than a schoolteacher."

"If she'd been a teacher, I wouldn't be in this mess, for sure," Solon said. He closed his eyes, and he could see the hen sitting in a cooking pot. Beverly had a big wooden spoon, and she was stirring him around and around.

41

THAT NIGHT, Clayton and Tracy slept in the dugout. They'd gone out there for some privacy, and when he suggested heading back to the house, Tracy had stayed put.

"I don't care what the others think," she said firmly. "I want to be with you. Alone. Wanda will take care of the baby."

So they stayed right there, wrapped together under a shared blanket. Clayton slept peacefully, content with Tracy nuzzled up against him. Twice during the night, she awakened him when she hurried off to check on Alice. The second time, she returned with the baby in her arms and tucked her between them. Clayton stroked the tiny body and listened to her soft breathing, and thought this must be the most wonderful feeling in the world, lying with the two of them in the dugout.

He awakened before Tracy and got up to have a smoke. It was still a good while until dawn, and he wondered what had awakened him so prematurely. He hadn't been having his habitual nightmare. This both pleased and surprised him. So many times over the years, he'd come awake feeling cold and frightened from the scenes that played over and over in his sleep.

As he stood there, pondering the changes in his life, he saw the shape of a buggy in the semidarkness, moving away from the house. It was the buggy that had brought Tracy and the baby. For a moment, Clayton felt irritated.

It had been a long time since he'd slept so soundly and peacefully. Who was causing the intrusion?

He was still watching the buggy, when he heard footsteps coming toward him. It was Solon.

"Wanda's leavin'," he said.

Clayton had been so happy to be with Tracy and the baby, he hadn't given much notice to any of the others. He knew there was a chance of some kind of confrontation with Beverly and Wanda under the same roof, but he hadn't really let his mind linger on the matter.

"Well, I can't really say I'm surprised," he offered lamely.

"I have to catch up with her and talk to her," Solon said. He looked back nervously toward the house. "Beverly told me to."

"She did?" Clayton said, surprised. "What for? Did you tell her about you and Wanda?"

"Not a word. She said she just knew. Said a person can't hide a thing like that. By damn, Clayton!" Solon shook his head in frustration. "I swear, I don't know whether I'm comin' or goin'. Maybe I'm makin' a mistake, gettin' married. Beverly can sure be a bossy cuss at times. Hell! You know I never cared much about takin' orders from anybody, let alone a woman." He felt about as miserable as a man could feel, standing there and watching Wanda and the buggy get smaller in the distance. Beverly had a real knack of doing that—making him feel all troublesome and confused one minute, then turning right around and captivating him with her charms. He wasn't sure from one moment to the next how he was going to feel. "Well," he sighed, "Beverly told me that Wanda seemed like a nice person, and that I should go to her and work things out. Can you beat that? I don't guess I'll ever know a dern thing about women. First she acts jealous, then she goes and tells me to talk to Wanda." He stepped away, then turned back. "What do you reckon it is I'm supposed to work out?" he asked, mostly to himself.

Clayton didn't say anything. Solon really didn't expect him to. Clayton didn't seem to have women figured out any better than he did. Maybe he was just supposed to tell

Wanda good-bye. Maybe that was what Beverly considered "working things out." Whatever it was, he felt obliged to go saddle up Doolittle and ride after her.

He put the horse into an easy lope, and soon he was riding up next to the buggy. Wanda looked at him, but she didn't speak. That threw Solon for a loss, and he couldn't find the nerve to say anything.

He felt foolish, riding alongside Wanda with his mouth clamped shut like a useless tool. He should have left well enough alone, he thought. After all, Wanda was leaving. She knew she was out of place there. Why was it necessary to prolong things? Solon couldn't understand why he sometimes had so much trouble talking to women. It was one of life's mysteries. Normally, he could hold a fine conversation with anyone, man or woman. It was only rarely that he ran across a woman he couldn't start up a conversation with. And he'd always been comfortable with Wanda, until now.

Wanda seemed to be taunting him and his twisted tongue. She kept looking at him with her big brown eyes, making it plain that the conversation was in his hands. Solon didn't know what to do. He wanted to pull on Doolittle's rein and steer the horse back around toward the house, but he couldn't muster up the courage. Wanda's dark eyes held on to him.

The longer they rode, the more miserable he became. He thought up little bits of conversation, then cast them off as idiotic. How could he tell her what she already knew? His neck began to sting. He stared nervously straight ahead of them. Texas was in that direction, he thought. If he had any nerve at all, he'd dig his spurs into Doolittle's sides and lope away. Wanda couldn't possibly keep up with him. He'd head straight for Dodge City and pick up as much whiskey as he could carry. Then he'd ride until he hit Texas, drunk all the way.

Everybody would feel sorry for him, for sure. Beverly would worry first, wondering if he was out there somewhere, hurt or sick, or maybe even dying. Then, when he didn't return for days, or even weeks, she'd pine away and cry for him, wishing he had stayed there in Ness

County. She would wish she hadn't been so bossy—that she would have let him make his own decisions and treat him the way a gentle and respectful woman should. And she certainly would regret making him tell Clayton about their plans for matrimony and sending him on missions like this one.

Maybe he could find some whiskey *before* he got to Dodge City, Solon thought. Phillip Dempsey had a little stopping place along the trail to Dodge, and sometimes he carried liquor. Then he wouldn't have to go all the way to Texas. That way, Wanda would just ride up and find him first, laid out on the ground, good and drunk. She'd feel so terrible, she might even let him lay his head in her lap and make over him, while Beverly was crying for him at home.

But life was full of maybes. Solon let go of his dreams and continued to ride alongside Wanda and her buggy, hoping that some inspiration would come his way.

They were a good four miles from the ranch, and the sun was making its morning debut, when Wanda pulled rein and set the buggy's brake. Wordlessly, she climbed down and walked over a little bush. Then, as if Solon was nowhere within miles around, she squatted and peed. Solon watched curiously, as her water ran out on the hard dry ground and soaked into the earth. When she pulled up her drawers, he tried hard to get a glimpse of that part of her anatomy, but her dress was too big, and Solon had to fill in the details in his mind.

A familiar stirring came over him. It was a feeling he couldn't stop or hide. Sheepishly, he climbed down from Doolittle and tied his reins to her buggy wheel, then stood there uncertainly.

Wanda spoke at last, and the words stung Solon like a bee.

"I'll let you dip your candle, if you want," she said in a straightforward manner. "That's what you're wantin' to do, ain't it?"

Solon felt embarrassed. "I wish you wouldn't say things like that. You make it sound like that's the only reason I'm here."

"Well, it's the truth, ain't it?" Wanda said, her hands

on her hips. "All you cowboys ever want is to dip your candle. I don't know why I thought you would be any different."

Wanda had never been prone to crying or showing her emotions like most females did, and the small lump that appeared in her throat felt like some foreign object. She had been foolish to let Tracy talk her into coming here in the first place, she thought. Nobody wanted a whore in their home. And certainly no decent man wanted to settle down with one. For one silly moment, Solon had seemed different from the others. Wanda had never let the word "love" enter into her mind, but she had thought that Solon cared about her. How stupid, she thought. How repulsive. Clenching her teeth into a tight smile, she said, "There's a blanket in the carriage."

Solon was confused. Just the day before, he'd given in to the fact he was going to marry Beverly. Though he hadn't let himself do much actual thinking about it, he'd still accepted the idea that she was the only woman he would ever bed down with again. Now, his body started shaking as he looked at Wanda. She had already begun to undress.

Solon tried to slow things down and reason things out, but his gun belt came away. He set it on the buggy seat, then spread the blanket on the ground. Pangs of guilt overcame him in waves, like floodwaters. Solon knew they would have to drown him, for right now, Big Ears Wanda Brackhage owned him, body and soul. He knew it, and he reckoned she knew it, too.

Afterward, Solon fell asleep on the blanket, but it wasn't the kind of sleep a man got at night. It was more like a pleasurable nap. He didn't know how long it lasted, but when he woke up, he opened his eyes to see Wanda, lying beside him with her eyes closed.

He jerked upright and peered at her nakedness, as the Kansas breeze floated over them, drying the sweat of their passion. He looked down at himself. His manhood looked as dead as a doornail, but the sight of Wanda was starting to arouse him again. He thought about getting up and leaving, but then Wanda started to stir. She writhed on the blanket and touched his leg with her own, and Solon was powerless to move.

When her eyes opened, she reached out for him and pulled him onto her. Solon immediately thought about fetching his britches for more money, then remembered that it was free this time.

She began to move against him, and his thoughts left the present. His body had a mind of its own, as it slid willingly atop her. Grasping a generous amount of her soft hair in his hands, he closed his eyes.

Life was good. He was racing toward the end of the rainbow, when the words from behind him stopped him as cold as a sudden winter storm.

"Turn around. I want you to see me when you die."

Solon stopped moving, and his head jerked up. He turned and looked into the barrel of his own Winchester. Beverly's face hovered behind it, her eyes wide with anger.

"B-Beverly! You put that rifle down, you hear?"

Solon stared at her in shock. He still held Wanda's hair in both hands, but all other signs of passion had ceased. It peeved him to think that she had managed to ride up and steal his rifle off Doolittle's back, while he hadn't heard a thing.

"I'll put it down, all right," Beverly sneered, "after I've shot you real good." She walked closer. Her face was red, and her bottom lip trembled, but she held the Winchester steady, its deadly barrel pointing directly at Solon's head. "You get off that bitch."

Solon had momentarily lost track of Wanda and what they'd been doing. Every thought he could muster was on the Winchester and the white-knuckled hands that held it, one finger squeezed against the trigger.

From underneath Solon, Wanda spoke out. Her voice was more calm than either of theirs. "I understand how you feel, but you better put that gun down before it goes off and hurts somebody."

Beverly drew in her breath at such bold talk. "You shut up, you wicked bitch! I wasn't figurin' on killin' you, but that's not to say I won't!" she spit.

Solon let go of Wanda's hair and rolled off of her.

Slowly he sat up, while the tip of the Winchester moved with him. Wanda sat up, too. She didn't bother to cover herself, and Beverly gasped.

"Now, Beverly," Solon said. "Let's talk this over. It don't mean anything—"

"It does, too," she said in a shaky voice. "It surely does mean something. It means I'm gonna shoot you."

Exasperated, Solon pointed his finger at Beverly. He started to say something else, but the gesture incensed her even more. Beverly cried out as she squeezed the trigger.

"Nooooo!" Solon yelled. He heard a click, but nothing happened.

It took a second or two for him to realize that, in her excitement, Beverly had forgotten to put a round in the chamber of the Winchester. He jumped up as fast as he could to disarm her, but Beverly moved too quickly.

She jacked the lever and fired again. The Winchester jerked and exploded, sending a deafening roar across the prairie. Solon jumped like a rabbit, expecting to feel a terrible pain somewhere. But he felt nothing.

Behind him, Wanda screamed out. "My God! You've shot me!"

In that instant, Solon became confused as to which way to look. Involuntarily, his head turned to Wanda. Blood was seeping between the fingers she held clutched against her right breast. She had fallen back down on the blanket, and her legs kicked the air.

It shocked him to see her thrashing about and screaming. Even with the kind of life she had chosen, Wanda had always been so calm and unruffled. Now, she was more like a helpless child than a grown woman. Her behavior unnerved him even more than the fact that she had been shot.

The sounds behind him broke his stupor. Beverly was operating the lever of the Winchester. He leaped at her and grabbed for the rifle, just in time. As his hand squeezed around the barrel and shoved it to the side, he felt the bullet being discharged and roaring past.

Beverly tried to yank the rifle free from Solon's hands, but he held on. She started to scream in frustration. Behind him, Wanda was crying out, too, calling for him to please help her.

As both women screamed at him, a sickening feeling stole through Solon. He felt weak with the knowledge of how close he'd come to being shot. He wanted to wrestle the rifle from Beverly's crazy grasp, but he also wanted to run to Wanda and comfort her. Finally, with one powerful yank, he pulled the Winchester and Beverly up close and held on to both. At the same time, he turned back and glanced at Wanda. The sight that filled his eyes stunned him. Her entire front was decorated with fresh blood. "My God," he blurted out to Beverly, "you've killed Wanda."

"Let go! You're hurting my hand!" she yelled, struggling to push him away.

Solon noticed that her finger was pinched between the trigger and the guard. He eased his grip enough to let it loose, but once her hand was free, she started to pound him with her fist.

"I should've killed you!" she glared up at him, squaring off to deliver another blow. Solon tossed the Winchester well out of reach, then wrapped his arms around Beverly's waist, pulling her tightly against him. "Stop it!" he said with as much authority as he could muster. "Do you hear me? You've killed Wanda."

The plea had no effect on the outraged Beverly. She scratched and clawed at him with both hands, trying to twist free from his grip. Solon desperately wanted to see about Wanda. This was all his fault, and she was dying while he and Beverly wasted time with this useless struggle. But Beverly would not stop her assault.

Finally, he braved her fists to let go of her waist and took her by the shoulders. He started shaking her.

"Please, Beverly! Calm down. We've got to check on Wanda. Don't you understand? She's dying!"

Suddenly, Beverly's raging anger turned into a deep heart-wrenching cry. She buried her face in her hands and turned away from him. Solon tried to rub the back of her head to console her, but she pulled away.

"Leave me alone," she sobbed. "Oh, my Lord! What have I done? What have I done to her?" She paused to peer over at Wanda. "Don't touch me!" she said.

Solon wanted to do just that. He wanted to touch her, but he knew he couldn't. Not now, and probably not ever. He looked back at Wanda, then down at the Winchester lying on the ground a few feet away. "I won't touch you," he said uncertainly.

Beverly's face was all wet. Slobber ran from her mouth and down her chin, and her hair had gotten all messed up in their battle. Her fine features were all puffy and red.

Was this the woman he was going to marry? Solon stared at her. Beverly almost seemed like a total stranger. He had never thought her capable of such behavior—especially of killing anyone. It unnerved him to no end.

He was pondering such thoughts, when Beverly walked away from him and went over to where Wanda lay. She gasped and put her hand over her mouth. Her eyes were wide as they ran over Wanda's bloody body. "I can't believe I did this!" she wailed. "Oh my good Lord!" She fell to her knees. "Solon, give me your shirt!" she called out. "And your canteen. Hurry."

Wanda wasn't sure she wanted to let Beverly anywhere near her, and it took some doing before she was calm enough to let Beverly inspect the wound. Beverly took the canteen from Solon and washed the blood away. Wanda hollered out as the water struck her skin.

Solon stood and watched the two, somewhat fascinated over the idea that a woman who had been giving him such pleasure just moments before was now being tended to by the woman who had just viciously tried to kill them both.

Beverly bent over to inspect the wound, then raised up with a look of relief on her face. "You're going to be all right," she said to Wanda. She looked at Solon. "She's going to be okay," she repeated.

Luckily for Wanda, the bullet had only grazed her right breast. The nipple had been shot off, as neatly as if a Philadelphia surgeon had done it with a knife. All that was left was a bloody red spot right in the middle.

Solon stared at Wanda's injuries. Relief swept over him, too, but the relief soon turned to wonderment as to how she was going to carry on business as usual with only one nipple. Maybe she could draw customers as a special attraction, he thought. But what would folks call her now? For a long time, she'd been known as Big Ears. He'd never understood why. Her ears were somewhat larger than normal, but they weren't big enough to warrant a special name.

Solon looked at the bloody spot on her breast. Just a few minutes before, he'd had his mouth attached to that spot, as fervently as a suckling newborn.

He couldn't help but wonder if Wanda would ever again be known as Big Ears.

✐ 42 ✐

BEVERLY STAYED long enough to tend to Wanda's wound. There wasn't much they could do, under the circumstances, but as soon as they had applied a dressing out of Solon's shirttail and the bleeding slowed, Beverly got on her horse and rode away, toward the house.

"Don't bother calling on me anymore," she said as she left.

Solon couldn't think of anything proper to say, under the circumstances. He felt a tremendous sadness building up inside as Beverly left, taking with her all those fine suppers and her pleasing company. He thought about her cooked beans with the little chunks of 'possum meat, and the hot pans of corn bread. He remembered her appetite at frolicking and generosity with it. She'd been the most ambitious woman he'd ever encountered in that area. And her conversation. She was a knowledgeable woman with an opinion, and he'd enjoyed many a long afternoon discussing every subject under the sun. Why, in some ways, she was about the most pleasurable woman he'd ever met. He would surely miss her.

Now, he wasn't quite sure what he was going to do. Wanda sat there, sobbing softly to herself. He felt a pity for her. Wanda had never been the crying type, and seeing her so defenseless threw him into a quandary. He'd had a big mess laid on his shoulders, he thought. It was almost too much to bear at one time.

He watched Wanda for a moment. She held her hand

against the exposed breast, with a piece of Solon's shirt still covering the spot. He wished he could find the nipple. Maybe they could go and get it sewed back on. It was surely the most magnificent one he'd ever seen, large and dark red in color. Wanda had giggled over his fascination with them, but it had pleased her, and she had taken great care to proudly show them off to him.

He knew Wanda was hurting, but still he searched a while before he gave up the fruitless effort and turned his attention to her.

He looked the situation over. She needed to see a doctor, he decided, and she wasn't in any shape to go on her own. At first, he considered taking her to Dodge City, but that was more than forty miles away. He wasn't sure if there was a sawbones in Ness City, or not. He'd never had call to use one. But, after consideration, he decided that they had no other choice but to go there. Surely, he'd find somebody who could take care of such things.

Sadly, he tied Doolittle to the back of the buggy. He took one last quick look for Wanda's nipple, then loaded her up in the buggy and headed for town.

They hadn't ridden more than a few hundred yards, when they came across a man on horseback. The man introduced himself.

"Good day," he said, lifting his hat. "My name is Professor Milo Tyler. I'm on my way to Ness City. Going to be putting on a big show there—a really big show. I like to arrive ahead of the troupe to set things up. You folks will surely want to attend."

He went right on talking in his excited, high-pitched voice, then suddenly stopped and stared at Wanda.

"I certainly don't mean to be forward, madam, but you seem to have some kind of wound to your chest."

Solon wasn't surprised at the man's direct statement. He'd approached them with a direct manner. He was surprised, however, at how long it had taken Professor Milo Tyler to notice Wanda's predicament. Her right breast lay exposed, except for the bloody piece of Solon's shirttail that covered a tiny portion.

"Er, yes. She's sort of had an accident," he mumbled. Wanda only sniffled.

The professor nodded wisely, then looked at Solon.

"And you, sir, have definitely acquired an advanced case of tapeworm infection."

"What?" Solon said with a quizzical look.

"Tapeworm infection," the professor repeated. He pointed toward Solon's belly. "It's a classic case, I can see."

Solon stared down at himself. He patted his belly. "This? Why, I reckon I got this from eatin' lots of good vittles!" The thought reminded him of Beverly, and that made him sad. He didn't know if he could face life without her beans and fried chicken. And those wonderful biscuits and that corn bread. Solon wondered if he'd ever again wake up to the aroma of biscuits baking and fresh eggs frying. "It's vittles, all right," he added.

"My good man, I don't wish to be argumentative, but I've treated hundreds, maybe thousands of cases of tapeworm infections. I know of what I speak. See how your stomach is all pooched out?" Professor Tyler gestured.

Solon couldn't help but glance back down at himself. He hadn't realized that his belly was growing so big. There was skin showing above and below the button in the middle of his stomach.

"I'll bet if I was to poke that stomach of yours, it would be hard as a melon."

All of Solon's concerns about Wanda's nipple and Beverly's departure fled from his thoughts. He felt his insides start to crawl and twist about. "Do you really think so?" he asked.

"Oh yes," Professor Tyler said with confidence. "I would stake my reputation on it."

Solon thought back. Every little twitch and pain he'd felt in his stomach over the last few weeks all came back to him at once. He felt a desperation coming over him. "What exactly is a tapeworm?" he asked.

"Well, obviously, it's a worm. It grows on your insides." With his finger, the professor began motioning as he talked. "It weaves its way into your intestines, and whatever you eat, the tapeworm eats. Why, I've seen them as small as a foot in length, and just last week, I extracted one from a man that was more than six feet long.''

Solon's stomach began to hurt. He felt a little feverish. ''Exactly how do you go about extracting one of these tapeworms?''

A twinkle appeared in Professor Tyler's eye. He gave a gentle smile. ''Oh, extraction is easy if done properly.'' He reached to the side of his horse, where a black bag was tied. He opened it and fished around inside, then his eyes brightened as he pulled out a bottle with his left hand. In his right, he held a capsule. He held them up for Solon's viewing.

''Just take this capsule, along with this bottle of medicine,'' he said. ''I'm going to give them both to you free of charge. I only ask one thing in return.''

''What's that?''

''As soon as you pass the tapeworm, I would like for you to bring it to me for scientific research.''

''For what? Say that again,'' Solon said.

''I would like for you to bring me the tapeworm.''

''I don't understand—'' Solon was beginning to perspire. He wasn't feeling well, at all.

''You see, my good man, I am conducting a study of this most special medicine, which I developed myself in a laboratory in Chicago. This bottle of Professor Tyler's nostrum will most assuredly relieve you of this terrible malady. You see''—he paused and looked directly into Solon's eyes—''the capsule will actually kill the tapeworm. The liquid medicine,'' his voice raised, ''will clear up any and all infections and put you on the road to recovery.''

Solon stared at the bottle and the big pill in the professor's hand. Professor Tyler added, more slowly, ''You see, the tapeworm will die, and you will pass it through your bowels.'' He rode closer to the buggy and handed his cures to Solon. ''I suggest you take the capsule right away.''

Solon studied the capsule, which now lay in the palm of his hand. The professor had shown up in the nick of time, he thought. He hadn't been feeling right as of late. That was a fact, and right now his insides felt like something awful was crawling through them. Carefully, he opened the bottle and wrinkled his nose as he took a sip. He was expecting the worst, but he found to his surprise that the medicine had a pleasing taste.

"Go on," the professor prodded, "take the capsule."

By now, Solon didn't need much prodding. He laid the big capsule on his tongue. His only thought was whether he could swallow the thing or not. He took a deep swallow of the medicine and felt the capsule go partway down his throat, then stop. His fears were founded. He clutched his chest.

"Take another drink—fast!" the professor ordered. "It can't harm you. It's most likely dissolving right now."

The professor was right. The second drink sent the capsule farther down to where there was no more pain in his chest. Once again, the medicine had a pleasing taste, and it sent a nice warm feeling throughout his body. He couldn't tell for sure, but he thought he was already starting to feel better. He took in a deep breath. "How often should I take this medicine?"

"Oh, you should keep at it for the next couple of hours. It won't hurt a thing. In fact, the quicker you get the poison out of your body, the better you're going to feel," the professor instructed.

Once Professor Milo Tyler had Solon taken care of, he turned his attentions to Wanda, who had been sitting quietly in the buggy, clutching her right breast. She cried softly and moaned with the pain, but put up no protest when the professor climbed up next to her and pulled her hands away. He removed the shirt bandage.

The professor jumped back, letting out a shriek. His eyes widened as he surveyed the round breast, perfect in every way except for the tip. Right in the middle was a dark, bloody spot where the nipple had been. He turned around and looked nervously at Solon.

"What happened to this poor woman?" he managed to say. "Did you do this to her? Did you bite it off?"

Solon had been taking another drink of the pleasing medicine, and he was beginning to enjoy the nice warm feeling that was coming over him. It was almost the same feeling he'd gotten when drinking Beverly's whiskey. At the professor's question, he yanked the bottle away from his lips, spilling some of the medicine down the front of his shirt. "What kind of fool thing is that to ask?" he said. "Of course I didn't bite it off!"

The professor held up his hand defensively. "Relax, my good man. The only other time I came across a case such as this, I was back in Illinois. Some fellows decided to rob a bank one day, and they blew up the safe. A man happened to be staying at the hotel across the street, and he was— er, in a compromising situation with a young lady. Well, when the dynamite exploded, it rocked the entire town. That poor man was so startled, he bit clean through the woman's—well, he bit it off. It looked very similar to this." The professor removed his derby hat and wiped the sweat from his head.

Solon gladly paid Professor Milo Tyler a dollar for a tin of miracle salve. Then, he gingerly daubed some onto Wanda's wound.

Soon, they parted company. Solon, with the tin of salve and the bottle of medicine, promised that he would take the tapeworm to the professor at the medicine show.

Solon felt happy to oblige the professor his request, for he was already beginning to feel quite content and well. He hummed an old sacred song as he got into the buggy and headed back toward the house.

Wanda rode along beside him, clutching her breast and still in considerable pain, even with the application of the miracle salve. Unlike Solon, she didn't feel any better, at all. About halfway home, she accepted a drink of the medicine, not even questioning the fact that it had been sold as a cure for tapeworm infection. Solon was clearly feeling so good, the medicine would surely help make her feel good, too.

43

CLAYTON HAD never known that life could hold such contentment. It seemed like all of his life had been filled with darkness and painfully few spots of light. The older he grew, the harder it became for him to recall the simpler days of his youth. It was an odd trick to play on a man, he thought. As a little boy, he had loved and respected his family. But nowadays, what frequently came to mind was his poor mama and how she had aged before her time.

It had taken him quite a while to get used to not wearing his sidearm, but he'd put it away for good. Baby Alice had replaced that part of him, almost overnight. He couldn't explain it, but he knew that he loved her more than anything in life. He wanted to hold her forever and drink in the sheer pleasure of looking down at her helpless, innocent face.

He and Tracy were sitting on the porch, having a discussion about Clayton's house, when Martin Frusher came by to purchase a pig.

"How do?" Frusher said to Tracy, tipping his hat.

"This is Miss Tracy O'Brien," Clayton said. "Soon to be my wife. And this," he held up Alice, "is my little girl."

Frusher looked surprised, but he smiled at Tracy and the baby. "Well, well," he said. "You know, Crist, with a family, you can't live like a bachelor anymore. You need furniture, for one thing." He picked up the pig and loaded it into his wagon. "I'll be back in a few days with a crib

for that young'un. I like to build things, and it'll give me
an excuse." He smiled, excited at the prospect of helping
Clayton.

As soon as Martin Frusher had left, Tracy turned to Clayton. "That's awful sweet of your friend," she said, "but it
ain't really necessary. Like I told you, I've got a whole
houseful of furniture back in Dodge City."

Clayton smiled. He was so happy, he didn't care where
their furniture came from. The more, the better. For the first
time since he'd gone off to war, he was going to have a
real home. A home with furniture. A home with a wife and
a baby, filled with love.

Just then, Tracy pointed. "Look, hon. It's Beverly ridin'
in. She don't look too happy, neither."

Beverly tied her horse to the post and marched right past
them on the porch. In a couple of minutes, she returned,
carrying her things.

"I must apologize for leaving so abruptly," she said,
fighting back tears.

"What's wrong?" Tracy asked, concerned.

Beverly threw back her head and said, "I won't go into
it, but if and when that low-down Solon comes back, please
tell him that he needn't bother coming after any of his
things. I'll send 'em over."

Tracy got up and put her arm around Beverly. "Please.
Won't you tell us what's happened?" She knew all too
well, though, what the problem must be. When she and
Wanda had come to Ness City, they'd had no idea that
Solon was involved with another woman. The situation was
a delicate one at best.

Back when Clayton and Solon had left Dodge City, the
loneliness had nearly eaten Tracy alive. She had met Wanda
at the post office, and they'd struck up a quick conversation. Wanda had confessed her feelings for Solon, silly and
improbable as it sounded, and the two women had formed
a friendship out of their shared loneliness for the men.
Tracy had asked Wanda to come with her, and Wanda had
been reluctant, until Tracy convinced her that she was as
good as any woman, and she ought to at least see if Solon
was interested.

Beverly couldn't hold back the tears any longer. She pulled away from Tracy and cried. "It doesn't matter. Not anymore." She stepped off the porch and mounted her horse. "I thank you for your hospitality," she murmured, and rode away.

When she'd left, Tracy nudged Clayton. "You could've said something."

Clayton gave Tracy a quizzical look. Right now, the only thing that held any meaning for him was Tracy and the baby. He searched his mind for something to say, but it came up blank. He was enjoying his life for the first time, and he really didn't care to think about anything else.

"She's your friend, Clayton," Tracy pressed. "I feel sorry for her. What do you suppose happened?"

Clayton shook his head. "Whatever it was, I figure it's none of our business."

Tracy sighed and got up to go inside. "I'm gonna get to work on the floors. They need a good cleaning."

Clayton nodded. He had Alice in his arms, and he was quite content to just sit there in the solitude and hold her. The baby seemed happy with him. Clayton wondered if his mama had been right about babies having some kind of sense about who their kin was.

When Solon and Wanda rode up, Clayton's thoughts were abruptly turned from the euphoria he'd just been experiencing. In fact, he couldn't believe what he was seeing.

Wanda was only half-clothed, and she leaned up against Solon on the buggy seat. Neither she nor Solon seemed all that upset.

"Beverly shot Wanda," Solon said with a smile. He stepped down from the buggy and stumbled. Still holding Professor Tyler's bottle of nostrum, he managed to catch his balance, then groggily turned to help Wanda step down from the buggy. She giggled.

Tracy was mortified at the sight, but Solon and Wanda refused to offer any explanations. They went into the house and sat down, laughing and recalling old times. The more medicine they drank, the happier Solon became and the better Wanda felt. By noon, the bottle was empty, and both were in fine form throughout the noonday meal. Wanda

refused to let Tracy look at her wound, but did agree to
robe herself with one of Clayton's shirts.

They remained there all the way into midafternoon, when
Solon suddenly felt a bad need coming on. His stomach
developed a severe case of cramps that came in waves.
Soon, he made a bolt for the door and ran out behind the
barn as fast as he could go. He barely got his britches down
in time.

He had never experienced such bad diarrhea. He would
barely finish with his business and get back to the house,
when it would start up again. By suppertime, he was feeling
weak. That was when Wanda's stomach began to cramp
and she, too, started making trips to relieve herself. It got
so bad, a couple of times they sat together.

Solon was on one of his solitary visits. He'd managed to
find a clean spot behind the barn. He didn't think he had
any more energy left, and there couldn't possibly be anything left for his body to discharge. Then, he looked down
on the ground and saw the tapeworm. It was nearly three
feet long and curled out between his feet.

He had just been cursing Professor Tyler, thinking he
must have given him and Wanda some sort of poison. But
now, as he stared at the tapeworm, relief came over him.
The professor had been right. This was why he had been
cramping so bad. Solon's life had been saved. He couldn't
believe his good fortune. The professor had appeared, just
in the nick of time.

He found a stick and picked up the tapeworm, then
washed it with well water and wrapped it up in a rag. Outside of being weak and incredibly sore, he was already
feeling better. The thought that such a nasty thing had been
living inside him—and no telling for how long—made Solon shudder. He wondered if Wanda, too, had a tapeworm.
He started to mention it to her, but then reckoned the professor would've known that. Still, it puzzled him as to why
she had such a bad case of diarrhea, too.

It was near bedtime before Wanda quit making her trips
to relieve her discomfort. Solon's had stopped sometime
earlier, and it was just as well, for he was too sore to go
anymore. They went to bed that night feeling exhausted,

but relieved that the ordeal was over and still inebriated enough to sleep soundly.

The next morning, Clayton and Tracy tiptoed around, so as not to wake them. Solon got up first, and he gave a brief account of what had happened. Wanda awoke shortly after, but she complained of a bad headache and went back to bed.

They were just finishing breakfast, when Martin Frusher and his wife, Debra, rode up wearing big smiles. Behind them were several buggies, wagons, and people on horseback. Everyone was carrying something.

Clayton stepped out on the porch and watched them. With a puzzled expression, he returned Frusher's greeting.

Frusher waved his arms at the folks around him.

"These are your neighbors, Clayton. Some of 'em you know, some you may have seen around." He glanced around at the other buggies and wagons. "Most of 'em go to church with me and the missus. Now, we don't mean to embarrass you, but we knew you didn't have nothin' in the house, and what with a new baby and all, we thought we'd like to help you out. So, we brought along a few things, if'n that's all right."

Clayton was nearly overcome with emotion. He nodded slowly, not trusting his voice to speak. Ladies wearing bonnets emerged from the wagons and filed past him, carrying baskets of bread, pies, and cured meats. Others carried pieces of furniture. The barber, Ollie Knowles, brought in a chair. Galen Peevy pulled a chest of drawers from his wagon. Martin Frusher brought a milk cow. And a carpenter, Curtis Adamo, offered a butter churn.

Clayton stood holding the baby. His mouth was hanging open as he watched the folks pass by with their gifts. The womenfolk paused to smile at Alice, and the baby was quickly whisked out of his arms and disappeared among them. Several men nodded, and a few stopped to talk a spell.

The kindness brought tears to Tracy's eyes. All the time she had lived in Dodge City, she had never seen such kindness as she was seeing right now. Dodge City was a hard town—not that there weren't a lot of good folks in it, but

she had come to think that most everyone in this part of
the country had become hard-bitten, with a skeptical edge.
She had often wondered if she, too, would end up old and
lonely.

But now she saw a different side of life on the prairie.
She saw women with their eyes full of concern and passion,
who put aside their thoughts—leastwise in front of her—
about her having had Alice out of wedlock. And the men
respectfully doffed their hats. There were stories about the
local school and quilting bees. She was invited to their worship services and into their homes for tea. Clayton had been
right about Ness County, she thought. It made her want
him even more. This was where she wanted Alice to grow
up, with Clayton as her father. It was funny how life turned
out, she thought. It had always been hard for her to accept
the fact that anything good could happen to her. She had
taken a long time to love and trust her first husband, Pug,
and then he'd been killed.

But then Clayton had come along, and in spite of herself,
she had loved him almost from the very beginning. Now
she was going to love Ness County as well.

Clayton invited everyone to stay for dinner. He offered
to cook for everyone. It was the first time he'd ever made
such a sociable offer to anyone, but he was ready to show
them his good feelings.

They declined, insisting that Clayton had enough on his
hands to worry about cooking up a big meal. As Martin
Frusher left, he heartily shook Clayton's hand and reminded
him to be sure and attend the big medicine show.

"We'll all be there," Clayton assured him. All except
Wanda, he thought to himself.

When everyone was gone, Clayton and Tracy looked
over all their gifts. They marveled at the generosity of their
friends and neighbors. Clayton was so overcome, he had to
fight to keep from weeping. He was sure that if he were all
by himself, he would have cried like a little boy. As it was,
his eyes grew misty as he looked around the room at the
sacks of flour, molasses, homemade preserves, potatoes,
and onions. Even though they still didn't have a table, they
now had three chairs. There were bags of beans, several

quilts, and fancy doilies. Out front, Martin Frusher had tied the milk cow to the porch. A widow woman, Estelle Adelman, had left seven laying hens scratching in the dirt.

Life was good. It was better than Clayton had ever dreamed of deserving. Since Tracy and the baby had come, he hadn't had any of the terrible nightmares. Maybe they had stopped forever, he thought. Maybe he would actually be allowed to live out his life right here, as a family man.

He ran the words over and over in his mind. A family man. He would go to church with his wife and daughter. He would proudly work in the fields—raise a big garden and tend to the livestock with pleasure. Never again would he set foot in a saloon or earn another dime from the blood of another man.

He went outside and stood there, surrounded by the goodness of others, and suddenly found himself remembering the words of the sinner's prayer. Tears crept into his eyes, but he didn't try to stop them. He could feel his parents' presence, right there with him.

Clayton couldn't help glancing upward. As he prayed, his body began to feel lighter, as if some burden had been lifted from his shoulders. His mother, from her throne in the hereafter, was praying with him, and he knew that God was listening.

This was an entirely new experience for Clayton, and it was a little scary. Long ago, he had accepted the fact that he was doomed to spend the hereafter among hell's fires. He'd never accepted that "blink of an eye" business. How could he accept such a promise, with so much blood on his hands? But now, the transformation that was taking place erased all those years of self-denial. He felt like a man redeemed.

He was still staring upward, when he felt Tracy's body next to his. Unashamed, he pulled her tightly to his side and let a teardrop fall into her hair. She put her arms around him. They didn't need to say a word. They had that special feeling of becoming one.

⚐ 44 ⚐

LIFE HAD become full of happiness. Clayton sometimes wondered if this was all just one big dream. If so, he wanted to keep right on dreaming.

He had an urge to pack up his new family and take them back to Tennessee, even though his father and mother were dead. He still had a brother and sister there. It would be good to see Wendelin and Joshua again, and he wanted so much for them to meet Tracy and to hold Alice. He wanted them to know that something good had finally come of his life.

A couple of years before, their cousin, Ginger Mae Ramsey, had sent him some clippings from the Nashville newspaper about his exploits as "the Gunny." Clayton had been dismayed to know that his brother and sister had read them. They were surely ashamed of him. Everyone back home probably knew all about his reputation.

But Tracy and Alice had given him a new chance to vindicate himself, to let his family know that he was a good man—a man with a wife and child. He couldn't help but pleasure himself with thoughts of the three of them riding down the Columbia River. They could meet up with family friends and visit the old homestead. When Alice grew older, he could take her to the places where he'd caught a big fish or gone swimming. She would want to hear stories about his mother and father, the grandparents she would never know.

Maybe, he thought, if he posted a letter to his sister and

explained everything to her, maybe she would write back and insist that he come home to visit or even to settle down.

But Tennessee would have to wait a little longer. Clayton's happy morning thinking was interrupted by the others. It was time to go to Ness City and see the big medicine show. Tracy had decided that they should spend the entire day in town. She made sandwiches and packed a picnic basket and blankets for them all to sit on.

Wanda wanted to go. Solon tried to protest. He was worried about her traveling—that, and the prospect of seeing Beverly. Wanda, however, pushed aside his weak arguments as nonsense and insisted. She was loaded into the back of the wagon, seated atop the stack of blankets.

Solon kept his promise and tucked the tapeworm in his pocket to show to Professor Milo Tyler. His backside was still a little raw, but he otherwise felt fit as a fiddle as he swung himself up on Doolittle's back.

In short order, they were on their way to town.

Ness City was bustling. Folks were all talking about the medicine show. Children ran through the streets, mindless of the adults that hollered at them to get out of the way of the horses and buggies that filled the street. Such entertaining events were rare, and there was a festive atmosphere all over town.

They hadn't been there more than fifteen minutes, when Professor Tyler spotted Solon and hurried over.

"My good man! You look wonderfully fit!" the professor said with a grin. He started poking Solon's stomach, his face serious as he prodded. Then, a twinkle appeared in his eye.

"It's gone!" He nodded his head. "The tapeworm's gone."

Solon, ignoring the wide-eyed stares of the others, smiled broadly. "Yup! It was the derndest thing I've ever seen! I'm tellin' you, I haven't felt this good in years!" He reached into his pocket and pulled out the rag. Proudly, he opened it, exposing the long tapeworm.

"Let me have that," Professor Tyler said.

Solon pushed it toward him, like it was a sparkling diamond. Both of them studied it. They would look at each other, then back down at the tapeworm.

The professor said, "I've performed this procedure many, many times before, but it never ceases to amaze me! I've got a sister. Lovely woman—Irene's her name—but every time I see her, she wants to know if I'm still going around the world, playing physician! A scoffer, I tell you! She's nothing but a scoffer!"

To Solon's chagrin, Professor Milo Tyler folded the cloth back over the tapeworm and tucked it into the pocket of his coat. He went on sanctimoniously.

"Well, Irene's wrong! Wrong as rain. Not only is she wrong about my 'playing physician,' as she calls it. The fact is, there's not a physician alive who has my nostrum for extracting tapeworms! No, I feel I owe something to the fine people in this great country of ours, and I will humbly continue traveling the back roads of this land, saving the poor suffering people, just like yourself."

Solon was sure the professor was going to tear up and start bawling any minute. He was so sure, he almost forgot his irritation that the professor had taken the worm and deposited it in his own pocket.

"Well, that's mighty fine, but what are you doin' with my tapeworm?" he asked.

The professor patted his pocket. "Scientific research, my good man. Scientific research. With your permission, I'd like to show this specimen to the good people of this town. And, if it's not too embarrassing to you, I'd like to call you up before the people—to show them and give them the proof they must have. "Skeptics!" He shook his head. "The world is full of Irenes and skeptics!"

"B-but, I'd kinda like to keep that tapeworm," Solon pointed out. "Maybe after the show, you could give it back to me?"

"Oh no, I'm afraid not. I must send it to my laboratory in Chicago. Why, my good man, how else do you think science can learn about such things?"

Everyone was listening intently to the two go on. Solon started to answer, when a loud voice interrupted.

"Well, well, well! If it ain't the Gunny, Clayton Crist!"

Solon closed his mouth. The professor turned to see who had spoken, and everyone went silent. Clayton felt a dread running through his body. He'd heard that same high-pitched voice before, full of bravado and arrogance. He reckoned it was a voice he'd never forget. Instinctively, he pulled Alice closer to him and cupped his hand over her small head, as he slowly turned to face Kid Martin.

Their eyes met, and Clayton's spirits fell. Many, many times since that day in Dodge City, he had closed his eyes at night and seen the Kid's face right before him, menacing and deadly, the eyes pierced with anger. What he saw held true to his dreams. The Kid appeared cool and somewhat amused, but there was still death locked in his gaze.

It was Solon who spoke first. "What the hell are *you* doin' here?" he asked. Gone was his fascination over tapeworms and such. He felt like a man watching one of his children go into the deep waters of a raging river. He stepped between the Kid and Clayton.

Kid Martin stared past Solon, never once taking his eyes from the depths of Clayton's own. "Hello, Johnson," he said calmly to Solon. "I see you still have a penchant for sticking your nose into someone else's business." A smile appeared on his lips. "I just wanted to pay my respects, is all."

Professor Milo Tyler, who had been forgotten in the conversation, spoke up.

"So, you gentlemen know each other? How wonderful. Mister Martin, here, is now in my employment. He puts on a fine show!" With his usual exuberance, the professor swung his arms about and began to talk about Kid Martin's exploits with a pistol. "I hired him in Wichita last fall. It was right before Christmas. He's a wonderful attraction! You must all see him perform today."

Solon was still standing between Kid Martin and Clayton. Tracy eased over and slipped her arm through his, then placed a protective hand on Alice. She couldn't help but notice the small tremor that ran through Clayton's body. "Maybe we should go back home," she said. "I don't feel well."

"Oh? What is it that ails you?" Professor Tyler asked,

stepping closer to her. "I'm sure it's something I could help
you with. Is it a headache?" He looked her up and down.
"I'm most certain you aren't suffering from a case of the
tapeworm, as did my good man, Mister Johnson. No, I
would guess that it's probably something you have eaten."

Tracy paid no attention to the professor. Her eyes, like
Clayton's, were fixed on Kid Martin. "It's not that kind of
sickness," she said quietly. "Come on, Clayton. Take Alice
and me back home. Please."

Kid Martin doffed his hat to Tracy. "Sorry to hear that
you're sick." His eyes slid back to Clayton. "Maybe you
oughta go home, Clayton. Take the little woman and go."

The anger rose up in Clayton like a stoked fire. He suddenly wished he was young again—not only on the outside,
but on the inside as well. Why, he'd kill this young squirt
and never think twice. After all, wasn't that what Kid Martin wanted? A challenge where only one man walked away?

But youth was gone forever, and Clayton knew it. He
hated Kid Martin and all others like him. He realized that,
up until now, he had hated his life. Kid Martin was just a
mirror of himself—a memory of what he himself had once
been.

More than anyone else in the world, Clayton realized that
this was a deadly business. Kid Martin would not ever go
away. He would always be somewhere close by, waiting.
And Clayton would not find peace until the Kid was satisfied.

As the truth came clear, all kinds of thoughts ran through
him. He didn't wear his pistol-rigging anymore. His days
had been occupied by thoughts of farming and cattle op-
erations and setting up a home with Tracy. Could he face
Kid Martin? Would he still have that intangible force that
separated him from the others? When he pulled leather,
would he again be consumed by that deadly driving force?
Or would he hesitate? Would he pause that last split second
to think about Tracy and Alice?

"Why don't you go and leave me be?" he asked simply.
He forced himself to smile. "Can't you see? I've got a
family now. I have a daughter. Her name's Alice. Fonda
Alice." He didn't know why he was doing it, but he turned

and exposed the baby's face. "She's mine. Look, I don't wear a gun anymore. I'm no threat to you, Kid. You can have it all. The world's yours."

No one spoke, not even Professor Milo Tyler. Everyone was watching the Kid.

His face broke out into a big grin. Slapping his leg with his hat, he exclaimed, "Well, I'll be damned, Crist! All this time, I've thought about nothin' but you. I thought about you when I was twelve, and when I was fourteen. Hell, I've thought about you nearly half my life!" He laughed some more before he turned to leave, then stopped and spoke to Tracy. "Ain't no need to be sick anymore, lady. I ain't gonna bother your man." He laughed again, a high-pitched sound that rose into the sky. As he went away, his shoulders could be seen quaking with laughter. There was an exuberance in his step.

Clayton's eyes followed Kid Martin. It was over, he thought with relief. The times *were* changing. The days of Kid Martin and Clayton Crist were coming to an end. Briefly, he thought back to the war. As then, maybe he was still indestructible. After all, modern times were upon them, and Clayton was still here. He had survived a life of hell and lived to hang up his gun and become a farmer.

They spent the day going in and out of shops. Clayton was amazed at Tracy's energy as she browsed through each and every store, talking to the Ness City merchants and examining their wares. Clayton's back started to hurt, and his arms stung from carrying Alice. She was so little, yet her burden eventually grew heavy. Clayton didn't mind in the least. He would find a place to sit and play with the baby, until Tracy was ready to leave for the next store.

That evening, Clayton and Tracy found Solon and Wanda where they'd left them several hours before, stretched out on the blankets and nursing a bottle of rye together. They all ate the last of their sandwiches and joined the people who were headed toward the big show.

When they reached the fringe of the large crowd that had gathered, Professor Milo Tyler came pushing through the people and grabbed Solon.

"Here you are, my good man! I was worried sick that

you weren't going to come. Now, the show can go on!''
Together, they disappeared among the crowd and headed
toward the makeshift stage.

The weather was warm and damp, drawing hungry flies
and mosquitoes. People fanned themselves and swatted and
complained. It had been a long day for most, and they were
all ready for the show to begin.

At last, a roar of applause went up. Two women, one tall
and skinny and the other short and shapely, came out onto
the stage. The short woman was carrying an accordion,
which she promptly began to play. The taller woman began
to sing in a loud, pleasant alto. They performed three lively
numbers, and then it was the professor's turn.

''Friends, I'm not gonna lie to you,'' he began earnestly. ''I
came here to hawk my wares. My intention was simply to
bring some comfort and healing to your lives. But, a serious
problem has been brought to my attention. I'm afraid I must
tell you that a terrible epidemic has struck this community,
and it must be addressed immediately. I—'' He paused and
coughed delicately into his hand. ''I don't know of any gen-
tlemanly way to address this problem, other than to be forth-
right. You see, on my way to your fine city, I encountered this
man.'' He gestured to Solon, who climbed reluctantly onto
the stage. ''This is Mister Solon Johnson. Upon encountering
him on the road, I noticed right away that he had the worst
case of tapeworm infection that I've seen in a long time.''

A hush went over the crowd, as folks stared at Solon.
He looked down at his feet, blushing deeply. He wished
he'd never come to Ness City tonight. He wished he'd
never met the professor, even though he may have saved
his life.

The crowd began to murmur, and exclamations followed.
Professor Tyler held up his hands to still the crowd.

''Rather than my usual health lecture,'' he said, digging into his pocket and pulling out the rag, ''I feel a
desperate need tonight to concentrate on saving this community from a dastardly health problem.'' As he talked,
he opened the rag and exposed the tapeworm. It dangled
from his hand.

Some of the women screamed out. Men stared wide-eyed, and little children quit fidgeting and running around. Every eye fell upon the long worm as it hung in the air, seeming to dance before their eyes. The professor suddenly pointed to a man of about sixty. "What's your name, my good man?" he asked.

"It's Luke Hopper."

"Well, Mister Luke Hopper. Even without a physical examination, I can see that you, too, are suffering from tapeworm infection."

Before Luke Hopper could utter a word, the professor pointed his finger at another man not far away from Hopper. "And you, sir! I can see that you have the same unfortunate affliction."

With the three-foot tapeworm dangling in his hand before the crowd, the professor soon had more than a dozen folks in the crowd designated as having the same affliction. The crowd reacted with alarm, and when Professor Tyler was finished, he sold seventy-seven bottles of his nostrum. Some, like Luke Hopper, bought two or three bottles. Solon became an instant celebrity, as folks came up and patted him on the back and told him how lucky they all were to have crossed paths with the professor. Maybe they would all be saved, they said, from any nasty complications of the tapeworm infection.

The professor announced that there would be a thirty-minute intermission. When the show commenced, he said, Kid Martin would be putting on what he promised to be the most spectacular display ever seen by civilization.

Clayton had to pull Solon away from the crowd. He was enjoying being the center of attention. He was a little disappointed, but when Clayton pointed out that he'd rather avoid seeing the Kid again, Solon reluctantly agreed to leave.

They were barely out of town, when Wanda began to giggle to herself.

"What's so funny?" Solon asked.

"You," she replied. "You and that tapeworm."

"I don't see what's funny about it. Why, the whole community could be sick over this thing! The professor told me that it's highly contagious. Did you ever stop to think that, just by being close to me, you might've developed one, too?'' Solon asked.

Wanda clutched her breast. "Stop! It hurts to laugh!" she said. "Oh, Solon! You never had a tapeworm!"

"I'm disappointed in you!" Solon said, wounded. "Didn't you see it for yourself when I showed it to the professor this morning?"

"I saw it, all right," Wanda said. She started laughing again. "But, I couldn't embarrass you in front of everybody. That's an old trick, Solon! I'm surprised you fell for it."

"Old trick?" Solon said slowly. "What are you sayin'?"

"Just that! The professor played an old trick on you. I'll bet he had you swallow a pill of some kind, and then he gave you some medicine that made your bowels move. Solon, that pill had a rubber worm inside. The medicine just made it pass through you quicker."

"Well, I can't believe what I'm hearin'!" Solon exclaimed. "You were right there! You saw him give me the stuff!"

Wanda held her breast with both hands and laughed. "I know, but I was in so much pain at the time, I didn't pay any attention!"

Solon sat there in shock. "I find that hard to believe," he said, shaking his head. "Why, you even took some of his medicine, yourself."

"Don't get your dander up. I was too sick to care! Besides that, the blamed medicine kept me runnin' half the night, myself!"

Maybe the professor *was* a damned phony, Solon thought to himself. If so, he ought to head right back into town and show him what he thought of his damned tapeworm nostrum.

"Well, you have to admit the medicine made you feel pretty good," Wanda said.

"Gave me the worst case of the runs I've ever had," Solon grumbled. He looked at Wanda. "At least it made us forget about our problems for a spell," he commented.

"It did, for a fact." Wanda smiled.

That night, Solon was still nursing his pride and wondering if what Wanda said was really true. He considered whether or not he should bed down with her, but then remembered that she would be leaving for Dodge City soon, according to her plans. That was just enough excuse for Solon to crawl in with her.

He lay next to her and felt depressed. Here, he'd managed to lose two women and a best friend. Life seemed bleak. He had expected to see Beverly in town that day, but there'd been no sign of her. And Wanda was leaving with her one good nipple.

For Clayton and Tracy, it had been a good day. They'd enjoyed shopping together and sharing the care of Alice. On the way home, they'd secretly laughed together as they listened to Solon and Wanda go on about the tapeworm. Later that night, when they curled up together, Clayton relaxed, while Tracy nursed Alice. The curves of Tracy's body fit nicely against his front side.

He felt like a huge weight had been lifted from his shoulders. It didn't take him long to fall asleep.

⚔ 45 ⚔

CLAYTON AND Tracy were married by the Reverend Daniel Bondurant in the Union Church. Wanda held Alice, while Solon stood up for Clayton. Once during the ceremony, Clayton glanced back over his shoulder. He couldn't believe it. Every seat in the church was taken. People were even standing in the aisles. For most of his adult life, he had felt alone, and now, here were all these people. There were many whose names he barely knew. Many were men who had fought on the other side in the war, Clayton's enemies on the battlefield. Some had the scars to prove it. A few had missing arms, and one man had but one leg to stand on. Nonetheless, they were all there, for him, just as if that war had never happened.

Clayton grew nervous. He kept waiting for something to come along and stop the good that was taking place in his life. He was sure something would crash through the ceiling from the sky, or that someone's voice would ring out from the crowd, protesting this union. He felt that surely, this kind of good fortune was not supposed to happen to him.

But nothing did fall from the sky, and no one hollered out in disapproval. Clayton and Tracy exchanged their vows.

The ceremony was brief, followed by a reception outside on the church grounds. Mrs. Joshua Milburn, the baker's wife, had made a wedding cake, and the newlyweds laughed and held hands as they cut the first piece. Fiddles were brought out for dancing, and the womenfolk presented Tracy with a parcel of their favorite recipes.

Late that afternoon when they returned home, Clayton felt like he had been transformed into a new man. He was filled with a new fervor and immediately set out with his plans to make the house into a real home. As he worked over the next few days, Solon began to grow a bit melancholy. He sat and talked while Clayton went about his chores. Something inside of him had changed, too, within the last few days.

"How does it feel to be a married man?" he asked Clayton one afternoon.

Clayton stopped working and wiped his brow with his arm. He glanced at Solon. There was no sarcasm in the question, and Solon looked sincere. He thought a moment.

"You know," he said, "it feels different. It really does. I didn't think anything would be different, at first."

Solon ran his tongue over his lips. He scooped up some dirt in his hand and watched as it fell through his fingers to the ground. He said, "I don't guess I'll ever marry. Dern women! I can't figure them out."

"What's to figure out?" Clayton asked, obviously not sharing Solon's views.

They had been friends for so long, it was odd how, in just an instant, they had become almost like strangers. All through the years, Clayton had listened to Solon go on and on, first about one thing, then another. Clayton had always felt a kinship to Solon, and they had agreed on a lot of things. But now, he was on a different page in life, and he really wasn't in the mood to hear such negative comments.

He said, "Look, my friend. I can only say that I ain't never been happier. You oughta get married, yourself. Settle down here. Lord knows I've got more land here to work than makes sense. Y'all could build you a house over yonder to the east."

"Who would I marry, even if'n I was wantin' to hitch up? Beverly won't never have anythin' to do with me again," Solon said gloomily. He couldn't keep his mind from drifting back to Beverly's good cooking. He was missing that more than anything.

"What about Wanda?" Clayton asked. "Tracy said she was eager to stay here and keep your old bones company."

Solon let out an exasperated breath. "I can't believe you'd even suggest such a thing! She's a whore, Clayton! Not that I hold it against her, but whores don't get married!"

"Well, I never heard that to be a fact," Clayton said. "I've known whores that got married. In fact, I ain't so sure that they don't make better wives. 'Sides, I remember you tellin' me that more than once."

Solon stood up. "This is crazy talk. Speakin' of Wanda, she and I'll be leavin' in the mornin'. I told her I'd see her back to Dodge. I think I'll stop off at Shorty Gillis's place and see if he needs any work done." He paused, and stared off in thought. "Hell, as bosses go, Shorty ain't such a bad sort. He could drive a body crazy, but I've put up with him before, and I reckon I can put up with him again. Anyways, Ray Bradford mentioned once that if I ever need a job, to come on down to the Outlet, and he'd give me one. There's talk that they're gonna open up the Outlet for settlement someday. I might just hang around 'til they do that."

Clayton didn't say anything. He just walked off toward the corral. There was a resignation about Solon that Clayton accepted. He wouldn't try to talk him out of leaving. After all, Solon had left before. He was always running off, and Clayton didn't worry over him like he used to. Though Solon still drank, he'd moderated himself in that area.

Age and time were changing both of them. Clayton suspected that Solon would do all right for a spell, and the next time life's path ran out on him, he'd come back to Ness City.

And Clayton was a family man now. He couldn't wait to get into his new life. Just that morning, he had told Tracy that, come Sunday, they would both take Alice to church. He'd even started talking about the baby's education, drawing a playful rebuke from Tracy. "Why, she's only a baby, Clayton!"

He was looking forward to taking the family back to Tennessee to visit what family was left there, and that night, he sheepishly brought up the idea of having another child in a year or so, which delighted Tracy. These days, Clayton's head was now filled with wheat prices and farming equipment. He promised to buy Tracy a kitchen table, and he encouraged her to invite the other women over for coffee.

The next day, Clayton was feeding the hogs. Tracy had brought Alice outside, and she handed him a jar of cool well water. Clayton didn't realize that a rider and his horse had ridden up behind him, until he tilted his head to take a long drink and noticed Tracy looking sharply over his shoulder.

"It's Martin Frusher," she said.

Frusher's face looked pale, and he had dark circles under his eyes. Clayton had noticed them before, but they were more pronounced this time. Something was wrong. He took another drink of the well water.

"Step on down from your horse," Clayton said. "Tracy's got a pot of coffee on the stove."

Martin Frusher was a tired and reluctant messenger. He shook his head. "I'll take a sip of that water, though." He drank half of it before he spoke of why he'd come.

"For what it's worth to ya, that Kid Martin feller is back in town, Clayton. He says he's comin' out here. I thought you needed to know that."

"He told you himself?" Clayton asked.

Martin Frusher nodded. "He told everybody. "I'm truly sorry, Clayton, but I'm the one told him where you lived. I thought the man might be a friend of yours, the way he seemed to know all about you, and all. I didn't know otherwise, until he started braggin' to everybody about how he was gonna show the world who was boss with a gun."

Martin Frusher shook his head at himself. He'd always enjoyed the fact that he and Clayton Crist were friends. He'd even written letters to his people back in Indiana to impress them with the knowledge that "the Gunny" lived here, and that they were neighbors.

"Maybe he won't come," Tracy said hopefully. "Maybe it was just talk." She looked uncertainly at Clayton.

"Maybe," Martin Frusher said, with no more confidence than Tracy had. "But, when I left to come out here, he already had a crowd of folks gathered around him. I'm real sorry, Clayton. I truly am."

"Don't be sorry," Clayton said. "You didn't do nothin' wrong."

Nervously, Frusher looked back over his shoulder, toward town. He'd been keeping an eye in that direction since he'd arrived, half expecting to see the Kid show up on the horizon at any second with his guns drawn. He took out a rag from his britches and wiped the sweat from his palms, twisting it in his hands. "That fool Kid. I told him he'd get him a one-way ticket to the graveyard if he came out here." He swallowed hard. "But you know how those young ones are, Clayton. They're all full of themselves."

"Surely, he won't come," Tracy said again to no one in particular.

"He'll come, all right," Clayton said. "Now, take the baby on down to the house." He smiled at Frusher. "I thank you for comin'."

Frusher hesitated. "Again, Clayton, I can't tell you how sorry I am."

"You've done nothin' wrong. Just been a good friend, is all," Clayton said.

When Frusher was gone, Clayton walked back to the house, and found Tracy standing by the window, holding his pistol.

"I'm not letting you have this," she said.

Clayton tried to smile. "I've got no choice, hon."

"Yes, you do. We've got a baby to think about. I'm not giving you your gun, and that's that." Tracy pressed the pistol in its worn holster against her chest. "If he comes, I'll talk to him. I'll tell him you're not like that anymore. Surely, he'll understand." Her lips trembled.

Clayton took Tracy by the shoulders and pulled her next to him. With his fingertip, he traced her eyebrows, then gently rubbed his fingers over her fine features. He wished it was all that simple. With some men, it would have been.

"I love you."

It was the first time he'd said the words only for her. No longer was the memory of Jolene lingering in the back of his mind, or thoughts of any of the others.

Tracy began to sob and buried her face in his chest. "Please don't go!" she said. "Don't do this to me and the baby. We could leave! We could go away before he gets here! Maybe we could go to Elmer and Maudie's. They'd let us stay there a couple of days." She grabbed his collar and tried to shake him. "I need you."

The scent of Tracy's hair filled Clayton's nostrils. Through the door, he could see Alice's little hand waving back and forth in the crib that Martin Frusher had made. His feet felt heavy, as if the soles of his boots had been nailed to the floor. He wished he could go back to the time before all the killings had started, but he couldn't. He had to reap what he, himself, had sown. Slowly, he pulled back and took her chin in his hand.

"I can't run away," he said. "Once I did, I could never stop running. He wouldn't let me. And what kind of life would that be? Give me the pistol."

"No!" she cried. "You can't have it! I've lost one husband, and I'm not going to take a chance on losing another."

Once again, Clayton pulled her head to his chest and rubbed her hair, letting it catch between his fingers. It felt soft and warm. He felt a surge of anger that this newfound happiness was being threatened. With harder force, he grabbed the pistol and pulled it from her.

"Take care of the baby," he said. "Stay in the house."

Tracy's eyes widened. "You're not leavin'?"

Clayton said, "I'm going to meet him. I can't let him come here. I won't take any chances—not with you and the baby."

He'd just stepped off the porch, when he saw at least a dozen riders approaching. Kid Martin led the group, riding an Appaloosa. Clayton wondered who the others were.

As he moved away from the house, he recognized Ollie Knowles, the barber who had recently cut his hair. Beside him was Norton Cravens. Clayton had sold Cravens a couple of hogs the previous Monday. Clayton frowned. What were they doing with the Kid?

As they neared the house, the other men split off and angled to the sides, but the Kid rode straight ahead.

Clayton had the urge to reach down and grab hold of his thighs to stop them from quivering. A queasy feeling had started in the middle of his stomach. A gust of prairie wind, cold against his face, reminded him that he was sweating. His fingers felt sticky.

Kid Martin stepped down from his finely muscled Appaloosa horse. A youthful smile was on his lips, but his eyes were fixed and deadly. He moved with a fluid grace that showed his confidence. Clayton's mind flashed back to Dodge City and the first time they had met. Clayton had sensed the danger in the Kid's nature right away, and now, as he stood not twenty feet away, Clayton knew for certain that death waited for one of them. He had the urge to pull leather, while the Kid was enjoying the moment, but he couldn't follow through with that urge. Instead, he stood there, listening to his own heart pounding, his breath quickening.

The townsmen were still sitting atop their horses. Ollie Knowles hollered, "Clayton, we rode all the way out here to see if we could put a stop to his crazy ideas, but nobody's been able to talk him out of it."

Suddenly, as if on cue, the men filled their hands with weapons. Joshua Milburn and Troy Irvin raised their shotguns. Another town merchant, Arthur Corrigan, aimed the only weapon he had, a Kentucky flintlock, at the Kid's back.

The smile that had been playing on Kid Martin's face faded when he turned around and saw the assortment of weapons that were trained on him. He looked confused and bewildered. "What's this?" he asked.

Ollie Knowles's voice wavered as he said, "Just what it looks like, Kid Martin! I'm tellin' you right now, you're not comin' in here and messin' with one of our own. We tried to talk you out of this, and gave fair warnin', but you wouldn't hear it. Now, I ain't never killed nobody, but I swear to the Lord that I'll shoot you, if you try anything." He pointed his Henry at the Kid's midsection.

Joshua Milburn, holding his shotgun with a steady hand, said, "Let Clayton kill the smart-mouth," he said. "I tell you, there's a difference in puttin' on a show! I reckon

Clayton's proved himself over and over against real live targets.''

"That's right," Jody Howar added. "We oughta let Mister Crist kill him."

A murmur went among the men, who all nodded their approval.

"No sir!" Ollie Knowles said. "I know how good Clayton is, but I've seen this Kid, and we ain't takin' no chances. Now, you either leave or die, right where you're standin'," he said to the Kid.

"Well, ain't this something," Kid Martin commented dryly. He threw up his hands, then let them drop at his sides and turned to Clayton. "You're a lucky man to have such friends. But, we'll meet again. You and I both know that."

Clayton saw the gleam in Kid Martin's eyes, and the hair bristled on his neck. The Kid had no intention of giving up this easily. "Put it away, Ollie," he urged. He looked around at the others—men holding rifles and shotguns that they used to hunt game for their families' tables. They were men who hadn't pointed a weapon at another man since the war. Some, he realized, weren't even old enough to have been in the war. A calm came over him. He noticed that his legs had stopped trembling. "Please, all of you. Put 'em away. Let me handle this."

Kid Martin watched with a silly grin, as the men reluctantly lowered their guns. His own demeanor seemed to relax, and he turned back toward Clayton. A gust of wind kicked up dust between the two. Clayton watched the Kid smile. He knew there would never be a better opportunity.

"Let's do it, Kid!"

The stories about the Kid's speed had not been exaggerated. His movements became a blur. As time seemed to freeze for the tiniest part of a second, the barrel of his .45 suddenly appeared, looming toward Clayton as big as the sky.

Clayton thought he caught a fleeting glimpse of the slug filling that big hole extending from the Kid's hand. Thunder and lightning reached down from the heavens, and together they collided against his chest. His mind was still frozen in the moment when he realized what was happening. A heavy pain knocked him backward. His lips didn't move, but his voice screamed from deep inside for Alice. A vision glided through his mind of his little girl, wearing a dress that Tracy had made, running and playing in the schoolyard.

He felt the impact of his body landing on the ground. The grasses rubbed against his neck and the back of his head. At that same instant, something inside of him took hold of his own Colt and aimed. In the same slice of time that he'd seen his vision of Alice on the school ground, his finger tightened on the deadly trigger, then he saw the Kid's knees buckle. In a heartbeat, the menacing eyes were changed forever. Kid Martin pitched forward to his death. As he fell, Clayton's own Colt exploded. The .45 slug struck the Kid needlessly in the shoulder, just as his body bounced off the hard Kansas earth.

Clayton grimaced. The pain in his chest made it difficult to breathe. He raised his head and saw the puff of smoke lazily drift upward from the barrel of the Winchester that Solon still held poised.

Clayton clutched his chest. There was a familiar ache underneath the small rectangular item that he touched with his fingers. Reaching inside, he pulled out the Testament, which General Lee had given him so many years ago.

There, barely touching the minié ball, was the Kid's .45 slug, buried among the pages.

⚒ 46 ⚒

THAT EVENING, Clayton buried Kid Martin next to a lone willow tree. He wept as he lowered the Kid into the cold ground. He made Tracy promise that, no matter what ever happened to him, she would always see to it that the Kid had fresh flowers over his grave. He thought about the Kid's mama. Would she ever know what had become of her son?

The next morning, Solon and Wanda set out for Dodge City. Five miles south, along the trail, they came upon Martin Frusher and Ollie Knowles, along with Joshua Milburn and Wilbur DeShazo, everyone, in fact, who had been there the day before. They had made a large pile of rocks. In front of the pile, they had put up a marker.

Ollie pulled a fistful of cigars from his saddlebag and passed them out. He had told his wife that he liked to give them to his customers. Good for business, he told her. In reality, Ollie liked to smoke them, himself. It was a good excuse for the missus, who likened cigar smoking to whiskey drinking, which she would not tolerate.

The men lit their cigars and blew out the smoke, letting it mingle with the Kansas breeze.

"I think this'll do it," Joshua Milburn said, coughing on the cigar.

"Dern right!" Ollie barked. "Not a one of you better breathe a word of this to anybody! We're gonna keep Ness County a decent place for our wives and young'uns, and take care of Clayton, to boot. Let him get on with his life."

The rest of the men nodded proudly. They stood around, smoking their cigars and talking about next year's crops. Finally, one by one, they left.

When the last man was out of sight, Wanda pulled a blanket from the wagon and spread it out on the prairie grass, then sat down.

Solon stood there a moment, gazing down at the marker.

"You mind tellin' me exactly what it says?" he asked. "I never could read much more'n a few words."

Wanda paused from unbuttoning her blouse. She nodded, then read:

HERE LIES THE GUNNY, CLAYTON CRIST
KILLED IN A GUNFIGHT BY KID MARTIN
1884